Thanks and acknowledgements
This book would not have been possible without the help
and support of the following people:

My fiancée - Chrysti, Ellen, Kelly, Ari, K.C., Chris M., Mark,
Zen, Christos, Vivian, Steve, Andy, Scott, Max, Christine,
Ron W., and my supportive family.

Chrysti, thank you for listening to my endless brainstorming.
It was a test of patience but without you this book would not
have made it this far.

Ellen, thank you for mentoring me and teaching me how to
become a better writer.

WILMAR LUNA

The Silver Ninja
A Bitter Winter

Written by: Wilmar Luna
Edited by: Ellen Brock

SILVER PENCIL BOOKS
100 CAMPUS TOWN CIRCLE
SUITE 103 #114
EWING, NJ 08637

ISBN-13: 978-1-7322213-0-7
LIBRARY OF CONGRESS CONTROL NUMBER: 2018906131

PUBLISHED BY: SILVER PENCIL BOOKS

FRONT COVER: JADE LAW | BACK COVER: ANTOINE COLLIGNON
EDITED BY: ELLEN BROCK

DEDICATION

Mr. Latini was my 9th grade Physical Sciences teacher. I bring him up today because I wanted to share a story of something he said a long time ago. On a particularly boring weekday, a few of my classmates decided they wanted to pick on me. They made fun of my hair, my pimples, and the way I dressed. Back then I didn't have the confidence or social skills to defend myself.

Luckily, Mr. Latini did not tolerate fools. He said, "You better leave him alone. One day, Wil is going to write a book about you clowns and he's going to have the last laugh."

I never wrote about those clowns and I never will. They did not matter to me and their words have long turned to dust. What mattered was that Mr. Latini stood up for me and had inadvertently held me accountable to an unspoken promise. I needed to write a book. I wrote several.

Mr. Latini, for those who didn't have the pleasure of attending his class, was an energetic young man of thirty-two or thirty-three, I don't really know. He had short red hair, a goatee, was well-built, with freckled fair skin, and glasses. He looked like an Irish nerd with an Italian last name. Mr. Latini was not a typical teacher. This was a guy who one day turned off the lights, dipped his hand in flame resistant solution, and lit it on fire. He waved his hand around like a torch while the class screamed in terror. He thought it was funny.

If he wasn't lighting his hand on fire, he was walking into the classroom with a championship wrestling belt over his shoulder. He'd march in with a cocky, smug swagger, parading around his belt like a wrestling superstar while my classmates called him a dork.

One time, he asked us all to gather around his desk where he had a chemistry set. "Now I want you guys to get really close. Neon gas is very dim so you won't be able to see it from far away." Though I wasn't a science whiz, I knew what neon was. I stayed back while the rest of my classmates brought their curious eyes closer. He flipped the switch and blinded the classroom with hot pink light. They yelled and shielded their eyes while Mr. Latini cackled madly. Good thing I was smarter than them.

These somewhat childish traits are what made Mr. Latini my most memorable teacher of freshman year. I didn't mind coming to his class because I knew I'd learn something new and I knew he'd look out for me. He made science fun.

A few months into my sophomore year, the principal made an announcement over the PA system. Mr. Latini had passed away. A teacher found him slumped at his computer desk. His heart had failed while grading papers, a birth defect. He passed peacefully and quietly.

The irony is, I didn't know Mr. Latini that well. There were other teachers in my later years who encouraged me to study vocabulary and pushed me to go to college. All Mr. Latini did was make an off the cuff remark about writing books. And I never forgot it.

Words have power. Don't waste them. A comment big or small can have a lasting impact.

This is why I dedicate this book to you, Mr. David Latini, Physical Sciences teacher from Nottingham high school. Though you were taken from this Earth much too soon, your words will live forever.

Introduction

In the year 2010, Dr. Ursula Wolf created the first hybrid single cell organism. Made of both organic matter and machinery, her creation became the first step into what would eventually be called: nanotechnology.

Several years later that same nanotechnology would be used to create the world's first . . .

SUPER-HUMAN.

CHAPTER 1:

From Hero to Zero

Three days ago a member of the Mubarizun of Allah walked into a soccer stadium in France and blew himself up. He waited for the home team to score before pulling the detonation cord on his suicide vest. Thousands of screaming fans were rushed to local hospitals with their limbs lost among the wreckage. Last week, an MOA zealot barreled a van through Times Square. Seven were mutilated and crushed under the weight of the madman's vehicle. It was the age of terror.

This was when she was once human. Before her name instilled fear. Before her body became a weapon. Before she inspired a revolution. She was Cindy Ames, a woman who wore her history through the aged, subtle scars on her left cheek bone and the bridge of her nose.

Tonight the Javits Center was host to a brand new conference called Future Technology Today. All the important political VIP's (except for the governor) were going to be in attendance. The security was so high that even the Emergency Services Unit SWAT team and K-9 unit were on patrol.

Cindy watched the SWAT officers from her security checkpoint near the main entrance. On a normal day, ESU would be all smiles when chatting with fellow LEOs. But tonight, they were severe and quiet with their fingers near the trigger. The threat of another MOA attack was real and everyone needed to be on point. Despite the tension, she was jealous of them. Two years ago, when Cindy used to call herself officer, she had an opportunity to train with the ESU SWAT team. The first time she had tried on a vest and helmet, she remembered being surprised at the heaviness of the gear and how awkward it was to push the stock of an M4 carbine into her shoulder. It was fun though, and made her feel badass whenever she carried it. She missed being a law enforcement officer, being a LEO was definitely better than being a security guard at Javits. Not that there was anything wrong with security, it just wasn't what she wanted.

An officer from the K-9 unit crossed her line of sight. She smiled at the Ger-

A Bitter Winter

man Shepard being led on a leash with its snout sniffing the freshly mopped floor. She once considered trying out for the K-9 unit but was too afraid of being bitten by police dogs in training. She saw the scars some of the guys had and didn't want to add more to her collection.

A young guy, a hipster type, with the classic horn rimmed glasses, thick beard, flannel shirt, and torn jeans approached her checkpoint. He had a backpack strapped to his shoulders and had willfully ignored a sign which read: *No backpacks, luggage, or bags allowed, no exceptions.* He took out his cellphone and showed Cindy his barcode to get in.

"Sorry, Sir. No backpacks allowed tonight."

"No worries, it's just for my laptop."

"You're going to have to leave your items with us. You can pick it up after the event."

"Um, I work for the press and I need this to take notes."

"What press?"

"It's a new startup in Bay Ridge."

He handed her a business card. She didn't bother to look at it. "Never heard of it. Use your cell phone for notes, leave the bag and your laptop here."

"This is ridiculous. I have a right to free speech. You ever heard of freedom of the press?"

She questioned whether this kid actually worked for the press, if he did, he would know MOA's sick preference for blowing people up with backpacks. There was no way she was going to let herself be blamed for a bomb getting through. The man shrugged off the straps of his backpack. "Hope you're enjoying your power trip." As he crossed the metal detector he muttered, "You rent-a-cop."

"Excuse me, Sir. I need you to come back."

Those waiting in line backed away from the checkpoint. The scrawny young man spun on his feet and looked at her as if she were baseborn.

"What?"

"Could you please repeat what you said?" Despite Cindy's head only coming up to his chest, the hipster seemed to have lost his nerve. "Something about a rent-a-cop?"

"It was a joke."

4

"You think I'm a joke because I'm a security guard?"

"N—no of course not."

She pointed at the numerous signs at the main entrance, hanging banners, and the security checkpoint itself. "The signs over there, there and there say no backpacks allowed. You know why? Because we don't want terrorists to blow us all up. But you seem to think the rules don't apply to you. So now you get the first class TSA treatment." She clicked on her radio. "Fourteen to Command One."

"Go ahead fourteen."

"I'm sending a guest over to the police checkpoint for a strip search. He tried to sneak a backpack through the south access point."

"10-4 we'll send someone over."

Cindy looked up at the mortified young man and glared at him. "There's nothing funny about backpack bombs. Follow the rules next time." She faced the crowd and shouted, "Next!"

By seven o'clock, there were people everywhere. If they weren't drinking overpriced lattes at the café they were milling about the vendor kiosks on the exhibition floor behind her. She was surprised that so many people had come. She expected this kind of turn out at Comic Con but not a technology conference. While she scanned in guests, a hand reached out from the crowd and tapped her shoulder.

She spun around and mentally prepared her usual speech, *Bathrooms are downstairs to your right, the presentation is*—her face suddenly brightened. "Hey baby!" She threw her arms around Jonas's neck. "I'm so happy to see you."

"I'm surprised I got the jump on you. You're usually like a motion detector." Jonas flashed his trademark boyish smile. His hair was the color of oil, freshly shaved on the sides, styled with gel on top. His jaw was buttery smooth from a clean shave and he smelled like the night they first slept together. There was something about his smile and calm demeanor that was infectious. She couldn't stay mad or grouchy whenever he was around. Hopefully this will still be the case once the honeymoon phase is over.

"Look at you all cleaned up and sexy like you're going on a date," she said with a smirk. "Who's the lucky girl," she teased.

"My wife." He smiled at her. "Smart ass."

She sighed. "I'd rather be hanging out with you than standing here."

"Having a tough night?"

"Work sucks today."

"You always say it sucks."

"I got snippy with a guest. Wasn't my best moment."

"What'd he do?"

"He disrespected me."

"Uh oh." He gave her a sideways glance. "Did you hit him?"

"They'd fire me if it wasn't in self-defense. No, I just sent him over to the police checkpoint for a strip search."

Jonas chuckled. "Oh well he's lucky then. You hit pretty hard for a little woman."

"If I see the guy I should probably apologize."

"Hell no." Jonas seemed offended she would even suggest that. "You made the right call. No one wants to explode tonight, especially me."

"Thank you." She adjusted the collar of his shirt. "Why didn't you tell me you were going to clean up tonight? I would've—" she leaned in. "—worn a thong."

Jonas raised his eyebrows with interest. "I have to present in front of all these people. The last thing I need is my flag at full mast."

She grinned mischievously. "We've been married two years and I still feel like I can't get enough of you. Working security at night and gymnastics during the day sucks."

Jonas lifted her chin. "That's going to change after tonight. Once I finalize selling my company to Raymond you can quit both jobs and do whatever you want." He rested his hands on her hips. "And we'll definitely celebrate. Do you still have that polka dot thing you bought?"

Her lips spread into a toothy grin. "That's what I would've worn," her voice became sweet like melted chocolate. "Anyway." She changed the subject and opened her eyes wide with amusement. "Did you see your giant photo?"

"The one they plastered on the steps?" He grimaced. "I look like an idiot."

"You don't look like an idiot." She giggled. "You look like you belong in a Hispanic boy band. Eres muy lindo, Papi."

"I can't wait till they take it down."

Cindy laughed. "I took a picture with my phone."

"Oh come on."

She tapped his arm. "You should get going. I don't want you to be late."

Cindy went up on her tip toes and kissed his lips. "Love you."

"Love you too."

After Jonas had gone, she continued to dwell on the idea of quitting her jobs. Well . . . maybe not gymnastics. Life would be a little too boring if she couldn't teach her students. It was nice to have a group of young girls who looked up to her and treated her with respect.

The voice from the head of security blasted out of her radio. "Command One to Fourteen."

Cindy squeezed the radio which had a number fourteen label taped on it. "Go ahead."

"Head of security wants you reassigned to the mayor when he gets here. Make sure he and his family have no problems getting where they need to go. If the mayor asks where the bathroom is, you take him there."

"He has a security detail."

"Doesn't matter. You're the point man."

"Shouldn't the shift supervisor—"

"They're dealing with a vehicle situation down at the loading dock. Handle it."

"Copy."

The photographers circled around the mayor's family like vultures eyeing a meal. His security detail, a group of men wearing suits and sunglasses, shoved anyone who got too close. A bored looking teenager shuffled in the middle of the group. Her hair was a collection of black squiggles barely controlled by a scrunchie. Blonde accents shot across the crown of her head to break up the black, a style inspired by a popular musician. Her name was Priscilla Montez, she was the mayor's daughter and also happened to be a student at Ninja Gymnastics.

"Mrs. Ames?" Priscilla jumped with excitement. "What are you doing here?"

"I'm . . . working security," she said with resignation.

"Oh my gosh." Priscilla looked horrified. "Does that mean you're not teaching gymnastics anymore? I thought we—"

"It's just a part time gig. Don't tell anyone okay?"

"Why not?"

"You know how you don't want photographers to bother you when you come to my class to practice your uneven bars? Same thing here. Can you promise not to tell anyone?"

"Of course!" Priscilla waved her family over. "Mom, dad, come here. My coach is working security."

"Great . . ." Cindy muttered.

Mayor Montez approached with a confident stride. He reached across his droopy chest and into his suit jacket pocket. He pulled out a printed ticket with a barcode and held it in front of his barrel belly. The photographers swooped in with their shutters clicking, bulbs flashing. Cindy put her hand over her face and scanned the mayor's ticket.

"Smile for the camera," a photographer yelled.

"No, thank you."

The photographers were caught off guard. Not many people turned down a photo op with the mayor. "Come on. Just a quick one of the two of you."

Cindy shook her head no.

Mayor Montez leaned in with a big, genuine smile. "No need to be shy," he said reassuringly. "The sooner we take the photo the sooner they'll be out of your hair."

Cindy felt sick to her stomach. She didn't want the guys on the force to see her picture on newspapers or social media. She didn't want them laughing at her for becoming a security guard.

"Can we not take the photo, Sir? I have personal reasons."

The mayor nodded and told the photographers they would take a family photo instead. Mayor Montez blocked Cindy from view and held onto the shoulders of his wife and daughter. Once the flashes were gone, he turned around and introduced his wife.

"You remember my wife, Carmen."

How could she forget Carmen? Despite being rich and the Mayor's wife, she was refreshingly down to earth. Unlike most wealthy parents, Carmen did not give Priscilla everything she wanted. All she gave her was a roof over her head and food in her belly. If she wanted new shoes or expensive clothes she had to earn it by working, volunteering, studying, or doing chores. It did not matter if you approached Carmen with holes in your shirt and two dollars in your wallet. She would happily welcome you into her luxurious home with open arms. "Mrs. Ames, it is absolutely delightful to meet you again." She extended her hand. "Where is your sister, Jadie?"

Cindy smiled and shook her hand. "She might stop by a little later."

"Wonderful. Priscilla simply cannot stop raving about the both of you and your class. I knew once she started putting on her father's underwear and tying a towel around her neck that gymnastics would be a perfect fit for her."

"Mom . . ."

"She would lift the furniture and make-believe she had super strength."

"Mom! Oh my God."

Carmen waved her hand. "Oh honey, relax."

"Priscilla if that's the most embarrassing thing you've done, I will happily trade places with you."

"Me too," Carmen added.

Priscilla shook her head. "Please kill me."

Mayor Montez turned to Cindy. "How long has it been since you've left the force?"

She grimaced, hard. "Two years now, Sir."

"That's a shame. I thought the uniform suited you."

"Me too," she said quietly.

"I bet you were a badass cop," Priscilla said.

The mayor's security detail barged into the conversation and informed the mayor they were clear to travel. Cindy radioed command to let them know she had the VIP and led the family to the third floor where Jonas's big presentation was fifteen minutes away from commencement. At the end of the convention hall was the elevated stage where Jonas would make his appearance. Standing near the base of the presentation platform were two men surrounded by their own security detail. Senator James Albright and a man whom Cindy had hoped never to see again. Police Commissioner Patrick Gates.

The mayor waved the men over. She didn't know Commissioner Gates was going to be here, didn't even see him check in. She tailed the mayor's bodyguards and used them as moving wall cover.

"Quite the turn out," Senator Albright said. "I wish this many people would turn up to the polls."

"Then we'd be out of the job," Mayor Montez said.

They laughed.

"You know." Commissioner Gates lowered his voice. "I'm eager to see this new toy I've been hearing about. Have you guys heard about this?"

They shook their heads.

"Supposedly this presentation is about a combat suit; thin, lightweight, completely bulletproof. I would love to get my hands on one."

"Don't come crawling to me with a proposal to increase your budget," Mayor Montez replied.

"Dad," Priscilla whined. "Do you really have to talk about your boring politics right now?"

"It's called work, Muñeca. Zip it."

She watched the commissioner from within the shadow of the broad chested guard. Being short sometimes came in handy, this was one of those times. Carmen walked up to Cindy and touched her shoulder.

"What are you doing hiding, Mrs. Ames? Don't tell me these men intimidate you."

"What? No. No." She stammered. "I don't want to get in the way."

"Nonsense." Carmen took Cindy's hand. "No need to be bashful. These men have the same flaw you and I do. They are human."

She tried to squirm away. "No, Carmen, please. I don't need to speak with them."

As Cindy gently, but firmly resisted Carmen's nudging, a tall, blonde woman shoved her way through the crowd and made a bee-line for the mayor. The guards spotted her right away.

"We got incoming."

The blonde woman stood at almost six feet tall. She twisted and sidestepped through the crowd while calling out, "Sis, Sis," before being tackled by two bodyguards. "Ow. What did I do?"

"Damn it, Jadie," Cindy muttered to herself. She left the shadow of the security guard and told them the woman was her sister.

The guards ignored her and looked to Mayor Montez for the approval.

"Dad, tell your jerk bodyguards to let go of my coach."

Mayor Montez waved his hand. "You don't need to bully my voters."

The security guards released her. Jadie rubbed her arms and narrowed her eyes. "Thanks a lot. Jerks."

The guards scattered and left Cindy out in plain view of Commissioner Gates. The man she hated, glared at her with an equal amount of hatred in his own eyes. The reason she wasn't a cop anymore was because of him and the reason his son wasn't alive was because of her.

"I didn't know they were hiring moro—" Commissioner Gates leashed his tongue in the presence of the mayor and his family. "—more personnel. You didn't mention Cindy was with you, Manny."

"She's not technically—"

Cindy cut him off. "I'm with the Javits center, Sir. They requested I guide the Mayor."

"Security." Commissioner Gates's face narrowed into a wolfish grin. "Good for you to still be able to find work befitting of your skills. Being a part of New York's finest is a tough, demanding job, it's not for everyone. I think you've definitely found your calling."

She was amazed by how easily the commissioner was able to call her a piece of shit without anyone noticing. She stared at his smug face and fantasized about cracking him across the jaw.

She took a deep breath and swallowed her emotions. "Well . . . I should get back to my post. Enjoy the show."

"You do that."

"Bye, Mrs. Ames." Priscilla waved cheerily. "See you in class later."

Cindy walked out of their line of sight and deflated. She didn't even want to watch Jonas's presentation anymore. She just wanted to go home and crawl into bed. The commissioner had stomped her last scrap of dignity under the heel of his glossy black loafer.

"Hey you okay?" Jadie put her arm around Cindy's waist. "Don't listen to that prick." Jadie waved a middle finger over her shoulder. "You want to hear something ironic?"

"What," she said without enthusiasm.

"Mayor Montez said don't bully my voters, but I never voted for him. Whoops."

Before Cindy could respond, a familiar voice boomed through the convention center loud speakers.

"Standing behind me is a technology the likes of which you have never seen. It is both robotic and organic. And before anyone out there gets too excited, it's not a Terminator."

"Jonas's presentation," Cindy whined. "I'm missing it."

"So let's not." Jadie dragged Cindy over to the presentation stage. "I'm excited to see what this thing is."

Jonas paced across the stage with a small microphone curved around his cheek.

"Imagine a suit no thicker than a hundred page paperback novel capable of being burned, shot, and hit with no damage to the user. A combat suit that you don't need to squeeze into but can still give you the strength to lift a car. You wouldn't believe it exists, but it does because my team at Lucent Labs has created it."

Jonas pointed to a giant capsule standing behind him. The cylinder hissed. Gasses spilled out from its exhaust ports and curled across the stage platform.

"I feel like I'm on a movie set," she said to Jadie.

"Yeah it's like, overly dramatic."

"He loves to make a big show. I wouldn't be surprised if he filled that thing with dry ice."

Jadie laughed.

Jonas strode to the right of the stage and pointed to the awakening machine. "Ladies and gentlemen I present to you, Stealth—" The lights throughout the convention floor went dark. Jonas's voice lost its amplified volume. "—umm, hello? Can anyone hear me?"

The spectators turned on their cell phone flashlights and murmured amongst themselves. The Lucent Labs team joined him on stage and checked the cables to investigate the power outage.

Cindy squeezed the broadcast button on her radio. "Fourteen to Command One." A loud buzzing rang from the speaker, possibly interference from all the cell phones nearby. She turned to Jadie and said, "I'm going to check out the loading dock to see if everything is all right. I want you to get Jonas and his friends out of here, just in case."

"You think it's serious?"

"No, but I don't want to take any chances. I'll call you once I know what's going on."

A sound, like a giant lawnmower sputtering its diesel engine, vibrated the walls of the convention floor and the wooden kiosks. The auxiliary lights powered up and cast dim light over the crowd. Cindy looked up at Jadie and smiled. "Probably just a brown out."

She went down the narrow grates of a stopped escalator and ventured to the locked doors accessible only to Javits personnel. She waved her badge keycard and continued through musty cement corridors where she walked past forklifts and stacks of plywood. The feral cats *employed* by the Javits Center took notice of Cindy and followed her shadow. After too many complaints from loading dock workers about rats jumping out of boxes, the Javits Center captured and vaccinated a feral cat colony to deal with the infestation.

Cindy found a cat sitting atop a spilled puddle of red paint next to a Javits moving van. She made a feeble smile and gingerly approached the animal.

"Hey there."

The cat stared at her and meowed.

"You're cute," she said in a gentle voice. "You don't care that I'm a loser."

The cat meowed again and swished its tail.

"I'm supposed to check on something down here but you make me feel better. So I'm just going to pet you for a little bit and get back to work, okay?"

Cindy knelt by the cat and noticed red paint over its paws. "Did you knock over a paint can?" She pet the animal which purred at her touch. "They're going to fire you for that. No more free food." A strong, nauseating smell of copper wafted into her nose. She sniffed the cat and didn't smell anything. She smelt the puddle and coiled back. "This isn't paint."

A Bitter Winter

There was a scarlet trail leading from the cat to a parked van. There she found the slain corpse of a woman next to the tires. Her eyeballs were bulging out of their sockets and her blouse was stained with an explosion of red ink. The head of security ID badge dangled uselessly from her chest.

"Oh my God."

CHAPTER 2:

A Taste of Death

The cats gathered around and licked the blood off the face of the former head of security. Cindy fell back and landed on her bottom. Her hand patted around the floor and stopped atop a slimy rock. Her fingers had poked into something soft and squishy. She looked down and shrieked when she saw her finger pushing an eyeball inside the skull of her shift supervisor. They were dead, they were all dead.

"Oh my God, Oh my God." Her hand trembled as she spoke into her radio. "Fourteen to Command One. I need—I need police officers at the lower level loading dock. 10-34 Young. Send a—" There was a hole the size of a quarter punched into the shift supervisor's head. She closed her eyes and held the radio with both hands. "—send a 10-54 Union."

The radio whistled and popped over a bed of buzzing noise. "Hello? Command One do you copy?" She couldn't hear anyone over the growling radio. "Are there any ESU units on this frequency? Hello?" She checked her boss and the shift supervisor's body for the master keys but they were missing. A sound of whispering in the windless corridors made her freeze where she was. There were men talking in hushed tones. Cindy pressed the radio to her chest and crouched next to the parked van.

"Did you hear something?" the voice said.

She steadied her breath but couldn't stop the pounding in her chest. Her neck and back ached from the stress flooding her system. She pushed against the driver's side door and listened. Heavy boots thumped over the crunch of loose asphalt. Each step jingled like keys or handcuffs. Was it the police? She leaned past the headlights for a better look.

A group of men, six from what she could gather, stood behind the open hatch of a delivery truck. A man wearing a bullet proof vest and gas mask climbed into the back of the truck and began prying open crates with a crowbar. Definitely not police, but they didn't look like Mubarizun terrorists either. For

17

starters, MOA members were poor and didn't have access to much equipment. These guys were unloading machineguns from the back of the truck. They must have been hired mercenaries, but who hired them?

Cindy tried to call 911 through her cell phone but she had no reception. She was connected to the Wi-Fi but for some reason the call wasn't going through.

"Probably a cat. You see how many are down here? It's like a cat house. Get it? Cat . . . house?"

"I got it you moron. And since when do cats sound like women?"

"Well they are puss—"

Cindy's radio screamed with distorted, ear splitting noise. "—up *static* Rep—me—ge." She frantically twisted the volume knob and shoved the speaker against her jacket.

"I knew there was something over there." The mercenary raised his gun.

Her sneakers squeaked against the floor. There were mechanical clicks of pregnant ammo box feeders being snapped onto their weapons.

"You were supposed to kill all the security guards."

"I did!"

Cindy bolted from the van and ran as hard as she could. She slid around a corner and crashed into the wall leading to the stairwell. The footsteps chased after her but she didn't dare look back. She tore up the stairwell steps and rammed through the heavy doors at the top. She slammed the doors shut and put all her weight against them. Her shirt became wet with fear as she waited for the doors to slam into her back but they never did. Did they stop chasing her?

A German Shepard lunged at Cindy with saliva spraying from its chomping maws; barking as it stood on its hind legs. She screamed and shielded her face. The officer from the K-9 unit yanked on its leash and gave the command to stand down. The dog immediately sat with its ears pointed at full attention.

"Sorry about Bishop," the officer said. "He's been acting weird."

"There's six gunmen downstairs, they've got guns, and—and I think they shot my boss, and they were chasing me—"

"Whoa, whoa, whoa slow down, take a breath, and tell me what you saw."

"I-I-I saw shooters at the loading dock."

"Shooters? Are you positive?"

She nodded.

His eyes went wide. "The mayor." The officer called on his radio only to be greeted by the same interference she encountered. "Something's wrong with the radio. Can you lock that door?"

"My boss was down there and she had the master key."

"Damn it. Okay. We need to find the mayor and get him out of here."

"I don't have a gun."

"That's okay, we got Bishop." He scratched the dog's neck. "Right boy? What's your name anyway?"

"Cindy."

"Cindy? Got it. You can call me Yang. C'mon, let's get going."

"We have to block this door first."

Cindy grabbed a nearby table and dragged it in front of the door. Officer Yang joined her and helped create a stockade of upside down chairs and plastic tables.

"Why haven't they barged through? They were right behind me." It was a rhetorical question she didn't mean to vocalize.

"Could be some kind of strategy. Maybe they know that if they come through here the ESU guys can shoot 'em from the upper level. Either way, we're moving out."

Officer Yang went up the escalator and urged her to follow. She didn't want to go, not without a gun, but he didn't leave her much choice. A security officer was supposed to get to safety, call the police, and give them an incident report. But they were also obligated to assist local police if asked. She eyed the exit doors a mere twenty paces away and for a brief, shameful moment, she considered leaving through them.

She had no gun, no badge, and no courage. Her hands were shaking and the sweat on her skin left her cold. Police Officer Ames didn't know what fear was. She would have led the charge instead of Yang. Security Guard Ames lived in fear, knew the kind of screw up Officer Ames was. The older she got, the less invincible she believed herself to be.

A gunshot rang from the floor above followed by the screams of thousands of guests. Their cries sounded almost identical to the people who died in the terror attack in France and those who were run over in Times Square. It didn't

A Bitter Winter

matter that she wasn't a cop anymore. What mattered was getting everyone to safety.

On the floor above Officer Yang and Cindy, the people stampeded down the escalator, pushing and shoving each other out of the way. She tucked her head and shouldered her way through the panicked herd. At the top of the escalator was the hall where Jonas's presentation had taken place, and where a massacre was currently underway.

Flashes of light were followed by the crack of gunfire. People landed on their knees and cupped the blood spilling out of their stomachs. Officer Yang drew out his service pistol and fired at a gunman shooting from an emergency exit. The gunman fell through the door with a scattered array of quarter sized holes in his chest. Another exit door thundered open. A gunman stepped through the entrance and aimed his gun at Cindy. All prior training had abandoned her. She froze in place, waiting for the gun barrel to explode. Officer Yang dropped the gunman before he could fire a single shot.

"Don't just stand there, Cindy! You're going get yourself killed."

Another gunman at the far end of the hall readied his light machine gun to fire. Officer Yang tried to take aim but hordes of running people kept getting in the way. He knelt down beside Bishop and unhooked the leash from his collar. "Bishop, arrest!"

Bishop's paws scratched along the carpet as he weaved between the legs of the running guests. The animal lunged at the gunman and chomped down on his arm. Bishop snarled as he savagely whipped the man's arm and tore fabric and flesh like paper. Officer Yang aimed his gun and was sucker punched by a gunman who had been hiding near the kiosks.

Until this moment, Cindy had been in a dream, carried by the whims of her nightmare. The threat to Officer Yang's life awakened her dormant training and reignited her innate desire to protect. She trapped the assailant's gun wielding arm with her hands and stretched it until the limb could go no farther. She delivered a palm strike to his elbow and burst the joint forward. His muffled howls bellowed from inside his gas mask. She tore off his mask and raked his face with her fingernails, kneed his stomach, and smashed his head with her elbows. Staggered and dazed, he fell to the floor.

"Holy crap," Officer Yang said. "You know how to fight. Thanks."

0

"I'm going to need a gun." Cindy bent down and picked up the assault rifle the gunman was carrying. To her great surprise, the gun spoke to her.

"Security breach, unauthorized user. Weapon is now locked."

"Are you kidding me?" She tried to pump the trigger but it wouldn't budge. "They have gun controls on this." She dropped the rifle and found a flashbang grenade on the unconscious mercenary.

Officer Yang fired at the gunman wrestling with Bishop. With the suspect dead, the dog returned to Yang's side. "Don't worry about the guns. We're getting out of here as soon as we find the mayor."

Officer Yang, in a lot of ways, reminded Cindy of who she had been. Decisive, brave, willing to put his life on the line for others. Fighting by his side reminded her of how much she wanted to be like him again.

Bishop sprinted over to the presentation stage and led Officer Yang and Cindy to the mayor's family and their security detail. Priscilla bawled inside of Carmen's arms. "Why are they doing this? Why are they killing all these people?" No amount of comforting from Carmen could stop her tears. Mayor Montez sat between his guards and nervously rubbed his hands together. He was quiet and isolated, even from his own family. Officer Yang approached the bodyguards while Cindy hung back.

Priscilla saw Cindy and her face suddenly filled with hope. "Mrs. Ames," she said as her cheeks glistened. "You used to be a cop. You can get us out of here right? You can save these people."

"We're going to get you all out of here." Cindy didn't believe her own words. She had lost her edge and had become useless in her time out of action. Deep down she knew their lives were dependent on Officer Yang and Bishop. If those two couldn't lead them through this mess, then they would all be dead. She thought about Jonas and Jadie. Were they still in the building? Did she need to go rescue them? Cindy checked her cell phone but it still didn't have any bars. The Wi-Fi must have been sabotaged.

Officer Yang got in her face. "Cindy? Did you hear what I said?"

"What? I'm sorry. I'm worried about my family."

"You got family here?"

"My husband and my sister."

"Mayor takes priority, then we find your people. Okay? I need you with me on this."

She nodded.

"We're going to move out as a group and make our way to the second level exit. Got it?"

"Yes."

"Good." Officer Yang turned to his dog. "Bishop, c'mere buddy."

The dog's ears perked up. Yang scratched Bishop's neck and tousled his fur. "I need you to keep an eye out for bad guys okay?" He patted Bishop's belly, stood up, and gave the command. "Search."

The group followed behind Bishop. He listened for the sounds of gunfire and kept the group away from those areas. As they walked past acres dead bodies, Mayor Montez grabbed Priscilla and covered her eyes. The expo had become a warzone. Kiosks were toppled over and used as make-shift cover for people who couldn't escape. The carpet was filled with brass casings, wood chips, and made wet squishing noises wherever they stepped. Cindy kicked herself for not having been able to do more to prevent the massacre. She should have known something was wrong at the loading dock, should have acted faster. It was such an obvious red flag. She couldn't believe how dense she was not to recognize the blood sooner.

Bishop stopped in the middle of the floor a mere twenty feet away from the fogged glass exit door. His ears stood on alert, eyes locked in front of him. Officer Yang told the bodyguards to keep an eye out. Though the space looked empty, Bishop could sense something was wrong.

"What does he see," Mayor Montez whispered.

"Trouble," Officer Yang replied. He loaded a fresh magazine into his Beretta; the bodyguard's did the same. The glass door opened. Seven gunmen stormed through the second level entrance with their guns pointed at the group. Bishop and Yang remained resolute and defiant. She wanted to be brave like them but couldn't seem to muster the courage. She stuck her hand into her security jacket pocket and threaded her thumb through the hoop of the flashbang grenade.

The lead gunman took off his gas mask. He had a spider web tattoo over his eye and a bald head. The gunman addressed one of the guards protecting the mayor.

"This wasn't a part of the plan, Boss. We shouldn't have lost this many guys." The bodyguard replied. "Yeah I know." He pulled out a Glock pistol from his jacket, spun around and blasted a hole into the forehead of the guard behind him. He shifted his aim then exploded Officer Yang's stomach. Another bodyguard revealed himself as an accomplice as he turned around and killed the last remaining bodyguard. With the security detail neutralized, the accomplice focused his aim on Mayor Montez.

"Dad!"

Cindy staggered back. Officer Yang and two bodyguards were dead. She had blinked and just like that, they were gone. Her only hope for survival had been taken away and now the mayor was next in line to receive a bullet. Time seemed to slow. Her senses became heightened. She could hear the firing pin slide back in the chamber, could smell cheap cologne, and tasted the salt from her own sweat. It was all up to her now.

She brought her foot back, harnessed the power of her hips, and threw a punch which rippled the accomplice's cheek. His gun popped off and shattered one of the thousands of glass windows surrounding the Javits Center. The rest of the gunmen took aim and she could feel their scopes lining up with her body. Cindy pulled the pin from the flashbang grenade and lobbed it into the group of killers.

"Grenade," they yelled.

A metallic pop blasted her ears. She quickly lost her balance and nausea rose up in her throat. The piercing tone reverberated inside her head. Blind and unable to see, she pushed on Mayor Montez's back not realizing they were next to the stairs. They rolled down the granite steps, groaning and yelling as their bones smacked against stone.

As the effects of the flashbang began to wear off, she could hear the hollering of the criminals on the level above and Bishop barking. "Get rid of the fucking dog!"

A dull thud echoed from the second level followed by Bishop yelping in pain.

"Ruuuun," Cindy yelled.

Mayor Montez huffed as Carmen and Priscilla sprinted for the exit. The mayor, drenched in sweat, wheezed from the burden of his own heavy weight and could run no more. She crashed into the winded mayor and urged him to keep moving. "You can't slow down, you can't slow down."

To which he replied, "I can't breathe."

A sharp, stabbing sensation punched her shoulder, followed by another. Her head snapped back and when she touched her lip, she wondered why there was blood on her fingers. The back of Mayor Montez's suit jacket burst into a wet rose. His face smacked the floor as more gunfire filled the lobby. Priscilla screamed for her father as Carmen pushed her through the doors where Cindy could feel the cold air blowing in. Her legs grew weak and she began to stumble until her palms slapped the floor. She looked over her shoulder with pain haunting her every breath. The bodyguard came down the stairs with smoke rising from his Glock. The rest of his team remained on the second level with their guns ready to fire.

The bodyguard grabbed onto his neck and ripped off his own face which had been a mask. Underneath, the man had a peppery goatee, long, balding stringy hair, and steely grey eyes. She remembered his face from two years ago, burned it into her memory after what he had done to her partner. The man's name was Ned Pickler, a.k.a. Death Dealer. He killed Cindy's partner in the line of duty and was the reason she had lost her job.

Despite the pain radiating from her wound, she dragged herself across the floor and left a smeared trail of her own blood. She crawled on top of Mayor Montez and shielded his body with her own.

"You," she said to Ned.

"Am I supposed to know you?"

Strings of red spittle flicked out of her mouth. "You killed my partner."

Ned shrugged. "I've killed a lot of people, Hon. Especially people who screw up my operations. I don't know you from Nancy." He raised his gun and pulled the trigger once. A hot punch burrowed into her belly. He fired again. Blood spurt from her chest. Her teeth chattered from the sudden chill spreading through her limbs. She wondered if Jonas was safe, wondered if Jadie had . . . if . . . if the lobby had always been this cold.

CHAPTER 3:

Tissue Engineering

Jonas watched the nurses rip open Cindy's shirt and pump her full of drugs to keep her alive. He followed the stretcher to the boundary of the Operating Room where a nurse stopped him from going farther. This wasn't the first time he had to watch his wife be taken to the OR, but it was the first time he worried it would be her last.

He spied Jadie leaning against the wall with her arms crossed and her head down. She clearly didn't want to be bothered so he wandered off to the waiting room. He paced back and forth while thinking back to those awful late nights when Cindy would be out on a dangerous night patrol. He'd kiss her goodbye, tell her to be safe, and then wait by his phone. He would play video games or watch TV to keep himself occupied but it never worked. She was always on his mind.

One night, she was late checking in. For five hours he paced around the house wondering if she was all right. When she came home, there were bandages all over her arm and cuts on her fingers. She had been ambushed during a vertical patrol, but to hear her talk about it made it seem as if it was just another day at the office. He didn't want to experience that kind of anxiety ever again. That's when he decided that SIRCA needed to be completed sooner rather than later.

Before he married her, the SIRCA prototype existed as a clump of spare parts and incompatible software. Once nanomachines became a reality, so did his dream. He spent all of his money and . . . unfortunately, all of Cindy's money, to build an invention which could define an era, like the wheel, or the plane. If only he could have finished the prototype sooner . . . They would have been in a cab heading home, talking about the craziest night of their lives. After a few minutes of fretting over Cindy, Jonas was eventually joined by his friend and employee, Michael Dresden.

A Bitter Winter

They met at MIT. Michael was studying computer science while Jonas was earning a Master's in mathematics. One day on his way to class, Jonas witnessed Michael trying to get a phone number from a girl. He watched as Michael fumbled over his words with sweat staining his underarms. The girl didn't want anything to do with a nervous wreck and politely let him down. Jonas felt bad for the kid, so he took him aside, told him how he could improve his game, and a friendship was formed (though Michael never really did get the hang of talking to women). If it wasn't for Michael—who'd known Cindy's family since childhood—Jonas never would have met her. He still didn't understand why Cindy and Jadie were the only women Michael never had a problem talking to.

"Hey," Michael whispered. "Just got off the phone with Sid. Everyone's home, safe and sound."

Jonas was relieved to hear his Lucent Labs team made it back in one piece. "What about the prototype?"

"Back at the lab."

"Did you bring what I asked for?"

"Yeah, I did." Michael dug into his pockets and handed Jonas a brown bottle and a plastic bag full of an assortment of medical tools. "I don't know about this."

Jonas studied the bottle Michael had given him. Inside the vial was an untested compound designed to accelerate cellular regeneration to an extraordinary rate. Unfortunately, it had not yet undergone any human trials.

"Maybe I won't need to use it," he said to Michael.

"If Raymond finds out he'll cancel buying us out."

Jadie barged in between them. "What are you guys talking about?"

Jonas quickly slipped the bottle into his pocket while Michael changed topics.

"I was telling Jonas how we're grateful you got us all out of there in one piece. If you hadn't convinced Jonas to exit the building, we'd probably still be there."

"Yeah . . . well I didn't get everyone."

"Uh." Michael cleared his throat. "Anyone want a coffee?"

"I'll take one," Jonas said.

Jadie shook her head no.

They sat around in the waiting room. Jonas held a paper cup in his hands while Jadie tapped her foot and continually sighed. Michael watched Impress news on his phone, feeding himself with updates on the Javits massacre. After a few hours, the three of them had fallen asleep from exhaustion.

"Mr. Ames?"

Jonas gasped and opened his eyes. A petite woman stood before him wearing a white lab coat and green scrubs.

"Sorry, I didn't mean to startle you."

"That's okay." He cleared his throat. "Are you . . ."

"Dr. Brock. I'm the surgeon who operated on your wife."

Jonas sat forward and wiped the drool from his lip. "What time is it?"

"It's almost four in the morning."

"Jesus." He rubbed away the crust on his eyelids. Both Michael and Jadie were still asleep with their heads resting against each other. "How is she?"

Dr. Brock looked down and clasped her hands together. "She's stable."

"But?"

"I'm not sure for how long."

"What does that mean?"

"Even if she somehow manages to pull through, the amount of shrapnel still left in her body could potentially reopen her wounds and cause her to hemorrhage."

"So take it out."

"It's too dangerous. The remaining fragments of shrapnel are located near major arteries. If we pull one out and the artery bleeds, we won't be able to stop it."

Jonas nodded. "So there's a risk she'll die."

"We've done all we can. It's going to be up to her now."

Jonas wasn't a medical doctor, but he knew what Dr. Brock meant. The boundaries of modern medical science had been reached and it still wasn't enough to save his wife. He needed to turn to something more extreme, more cutting edge.

He quietly stood up, careful not to wake Jadie and Michael.

"I'd like to see her in private."

"Of course."

A Bitter Winter

Cindy's room was dark and quiet with a single wall light starkly illuminating her head. Oxygen tubes breathed into her nose and IV lines pumped her forearm with morphine. An EKG monitor chirped beside her bed, displaying readings of a dangerously low heart rate on an LCD screen. Even with some of her make up still intact, her skin looked pallid and drained of life. As he approached the bed he could still smell the perfume lingering on her skin: Cinnamon, spruce, and pomegranate. She smelled like Christmas and the fond memories of nibbling her lips under the mistletoe. He kissed each of her knuckles and held her warm hand against his cheek.

He emptied his pockets onto a nearby table. He laid out cotton swab sticks, an empty petri dish, scissors, latex gloves, tape, and an amber colored bottle. The sealed container had a handwritten label that read CRC-T298. Cellular Regeneration Catalyst Trial two hundred and ninety-eight.

After almost three hundred attempts, Jonas's employee, a bioengineer by the name of Dr. Charlie Hudson had successfully created a compound which regrew muscle and skin tissue on a mouse that had been nearly split in half. In four weeks, the mouse was able to scurry around as if it had been freshly born. Though the test was illegal and the mouse later died of complications, the research data gained was invaluable. Charlie iterated on the compounds and claimed to have solved the tumor issue caused by his formula.

Still, like all untested prototypes, there was a risk. He had to decide whether he believed Cindy was strong enough to recover on her own or give her a potentially dangerous formula to accelerate her healing. The thought of doing nothing was unbearable. They were still newlyweds in a sense, less than two years. There were so many things he still wanted to experience with her, so many places to visit, he didn't want to do these things without her by his side.

He lifted Cindy's hospital gown. There were several layers of bandages wrapped around her stomach and adhesive patches stuck to her chest. Jonas snapped on a pair of latex gloves, grabbed the scissors off the table, and carefully cut through the bandages. He pulled off a layer of linen and exposed the gauze pad. He dug his latex covered fingernails beneath the rounded plastic layer and carefully peeled it back. Underneath the browned bandage was a gaping bloody hole still fresh from surgery.

Jonas turned away and coughed into his elbow. He grabbed a cotton swab and carefully brushed along the circumference of her wound until the tip browned. Then he deposited the collected samples into the petri dish. He unscrewed the formula cap and poured clear liquid onto the sample. Pink foam bubbled inside the disc and fizzed like soda. Jonas grabbed a new cotton swab and mixed the liquid until it solidified into a mucus like goop. He lifted the stick and watched slime drip off the white fuzzy tip. Already the compound began to harden into a flaky, unusable crust. He had to apply it quickly.

As he carefully brought the formula over to Cindy, someone knocked on the door.

"Mr. Ames. Jadie would like to see her sister."

The petri dish had layers of crust floating on its surface. Barely two seconds had passed and already it was turning into useless powder. Jonas shot up from his seat with the cotton swab dripping from his hand. He grabbed his chair and dragged it across the room. The door slightly opened and he slammed it shut in response. Jonas wedged the chair under the door handle and backed away.

"Mr. Ames, please open the door."

Jonas ran back. Islands of hard, useless powder formed within the petri dish. He vigorously stirred the cotton swab and slathered it onto Cindy's gaping wound. A pink foam bubbled from within the hole and hissed. The EKG monitor spiked. Cindy's heart rate gradually began to increase.

"Come on, come on, just a little more."

"Mr. Ames, open this door right now or I will call security."

The EKG chirped faster. As the formula boiled inside her wounds, Cindy writhed. Her head jerked from side to side with torture visible on her pinched face. Still, Jonas applied more formula. The chemicals sizzled her skin like grease on a skillet.

"Jonas what are you doing in there," Jadie yelled.

"Open the door!"

He pet her hair and profusely apologized. "I'm sorry. It'll be over soon, I promise."

The formula dried into an elastic layer of skin as thin as soap scum. He restrained his wife and applied more formula in order to create a canopy of artificial skin. In a few seconds, the freshly birthed cells would begin knitting her skin together. The EKG rang the alarm and alerted the medical staff to come immediately. Cindy arched her back and screamed as if she were lit on fire. She thrashed and snapped the IV line out of her arm which spewed morphine all over her bed and gown. Jonas backed away to the wall, terrified of the spasms taking control of his wife.

Cindy went limp. The EKG let out a steady, unbroken tone.

"Cindy?"

A security team burst through the door followed by Dr. Brock. She saw the flat line on the monitor and glared at Jonas as he stood against the wall.

"What did you do?"

"I tried to save her."

"Get him out of here, now!"

*　　*　　*

"Mayor Manny Montez is in critical condition after a terrorist attack at the Jacob K. Javits center left sixty dead and at least a hundred people wounded. Officer Yang Shen from the K-9 unit was among those dead, survived by his K-9 partner, Bishop who suffered a fractured rib. Counter terrorism experts suspect MOA, also known as the Mubarizun of Allah, may have been behind tonight's attack. The Black Rook, leader of MOA, has yet to claim responsibility for the attack. After the break, we interview NYPD Police Commissioner Patrick Gates for more details on this horrific attack."

"Jonas." Cindy moaned with her eyes closed. "It's so loud. Turn off the TV."

She awoke suddenly as if startled from a dream. TV commercials droned on in the corner of her room. Light stung her hazel eyes. The wind howled as it whipped the snow outside. Ice crystallized on the window, crackling and crunching as fat snowflakes splattered against the glass. The air had a strange smell to it, like drugs and linen wrap. The annoying beep of an EKG monitor rang in her ear.

She uttered a feeble groan. Her memory was clouded by a soupy fog. She knew this was a hospital room but didn't remember how or when she got there. She looked up at the TV and saw Commissioner Gates being interviewed by a reporter. The lower third read: Massacre at Javits. Her memory came back on a river of corpses. She remembered Officer Yang, and the mayor, and relived that sickening feeling of powerlessness all over again. She winced as she reached for the remote holstered by her bed and raised the volume.

"I want to make it very clear that this was a well-coordinated, well-funded attack. They had jamming devices, body armor, and robust military grade equipment. These guys came to play hard ball and managed to slow down our units with roadblocks and diversions which significantly delayed our response time."

The reporter asked, "How did the mayor stay behind while you and Senator Albright escaped?"

Commissioner Gates took a moment to think on his answer. "Senator Albright had plans to leave before the start of the presentation. I offered to walk with him to the exit and that's when the shooting started. I was not allowed to return to the premises once we had been evacuated."

"There were reports that a Javits security officer had delayed the terrorists long enough for the Emergency Services Unit to intervene."

"False. Officer Yang and his K-9 Bishop were the real heroes tonight, never forget that. No further questions."

That dickhead. She turned off the TV and held the remote in her hands. Maybe he was right. Had she been able to save the mayor then she would've been the one giving the interviews. Cindy leaned her head into the pillow. She brought both hands to her face and allowed herself to sob.

"You fucked up," a gravelly voice spoke.

Cindy snapped her hands away and looked around the empty room.

"Hello?"

She wiped her eyes and glanced at the TV thinking she had forgotten to turn it off, but the screen was black. She looked at a corner of the room where there was an unnerving pillar of blackness. Little hairy insect-like arms emerged from the black, writhing against the walls, creating legions of spiders which crawled up to the ceiling. They're not real, they can't be real. She tried to squirm out of her bed but her legs seemed frozen.

A man stepped out of the blackness with ropes of tar dangling from his webbed, pink skin. He wore a burned navy blue uniform covered in ash and soot over his burnt body. In his mangled hands the bones of his fingers could be seen between the gaps in his flesh, he held a Glock pistol.

The lines of the EKG monitor beeped closer together. The man crossed the foot of her bed with dead, cloudy eyes. His face was peeled and deformed with random tufts of hair sprouting from the fleshy craters of his bald head. She began to hyperventilate and let out a quivering moan of fear.

The uniformed man raised his gun and pointed it at her.

"You died," she whimpered. "You're not real."

"You owe me." His voice carried the growl of a lion, almost demonic in pitch. A red hot bullet screamed out of his gun and punched her chest. She blurted out a blood curdling scream which fattened the veins in her neck. More bullets ripped open her flesh and left her in an excruciating loop of agony. Alarms rang from the health monitors. The door to her room slammed open and as she heard the people enter, she screamed louder and thrashed in her bed. A hand reached for her head. Cindy ripped away and screeched until her throat burned raw.

She threw her elbows across her chest, fighting off the hands trying to restrain her. The room caught fire. Flames crawled along the walls, crossed the ceiling, and dripped down to her hospital gown setting it ablaze. She smacked her legs to put out the fire and tore open her hospital gown. The embers latched onto her arm and roasted her skin into boils.

"I'm burning, I'm burning!"

"Okay," Another woman's voice spoke aloud in a soothing manner. "I'm just going to increase your dosage and then you'll feel much better."

The fire sucked away as if someone had turned off the stove. Her burnt partner had disappeared and her arm was smooth and untouched. There were people standing around her bed and an older couple whom she recognized as her parents. It had all felt so real. Her eyelids grew heavy. Time became separated by black flashes as her eyes slowly closed and snapped open. She tried to resist, tried to stay awake despite her body growing weaker. She was afraid that if she fell asleep, the burned man would return.

Her mom told her not to fight it. She promised everything would be okay, that mom and dad were here. Cindy rolled her eyes and succumbed to the pull of sleep.

CHAPTER 4:

Fragmented

Cindy returned home to Forest Hills, in February, a time where the winter makes the northeast miserable. She flared the bedroom curtain. Sunlight poured in and bathed the bedroom in soft light. She watched the neighborhood kids pelt each other with snowballs and felt longing for a time when she would have been the one out there flinging snowballs at her sister. They released her from the hospital two weeks ago with orders to maintain daily physical therapy in order to rebuild the deteriorated muscles in her shrunken legs.

Seeing the snow reminded her of the dump she used to live in during her probationary officer days. She could only afford rent for a cramped apartment in West New York where the radiators ran hot and could not be shut off or turned down. One time, she went to her neighbor's apartment to ask for some half and half for her coffee. When they opened the door, snow blasted out the doorway. They had left their windows open in the middle of a blizzard because it was too hot inside their apartment. She thought it was hilarious.

So winter sucked, but the spring and summer was magical. Cindy and her neighbors would wait until the sun was red and peeking from behind the buildings. They would go up to the rooftop and haul coolers filled with beers, soda, and food. They would decorate with hanging lights and gather around a smoking grill where someone volunteered to cook juicy hot dogs and hamburgers. But her favorite dishes were the tamales and tostadas brought by the Latino neighbors. They drank from ice cold beers and shared funny stories until the sky became purple with boredom.

Forest Hills was nothing like that. For starters, she and Jonas lived in a small, but pricey Tudor mansion. He didn't know his neighbor's names and didn't utilize the backyard to throw parties. They had a driveway instead of a parking garage and the second floor to their house was theirs alone, meaning no squeaky beds and moaning neighbors to keep them up at night. Though she loved the space and the ability to adjust the thermometer, she still longed for a community. At least then, whenever she became ill, a neighbor would come over with chicken soup or medicine and she would repay the favor with whatever they needed. Jonas made her happy, but he wasn't an apartment building full of friends.

Cindy closed the curtain and sat up. Sharp pains hooked into her stomach with each subtle movement. She lifted her shirt and touched the misshapen holes carved into her stomach. Each scar was a gift from Ned, unique in their grotesque shape and size.

She found it disturbing that before she lost consciousness, there had been Christmas decorations on her neighbor's house and a Christmas tree in the corner of her living room. She didn't get to see the New Year's Eve ball drop and didn't know it *was* a new year until Jonas had told her.

Sixty two days had gone by and she had missed all of it. Being absent from your own life was more terrifying than a squad of heavily armed hit men. What happened during those weeks that she was gone? She imagined falling asleep as a pre-teen and then waking up as an old woman. She would have never experienced a first kiss, driving, going to college, or even becoming a woman. Anxiety and fear closed around her weakened mind and blocked out rational thought. *You're worthless, a coward, a complete and utter . . .* she heard a dog bark. Not a big dog, but a small one, like a Chihuahua. An annoying little yipe.

The bark repeated a few more times and was joined by lively trumpets, drums, and a man singing El Baile del Perrito at full volume. The bass boomed with such vigor, the photos from her honeymoon danced across the wooden dresser.

"Oh no," she said. "He's cleaning."

The lyrics marched into her ears with its irritating repetition and that annoying bark. The Spanish lyrics literally translated to: the dance of the dog, the dance of the dog, everyone wants to dance. Cindy grabbed her crutches, shoved them under her arms, and followed the jaunty tune to the living room.

Jonas stood behind the vacuum cleaner, bouncing his shoulders as he pushed and pulled the vacuum. Each time the dog barked, Jonas would shimmy his ass left then right with the vacuum motor changing in pitch as it rolled back and forth.

"Jonas."

The dog barked. Right then left. Left then right.

"Jonas."

He looked up from the vacuum and finally saw her. He smiled and pushed the vacuum closer to her feet. He yelled over the suction and music, "I thought you were sleeping in?"

"I was trying to."

"What?"

A little louder. "I was trying to."

Jonas spun around with the vacuum and twerked in sync with the barking.

"Oh my God." She giggled. "Something's wrong with you."

Jonas turned off the vacuum and danced his way to Cindy. He carefully took away her crutches and draped her arms around his neck. He gyrated his hips while holding onto hers. She couldn't help but smile. "You're silly."

He danced her in a circle but was careful not to move her too hard. The man had moves. She didn't know if it was because he was Latino or if someone in his family taught him how to dance, but Jonas had great rhythm.

She found herself mesmerized by his brown eyes and his sexy smile. He had a nice slim torso but not much of a muscular build. Not that it mattered, she liked his butt . . . and his intelligence, of course. When the song ended, she tried to pull him in for a kiss and instead fell when her legs slipped from under her.

"Whoops." Jonas grabbed her underarms. "Someone's been drinking."

The room began to spin. Her breaths became quicker and shorter. The thumping in her chest made the veins in her head throb with blood. She began sweating profusely as she remembered being overwhelmed by hitmen. She clutched Jonas's sleeve and almost ripped it from holding so tight.

"Hey . . ." Jonas held her steady. "Are you all right?"

She thought of Officer Yang and Bishop and the powerlessness she felt when Ned turned the gun on him. But the most powerless feeling of all was when Ned didn't remember her. Was she that worthless? Jonas carried her to the couch and sat her down.

"You feeling better?"

"I'm fine."

"You don't look fine."

A Bitter Winter

Amazing how quickly a bad memory could sour her mood. "I feel like I shouldn't be here."

Jonas rubbed her arm. "What do you mean?"

She rested her head against his soft chest. "Before I got shot, I asked Ned if he remembered me. And he looked at me and said, 'I don't know you from Nancy.' I was so meaningless, that it didn't matter whether I lived or died. And it makes me feel like I should have been in the morgue instead of Officer Yang."

"Cindy." He kissed the crown of her head. "Don't say things like that."

"I'm just telling the truth. I couldn't protect the mayor, couldn't protect Officer Yang, I couldn't do anything. I was the statistic, the meaningless extra who gets killed in the movies by the bad guy."

"You did what you could."

"Officer Yang and Bishop were the real heroes. All I did was get in the way and let everyone down." Cindy thought about how she ended up in Javits in the first place. After being fired from the force, she had planned to sustain herself with money from her gymnastics school, but it wasn't enough. Jonas had taken her police savings without asking. She pulled away and glared at him.

He seemed confused by her change in demeanor. "What?"

"I need to talk to you about something, a few things actually."

He sighed. "It's going to be one of *those* talks, isn't it?"

"The only reason I was working at Javits was because I needed to pay for a house I couldn't afford on my own."

"Are we really going to argue about this again?"

"You stole all the money from my savings account and used it for your inventions. You spent all of my money, yet I was the one who had to work two jobs."

Jonas clenched his jaw.

"So I ended up getting shot because you couldn't support this household anymore," she said. "I think what upsets me the most is that you didn't ask me. You just took it thinking my savings belonged to you."

"So you're going to put all the blame on me?"

"I really want to."

Jonas slumped forward. "I already apologized, Cindy. There isn't a day that goes by where I don't feel terrible for what I did. If you want to blame me, blame me. But I promise I will make it up to you. I know I'm very lucky you chose to stay with me."

She felt better for finally getting that off her chest, but there was still one more thing. Jonas wasn't the only one who had done something shameful.

"What now?" he said.

"I have a confession."

"Go on."

She toyed with her fingers. "I'm only bringing this up because I have a guilty conscience."

"Just tell me already."

Cindy grabbed her crutches. "We need to go to the basement."

"What's in the basement?"

"Hopefully not another fight."

Cindy led Jonas downstairs, one wobbly step at a time. He flipped the light switch which turned on a single lightbulb. Not much was down in the basement except for some cobwebs, old computer monitors and printers from the nineties. Why he kept this junk she never understood. Stacked along the walls and shelves were dusty boxes filled with old Halloween and Christmas decorations.

"Why are we down here?"

She pointed to a shelf. "Pull that out."

"This one?" Jonas gave the shelf a hard tug. He tripped backwards as the shelf rolled forward. "I don't remember putting wheels on this."

"I did."

The shelf led into a hidden room the size of a closet. A motion sensor light flashed on and illuminated a corkboard wall. Dozens of photos and newspaper clippings with hand written notes were pinned to it: *Burned corpse wearing an NYPD uniform found in freight container. Rise in shootings linked to Death Dealer smuggling operations. Police seize thirteen million dollars in drug money, possible link to Death Dealer.* There were maps of each of the five boroughs with red lines drawn between them. The Bronx, Queens, Manhattan, Brooklyn, Staten Island, all had red x's with a note that read, *Dead end. Interview with suspects imply Ned's base of operations is not within city limits.*

"What is this," Jonas said.

"I've been lying to you when I said I was working late night security jobs. I've actually been collecting intelligence."

"It looks like a serial killer lives down here." He grabbed a notebook and rifled through the pages. "Every page is full. There's even notes in the margin." He looked at her. "This is all about Ned. How long . . . ?"

"Since the day I got fired."

"Two years, are you insane?" He pored through the pages. "Brownsville, East New York. You could've gotten yourself killed going to these places. You were stabbed in Brownsville for crying out loud! We agreed, no more police work."

"You stole money from me and I went looking for the man who killed my partner."

"It's not the same thing and you know it," he snapped. Jonas put the notebook down and took a breath. "So why did you show this to me? You could've kept this room a secret and I never would have known."

"If you want me to forgive you, you need to forgive me. It's a new year, I want to wipe the slate clean."

"Let's say I agree. What happens to the stuff in this room?"

"I want to be the one that catches Ned, but I don't think I've got what it takes anymore. I'll turn this over to the police."

"If you get rid of this stuff, I'll call it even."

She glanced at the photos where two years of sleepless nights were stuck to the walls with tape. The thought of getting rid of it all seemed preposterous.

"Cindy . . ."

She nodded her head. "Okay."

An hour and a half later, Jonas helped Cindy shower, get dressed, and sat her at the dining room table where breakfast was served. She told Jonas that her documents were to go to the police. What she didn't tell him was that she was planning to hand deliver them to Commissioner Gates. If anyone would utilize a how-to guide on catching Ned, it would be the father who lost his son to him.

Jonas pointed to her plate of strawberry crepes with whipped cream. "Dig in."

A juicy release of strawberry fruit and banana filled her mouth. She moaned with pleasure. "Oh God," she said with one hand covering her mouth. "You are such a good cook."

Jonas grinned. "Way better than the protein shakes you usually drink."

"You're going to make me fat." She smiled. "Thank you for breakfast."

The front doorbell rang and interrupted her sip of orange juice. She looked at Jonas. "Are you expecting someone?"

"Umm . . . No." He wiped his mouth with a napkin and stood up. "Wait here." Cindy put down her glass. She grabbed a butter knife and hid it under the table.

Jonas opened the door and let in the cold air and brilliant light. "Hey what are you doing here?" Jonas shook Michael's gloved hand. "Come in, come in."

Michael had dressed as if he were going on a Siberian expedition with a sled of Huskies. Cindy let out a sigh of relief and set her whipped cream covered knife back on the plate.

"Hey Cindy." Michael waved happily as he took his jacket off.

"Hey you!" Cindy spread her arms wide for a hug.

He waved his hands with a sarcastic flair. "No, no please. Don't get up." Michael trekked across the living room carpet and left a track of snow prints. He bent over and squeezed Cindy in his arms.

"How are you feeling? Any side effects? Mutations? Have you turned green and burst out of your clothes yet?"

Jonas made a slashing motion across his neck. Cindy looked at him, confused, then turned to Michael. "What are you talking about?"

"Oh, just . . . you know. Feels like you're getting strong. They putting steroids in your medicine?" He pretended to lift weights and growled.

She smiled. "Just painkillers."

"Is that body wash I smell? Did you actually shower today?"

"It was about that time, you know."

Jonas meandered over to the kitchen fridge. "You want something to drink?"

"No thanks. I'm not going to stay too long. Just wanted to make sure you were taking care of my ex-girlfriend."

"You wish." Ah, Michael. He always had an uncanny ability to make her smile and forget about the things troubling her. The only problem was, she knew he had a crush on her and though he wasn't an unattractive man, she never felt a strong passionate connection to him. Physically he was fine, piercing blue eyes, short, faux hawk styled black hair. And though he was intelligent and funny, she could never shake the little brother vibe she got from him. Jadie liked him, but he never seemed interested in her which was, in her opinion, absolutely bizarre.

Jonas closed the fridge and glared at Michael.

"Oh, I almost forgot." Michael pulled out a get well card from his pocket and handed it to her.

She hid the card before Jonas could see it. She wasn't sure what Michael had written on it and didn't want to risk Jonas getting jealous. From under the table she peeked at the card and read it.

If bullet wounds have an ass, kick it.

With love, from your friend,

Michael.

P.S.

No seriously you can't die on me. I don't want Jonas to take all the girls again.

She thanked Michael and kissed him on the cheek. "So quick question. You guys never finished the demo. Is everything going to be okay?

"Uh, yeah, we'll be fine" Michael said. "But I do need to chat with Jonas about work stuff."

Jonas grabbed his coat and went to the front door. "Let's walk."

"Bye Cindy." Michael hugged her again. "Call me when you're feeling better. I'll take you out to dinner, my treat."

"Deal. Thank you for coming."

Now that Jonas was gone and she had the house to herself, it was time to give Jadie a call.

CHAPTER 5:

Empty Apologies

No matter how hard she tried, Cindy couldn't shake the memories of Javits. Her thoughts would reach over and touch her shoulder, causing her to relive her painful near-death experience in vivid detail. Trauma, she learned, was not only physical pain, it was a mental lashing which left her paranoid and afraid of the world. Dying was easy. Once the pain was over, it was over. Living, carried guilt. She would never forget the way Priscilla looked at her when Mayor Montez was shot in the back.

In hindsight, she never should have punched the mole bodyguard or popped the flashbang grenade. Doing so bound her to an unspoken oath: *I will save you and your father.* Her failure to do so left her feeling like a liar. She had to apologize to Priscilla for letting her down, for making her believe her gymnast teacher was some kind of hero.

Before Cindy could drop off her Manila folder filled with information on Ned to the police, she asked Jadie to take her north, to Gracie Mansion, the mayor's home which resided on the walled off coast of the East River. Unlike the neighboring apartment condos and brownstones, Gracie Mansion was a villa. A two story Federalist style home where the floor boards once creaked under the boots of Alexander Hamilton. She imagined what the building and city looked like the day it was built, when horse carriages trotted down cobblestone paths. After checking in with security and receiving permission from Carmen, Cindy went upstairs to visit Priscilla.

Her room had a big screen TV mounted on a wall and a laptop sitting atop an antique desk hundreds of years old. There were posters of boy bands, comic book superheroes, and spelled out wooden letters that read: *I'm not here to be average. I'm here to be awesome.*

Priscilla sat hunched on her bed. Even with the sunlight pouring in from the windows, the room seemed a mournful blue. Cindy shifted on her crutches and suddenly she wasn't sure what to say.

"How are you?" She kicked herself for such a stupid question.

"Fine."

"I just wanted to come by and apologize."

"For what?" Priscilla sounded disinterested.

"For not being able to protect your dad."

"Oh." Priscilla sank into her chest. "You didn't have to come all the way here to say that."

"I know. But I wanted to make sure you were all right. Going through something like that is . . . scary. Gives people bad dreams."

"Did my mom tell you I've been having nightmares about him?"

She shook her head no. "I just know that they happen sometimes."

"I'm scared to go to sleep because I'm afraid I'm going to see his chest explode. He's like a zombie and he's always trying to grab me, like he wants me to become like him. I hate it."

Cindy shifted back and forth on the pegs of her crutches. The guilt squeezed her chest. No teenager should have dreams of their parents dying, now she felt worse for stirring up bad memories. It was all so wrong, visiting Priscilla was a bad idea.

"The nightmares will go away with time."

"No offense, Mrs. Ames but it's been two months. I don't want to talk about it."

Cindy nodded. "Okay."

"And honestly, there's nothing to apologize for. You did what you could and I appreciate that. I just wish a professional could've been there to save my dad."

Cindy winced as if she had been slapped in the face. "Because what could a part-time security guard do?"

"Yeah."

She lowered her head and lurched out of Priscilla's room. Carmen and Jadie had been waiting outside, discussing how the attack on Mayor Montez affected both Cindy and Priscilla. When she came out, they turned to her and asked how the meeting went. "It was fine." Carmen offered for an aide to take them home, but Cindy declined. Instead she went downstairs with Jadie and stepped into the brisk, winter air.

Jadie kept pace with her as she hobbled down the driveway. "I'm going to guess the conversation totally wasn't fine."

"Yup."

"So what happened?"

"She told the truth."

"Which was?"

"That I'm a sorry sack of shit."

"Pretty sure she didn't say that."

"She didn't need to."

The pegs of Cindy's crutches landed on a glassy sheen of asphalt. She slipped and fell on black ice, smacking her chin before Jadie could catch her. She imagined Priscilla looking out the window, seeing her teacher rolling about the ice like a useless baby. She imagined Commissioner Gates and her former colleagues on the force looking at her, laughing at her, making fun of how stupid she looked.

"Damn it," she screamed.

Jadie reached for Cindy's arm which she quickly tore away. "Get off."

"Sis."

She clawed into the slick asphalt. "I'm fine, just leave me alone."

But Jadie ignored her and helped her up anyway. Cindy was forced to utter a begrudging thank you.

"Next time let me help instead of being all melodramatic."

"I want a drink. Haven't had one since I got married."

"Dude, it's like, not even three yet."

Cindy's crutches left hollow dots in the slush filled driveway. "You coming or not?"

The sisters boarded a train heading downtown towards the monolithic obelisk called One World Trade center. They swayed from side to side with the gyrations of the train and leaned forward when it braked before pulling into station. The doors opened and a group of men holding conga drums paraded into the car. They sat down in between two opposing doors and erected their drums. The car door chimed. "Stand clear of the closing doors please."

The train jerked forward, causing everyone to stumble backward. The musicians patted their drums and sang the names of each stop. "Next stop," The musician announced, "Fulton Street. Have a great day ladies and gentlemen and God bless you all." This was typical New York City. It didn't matter if you were having a crappy day or were in a bad mood. Someone will eventually interrupt your life and either make you smile or more pissed off. She gave the drummers two bucks and left with a slight smile on her face.

They arrived at a bar called Murphy's. Jadie had never been, but Cindy's partner, Dan dragged her here after they graduated academy and again when they were no longer probationary officers. Not only did Murphy's boast a diverse selection of Irish brews, but it also had the convenience of being only a few blocks away from police headquarters. Jadie opened the wooden door to the bar which let loose The Dubliners – Whiskey in the Jar. Banjos thrummed over speakers as singers with authentic Irish accents sang into their microphones.

Jadie locked down two barstools and helped Cindy to her seat before sitting on her own. She dropped their purses to the floor and squeezed them between her boots. Jadie smiled at the cute bartender and raised two fingers. He smiled back and gave her two beers.

Cindy clinked Jadie's bottle and said, "Thank you. For keeping Jonas safe."

"You're thanking *me*? Ho, ho, are you already drunk and I'm just late to the party?"

Cindy guzzled a quarter of her bottle. "Not yet. But I'll get there." She placed her bottle down and shook Jadie's forearm. "Seriously though. Thank you. It means a lot to me."

"Wow, you are being serious. Okay, then yes, you're welcome." Jadie took a swig from her bottle. "Wish I could've helped you though."

Cindy guzzled the rest of her drink. "Oh I'm beyond help." She held up the empty bottle and danced it in front of the bartender. He popped another one open and handed it to Cindy.

Jadie took a sip and held the bottle in her hand. "You know dad's going to be pissed if he finds out that we're drinking."

"I wasn't planning on telling him. Were you?"

Jadie shook her head no.

"I don't care if dad finds out anyway. It's Jonas I'm worried about."

"Yeah well you might want to slow down, just a suggestion."

Cindy needed to drink, only a little bit though. Just enough to give her some liquid courage before her next potentially boneheaded decision. She eyed the Manilla folder in her purse and convinced herself that giving this to Commissioner Gates could lead to beautiful, wonderful things. But with the energetic music in the background and the patrons cheering at the super bowl on TV, Cindy found herself saying "this is my last one," two, three, four more times throughout the afternoon. And the more she drank, the more the keg storing her pent up rage began to leak.

She saw the way the men were checking her sister out. Jadie fit the description of a super model, tall, leggy, blessed with long wavy blonde hair, radiant blue eyes. All the physical traits she wanted for herself. Cindy glared at her reflection in the bar mirror and hated the ugly, withered woman who looked back.

"Useless bitch."

Jadie spun in her seat. "Excuse me?"

"Not you." Cindy blinked a few times. "I think I need to stop."

"Ya think?"

A douchebag sat next to Jadie. Cindy thought of him as a douchebag because he sat down all smooth, sliding his arm across the bar counter with a stupid razor cut through his eyebrow. He spoke softly and slowly, like a typical punk looking for a garage to park his car. And the only thing he had to say to set off her internal warning alarm was, "Buy you a drink?"

Cindy leaned over the bar counter. "Don't talk to her."

"What'd I do," he said.

Jadie turned around and raised her finger. "Sis, don't start."

"He looks like a scumbag."

"That's unusually judgy of you."

"He's unoriginal. Buy you a drink? C'mon."

"God your breath is . . . retched. Was there dog shit in your beer? How many did you have?"

Cindy slowly drifted her eyes over to the bar counter where eight empty beer bottles stood. She then turned her wobbling head to Jadie.

"Those aren't mine."

"Don't make me regret bringing you here, Sis. The last time you got like this you walked up to a girl in a diner, flexed those bulging biceps of yours, and punched her in the face for calling me a whore."

"I do not recall."

"Good thing no one else did because you wouldn't have been hired as a cop."
Cindy angrily stumbled off her stool. "You saying I'm not good enough to
be a cop?"

"No, God, relax." Jadie helped Cindy back onto her seat. "Don't embarrass me."

"Look." Cindy held out her hands. "Do you see a drink in my hands? Do you
see a drink? No. Why did she call you a whore anyway? I don't remember."

"Because she ended up like you."

"She lost her job? How do you know that, you asked her?"

"No, stupid," Jadie said annoyed. "She got plastered."

"Oh."

"You're the older one, why am I babysitting you?"

"What are you now, like twenty two?"

"Twenty six."

"Only two years older than you."

"You should act like it."

Cindy pushed away her unfinished beer bottle and faced the door which
tilted and swam with the motion of her head. "He should be coming any
minute," she muttered quietly. While the patrons cheered over a touchdown,
several men with badges pinned to their chest entered the bar. At the rear of
this group of high ranking officers was Police Commissioner Patrick Gates. He
was chatting and laughing with the chief of police.

The entourage made their way through the crowd and sat down at a corner
table with a reserved sign on it. The officers sat around the commissioner and
ordered their drinks. Cindy stirred in her seat and tapped Jadie's back.

Jadie spun around. "Why are you being so annoying?"

It seemed Jadie hadn't noticed who entered the bar. "I need my purse."

"Are you going to do something dumb?"

Cindy snorted. "No."

Jadie gave Cindy her purse. Jadie then turned and smiled to her new friends.
She opened her purse and pulled out the creased manila folder.

"I'll be back," she said barely able to keep her head straight.

"Where are you going?"

"Bathroom."

"All right." Jadie prepared to leave her seat.

"No, no, it's okay. You don't have to come. I'll be fine."

"You sure?"

"I promise."

"Okay," Jadie said suspiciously. "If you're not back in ten minutes I'm coming for you."

Cindy hopped off her barstool and balanced uneasily on her crutches. As she steadied herself, the creepy guy sitting beside Jadie said, "So how did a sexy woman like you end up in the Coast Guard?"

Cindy rolled her eyes and forced herself into the crowd. Navigating through the bar with too many drinks polluting her head left her confused and disoriented. People's faces were blurry and all mushed together. No matter how hard she tried to walk straight, she ended up zig zagging and bumping into tables. The bar crowd roared as the play by play announcer yelled, "Interception! He's going to the forty, the thirty, he's going all the way!"

She felt as if the announcer and the crowd were cheering for her. The whole world wanted her to confront the commissioner.

"Oh no." Assistant Chief Mohammad Hasan rose from his seat. Back then he was a Deputy Chief and she was a probationary officer straight out of academy, a "probie," at the Midtown South Precinct. She held an enormous amount of respect for Assistant Chief Hasan, even when he had to punish her for not meeting department arrest quotas.

"Cindy." Assistant Chief Hasan held out his hand. "Whatever you're thinking of doing. Don't."

"I just want to show him something."

"Go home, Cindy."

She threw a crumpled manila folder between a circle of beers. "Open it."

Commissioner Gates glanced at the folder then back to Cindy. "Take his advice. Go home."

"Not until you open it."

Police Commissioner Gates gestured for the Chief of Police, Glenn Olsen to open the folder. Chief Olsen released a flutter of papers with his meaty fingers. He stuffed the documents back into the folder and handed it to Commissioner Gates.

"What is this?"

"Arthur's kill." Cindy slurred. "The ship graveyard."

"I know what it is. Why am I looking at it?"

The *executives* as they were known, leaned over Commissioner Gates' shoulders. They furrowed their brows and touched their chins as if trying to figure out a non-existent riddle.

"In the two years since you fired me, I gathered enough Intel to help you track down the man who killed my partner. Your son, Dan. I would've turned it in sooner but I didn't have enough information."

Commissioner Gates shuddered as if a ghost had passed through him. His interest in the folder suddenly grew. "How did you get these photos?"

"Friend of mine has a drone. He showed me how to fly it." Cindy wobbled back and forth on her crutches. "It's pretty easy." She leaned over to Assistant Chief Hasan and loudly whispered, "I think he still has a crush on me."

"Who?"

"Don't talk to her, Moe." Commissioner Gates tapped the photos against the wooden table and stuffed them back into the folder. "Thank you for turning these over. I'll take care of it."

"No, uh uh." Cindy reached between the bottles and knocked over two beers. Chief Olsen shot up from his seat with a beer stain on his crotch. He grabbed a handful of napkins and shoved them onto his soaked dress pants. Cindy snatched her wet manila folder and clutched it tightly to her chest while fumbling with her crutches. "Let me help bring him in. I did all the work, I deserve to be there. Just give me my badge back for a little while, put me on a taskforce and I'll resign after we catch him."

Commissioner Gates slapped the table which caused the remaining bottles to rattle. "Cindy, let me make something very clear to you. If you hadn't fucked up, Danny would still be alive and that lunatic would have never gotten his hands on him." He pointed to her beer stained blouse. "You're not fit to wear a badge."

She clenched her teeth. "I trained with the SWAT team for two months on your recommendation. Remember?"

"You weren't a washed up has been back then."

She threw aside her crutches and crawled onto the table. Chief Hasan and

Olsen grabbed Cindy's arms and stopped her from getting any closer. The patrons cheered as the announcer yelled, "Fumble!" They pounded their tables like war drums as the runner sprinted towards the end zone. The band played a lively tune in celebration of the touchdown which ended the game. The energy of the bar sped up the flow of boiling blood in her veins.

"Has been?" Cindy pushed against the chiefs and stretched as far as she could to get close to the commissioner. "Where the fuck were you when I took a bullet for the mayor?"

"I was hoping you would die."

In that moment, the bar darkened. It was only her and the commissioner. The music reduced to beats and drunken, incoherent revelry. She tilted her head back and spat in the commissioner's face.

"You disrespectful little bitch!" Commissioner Gates burst from his seat and flipped the table over. Bottles exploded like grenades as he lunged for her throat. Chief Olsen braced the commissioner and kept his hands away from Cindy's face. Chief Hasan put Cindy in a bear hug and tore her away. She thrashed and screamed in his arms.

Jadie shoved past the patrons. The music stopped and Cindy was slammed to the floor with her hands behind her back. Chief Hasan clicked the handcuffs onto her wrists and now she knew how a drunk person felt whenever she arrested them. Embarrassed and ashamed.

"I'm sorry," Chief Hasan said in a gentle tone. "It's for your own good."

Commissioner Gates pushed Chief Olsen out of the way. "Throw her in a cell till she learns how to cool off." Out of the corner of her eye, Cindy noticed a few bar patrons were secretly recording the commissioner with their cell phone cameras. Commissioner Gates appeared giant from the floor; and she was so very, very small. "Here let me get you started." The commissioner took someone's bottle of beer and poured it over Cindy's head. "Fucking bitch."

Foam splattered over her head and ran down her face. Commissioner Gates fixed his tie and smoothed out his ruffled hair. Chief Hasan lifted Cindy to her feet and brought her before the commissioner.

A Bitter Winter

He made sure to hold her gently even though she didn't deserve his sympathy. She also saw Jadie towering over the crowd, whispering, "Oh shit" as if she could have prevented Cindy from doing what she did. The commissioner wiped his cheek with a napkin and gestured with his head.

"Get her out of my sight."

CHAPTER 6:

Washed Up

Alone on a steel bench with no cushion or sheets, Cindy was on her back staring at a stone ceiling, shivering in a cold cell. She was placed among the faceless wretches she used to put away: the poor, the wicked, the ignorant, the greedy, the hopeless, the fallen. The corridors thundered with the clash of barred doors and rattled with the jingle of keys.

The rats squeaked between cells and roaches skittered along the brick walls. Officially this place was named the Manhattan Detention Complex, but everyone called it the Tombs. Though the jail was cold, smelly, and utterly repulsive, she still thought it was better and safer than Riker's Island. A trip to Riker's Island in her condition would have been a death sentence. Maybe that's why they put her in a cell by herself.

Piece by piece her identity had fallen apart and melted in the palms of her hands. She had become one of them, one of the bad guys. She remained on her back, rubbing her cold arms with her hands. She closed her eyes and thought about what Commissioner Gates had said. *It was your fault Danny died. Your fault.* The worst part of it all? He was right.

Two and a half years ago, Cindy told her partner, Dan that she wanted to become an undercover narcotics detective. She fantasized about infiltrating a gang in order to takedown a kingpin. Dan, who was also the commissioner's son, laughed so hard he choked on his own spit.

"Why are you laughing at me?"

"Do you really think a small, pale, white girl like you can go undercover as a smuggler? An enforcer? Not in this town. Your options are going to be A. girlfriend B. meth addict or C. hooker. Just because you speak Spanish don't mean you got what it takes to infiltrate a gang."

"Yes I do. I'm tougher than I look."

"It ain't about fighting, Cindy. Or being hard. It's about you being a white woman. Even if you got a Hollywood make up guy to make you look like trailer trash, ain't no gang around here going to take you in."

"I can prove myself."

"You're naïve. The only thing that's going to happen is this." Dan pressed two fingers into her temple and pulled the trigger. "So unless you want to open your legs to a bunch of Johns with STDs, you ain't ever gonna go undercover."

Having grown up with a competitive little sister, Cindy didn't take well to someone telling her she couldn't do something. Even though Dan was right, she was going to figure out a way to infiltrate a gang, any gang. But in order to do that, she needed to do something drastic. She needed to execute something so big that the executives would put her next in line for promotion. She got in touch with a few contacts she had made over the years and made preparations for the biggest drug bust in the city's history.

After verifying the confidential Intel through cursory stakeouts, Cindy passed the information to the DEA and State Police who then shut down a Meth lab worth over thirteen million dollars. Her plan worked better than she had expected. Deputy Chief Hasan was so impressed by her work that he began talking to the higher ups about considering her for promotion to detective where she could then transfer into the ESU unit. Once the idea of joining the SWAT team entered her head, going undercover to join a gang lost its appeal. Breaching barricaded buildings with a team of commando officers was a much cooler proposition.

The clanging of a cell door pulled Cindy out of her memory. She wiped the tears from her cheeks and sat up on the bench. Assistant Chief Mohammad Hasan had entered her cell. He joined her on the bench and leaned forward with his hands clasped between his legs.

"What are you doing here?" he asked.

"That's a rhetorical question, right?"

"I know why you're here, but I don't know *why* you're here. The Officer Brynfire I knew would have never spat on the commissioner's face."

"It's pronounced Brannifer. Not Brin-fire."

"Don't get smart with me, *Brannifer*. You're neck deep in shit and I'm the only one willing to dig you out."

She swallowed hard. Losing Chief Hasan's respect would ruin the entire legacy of her career. When the commissioner publicly embarrassed her, it spread throughout the ranks and made her life miserable. Chief Hasan risked his job by being the only one who didn't jump on the anti-Cindy bandwagon. "I was intoxicated, still am, a little."

"Oh I'm aware. But why? Why are you doing this to yourself?"

She shrugged.

"Thing is, Cindy. When I was Deputy Chief of Midtown South, you were a huge pain in my ass. You didn't want to meet your quotas for the stop and frisk campaign and didn't arrest perps under the broken windows strategy issued by the commissioner. You helped contribute to my precinct missing its target goals which in turn, made me look incompetent in front of the executives.

"Granted, I did recognize those policies were . . . how should I say this . . . unfair to certain ethnic demographics. Even though I wanted to fire you, I respected your conviction. But I couldn't let the rest of the force think this was acceptable. So I had your commanding officer reassign you to the most dangerous precincts and put you on vertical patrol to make an example out of you. Little did I know that you would reach out your hand to the disenfranchised communities and show those people that the police were not something to be afraid of. People in Brownsville, who never in a million years called the police, asked for you by name. A white girl of all people, the enemy. And to add even more insult to injury, you earned a medal during one of your vertical patrols.

"You left such a good impression in those troubled precincts that the commanding officers asked for you to be permanently reassigned to them. Some of them even requested you host training seminars on community development. So in retrospect, transferring you to another precinct was a useless form of punishment."

Cindy quirked her brow. "They asked for me?"

"Of course. You see what makes a good cop is not how many people they arrest or how many violent offenders they put behind bars. A good officer, a great officer, makes the people they protect feel safe. They wanted you because you made them believe you cared."

"I did care about them, I still do."

Chief Hasan smiled. "My favorite story to tell is one of an officer and a knife wielding man in a hospital. The man had been threatening to kill the staff and patients with his butcher knife. You had arrived on the scene and the man pointed his weapon at you and said he was going to kill you. There were no civilians behind him, so you were in the clear to shoot him. Instead you put your gun to the floor, sat on a desk, and talked to him.

"The man paced back and forth waving his knife around while you talked, and suddenly, he turned the knife over with tears in his eyes, and handed it to you. You threw the knife aside and hugged him as if he were your family. I always wondered how you convinced him to do that."

"I told him that I didn't believe he wanted to hurt anybody. I asked him why he was so upset and he said that he lost his job and couldn't afford the medical bills. I told him that if he gave me the knife, I'd make sure he'd get the help he needed and I guess he believed me."

"Because he knew you were telling the truth. If it were Dan or another officer, that man would have been killed."

Anguish pinched Cindy's face. Listening to the retelling of her past brought up feelings of regret and shame. "Why are you telling me this?"

"I bent the commissioner's ear and convinced him not to press charges against you. If he hadn't done what he did in front of all those cell phone cameras, you'd be going to prison. But because no one recorded you spitting at him, it's going to be our word versus the footage of him dumping beer over your head after you were already restrained."

She didn't understand why he was once again sticking his neck out for her. She couldn't cut it as a cop and she wasn't worth fighting for. "Why do you care," she said. "I'm not a police officer."

"It doesn't matter whether you're police or not. You don't belong here. I didn't suffer all those headaches just to watch you turn into a drunk. I know you feel guilty for what happened to Dan, but you have to let it go. You both knew the risks of the job and it could have happened to anyone. Don't let his passing ruin your life."

The entire cab ride home, she didn't dare look at Jonas and he didn't bother to say a word. Most people would have been grateful or honored if their former boss got them out of jail. And though Cindy was appreciative for what Chief

Hasan did, she would have rather stayed in the Tombs than have to face Jadie and Jonas. As the cliché goes, out of the frying pan and into the fire.

They arrived home around eleven pm. Michael and Jadie waited in the living room while Jonas carried Cindy to the bedroom, still not saying anything to her. He set her down on the bed, turned around, and quietly shut the door behind him. She dragged herself over to the foot of the bed and watched the shadows of his feet cross into the living room.

"Why did you take her to a bar?"

"She wanted to go," Jadie said.

Cindy aimed her ears towards the living room.

"It's not Jadie's fault," Michael said.

"Stay out of this."

"She took a fucking bullet for the mayor," Jadie said. "She earned the right to do whatever the hell she wants."

"How is it that you, of all people, managed to stay sober?"

"What's that supposed to mean?"

"You're a family of alcoholics," He said in a condescending manner. Jonas wasn't the type to yell and if he did it was rare. He preferred to sling insults at people's insecurities.

"Fuck you, dude. I'm leaving."

"So leave. The both of you."

She heard the front door close and that's when Cindy knew Jonas would be coming to the bedroom next. She chewed on her fingers and listened to the footsteps approaching the bedroom door. The light from the living room spilled into the bedroom. His shadow loomed over her before he closed the door.

"Jadie and Michael left," Jonas said.

She took her fingers away from her mouth and remained quiet. Jonas slinked into the dark bedroom and walked to the side where he slept. The bed creaked under his weight. "I'm trying to decide which is worse. The fact that you got drunk or the fact that you spat on the New York City Police Commissioner." He began to unbutton his shirt.

"Probably spitting."

"This isn't a joke."

She turned her back to him.

"Hey." He grabbed her shoulder. "We're having a discussion."

She shrugged his hand off. "No, you're going to lecture me."

"You want me to pretend tonight didn't happen?"

"Sure, give it a shot."

"Cindy," Jonas growled. "You promised me you wouldn't drink again."

"Things got out of hand." She sat up and felt the sting of shrapnel cut into her tensed stomach. "I was going to give my documents to the commissioner and I needed to calm my nerves." She rubbed her aching belly. "I got a little carried away." She then narrowed her eyes. "And you're going to apologize for what you said to Jadie."

Jonas shook his head. "Don't change the subject. We're talking about how you've started drinking again because of Ned and what happened to your partner. It's not like Dan's even worth the trouble."

Her eyebrows scrunched together. "What did you say?"

"Okay, I guess I'm going to say it. Your partner was not a nice guy. First day you met, he came in drunk and threw up on your desk. He stole money from detainees; made comments about your body; and blamed you for hurting a suspect that he beat up. This is the guy you got yourself thrown in jail for."

She raised her hand. "That was when we first met, okay? He changed a lot since then."

"I don't care about Dan," he snapped. "I care about you. Ever since he died you haven't been the same. You used to be so confident and happy and sociable and all these wonderful things I loved about you. Where is that person?"

She rolled her eyes. "It's like Groundhog's day with you. We keep having the same conversation over and over. I'm allowed to be angry for losing my job."

"Bullshit! This isn't about your job. You learned what failure was and now you don't know how to live with it. And the worst part is . . . you're beating yourself up over the death of—of an asshole."

She slapped him.

Jonas sat there, confused, with a red handprint fading on his skin.

"How dare you." Rivulets of mascara rolled down her face like black ink. "He burned alive because I didn't keep my mouth shut about who found the lab. It was my fault he died. You get it? My fault. My fault!"

She couldn't hold it together anymore. She crumbled and couldn't stop the tears from coming out of her eyes. "What was the point of surviving . . . if all I've done is teach gymnastics and work fucking security!" She hid her face and sobbed. Jonas took her into his arms and guided her head to his shoulder.

"Shh, shh, shh. It's okay."

"I should've never been a cop."

"You were a great cop."

"No I wasn't."

"You were to me." He combed his fingers through her hair. "I'm sorry for what I said."

"I didn't mean to slap you," she said. "I'm sorry too."

"That's okay. I already called the cops on you."

She looked up at him with water still spilling out of her eyes. "What?" Then sniffled.

"The SWAT team's going to put a battering ram through our door any minute and they're going to see a white girl hitting a Spanish guy, and the Spanish guy is going to get arrested."

She chuckled but only because she wasn't sure how to react. "What are you talking about? They wouldn't send ESU for a domestic disturbance. Now if you had me at gunpoint . . ."

"Okay, it was a bad joke, I got it." Jonas sighed. "Listen, about Dan and everything that happened. I want you to know that when I took your money, it was to prevent something like this from happening ever again. I was afraid what happened to Dan would happen to you."

She wiped her eye. "SIRCA?"

"Yes."

"When am I going to see my investment?"

He smiled. "Come by the lab tomorrow."

CHAPTER 7:

A Future Foretold

Cindy braced herself in the shower. Her frail muscles struggled to support the diminished body once capable of squatting four hundred pounds. Her shriveled legs quaked as she slowly scrubbed a loofah against her skeletal ribs. Soap slid off her punctured white skin and swirled down the drain. Last night had been an embarrassment of epic proportions. She could add spitting on the commissioner to her list of regrets.

The water hit her bullet scars and split into two streams. She pulled the skin of her belly and stretched the malformed scars into narrow slits. The holes seemed smaller than yesterday. A sudden itch scratched at her throat. She grunted then coughed but couldn't clear the irritation. She coughed more forcefully and felt something hard come up from her windpipe. She spat into her hand. There was a gold pebble sitting in between the lines of her palm. It rolled drunkenly between the water droplets as she pushed it with her index finger. Cindy raised her hand to the light and squinted at the strange object.

"Shrapnel? That's impossible."

She turned away as another coughing fit wracked her body. Little rocks bounced atop her tongue. She spat them out one by one and listened to them rattle down the drain. She rubbed her finger across her bottom lip, no blood, no wounds, just the taste of burnt metal. Stranger still, was how much better she felt with them gone. In fact, aside from being forced to walk on crutches, she felt great, incredible even. She turned off the shower, wrapped a towel around her chest, and decided to dress up a bit for Jonas.

She powdered her face, painted her eyes, and wore an irresistible perfume called Christmas in July, Jonas's favorite. The woman in the mirror looked much more glamorous, confident, sexy even. She slung her purse over her shoulder, leaned on her crutches, and ventured off to see a man about his new creation.

A Bitter Winter

The front reception area of the Latini building swarmed with men from a company called: Here to There, LLC. Armed with hand trucks, they hauled refrigerator sized cardboard boxes to a delivery truck parked in front. She hobbled past the movers and made her way to the elevator. Before she could press the button, the elevator opened and Michael emerged smiling.

"Wow, look at you all dolled up."

"I don't look homeless all the time." She smiled warmly. "What's with all the dudes?"

"Those are the movers." Michael led Cindy into the elevator. He waved his ID card in front of the RFID reader and pressed the LL button.

"Are you and Jonas going on a date or something? You're like, on another level of hot right now."

She punched him. "Shut up."

"Ow." He rubbed his arm and smiled. "I'm serious."

"Have to distance myself from last night."

"Ah yes. Last night. That's going to be a story for the ages."

"God I hope not." She quickly changed the subject. "Jonas said I get to see your new invention today. Is he here?"

"He's running around getting things done for Raymond. He'll be here soon." He turned and smirked at Cindy. "Trust me, your money was well spent."

"For a bulletproof armor? It'd better be."

"Oh, Cindy . . ." Michael feigned offense. "You have no idea."

The elevator doors slid open into a corridor of reflective silver panels and glossy liquid cement floors which were so clean, she could see herself in the reflection. A blue light ran the length of the hall, cutting the silver panels in half. She had ideas for what Jonas's workplace would look like, but an industrial basement was not it.

They meandered past rooms which housed general storage and abandoned prototypes. The movers unplugged cables and put plastic coverings over racks of servers. At the end of the hallway they turned and approached a reinforced steel door. It looked like a bank vault, all steel, dotted with huge rivets and heavy metal plates. Michael placed his keycard on the reader and the entrance thundered with the click of a bolt.

"Jeez," Cindy said. "With all that armor I thought you'd need to do a retinal scan or something."

"Normally we do, but we turned off the additional security so the movers could get in and out."

Through the shielded door they entered a space called the Main Lab. A farm of five computers sat in three rows; two in the front, two in the middle, one in the back. They overlooked a glass observation window which peered into a giant chamber similar to a hangar. To the left, another Server Room, to the right a Biomedical Lab.

"Sid, John, Charlie, we have a visitor."

The team strolled in from different parts of the lab as if entering from different walks of life. They were a group of middle aged men approaching their wise man years. John Wright was tall and lanky with long peppery hair. He looked like a traditional geek, the kind that invests in pocket protectors and probably has a collection of toys at his desk. Charlie Hudson was short and stout with horse shoe pattern baldness. Charlie seemed more reserved and bashful. He carried an awkward smile and avoided leading the group by hanging in the back.

So far they all matched how Jonas described them. But the man she was most eager to meet was the legendary Sid Carmack. Cindy often struggled to get Jonas to talk about anyone, including his own family, but when it came to Sid she could never get him to shut up. He was Jonas's mentor at MIT and was responsible for guiding Jonas into the creation of Lucent Labs. She always wondered what it would be like to meet the man who taught her husband everything he knew.

Sid had a surprisingly unassuming presence. He didn't command attention like John did but he also wasn't ultra-shy like Charlie. If the word patience could have a physical embodiment, he would be it. He had receding, short greying hair and a prominent forehead. How interesting to meet the man Jonas called his American Grandpa.

Sid tentatively approached. "Is Mrs. Ames allowed in here, Michael?" He spoke softly.

Michael looked at Cindy. "Do you know what Jonas is working on?"

"Some SIRCA majigger thingy? It's a suit . . . right?"

"She's allowed in."

"Very well." Sid held out his hand to shake Cindy's then abandoned the idea when he noticed her crutches. "Oh. Umm. Perhaps a friendly fist bump?"

Cindy held up her fist and Sid gently tapped it. "Sid Carmack."

"Oh I feel like I know you guys already. Jonas talks about you all the time."

"Me?" Sid blushed.

"I think she's referring to all of us, Sid." John Wright bounded forward. Unlike Sid, he kept his arms loose and walked with a confident swagger which matched his firm handshake. "It is a pleasure to finally meet you."

The last one to shake Cindy's hand was Charlie. He didn't say much, actually he didn't say anything at all.

"You're the vow of silence guy, aren't you?"

Charlie smiled and nodded.

"Is there a reason why?"

"He hasn't told us," John said. "It can be annoying sometimes but we've learned to live with it."

"Fascinating."

Sid put his hands together. "What brings you to the lab, Mrs. Ames?"

"Jonas wanted me to come by and see a demonstration of the suit."

Dr. Carmack seemed confused. "He hadn't mentioned we were going to do a demo. I'm not sure we're even prepared."

"Typical Jonas move," Dr. Wright said with a dramatic flourish of his hands. "He doesn't tell us we're going to do something until the last minute."

"I know we shouldn't but . . ." Sid gave the team a knowing look.

"Are you thinking what I'm thinking," John said.

Michael nodded in agreement. "Jonas might get pissed though."

Cindy snapped her head as they all spoke. "What are you guys talking about?"

"We would like to show you the demo now rather than later."

Dr. Wright laughed. "Come on, let's fire it up."

Sid rubbed his hands together. "Yes, yes, great idea."

They migrated over to the giant hangar known as the Workshop, which also happened to be Dr. Wright's domain. He skipped ahead of the group and bent down behind the capsule she had recalled seeing at the Javits center. There were several clicks, followed by the sound of spooling generators. Fluid pumped through the rubber tubes wrapped around the capsule and brought the machine's generators to idle.

John shouted over the spinning cooling fans echoing throughout the chamber. "Until we switch on the solar rechargeable batteries, SIRCA needs this unit to power its systems."

Cindy looked to Sid. "What does Circa stand for?"

"Stealth, Infiltration, Reconnaissance, Combat, Armor."

"That's not how you spell circa."

"Ah, yes. We know."

Michael entered a few commands into the keyboard and pointed at the machine. "Here it comes."

One by one a column of LED lights lit up. The machine hissed gas, startling her. The doors to the capsule slid open and unleashed a rush of cold air. Inside the brightly lit chamber, smoke pushed onto the shoulders of a tall, androgynous, silver humanoid. It had no face, no genitals, or muscles. SIRCA reminded her a human sized Oscar trophy.

Michael smiled from behind his computer. "What do you think?"

The scientists eagerly turned their attention to her.

"That's it?"

Their smiles quickly dropped.

Cindy scrambled to take her foot out of her mouth. "I mean, I'm not trying to be a jerk. I just thought it was going to look a little more . . . sophisticated."

The keyboard rattled under Michael's blindingly fast fingers. "Don't be fooled by its simplistic appearance. There's a lot going on under the hood that you can't see with your eyes. For starters, the liquid silver shell can absorb rain water and convert it into sustenance."

"So I could jump into a swimming pool and never be thirsty?"

"Correct. Except for salt water which clogs the filters."

She nodded approvingly. "Okay, now you have my attention."

Michael pressed the up arrow key and the machine stepped forward. Its metal boots clomped against the concrete floor. "Underneath the polymorphic alloy skin is an endoskeleton capable of enhancing your speed, strength, and reflexes."

"So which one of you had to wear it?" She said with a smirk.

John Wright raised his hand. "The obligation fell to me since I built it. But to be clear, I only tested the endoskeleton and not the polymorphic alloy. I can say with confidence that the endoskeleton can lift an eighteen wheeler with ease."

"If it can do that, why do you need the liquid metal part?"

Michael chuckled. "You still don't get it do you? The liquid silver is a fluid, metamorphic, dynamic organism. It can deflect bullets, change shape, create weapons out of thin air, the list goes on and on." Michael shook his head. "You know what? Let me show you. John didn't Charlie spill something in the workshop?"

John glared at Charlie who bashfully lowered his head. "Last week I think."

"Check it out, Cindy. As a former cop, you'll appreciate this."

A miniature diode emerged from the crown of SIRCA's bald chrome head. Beams of light shot out from the little crystal and danced across the floor like a 3D printer assembling a sculpt. The light formed a hologram of the lab, how it was last week, with two identical mannequins representing the scientists. Dr. Wright walked through the holograms. The images burst into a swirling dust storm of particles before reforming. He joined Cindy and said, "Cool right?"

"I have to admit, that did look cool."

"This is the forensics investigation tool, but we call it FIT," Michael said. "SIRCA can scan a crime scene for footprints, liquids, chemicals, dirt, debris, and recreate what happened in an environment called augmented reality. The two lab coat wearing models in the simulation are John and Charlie."

"I'm the handsome one." John pointed to the model on the right. It was identical to the other.

"If I play it back . . ." The mannequins replayed what happened earlier that day. The model representing Charlie entered from the left and tripped over its feet. The simulation paused with the coffee lid popping off the top and liquid spewing out. FIT identified what kind of coffee it was and also pointed out that Charlie's shoe had been untied, causing the trip.

"John, is it safe to say that Charlie came into the lab with an order of French Vanilla coffee, then tripped over his laces and spilled said coffee over the floor?"

"That is exactly what happened."

"That's amazing." This feature alone would be enough to track down Ned like a bloodhound. She had to have it. Cindy marched forward on her crutches and was stopped by Sid who gently held her back.

"My apologies, Mrs. Ames. We can't risk you tripping and falling into SIRCA."

She turned and stared at him. "I'd love to put it on."

"So you admit it's cool," Michael said with a smirk.

She pointed at the machine and stammered, unable to form words. "What, what else does it do? Can it fly?"

"Fly? No it cannot." Michael entered more commands. "Sid can you change the WiFi password on the test network?"

Dr. Carmack took out his phone and thumbed through the options menu. "The old password was shaken not stirred, no spaces."

"We didn't need to know that, Sid," Michael said.

"Ah, right."

The diode retracted into SIRCA's helmet causing the holograms to flicker away. The machine stood still then raised its chrome hand. A black orb emerged from the silver skin adorned with a glowing LED ring. SIRCA grabbed the orb with its other hand and twisted it. "Attempting remote hack," it said in a loud mechanical voice. The glowing ring flashed green. "Remote hack complete. Password, the world is not enough."

"You're obsessed," Michael said.

"Wait." Cindy interjected. "You can hack into people's Internet with that thing?"

Michael crowed with mock laughter. "Internet is for amateurs. It can access anything with a WiFi or Bluetooth connection."

"That's—I—wh—" She caught her breath. "This is crazy." She turned to John. "You wore that thing? What does it feel like?"

"Oh." John bashfully rubbed the back of his neck. "Like I said before, only the endoskeleton, not the alloy skin. That part remains a mystery."

Cindy clacked forward on her crutches. "I'll put it on for you. It'll be fun."

"Whoa, whoa, whoa." The team formed an immediate blockade. "That's not a good idea."

"Why? It's just a suit."

Sid cut into the conversation. "Just a suit she says. The audacity! Is the space shuttle just a ship? Is brain surgery just a procedure? Dr. Hudson's formula alone could win a Nobel Prize. SIRCA is a gateway to the pinnacle of human perfection."

"Basically," Michael said. "It will change you, physically."

"Wait so" —Cindy looked down at her rail thin legs— "would my body go back to normal even though I'm all . . . scrawny?"

"You'd swell up until your clothes barely fit. Instant cross fit athlete. Abs included, healthy diet sold separately."

The excitement drove Cindy mad. A high tech suit capable of rebuilding her old body and tracking down Ned? Jonas should have said this is what he was going to use her money for. She would have even tried to get him more money somehow. She needed this suit.

Sid called for Cindy's attention. "I don't think anyone would complain about having a perfect body, especially those of us who sit in front of computers all day." He patted his belly. "But Charlie's formula, which is a vital component of SIRCA, has, in the past, created an accelerated form of cancer in lab rats. Charlie claims to have fixed it, but we are leery of testing."

And there was the catch. The idea of a perfect body lost its appeal once the C word was mentioned. She had visited too many hospital beds and watched too many quiet deaths to risk that for herself. "A, that's scary. B, how can Charlie say it's fixed if he can't speak?"

"E-mail."

Cindy returned her gaze to the suit. "Well I'd still love to test it, though obviously without the cancer part."

"That would be a no," Sid said.

Charlie, the one who had been silently standing amongst them also nodded his head in agreement.

"See, even Charlie says no and he made the formula," John said.

"Even after we fix the cancer issue, there's no way Jonas would let you wear his baby," Michael said.

"I paid for it."

John walked over to the computer and typed something on the keyboard.

"We're getting off topic. Let's show her the grappling hook and power down before Jonas gets back."

SIRCA's forearm began to deform. A metal canister rose from its skin like a bubble emerging from water. It stretched and changed shape until it took the gun-like appearance of a grappling hook launcher. SIRCA raised its arm and fired at a bull's eye against the far wall of the Workshop.

The sound of crashing metal shot electricity through her limbs. Though her body remained in the lab, her mind had gone to a different place in a different time. The growl of an engine revving filled her ears. Tires squealed and the smell of burnt rubber permeated the air. She could hear water lapping and the blood curdling screams of Dan burning alive. Ned and his friends laughed as they sat and watched the carnage.

Hands grabbed at her arms. She threw her elbows in a berserk fury and scratched at the faces of the men trying to kill her. They threw her into a black tunnel and locked the door. She screamed and pounded against the indestructible walls. She could hear her partner suffering, hear him begging for his life, and she could smell his burning flesh.

"Cindy." A voice spoke, calm and tender, out of place in this raging inferno. "You're at the lab. You're safe. No one is going to hurt you."

She moaned in fear, trapped in a past she could never change. The voice, distant and gentle, began to count down from ten, breathing deeply and slowly between each count. The sound of his voice pulled her from the nightmare. Dan and the burning freight container began to disappear until she could see the lab again. She listened to the man's voice and mimicked the pace of his breaths. Her controlled breathing slowed the pounding of her heart to a dull thud. Each breath took away the darkness and brought her back to the sterile lighting within the lab.

"Deep breath in, hold, slowly exhale."

Her mind returned to the lab. She saw both Michael and John were missing their glasses and wondered why they had fingernail scratches on their faces. She ran the back of her hand across her cheeks and got mascara all over her face.

"Feeling better?"

The man's voice startled Cindy. She looked at him and said,

"You're not Jonas."

CHAPTER 8:

Tomorrow is Never Promised

He introduced himself as Raymond Levreux but she already knew who he was, along with the rest of the world. Raymond had made his fortune developing Credit Guard, the first system to truly abolish identity theft scams by using an authenticator with every transaction. With his vast wealth, Raymond acquired a conglomerate of both big and small tech companies. One such company was Lucent Labs. She had seen Raymond at the Javits conference center and on Impress News but never got a chance to say hello. She was embarrassed to be sitting in front of the richest man in the world after having had a PTSD meltdown.

Raymond gave Cindy a paper cup of water. She wasn't thirsty but drank until her nerves settled. She handed the cup back and thanked him. Raymond knelt down and waved off the Lucent Labs team who were loitering around like vagrants.

"I've been in your shoes before, except with less makeup," Raymond said.

She wiped at her eyes. Her fingers became black with product. "Jonas isn't here is he? I don't want him to see me like this."

"He is not."

"Oh God." She opened her purse and dug through her make up kit. "I have to put this shit on again."

"Cindy, right? I don't think putting on makeup should be on your list of priorities, unless it makes you feel better." He chuckled softly. "Just my humble opinion." The sweet sound of his voice calmed her down.

She stopped before she could rub eyeliner on the edge of her eyelid. "You're right. I'm sorry . . . I'm just . . . augh, so frazzled." She took a napkin from her purse and wiped her face.

"No need to apologize. I understand completely."

He offered his hand and Cindy took it.

"Were you in the military," he asked.

"NYPD."

"You must have seen things."

Understatement of the year. "I did."

"Still bothers you?"

"Isn't it obvious?" She laughed at herself and he smiled.

"I didn't want to assume."

Raymond reached into his breast pocket and pulled out a business card. He gave it to her and she looked at it, confused. Why would Raymond waste his time with someone insignificant like her?

"Our little secret," Raymond said. "Feel free to call if you need an ear familiar with the road you're on. I will make time to speak with you."

"Wow, really?" The card was surprisingly heavy. A holographic 1C logo appeared and spun above its jet black surface. She tried to hand it back. "You don't even know me."

He pushed the card into her palm. "PTSD is a frightening road which shouldn't be walked alone. Besides, Jonas is my employee and you are his wife. My help is now available to you."

He had such a relaxed and tranquil demeanor that to say no made her feel rude. She put the card in her purse and whispered a small thank you. Jonas entered the room at the tail end of their conversation. Her tears had long since dried but Jonas knew something had happened. He held onto her cheeks and dappled her forehead with kisses.

"Are you okay?"

Raymond pivoted away from the couple. "She had a scare is all. Tripped on her crutches. Nothing to be worried about."

"I didn't know you were here already, I'm sorry."

Cindy shook her head. "It's okay, it's not your fault."

Raymond patted Jonas on the shoulder. "The movers will finish transferring the equipment tomorrow night. Feel free to take off early if needed."

"Thanks, Ray."

"Pleasure to meet you, Cindy."

She had enough excitement for one day and decided it was time to go home. Jonas had made plans to go out to dinner with his team and offered to cancel them in order to take her home and stay with her. She declined and encouraged him to go celebrate with his coworkers. She wanted him to enjoy himself and not miss out on bonding with his team. He reluctantly agreed and asked her to call if she needed anything. Cindy kissed him goodbye and called Jadie who picked her up. They bought Chinese takeout and went back to Forest Hills.

After they arrived home, Cindy dug into her take out container with a pair of chopsticks. "How was class today?" She pinched handfuls of pork fried rice into her mouth. "They miss me yet?"

Jadie dug into her plate of marinated General Tso's chicken with a fork. "You kidding? They ask me when you're coming back every day. I mean nothing to them."

"Get shot six times and they'll ask about you too."

Jadie took a sip from her beer. "I'd rather be awesome instead."

Cindy drank from her water bottle and thought about Raymond and Chief Hasan and her brief stay at the Tombs. This wasn't the life she wanted for herself. Did she want to be known as the sloppy drunk who spat in the commissioner's face or the coolest teacher her students have ever known? The sale of Lucent Labs to Raymond would give her the freedom to quit security and focus on her gym. And Chief Hasan was right, she wasn't the type of person to disrespect a police commissioner, no matter how rude. The alcohol had betrayed her once again.

Cindy rolled a chunk of pork with her sticks. "I have news you'll be interested to hear."

"What's that?"

"I'm going to trash the left over photos and documents I have in the basement."

Jadie's fork rattled on her plate.

"Seriously?" She seemed ecstatic by the news.

"Yeah, my stay at the Tombs has put things into perspective."

"There is a God."

Cindy pinched some rice into her mouth. "I mean what has chasing Ned gotten me?

"Nothing but trouble."

"Exactly. I don't want to be a drunk. I don't want to be a bitch. I need to stop feeling sorry for myself and move on with my life."

Jadie took a big gulp of beer. "Trust me, I get it." She burped. "'Scuse me. But this is like the best news ever. I think this will be good for you."

"Yeah I think so too."

"Are you really over Ned though?"

"It's going to take time, but I'll get there."

"It'll be nice to have you back to your old, obnoxious, arro—"

Someone knocked at the door.

"—who's that," Jadie said.

"Don't know." She glanced at the door then to Jadie. "Would you mind—?"

"Sure."

"Thanks."

Jadie stood up from the couch and wiped the crumbs off her pants. She walked over to the door and stood on her tip toes so she could see through the arc of glass near the top of the door. "Huh."

Cindy threw her arm around the back of the sofa. "Who is it?"

Jadie furrowed her brow. "It's that guy I met at the bar."

"You told him where I lived?"

"No, of course not. I'll get rid of him."

Jadie turned the lock and spun the knob.

The door flung open as if the SWAT team were raiding her house. The man Jadie met at the bar charged through the entryway with a shotgun primed to fire.

"What the f—" Cindy's cries were interrupted by Jadie yanking the weapon out of the creep's hands. She punched him across the jaw and sent him to the floor.

"My dad was a Marine." She pumped the shotgun. "What about yours?"

Another man crept in through the front door with a Sig Saur handgun pointed at her head. "Uh, uh. Put it down, blondie."

"Damn it."

Jadie slowly placed the shotgun on the floor. The gunman slithered into the living room while his friend rolled on the floor, holding his jaw. He gestured at Jadie with his gun, ordering her to turn around. He secured her wrists with a pair of handcuffs and pushed her into the floor. Cindy forced herself onto her crutches and ambled next to the couch. The gunman looked at her and laughed.

"Sit down before you hurt yourself."

She squeezed the handholds of her crutches. The padding squealed and popped nside her hands. She approached, one jerky movement at a time.

"What are you gonna do, fight me?" His gold tooth shimmered as he laughed.

She flung her right crutch which spun like a boomerang. The crutch bounced off the gunman's forearm and landed on the floor. He pushed his pistol arm forward and took aim at her head. She held her remaining crutch over her shoulder and walloped the side of his skull. The gunman fell, clutching his eye now filled with blood. She didn't know where her newfound strength had come from and didn't care. She mounted the gunman like a saddle and punched his head until blood squirted onto her chin.

"No one touches my sister!"

"Sis, behind you!"

The man's arms wrapped around her ribs and pulled her off. She flailed her arms and screamed as loud as she could, fighting him with her growing strength. The bar creep grabbed a handful of her hair and smashed her face to the carpet. She pushed her hands into the floor but lost whatever inhuman power she had left. The bar creep rolled Cindy onto her back and whipped the side of her head with the butt of the pistol.

———————

She awoke in the back of a stranger's SUV with a throbbing headache. In the driver's seat, the guy who hit on Jadie at the bar, put his pinky in his mouth. He made little mouse-like squeaks as he sucked on his teeth.

"I think she knocked out my tooth," The driver said.

The sky was like a coal burnt down to ash, grey with specks of black. Snowflakes turned to streaks of cocaine against the brush of a windshield wiper. Jadie was on Cindy's right, hands cuffed behind her back, pissed beyond words.

The front passenger yelled at the driver. "At least you only lost a tooth. Look at my fucking face!"

"Should've known there'd be a second dude," Jadie muttered.

A Bitter Winter

"It's not your fau—mm." The split in Cindy's lip stung when she spoke. The taste of copper soured her mouth. "I shouldn't have asked you to open the door."

"That's the last time I do you any favors."

"I'll get us out of here."

The passenger handed his cell phone to the driver. The driver placed the phone to his ear and spoke. "We got the girls."

"Lean over," Cindy whispered.

She bit into Jadie's aromatic hair and fished out a hairpin, along with a few hairs.

"Ow."

"Hey!" The passenger with the bloodshot—now swollen—eye pointed at the sisters. "Knock it off."

The hairpin slid into the back of her throat and nearly made her choke. She coughed once and cleared her throat to bring the hairpin back up. She spat it into Jadie's hands and waited for the car to go dark after passing a streetlight. In the brief second of darkness, Cindy took the hairpin and began twisting it into a lock pick.

The driver was still talking on the phone, licking the hole where his tooth belonged. "We didn't know she was there . . . Yeah, we tried . . . All right we'll be there in an hour or so, weather's pretty bad." He hung up the phone and handed it back to the passenger. "He's pissed that we didn't wait for the sister to leave."

"I told you."

"We had guns for fuck's sake."

"You didn't want to shoot the blonde."

She jabbed the hairpin into the handcuff lock and rotated it around. The driver suddenly looked at them through the rear view mirror.

Cindy yelled out, "My arms hurt," in order to distract the kidnappers.

"Shut up," the driver said. "Nobody cares about your arms." He glanced at Jadie and smiled with his missing tooth. "Just so you know, I really liked you."

"Fuck you," Jadie replied.

"It's not personal, baby. We were spying on the commissioner. If you two hadn't shown up you wouldn't be in this mess. In fact, I'd probably be licking whipped cream off your nipples about now."

"I'm out of your league, shit head."

"Let my sister go," Cindy spoke loudly to mask the quiet clicking near her back. "Ned doesn't want her."

"Too late, you're a package deal now." He looked to his friend. "Show her the thing."

The passenger took out a folder and dumped papers and photos of Ned onto her lap. She didn't know how these creeps got ahold of the Intel she gave the commissioner.

"The commissioner dumped your shit in the trash and we found it. You seem a little too interested in our boss and he don't want you to interfere."

The handcuffs popped and came loose. She pried the cuffs off and grabbed Jadie's wrists.

"My husband is going to look for us," Cindy said.

"Oh he'll find ya. He'll just need to read the ingredients off a dog food can." The passenger laughed and high fived the driver.

Cindy popped the lock on Jadie's cuffs. They were free. A shock of adrenaline trembled her nervous fingers. She steadied her breath and maintained focus. She checked the door and pulled the handle, locked. With the hapless thugs focused on the snowy road, she leaned into Jadie and muttered, "Put your seatbelt on."

Both sisters clicked themselves into their seatbelts. In the passenger seat, the man with the swollen eye turned on the radio and began searching through the channels. As she positioned her hands behind the driver's seat. She looked to Jadie for the OK. Jadie nodded.

The bar creep with the missing tooth said, "Do you think we're gonna get paid ex—hurghk!"

"Oh shit!" The passenger screamed as she choked the driver's neck. He pulled out his pistol and aimed for Cindy's head. Jadie threw herself onto him and pushed the gun away. The Sig Saur popped like a bottle of champagne. The driver's brains splattered against the window. The SUV swerved and listed on two wheels. The seatbelts snapped to their locked position as the truck rolled over a snow embankment and crunched on its roof.

Blood rushed into Cindy's head. Glass littered the crumpled ceiling like crushed ice. She could smell gasoline and hear the clicking sound of a dying engine. There was blood all over the driver's side window and dashboard.

"Jadie . . ." she groaned. "You okay?"

A mask of blood covered Jadie's unconscious face. Cindy pressed the seatbelt release button and dropped on her head. She looked out the window and saw a rogue spark light a pool of gasoline.

"Of course."

She crawled over to Jadie who was upside down and dripping blood. She tried to pull her down but the stupid seatbelt kept her locked in place. Black smoke crept into the cabin and made it difficult to breathe. Cindy stretched as far as she could reach and jabbed her thumb into the red seatbelt release button. She caught Jadie before she could hit her head. "I got you," she said. "Hang on."

Though she tried to keep calm, she felt powerless without her legs, and was frightened by Jadie's condition. Her breathing became erratic. The smoke seeped into her lungs and made her cough. How the hell was she going to get out of this mess?

"People who panic, die," she told herself.

She grabbed onto Jadie's collar and pulled as hard as she could. Jadie's boot thumped against the front passenger seat with a dull thud.

"Why'd you have to be so damn tall?" She turned and yelled out the broken window, "Somebody help me!"

She wriggled Jadie's leg from side to side but the boot wouldn't budge. The toe and heel were wedged tightly between the bottom of the front and rear seat. The small gasoline fire grew into a blaze, warming the car like an oven. Cindy undid the straps of Jadie's boot and wiggled her foot out. Once freed she hauled herself and Jadie across the mangled roof. The little glass diamonds cut the pads of her fingers and glittered within Jadie's hair. Her biceps and triceps trembled from exhaustion, but she kept going.

"Hey!" the thug with the swollen eye had regained consciousness. "Where you goin'? I can't—I can't get out."

A ring of fire blocked her route of escape. She grabbed a handful of snow and threw it on top of the fire. The flames shrunk, then grew back as if they were trick candles.

"Please get me out of here. Don't let me die."

Cindy ignored his cries and continued throwing more snow onto the flames.

"I can help you," he said. "Please, I'm begging you."

She looked into the car. The flames were drawing closer to the man who looked the same way Dan did when he died, terrified. She shuddered at the thought of hearing this man's screams once the fire reaches him. She didn't want anyone, not even her enemies, to go through what Dan did. She left Jadie outside and crawled back in through the window.

"If you don't help me, I swear to God I will hunt you down and kill you."

"Yeah, yeah, you got it. I'll do anything you want," he replied.

"Promise me."

"I promise!"

The button for the seatbelt release had gotten jammed and the strap was digging into his shoulder, trapping him in his seat.

"I'll need a knife to get you out and none of this glass is going to work."

"I got a knife in my coat pocket, you can use that."

The knife was where he said it was and the edge was razor sharp. She sawed the knife back and forth against the fibers of the strap until it snapped in two. He escaped from the harness and crawled out of the broken passenger side window. Once he was free of the wreckage, he took off running.

"Hey. Hey! You fucking asshole!" She stabbed the knife into the seat. "I'm going to remember your face. And I'm going to kill you!" She quickly backtracked through the window and accidentally dipped her hands in a pool of gasoline. She shook them off as best she could and rejoined Jadie outside. She grabbed Jadie with one hand and shoveled snow onto the fire with the other. The flames leapt onto her hand. She howled as her skin blistered and split open, even as she buried her fist in the snow. Having a taste of what Dan felt stirred up emotions she didn't have time to deal with right now. She swallowed everything down, including her excruciating pain, and forced herself to keep fighting. With the fire momentarily tamed. She used what little strength her frail body had left and dragged Jadie to safety.

The SUV had turned into a blackened, hollow husk, but at least they were clear of the inferno.

"Okay." She panted out of breath. "Time to wake up."

Jadie's chest had stopped rising.

"Jadie?" Cindy put her ear next to Jadie's mouth and counted to five. She did not feel any breath on her face. "Oh fuck." She climbed atop her sister's stomach and placed her mangled hands slightly above the sternum. She threw her body forward and managed to accomplish a shallow, useless chest compression.

Without being able to keep both hands locked, she lacked the necessary force to revive her sister. She tried again and again, with each attempt weaker than the last. Her tears dripped onto Jadie's dirty skin.

"Somebody fucking help me!"

The blizzard howled and carried her voice into the dark streets. She pinched Jadie's nose and breathed into her lungs. Jadie's pulse continued to weaken, slowing with each passing minute. Cindy punched her chest and breathed her entire being into her sister.

Clumps of ice formed on her hair and thickened over her shoulders. She shivered from the wicked cold and was losing endurance with each compression. "Jadie please." She breathed into her mouth and weakly pressed down on her chest. Cindy went on for as long as she could, but eventually the fatigue proved to be greater than her will, and she collapsed. She heard the crunch of snow under dozens of footsteps and looked up from her resting position on top of Jadie. She was surrounded by men wearing gang colors.

CHAPTER 9:

The Last Straw

So this was the price for a new life without Ned: a burned hand wrapped in bandages, a miserable cup of coffee, and a sister with a cerebral edema, a swelling of the brain. In order to *forget* about Ned, she had to accept the fact that Jadie might be stuck on a respirator and IV for the rest of her life and he would go unpunished. No. She shook her head. There was no forgetting him now.

Her body trembled, not from cold or fear, but pure, white-hot anger. She didn't know when or how she was going to get Ned. All she knew was that when the time comes, she will rip his body apart piece by piece. She will make him suffer and die a thousand deaths, in a never ending cycle of hellish torture.

The door opened. For a brief moment, she regained control of her thoughts and swallowed the rage, deep, deep inside. Now was not the time to let it loose. Michael opened the door and quietly walked across the room while staring at Jadie. He let out a mournful sigh and stopped in front of Cindy. She hid the monster growing inside her and nursed her cup of coffee.

"Are you okay?" Michael pulled up a chair.

"I'm super."

"Jonas told me what happened. I wanted to see you as soon as I could."

"Thank you." Her words were obligatory and hollow.

Michael shifted uncomfortably in his seat. "Is your hand all right?"

She sipped from her cup again. "It's fine."

"How did you get here? Jonas told me you guys were kidnapped and then a car flipped over but he didn't say how you brought Jadie."

She rubbed her brow to signal that she didn't feel like telling the story, but Michael didn't get the hint, he never did. "A gang called the BBRs showed up. I thought they were going to kill me for a gang initiation, but they ended up helping instead."

"That's unusual."

"It is and it isn't. Kids in gangs are like Pitbulls, they reflect the owner. I

A Bitter Winter

showed one of them how to do CPR and told the others to call an ambulance. I don't know why they were out in a blizzard and I don't care."

"I can't believe this keeps happening. First you, now Jadie. When is it going to stop?"

"When I split open Ned's skull with my fist." Her voice was cold, borderline apathetic.

Michael coiled back. "Whoa."

She blinked rapidly and immediately waved her hand in front of her face. "I'm sorry." She touched her head. "I have a lot on my mind right now."

"Clearly."

She let out a shuddering breath and confessed a secret desire. "I wish I had that suit."

"SIRCA?"

She nodded.

"I . . . can't argue with that."

"What would've happened if I had worn the suit? And be brutally honest."

Michael seemed surprised by her question. He pushed his glasses up his nose and answered. "Well for starters you would have been bulletproof. From the time they opened the door to the time you realized you were in danger, SIRCA could have been activated. Your legs would have regrown their muscle tissue and your strength would have increased exponentially. Tackling you would be like trying to tackle a utility pole."

She remembered how quickly her strength had faded. If only it had lasted a little longer, things would have ended differently. Michael rattled on. "If they got you in the car and you changed then, your hand wouldn't have burned and you could have punched your way out of the car like the Hulk. You would've easily been able to pull Jadie to safety." Michael adjusted his glasses. "It is after all, designed for combat."

His words were insensitive, but that was what she wanted, the honest truth.

"I want it."

"Umm." Michael fidgeted in his seat. "I don't think that's a good idea."

"So you're okay with seeing my sister like this?"

"I—what?"

"You say you care about me. But when I ask you for tools to get the motherfuckers who did this to my sister, you say it isn't a good idea?"

"Whoa." Michael waved his hands in surrender. "That's a little unfair. You know I would do anything for you. The suit is not mine to give."

"You programmed it."

"I programmed some of it. John built the endoskeleton, Sid integrated the neural network, and Charlie created the formulas. That doesn't mean any one of us owns the suit. You know who does? Raymond. Even Jonas doesn't have a say."

"I guess I'll have to call Raymond then, he gave me his card after all."

"Don't do that, Cindy. You don't know what you're getting yourself into."

"You know, I was hoping I could count on you, considering we grew up together. But if you don't want to help me, I'll find someone who will."

Michael shot up from his seat and flared his nostrils. "Under different circumstances I would have called you an asshole, but I won't because I know you're going through a difficult time. And by the way, just because Raymond gave you a card doesn't mean he's going to let you have a suit worth billions of dollars."

She watched him close the door and took another sip from her coffee. A friend, a real friend, was someone who cared about her feelings and would have done anything to help her. If Michael had been drafted into the military, she would have enlisted alongside him so he wouldn't go alone. The fact that he chose not to help when Jonas and Jadie would, left her immensely disappointed.

Jonas arrived a few minutes later. He brought with him a trail of balloons which bumped into each other as he walked in. He was also carrying a bundle of fresh clothes for Cindy to change into. Jonas set his gifts onto a nearby table then took Michael's place in the chair. Before her mind knew what her body was doing she found herself in his arms, spilling some of the emotion she had been gulping down.

"It's okay." He wrapped her in his arms and warmed her body with his.

"It's not. It's definitely not okay." She looked up at him, her eyes stinging with liquid. Jonas touched her cheek and told her to cry as much as she needed to. She balled her hands into fists and pounded her thighs.

"I'm sick and tired of being a fuck up."

"You're not."

"Look at that bed and tell me I'm not."

"You weren't the one driving."

"I'm the older sister. I'm supposed to keep her safe no matter what. That's my job. You have brothers and sisters, don't you get it?"

"I do, but you can't protect them from everything, even themselves."

Jonas grabbed a tissue from his traveler's pack. He dabbed Cindy's eyes and wiped her nose. He kissed her forehead and told her, "Your eyes turn green when you cry."

"Really?" She wiped her cheek. "That's weird."

"You should cry more often so I don't feel like a wimp when I get upset during a movie."

She sniffed once and let out a sigh. "Movies aren't real."

Jonas grazed his thumb against the childhood scar near her eye. "Don't be so hard on yourself. If it wasn't for you Jadie wouldn't have made it here. You kept her alive"

"So she could be a vegetable for the rest of her life?" Cindy dropped her head into her hands. "Oh my God. I don't want to call my parents. I can't put them through this again."

Jonas saw her bandaged hand and grabbed her wrist. "How bad is this?"

"You don't want to know." She held onto her wrist. "It hurts so bad. I think the doctors said it burned down to the bone. I can't even move my fingers."

Jonas grimaced then dug into his pocket. He pulled out a brown bottle, an empty petri dish, cotton swabs, scissors, tape, and latex gloves. "I didn't want to use the last of this but it looks like you need it."

"What is that?"

"This." Jonas held up the bottle. "Is a cell regeneration formula. I should have enough to heal your hand."

"Then give it to Jadie."

"I can't. This is for external use only." He grabbed the scissors and held Cindy's hand. "I can give it to you."

She tried to pull away, "I don't want it."

"This will fix your hand."

"Figure out how to give it to her."

"I told you, it won't work. This is applied on the skin, not the inside of someone's skull. Anything internal is going to require stem cells and I don't have that capability. Now give me your hand." Jonas cut through the bandages. The wraps split open and exposed her raw, ointment lathered skin. He carefully pulled the bandages off causing Cindy to hiss as the air touched the top of her webbed, patchy hand. She looked away from the charred bone visible through the missing flesh of her fingers.

He mixed a sample of Cindy's skin tissue with the formula. He applied the clear, viscous liquid to her hand with the end of a cotton swab.

"I have a confession to make," he said. "This isn't the first time I'm giving this to you."

She jumped forward as pain shot through her hand "Ah!" She tried to pull her hand away but Jonas wouldn't let her.

"I know it hurts. Just hold on."

"Ow, ow, ow, please take it off. Please."

Her hand fizzled like a fresh bottle of soda poured into a glass. Her torn, pink, bloody flesh began to change. The frayed edges of her skin died off and turned into flakes of ash. Gaps knitted together and generated canvases of new flesh. Cindy's hand looked as if it were covered in volcanic ash. Jonas brushed his hand against hers and released a cloud of dust. She was shocked by what she saw next.

Her skin looked flawless and glistened as if it had been freshly washed and moisturized. Even the tiny hairs on her knuckles had regrown. Flexing her fingers brought the lingering effects of pain, but it was only a dull ache. Jonas brought his lips to her knuckles and kissed them.

"Good as new," he said with a smile.

"That's incredible . . ." She turned her hand and was amazed by how pink and smooth it was. "This isn't the first time?"

"How do you think you got out of the hospital?"

"But how did you . . . I was unconscious."

"Correct."

"Is this the final, tested version?"

Jonas's mouth fell open. "Uh, no."

Cindy's internal bottle of anger sprung a leak. "Are you—"

"Okay, relax. Calm down."

"Don't tell me to calm down." She jabbed his chest with her finger. "Your coworkers told me this formula could turn into an aggressive, mutated form of cancer. And you gave it to me."

"What are you freaking out for? You're fine."

"Did you know the formula would work?"

"I assumed it would but no, not one hundred percent."

"Have you tested it?"

"Only on mice."

"And?"

"Most of them died of tumors, but Charlie assured me he figured out the problem and fixed it."

"You don't know that," she yelled.

"I was saving your life!"

His voice thundered loud enough to wake the dead. Cindy leaned back in her chair and crossed her arms in front of her chest. She didn't want to be saved. She wanted to trade places with Jadie and give her a chance to live her life. He shouldn't have wasted his magical formula on her.

"I wasn't—I'm not ready to let you go," he said softly.

"You should've let nature run its course."

"Why would you say something like that?"

Cindy pointed at Jadie. "She wouldn't be in here."

A morbid silence befell the room. They sat across from each other both avoiding eye contact. She had expected, hoped, Jonas would say something to the contrary, but he didn't. His unanswered reply confirmed what she had always feared.

"So you agree it's my fault."

"No I don't."

"You didn't say anything."

"I was trying to think of a reply."

"Shouldn't take that long."

"That doesn't mean anything," he said annoyed. "Look, if you want to be technical about it, yes, you made a mistake. Everyone does. You're the only one who can't seem to accept when you do. You act like your mistakes are the end of the world."

"You don't get it." She swallowed hard to avoid getting emotional. "I survived, right? I keep on surviving. And what do I have to show for it? Nothing. I survive—someone gets hurt. First it was Dan, then it was Officer Yang, then the mayor, now Jadie. If I don't stop Ned—" her voice began to crack. "—I'm afraid you'll end up next." And suddenly, without warning, she spat out a secret she didn't know she had. "I'm—I'm at the edge, Jonas. If something happens to you, I'll lose it and I don't know what I'll do next."

He touched her arm. "Nothing's going to happen to me. Raymond has a lot of security."

"Raymond does, we don't." She leaned back and recalled the demo she saw at the lab. She hoped Jonas would be more understanding than Michael about the suit, he had to be.

He furrowed his brows at her. "What?"

"You should give me the suit. I can protect us."

"Okay you're talking out of both sides of your mouth. First you yell at me for giving you an experimental formula which is part of SIRCA, now you want a prototype military-grade weapon?"

"Why stop at the formula? If I'm going to die of cancer, at least give me a chance to kill Ned."

"You're not going to die of cancer."

"You don't know that. I'm your guinea pig."

Jonas shook her hands. "Listen to yourself. You're talking crazy. Giving you the suit is too dangerous."

"The formula was too dangerous!"

"This is different. Charlie's formula isn't designed to make you violent or keep your body going when it should be dying. SIRCA was made to kill. If you wait another year, I can have the civilian version ready by then."

"I can control it."

"And it can control you." Jonas stood up from his seat and walked away.

———

A Bitter Winter

Midnight. All was quiet in Forest Hills. The storm had passed and the snow had settled into an unbroken sheet of white. Crystals of ice tapped against the glass windows. Cindy laid in bed and stared at the ceiling with her fingers interlaced over her stomach. She watched the shadows of a tree branch stretch across the ceiling and dance with the wind. Jonas was asleep with his back facing her.

She reached for her cell phone on the nightstand. The bright screen stung her eyes as she browsed through the photo gallery of her and Jadie. One was of a beautiful waterfall in Hawaii and the two of them jumping from the top. Another was of them in their bikinis, tanning on the beach while sipping piña coladas. Well . . . Jadie was tanning, Cindy was burning. The last photo was of them at a restaurant on the Avon Beach boardwalk in Jersey. Jadie posed for the photo by puckering her lips while holding a French fry near her mouth. No makeup, no worries, just a cute hat and a beautiful ocean behind her.

Now all she could see when she thought of Jadie were the ventilators and IV lines. The bruises and the cuts. The mistakes and the failures. She obsessed over the suit. Fantasized about putting it on and watching her body grow bigger and stronger. She didn't expect Michael to understand, he was an only child, but Jonas should have understood. She needed him to have her back.

She sat up and pulled the blanket away from her legs. She grabbed onto her pajama bottoms and hoisted her uncooperative legs to the floor. Palm by palm she moved along the wall and made her way to the dresser. She quietly slid it open and took out a cashmere sweater, skinny jeans, socks, and put them on top of the wooden dresser. Jonas's carbon fiber wallet also sat atop the dresser. On the back it had a clip to store money, inside the pocket was a GPS tracker, and in the credit card slots was an access card with the Lucent Labs logo stamped on it.

Cindy snuck out into the living room and got dressed. She hoisted herself up on her crutches, stuck the access card in her pocket, and took Jadie's keys which had not moved from the kitchen counter. She opened the door to a quiet, frigid, and windless night.

CHAPTER 10:

Once Human

In the northeast, sometimes the snow would never come. The winters would be cold but mild, a mere inconvenience. And sometimes the winter would be brutal. Entire cities would be enveloped by a swirling fog of snow. Businesses would close, trains and flights would be cancelled, and the world would slowly grind to a halt.

For Cindy, this was the beginning of a bitter winter. Everything she held dear was slowly being taken away. Jonas would be next, then her parents, and finally herself. *I'm being paranoid,* she thought, but with the way her luck has been lately who wouldn't? She would never forget the dizzying sensation of being trapped in a car rolling to its grave. Or how utterly helpless she was to protect her sister.

Had this been another regular winter, she knew exactly where she'd be right now. She'd be in bed, half-naked, with her pre-accident athletic body. Jonas would be next to her, reading a boring chapter on the application of nanomachines. And then, after removing her bra, she would reach below his stomach and entice him with a little bit of late night fun. How lovely it was to remember a time when her life had not decomposed into a complete pile of shit.

She pulled up to the gate blocking the entrance of the Latini building parking garage and waved Jonas's access card. As the gate opened and she pulled into a spot, she realized there would be no turning back. Raymond said the movers would come tomorrow to haul the suit away. If she decided not go on, there would be no second chances.

Armed with her crutches, she made her way through the Lucent Labs corridor and arrived at the vault door leading to SIRCA's housing. If Michael was right, the access card would be all she needed to gain access, no retina scan. She swiped it and quietly celebrated when the door unlocked.

The motion sensor detected her presence. One by one the fluorescent lights flickered on. Sterile light cast down onto the metal desks and a lone remaining computer. Through the glass window separating the Main Lab from the Workshop, the containment unit stood alone, with its lights and systems on standby. She woke the SIRCA control terminal from sleep and was immediately dismayed.

"Password? Shit."

She typed in James (Jonas Ames) for the user login and input the password he uses for his laptop—Gr4yf0x93. The login attempt failed. She didn't know how many tries the computer would allow and decided to hold off. Maybe there was a password written down somewhere.

Aside from a computer and chair the lab was stripped clean. She could find nothing related to the SIRCA control terminal or its password. The facility had been stripped clean and only had the bare essentials to keep it running. She found a random network card adapter, dusty Ethernet cables, and a tiny screw.

"Tell me I didn't come all this way just to be stopped by a stupid password."

She checked out an area of the lab called the Server Room. The enclosed space whined with the sound of hundreds of fans blowing at once. Towers of flashing lights stood in a row blinking with hidden purpose. Again, no notes, no password, nothing.

As she turned to head back to the main lab, she spotted a laptop hidden in a corner of the room. Wires dangled above it like vines and an external hard drive flashed its status light. A picture of Cindy and Jonas was taped over the laptop web camera.

Cindy tapped the spacebar which woke the laptop from sleep. She hen-pecked Gray Fox 93 and cheered loudly when the computer unlocked. A status bar sat in the middle of the screen, transferring files from a folder called SIRCA BACKUP to the external drive. Cindy left his back up alone and opened his password manager app.

Using her name and wedding anniversary as the master password, Cindy gained access to all of his passwords. His bank, his e-mail, his network and router login for home, his randomly generated passwords for websites he used only once, and even credit card information. Convenient, but extremely dangerous in the wrong hands. She typed SIRCA into the search field and was surprised by how simple the control terminal password was.

She returned to the Workshop and typed in: T3rminat0r.

Welcome.

"Yes!" She pumped her fist in the air. "I can't believe that worked."

She clicked on the SIRCA icon which booted up the control panel. A graphic of the containment unit appeared with a silhouette of a humanoid shaded in grey and another shaded in red. The graphic seemed to imply that there were two objects inside the containment unit but she wasn't sure.

"Okay. This is going to be trickier than I thought."

Navigating through every menu in the SIRCA interface left Cindy bewildered. The words on their own kind of made sense. UI, Array, module, list, widget, div, well, maybe not div. She learned that widgets must have been another word for switches or modules, because when she clicked lights on, the containment unit lights turned on. She expanded the widgets and unearthed even more widgets which sounded more complex than her initial list. A.I., Renderer, Physics, DataCore, Head Tracking, Heat Maps. And other words which made no sense at all, Nnet, Plyamr, APU, Aug-Real.

She scrolled through the options using the arrow keys and found a promising widget called Con. Unit Ctrls. The selections were fairly simple, open bay one or open bay two. She selected bay one. The capsule hissed. Star-like LED lights turned on from within the struts and pipes and cast an eerie glow. The doors slid open and released a cloud of gas which rolled across a cement floor full of nicks, burns and eroded caution paint, remnants of whatever tests they had conducted here. The interior lights flashed on and illuminated the silver suit. Its metallic skin was clean and pure, and within the reflection, her forehead and jaw stretched into waves like a funhouse mirror.

She stood in front of the containment unit, enveloped by its light. She could hardly see the machine because it was so bright inside the chamber. SIRCA, in simplest terms, was a blank androgynous mannequin of chrome. There were no lines which hinted of armor plates. No bumps or ridges from an endoskeleton. Hell it didn't even have a zipper. Cindy clacked forward on her crutches and gazed at the machine.

"You better be worth the trouble."

She glanced inside the containment unit.

"Okay, how do I do this?"

She stretched out her hand and touched SIRCA's waist which felt as it looked, smooth and solid. She felt around the back and couldn't find any latches or buttons to open. When she removed her hand, a trail of stringy mucus-like fibers dangled from her palm like glue.

"Ew, gross."

Shimmering silver covered her palm like a lake. She wiped her hand against her sweater and accidentally spread the metallic goo to her clothes.

"How is this a suit?"

An alarm rang inside the capsule. Red lights flashed over the sound of an automated voice, "Intruder alert, intruder alert." SIRCA melted into a puddle of mercury.

"Lovely."

With the alarm blaring, she went in search of a container large enough to hold SIRCA. *What a waste of time,* she thought. The suit was supposed to be wearable, it was supposed to make her stronger, not turn into a useless puddle of goop. This entire trip was pointless. She rushed over to the Bio Lab and found little more than empty counters and a pen. She opened every cabinet and managed to find a measuring cup with a chipped lip. She balanced on her crutches, took the cup, and turned towards the workshop where the containment unit flashed its red lights.

Sitting between her and the entrance to the workshop was a large liquid puddle. She had not seen it when she came in and leaned in for a closer look. The puddle was SIRCA, and it had moved from the containment unit. She gasped and nearly dropped the cup.

"No way."

She went around the island in the middle of the Bio Lab. The puddle slithered across and made gurgling sounds like boiling water as it blocked her route. She went the other way and the puddle followed. Then the puddle split in two and cornered her within the lab. There was no way she could continue believing SIRCA was just a suit. Jonas's creation had something more frightening than the ability to move, it had intelligence.

The hand she used to touch SIRCA began to burn. The pain started from her wrist and shot up the length of her arm as her fingers curled together. Slowly her sleeve tightened around her arm as if it were shrinking, but it wasn't shrinking, she was growing. Her head pounded from fear. The machine was physically changing her body and she didn't know what to do. The glass cup in her hand squealed and popped. Her closed hand had transformed into a metal fist. "What the f—"

The growing metallic muscles of her forearm split open her sleeve while her right arm remained thin and bony. She clawed at the liquid metal and tried to pry it off with her fingernails. The machine bit down on her skin and stung like a snake bite.

"Oh no. Oh shit."

The puddle burst wriggling tendrils from its viscous surface that raced to Cindy's feet. She screamed and hobbled over to the main lab with the creature chasing after her. She slipped and her crutches skittered to the other side of the room. The silver tendrils coiled around her boots and dragged her across the floor. She frantically tried to crawl with her hands as the creature reeled her into its maw.

Her ankles and calves exploded the stitching in her jeans with a loud tear. She military crawled past the central island and gained precious distance from the machine, but then it pulled her again and erased all progress. She screamed and rolled onto her back. She wedged her thumbs into the collars of each boot and wiggled her feet out. The machine sucked in her shoes and dissolved them like acid. The puddle merged into one giant mass and chased after Cindy with its Medusa-like tendrils wriggling in the air.

"Get away from me!"

SIRCA whipped one of its multiple arms and pulled on her pants, exposing a hint of her pink underwear. She breathed so hard and so fast she became lightheaded and dizzy. SIRCA chilled her skin as it crawled through her jeans and filled her atrophied legs with pipes of synthetic mass. Her pants tore open and revealed a pair of silver, muscular legs.

Her trapezius muscles pushed out from her spine and sundered her sweater into two pieces. Her arms grew too big for her sleeves and burst the fabric into ragged flags of thread. Her moonlit skin greyed into chrome and thickened into a hardened shell. The fibers and thread of her clothing sparkled and then disintegrated as if they were being deconstructed by a swarm of LED wearing moths. In its wake, her skin became a shimmering, flexible alloy. She arced her back and screamed in agony as SIRCA cracked her bones and reshaped her body. A dizzying surge of strength exploded through her limbs like a bolt of lightning. She smashed her hand through the floor. The cement cratered and spewed puffs of dust. Her feelings of anguish slowly morphed into ecstasy. She moaned and jerked her legs as if caught in the middle of an orgasm. Once it passed she gasped and caught her breath.

"Holy shit." She panted. "What's happening to me?"

There wasn't much left of the puddle. It continued to slurp and gurgle, almost as if it were sacrificing itself to give Cindy its power. There was no use fighting it now.

"Fuck it."

SIRCA climbed her mountainous trapezius and journeyed past the fattened veins in her neck to the bottom of her smooth, delicate jaw. Silver threads shot out from the gooey metal and sealed her head in a cocoon of metallic silk. The strands fused into a solid shell, creating a visor-less motorcycle helmet, but with two empty eye holes in the shape of parallelograms.

She quickly discovered that the eye holes were not actually holes but pieces of glass. With no vents for oxygen, she breathed in her own carbon dioxide. She gasped and wheezed, pushing her fingers against the bottom of her helmet. She searched for latches or buckles but could find neither amongst the smooth surface of the helmet.

She grabbed onto its sides and desperately tried to rip it off, but doing so was like trying to rip her head from her neck. Her upper lip grew wet from her hot breath filling the helmet. She cried out and smashed her head into the floor. The concrete cracked and fractured with each successive hit, but the helmet did not dent or scratch.

Her frantic attempts slowed to a lethargic, half asleep pace. She collapsed on the floor with the sound of a pan falling in a kitchen. As the last supply of oxygen dissipated from her system, she saw two men enter the lab before completely losing consciousness.

CHAPTER 11:

End of Watch

[Loading . . .]

[Lucent Labs, S.I.R.C.A. BETA v098.7—Unauthorized user detected—Initiating termination protocol. Error code 22 0x16, Error bad command. | Activating life support. Systems override: MDresden. Life support online.]

Her eyes stung as they adjusted to the star pattern of lights beaming against her face. She read a scroll of text floating in front of her vision. Beyond the text she could see the ceiling, walls, and computer equipment.

[SYSTEM STARTUP: Polymorphic armor – Online | Endoskeleton – Online | Synthetic Muscle Augmentation – Online | Life Support – Online | APU – Online | Artificial Intelligence – Online | Gecko Grip – Online | Acceleration Boost – Online | H. U. D. – Online | Mag Drivers – Offline | Stealth Camo – Offline | EWS – Online | Neural Network – Online | AR – Disabled | GPS Uplink – Disabled | CPU Assisted Reflexes – Online | Tissue Regeneration – Active | Initializing registration.]

"User," A robotic female voice spoke into Cindy's ears or maybe her brain. "Please wait while SIRCA completes installation."

A refreshing gust of air pushed into her helmet. She breathed it in and felt more alert and energetic. "Hello?" Her voice hissed like a ghost's whisper filtered through a radio speaker, deep and mechanical. She cleared her throat and spoke again. "My voice."

"Stealth, Infiltration, Reconnaissance, Combat, Armor has successfully identified and bonded to your DNA. You are now the pilot. Please note this process cannot be undone without the assistance of a system administrator."

"Pilot?" Cindy said, more alarmed. "Who is this?"

"I am SIRCA. Pilot, please state your identity."

"My identity?"

"You said, 'My Identity.' SIRCA will register you as 'My Identity' is this correct?"

"No."

"Pilot, please state your identity."

"Cindy."

"You have said, 'Cindy.' SIRCA will register you as 'Cindy' is this correct?"

"Yes."

"You are now registered as Cindy. Welcome, Cindy."

She turned away from hanging lights and raised her hand to shade her eyes. She gasped at the sight of her silver skin. Did it work? Did she actually manage to put on the suit? She felt resistance as she moved her arms. There were mysterious cables connected to her limbs and back.

"What is this?"

"Cindy," the robotic voice chirped. "Please state your objective."

"My objective?"

"Please state your objective."

"I don't know."

"I'm sorry, I didn't quite get that. You must establish an objective in order for me to assist you."

She didn't know how to answer. A few seconds ago she couldn't breathe. Now she had to state an objective. After a brief delay, SIRCA spoke again.

"You can use commands such as: terminate, capture, recover, infiltrate, or recon."

"Well then. I guess I want to terminate Ned Pickler."

"Primary Objective established: Terminate Ned Pickler. Calibrating HUD."

The lights obscuring her vision dimmed. The numbers and various displays floating in mid-air became brighter and easier to read. Suddenly, she was lifted by the bundle of cables and hydraulics connected to her spine and shoulders. She went from resting on her back on some kind of hydraulic bed to being suspended above the floor like a marionette. Michael and Raymond greeted her.

"Well this is a surprise," Raymond said. "I did not expect to see you again so soon, Mrs. Ames."

Michael was less enthused. "What . . . did . . . you . . . do."

Floating boxes filled with data appeared over Michael. SIRCA listed his details: name, age, height, weight, and glasses prescription. She looked at Raymond, curious to see what the suit would say about him, but the scan failed. [Error code 1065 0x429 Database does not exist]

Michael took off his glasses and pinched the bridge of his nose. "Jonas is going to kill me." He then addressed Raymond. "We need to remove the suit before it bonds to her DNA."

"Too late."

"Goddammit!"

"Michael," Raymond said. "Relax." She could see her silvery reflection within his green eyes. "She looks marvelous."

Cindy looked down and a face plate she didn't know she had clinked against her chest. She couldn't believe how solid she looked. With her feet still floating in the air and her shoulders suspended by cables, she bent her leg and swayed it from side to side. Her metallic thigh stretched and bulged.

"Michael," she gasped. "I can move my legs."

He raised an eyebrow. "Does it feel strange?"

"A little." She moved the other leg and shuddered with excitement. "I feel like I'm in someone else's body. Doesn't feel like it's mine."

"That's because it isn't."

"Michael," Raymond snapped. "Cindy, how is it that you are wearing the suit?"

She straightened her leg. "I snuck into the lab and touched it."

"Did you take Jonas's keycard," Raymond said.

"Yes."

"There was a password on the control terminal," Michael replied. "How did you gain access?"

"With luck and determination."

"Why?"

"To terminate Ned Pickler."

Raymond looked confused. "Who is Ned?"

"The man who ruined my life."

"Jesus, Cindy. You've gone too far this time," Michael said.

"Now, now, Michael." Raymond put his hands behind his back and paced in front of Cindy. "Though I respect your tenacity, I cannot allow you to keep the suit, Mrs. Ames."

"I'm not giving it back."

"You must."

Her bicep bulged. The cables suspending her body tensed against her newfound power. The plugs popped off her armor and released their hold. The eyeholes of her helmet flashed on in a radiant, cyan glow. The feeling of power was intoxicating. She wasn't going to hurt them, but she wasn't going to be stopped either. She earned this suit and had every intention of using it.

"Holy shit," Michael said.

"I didn't come all this way and suffer all that pain just so you could take this away from me." Her newly developed synthetic muscles flexed. "Don't think I won't push you out of my way." She relaxed and noticed her body shrink to its normal size, *impressive*. Now that she had properly warned them, it was time to try diplomacy again. Having Raymond and Michael supporting her would make her goal of catching Ned much easier. "Now, if you'd let me explain myself. Maybe we can come to an agreement?"

Raymond seemed quite surprised. "I would most certainly prefer you not push us. Please go on."

"I met Ned two years ago . . ."

"South King." A woman with a thick New York accent spoke through the police band radio. A dispatcher for the Midtown South precinct.

A patrol car from Midtown South replied, "South King, go ahead."

"Have you heard from South David?"

Cindy's radio blared from the holster near her chest. Her hands and feet were bound by rope and her mouth was gagged by a moldy sock. Dispatch was calling for South David which was her and Dan's unit designation, but she couldn't reach the radio.

"Not since we left base at fifteen hundred. Is there a problem?"

She kicked the trunk lid of the car she was trapped in. "Mmm, mmmpf!"

"They haven't been responding to my calls."

"Maybe they're having radio trouble."

"Mmmmm!"

"If you see South David, please tell them to check in."

"Four."

The static-filled voices through Cindy's radio ceased. She breathed loudly through her nose and hit the back of her head against the trunk compartment. She and Dan were ambushed during a routine subway foot patrol. As she tried to pull her wrists apart, she wondered if Dan had been captured too. She tried to roll on her side so she could squeeze the transmit button on her radio. But the button required pressure from both thumb and forefinger.

The car eventually came to a stop. Four doors opened and closed with enough force to jolt the trunk. She could hear footsteps and men talking outside. With the blindfold on, she focused on her other senses to figure out where she was so she could call for back up. The trunk clicked open. The sound of a foghorn crowed in the distance. A smell of fish and river water forced into her nose.

"Hello little princess. The king says you've been very naughty."

She kicked her hands and feet in a vain attempt to resist.

"Get her out of there."

The blindfold slipped and she was able to see the man's face. He had a tattoo of a spider web around his eye.

"Uh, uh, uh." He pulled the blindfold back over her eye. "No peeking."

The man scooped his big hands under her legs and back. His shoes crunched over pavement as he carried her and a ship's bell clanged close by. Obviously she was at a dock or harbor of some sort, but without more information she couldn't identify where. She could have been in Red Hook, or Chelsea Piers, or even across the river in Newark, New Jersey. Another hand touched her chest and removed the squawking radio from her person.

They carried her for a short distance and then dropped her onto a hard metal floor which sent pain up her spine. The man breathed on her face before placing the tip of a sharp object on her cheek.

"You know what that is?"

She nodded.

"I won't cut you as long as you don't act up. Your partner learned that the hard way."

The man rolled Cindy onto her back. He ran his knife through the ropes and weakened the binding enough so she could break free. But before she could escape, the man left and slammed a heavy door shut. The sound clapped her ears and left her disoriented. She pulled the ropes away from her body and took off the blindfold and gag. Her mouth tasted like smelly foot fungus and made her want to vomit.

She scrambled to her feet and carefully inched through the darkness, feeling for something, anything, with her hands. She bumped against a cold wall with a hard rusty texture to it. She ran her fingers along the grooves of corrugated steel and followed the wall until she found another wall and another wall. Her prison was a narrow rectangle made of steel. They had trapped her in a freight container. She banged her fists against the thick plates. "Let me out!"

"Hey," A man's voice screamed through a speaker mounted inside the freight container. "Knock it off or I'll kill you and your partner right now."

"Who are you? Why are you doing this to us?"

"Little girl, you know who I am. You stole thirteen million dollars from me."

"What are you talking about? I never took anyone's money."

"You don't remember bragging to your precinct about giving the DEA and State Police information on a drug lab in the city? My drug lab. You talked so much shit, everyone from here to fucking Mexico knew that a little pussy cop made a fool out of me. You remember doing that shit? Huh? Thirteen million fucking dollars!"

Fingers of dread pulled on her skin. This must have been Death Dealer, the owner of the drug lab. She only bragged about her involvement to people on the force. Did he have a spy in the NYPD? "I'm—I'm a police officer," she said nervously. "You can't touch me or my partner."

"You know, just because we're criminals doesn't mean we don't have rules. Everyone knows you don't sweat losing two, three, five thousand dollars. Those are operating losses. No one even blinks an eye at losing twenty thousand dollars anymore. At a hundred thousand dollars, though, things change, people get hurt. At thirteen million dollars, people disappear.

"The gangs told me not to touch you guys and I wasn't going to. But then you had to go run your mouth. You had to rub it in my face that you made me lose five fucking years of investment. Now I have to start all over again, from scratch! And it's because of you and your roided out partner. So now one of you is gonna disappear. And the one who lives gets to tell the other pigs that the big bad wolf is gonna blow down their houses."

The diesel engine of a truck snarled and roared, growing louder until the walls of the container rumbled. She slowly backed away from the wall and in that instant the panel imploded inward. She screamed and ran to the other side. The thunderous blast rang her ears as the entire container quaked and shifted under her feet. Through the speaker, she heard Dan's voice yelling and cursing at their captors. "Stop it! Please, God, stop!"

Ned and his cronies cackled like hyenas. The reverse alarm from the truck kicked in, *beep, beep,* and then its brakes hissed. The engine roared again. She braced herself against the wall and tightly shut her eyes. The container shifted and rolled, filling her ears with the sound of twisted metal. Gripped by fear, she lost control of her bladder and peed her pants. The tires squealed, she could smell burning rubber and also sensed the container grinding against the pavement. Suddenly, her feet flew up past her chest as if someone had tripped her and she knew she was airborne. She slammed into each corner, hurting her back, knees, and shoulders with each painful tumble. The container slid to a stop and she didn't know whether she was facing up or down, left or right. All she knew was that tonight would probably be her End of Watch.

"Someone help me!"

An odor of gasoline seeped in through the locked door. The box became warm like the inside of a car during a hot summer's day. She touched the wall and singed her hand from the intense heat. Flickering orange light seeped through the gap between the doors. Sweat formed on her brow and rolled down her neck as she screamed, "Get me out of here!"

The bolt which secured the door clacked open. Rusty hinges squealed as a gust of fresh air burst through the opening. She sprinted through the door and felt relief as the night sky cooled the moisture on her skin. She was so happy to be alive that she was ready to kiss the garbage-filled ground with her lips. Then she looked up, and her happiness rotted into fear. Only a few feet away, a container identical to her own, burned like a dry log. And Dan . . . Dan was still trapped inside, screaming. She ran to the garbage pile and found a rusty pipe. She heaved it over her shoulder and whacked the flimsy lock.

Dan burst through the door wearing the flames of his melting cage. "Cindy!" He charged blindly across the garbage filled dock. Loose scraps of paper and plastic garbage bags caught fire.

"Dan!" She tried to get closer but the heat was too intense. "Daaaan!"

A Bitter Winter

The fire turned into an inferno. She could no longer tell the difference between her partner and the garbage burning around him. She could do nothing but listen and watch the flames. It was horrible, so unspeakably horrible.

Even after all these years, speaking of Dan brought Cindy to the verge of tears. "I . . ." she swallowed hard. "I tried but I couldn't—"

"You can stop." Raymond held his chin, his green eyes unblinking. "A justified reason for revenge, but something doesn't add up. Why did your container suddenly unlock?"

"They wanted me to watch." Her resolve returned and hardened like the steel of her new skin. "These people are animals. And now they hurt my sister. You can't expect me not to respond."

"Although noble . . ." Raymond grimaced. "That's a sixteen billion dollar nanosuit you're wearing. To put it into perspective, I could buy a hundred F-18 military fighter jets and still not match the price of one suit."

"Meaning it's excessive for what you need it for, Cindy," Michael interjected. "A suit like that isn't designed to fight petty crime."

"Petty crime?" She flexed her fingers.

"I mean. It's—it's for combat zones. You know, military, CIA espionage. That's what I mean, I'm not saying what you want is petty."

She relaxed and turned to Raymond. "You want to make a deal or not?"

"What do you have in mind?"

Michael turned to Raymond. "You can't be serious."

Raymond made a shushing motion.

"I want two things: The first one is obvious, I want Ned, dead or alive. You let me leave with this suit and I will hunt him down. The second thing I want is for my sister to be cured. She has swelling in her brain from an accident caused by Ned's goons.

If Jonas's formula could heal my wounds and the suit can turn me into this; then there has to be a way it can help Jadie. You do that and I'll be your guinea pig."

"Reasonable, but not good enough." Raymond rubbed his chin.

"Thank God," Michael said.

"Unless you agree to complete certain, suit related tasks for me."

"No!"

She found Raymond's change of heart, suspicious, but intriguing.

"Like what?"

"Assignments related to national security."

"No killing."

"You would not be asked to. But if you refuse my assignments, I will consider that a withdrawal from our agreement. SIRCA would be returned to me."

A sixteen billion dollar suit to track Ned in exchange for some counter terrorism. Sounded like a reasonable price to pay. She wasn't sure she could trust Raymond but if he tried anything fishy, she could use the suit to take him down. For now, having allies was more important. She offered her hand.

"One more thing," he said as he grabbed her hand. "Jonas must never know. I do not think he would approve of our little arrangement."

They shook on it.

"What the hell do you two think you're doing?" Michael reached into his pocket and took out his phone. "I'm calling Jonas."

Cindy watched Raymond argue with Michael. "You're going to miss out on a prime opportunity." She was amazed by how charismatic and cool-headed Raymond could be even with Michael freaking out. They were qualities she hoped to one day develop for herself.

"What, an opportunity to see SIRCA rip her body to shreds? We haven't tested it!"

"If you agree to help Cindy with SIRCA, I will grant you full control over the development of the project. Jonas would be reassigned to finding a cure for Jadie and you become Cindy's personal caretaker."

She made a face. Thankfully, no one could see it behind her helmet.

"Wait." Michael lowered his phone. "What are you saying?"

"You're a smart man, Michael. Do I really need to spell it out?"

"What if the suit hurts her?"

"Then it will be your responsibility to make sure it doesn't." Raymond smiled. "I think the work you've done on SIRCA has earned you the right to take command of the project. Besides, I'd love to see the energy blade concept you've told me about."

"Remember what we talked about at the hospital? What I said about our friendship?" She touched Michael's jaw. "I'm sorry for hurting your feelings. You really are a good friend to me and I hope you'll consider helping me with this." She felt terrible for manipulating him, but she needed this suit. "We could talk about the good ol' days."

Michael blushed. "I guess."

"Then it's settled," Raymond said. "SIRCA has its first test pilot."

"Quick question. Jonas is going to ask me why the containment unit alarm went off." Michael adjusted his glasses. "What am I going to tell him?"

Cindy shook her head. "The bigger question is what am *I* going to tell him?" She pointed to her strapping chrome body. "I don't think a pair of glasses and a trench coat is going to cut it."

Before they could head back, Cindy purchased a can of beer from a twenty four hour convenience store and downed it before getting in Jadie's SUV with Michael. It was an awful, cheap beer, borderline skunked, but she wasn't drinking it for the taste or pleasure. She needed to convince Jonas that instead of stealing his prototype military weapon, she had been out getting drunk . . . like she used to do.

"Let me make sure all the metal is gone." Michael brushed his hand against her back while also driving the car. He spot checked her boots and hands "Looks like the suit deactivated properly."

"Just so I understand. I have to touch a spot on my forearm? Like, literally on my skin?"

"Yeah, try it out."

Cindy pulled up her sleeve and pressed the mentioned spot on her forearm. A grid of nine glowing dots appeared as if underneath her skin. "That is weird."

"It's technology." He then pointed to the dots. "So if you draw a C, like you did at the lab, the suit comes off. If you draw an S, which really is more like a reverse Z, you'll engage the suit. Kind of like your cell phone pattern lock."

"Okay," she said. "Makes sense."

"If Raymond is really going to give me full control, the first thing I'm going to do is program it so you can turn SIRCA on and off with your thoughts. The pattern recognition is just a temporary place holder."

She smiled at Michael. It was so easy to manipulate him. A tap on the shoulder here, a smile there, and he became like putty. She would never sleep with him, or kiss him on the mouth, but she would go far to keep him on her team. If something went wrong with SIRCA, he would be the only one capable of fixing it. "I had no idea you were this intelligent. That's a very sexy quality to have."

The car swerved.

"Whoa, easy." She grabbed the steering wheel and straightened it out. "One accident was enough."

"Sorry." He blushed.

"How did you program the suit to literally rebuild my clothes? That was pretty amazing."

Michael chuckled. "Well I told everyone on the team that we couldn't have pilots left naked once they were done using the suit. So I programmed SIRCA to remember how it disassembled clothes in order to be able to rebuild them later. I don't know if you saw it, but your clothes sparkle when it's being disassembled. They're LEDs from the nanomachines."

Her eyes opened wide with excitement. "Oh my God, I just got the greatest idea. I'll go to the most expensive clothing store in the city. Try on some clothes, turn on the suit, and then have like a . . . seven thousand dollar outfit in the database."

"That's . . . I never thought about that."

"It's a great idea, right?"

"Wouldn't that be considered theft?"

She patted his arm. "I'm joking."

"It's nice to see you smile again."

"I don't know what it is. Either I'm super excited about the suit or it's having some weird side effects. Who knows, maybe I'll stay like this."

"I hope so."

Michael parked in front of her house. He retrieved Cindy's crutches from the back and handed them to her. She pretended to hobble along, exaggerating how hard it was for her to walk with crutches. She wanted to make sure she looked visibly drunk from a distance, just in case Jonas was watching. Sure enough, as they climbed the steps to the porch, the door swung open.

"Where have you been," Jonas whispered. "I've been trying to call you since midnight. Do you have any idea what time it is?"

A pang of guilt hit her. She knew he was going to be pissed but she had to do it, she had to pretend to come home drunk again. She threw herself into his arms. "Babeeeee," she slurred and let the crutches fall. "I missed you." She rammed her lips to his face and bathed him with sloppy kisses tasting of stale beer. Jonas craned back and pushed her forehead with his palm. She pushed her head past his resisting palm and said, "Didjou missme?"

"Not this shit again."

"It was just a drink. One itty, bitty one." She pinched her fingers together. "Very tiny. Muy pequeño."

Jonas looked at Michael. "Did you do this?"

"Me? No. She called me to pick her up. Luckily I was already on my way back from the lab. Um, false alarm by the way. The containment unit is fine. A brownout tripped the alarm."

Jonas turned to Cindy and glared at her.

"Why did you call him instead of me?"

"Because . . ." she elongated her words. "You were going to get mad at me."

Jonas sighed. His eyes softened as he returned his attention to Michael. "Thanks for bringing her home."

"No problem, man. I'm going to—" He pointed over his shoulder. "Go home."

"You can stay the night if you want."

"Nah, I'm good. I'll see you tomorrow."

"Babe," Cindy said. "I have to pee."

"All right," Jonas growled. "Come on."

CHAPTER 12:

Test Trial

In the growing light of the morning, Cindy rolled under the blankets, clutching her belly. Her stomach felt bloated, as if a rock were forcing its way through her intestines. She whimpered softly and grabbed onto the headboard with one hand. She tightened her grip and accidentally crushed the wood within her hand. She turned her palm up and stared at the woodchips with astonishment. *How . . .*

A feeling of nausea overwhelmed her followed by the throbbing, agonizing pain in her stomach. She scrambled out of bed and ran for the bathroom. She coughed and heaved into the toilet but only a few drops of spittle came out. She tore a square of toilet paper and wiped her lips.

Jonas knocked on the door. "You okay? Need me to buy you some medicine?"

"I'm fine," she said.

"Are you hung over?"

"I'm . . . I'm fine. I'll be out in a minute."

"How did you get into the bathroom without your crutches?"

Her eyes went wide. "Um. I, I crawled."

"Why would you crawl?"

"Could you put them against the door for me? Please."

"Okay."

She rose to her feet and noticed a heavier weight pressing down on her ankles. Her pajamas proved tight around her arms and legs when only yesterday they had hung loose. She twisted the faucet and submerged her face into the basin. She slurped handfuls of water and spat out the foul taste in her mouth.

When she looked in the mirror, she spotted a strange bulge on both sides of her neck. "What the . . ." She slowly pushed the collar of her shirt and turned her head. Her neck muscles had grown in size and shape. "Oh, wow." She took a few steps back from the mirror and pulled up her pajama shirt.

"Oh . . . my . . . God."

A Bitter Winter

A column of muscles popped out of her flat stomach, they bulged and twisted with the movement of her hips. The bullet holes which had scarred her body were completely erased, as if nothing had happened, yet her older scars still remained. She couldn't even flex her arm for fear of tearing the sleeve with her bicep. Taking one more step back, she pulled down her pants and gasped when her thick, muscular gymnast thighs spilled out.

"Holy shit, girl." She smiled at the mirror. "You are sexy as fuck."

She would have continued admiring her new body except for one, disturbing new addition. A red, agitated splotch had replaced one of the bullet scars. The spot had raised bumps and looked like a rash or maybe a form of hives, she wasn't sure. It didn't itch but it was sensitive to the touch. "Well that's new." She opened the medicine cabinet and applied a skin cream to the red spot. Jonas knocked on the door again.

"Are you sure you're okay?"

"Jonas, I said I was fine."

"We need to talk when you get out."

The tone of his voice instantly put her on the defensive. "Okay, jeez. Go eat breakfast or something." She pulled down her shirt. "What's with him?" She muttered.

Cindy grabbed her crutches which Jonas had kindly placed against the wall and lumbered over to the bedroom to change into something looser. Did she grow overnight? She found an oversized sweatshirt with the words Jersey Strong printed on it and a pair of large sweat pants. Hopefully he wouldn't notice the weight she put on. She met him out in the living room where he was already dressed in his winter gear.

"You're going to work?"

"Yes."

He still seemed a little grumpy so she gave him a playful smile and a kiss on the lips. If only he knew how great she felt right now. How eager she was to take his clothes off and her own. So she showed him by kissing his neck.

"Stop."

"Oh come on." She made her way up to his cheek, then his lips. "Don't you miss me?"

Jonas pulled away and left her standing like a fool. He grabbed a brochure

122

from the counter and picked her crutches off the floor. He gave them both to her. "I think you need to go to this."

She took the pamphlet and read it. "Alcoholics anonymous for women? What the hell is this?"

"This is the second time you've come home drunk and I'm worried that you're using alcohol to cope with your feelings."

"I don't believe this." She threw the pamphlet on the floor. "I don't need to go to AA."

"Don't think I forgot when you slapped me and the state you were in when it happened."

She realized her mistake in pretending to be drunk last night. In fact, considering her history, faking drunkenness was the dumbest decision she had ever made.

"Are you listening to me?"

"Just go to work."

"Promise me you'll go to the meeting. I don't want to come home and see you hung over."

"I wasn't hung over."

"I heard you retching in there."

"I wasn't . . . hung over." She turned her back to him. "Just leave already."

"I'm worried about you."

"There's nothing to fucking worry about!"

She stormed off into her bedroom and slammed the door shut. She didn't blame Jonas for feeling the way he did, but why did he have to act so damn righteous? Just because he didn't drink or smoke didn't mean he was always right. If he really wanted her to go to AA, he should volunteer to come with her. She sighed and told herself the charade was only temporary. Once Ned was terminated, she could do damage control on her relationship.

———

A Bitter Winter

She borrowed Jadie's SUV and drove to an abandoned rail yard hidden within the woods of Northern New Jersey. She wanted to be able to test the suit without risk of harming anyone or anything, and this train yard in the middle of nowhere was the perfect spot. It was a long drive down winding roads which followed the contours of the hills and valleys. She turned onto a snow covered dirt road and bounced past barren trees incapable of obscuring the sun with their naked branches.

A light snow fell over the train yard. Dilapidated train cars sat detached from one another on crooked tracks abandoned decades ago. Their hollow, rusted shells left the interiors exposed, allowing snow to accumulate on iron brackets where passenger seats used to be mounted. Even this desolate place held sweet memories of her sister. When Cindy first got her license, she and Jadie drove around aimlessly and sang along to pop music. They found the dirt road by chance and Jadie was the one who suggested they explore.

On weekends or three day vacations, they would drive up here and camp out. Sometimes they roasted marshmallows and other times they drank beers and talked about life and dreams. Just the two of them. The train yard was their secret club house and no one else was invited.

She walked along the perimeter of the rail yard, listening for voices or footsteps. She found no trace of civilization, except for empty beer bottles and cigarette butts. Otherwise, this place was still abandoned. She pulled the sleeve of her coat and touched her forearm. The grid of glowing dots appeared on her skin. She traced an angular S with her finger and waited for the system to confirm the pattern.

Her hand began to tremble. She rotated her wrist and saw lakes of mercury pool atop her skin. The silver liquid went under her sleeve and spread up her arm. Her coat slowly stretched across her back as the layers of the suit began to erupt. SIRCA tore and consumed her clothes and left behind a wake of glossy chrome skin. An intoxicating strength charged through her limbs as the machine took shape and left her breathless.

Unlike the androgynous form from before, SIRCA now took on the shape of its pilot. It masked her genitalia with molded armor plates and replicated the muscle structure of her own body through the synthetic muscle fibers that gave her endoskeleton its strength. The suit appeared deceptively skintight, but Cindy's true flesh was buried beneath thick layers of armor, padding, and nanoweave fiber. She exhaled after a rush of ecstasy and pain left her body.

"Wow, still have to get used to that."

She took a step in her brand new cybernetically enhanced body and heard the subtle whirr of servos rotating in her joints. When her foot landed, soft cushions of air pushed against her feet and left her oddly comfortable. The Heads Up Display, also called the HUD, became active. A compass appeared in the top center of her HUD, north was 000, east was 090, and so on. The compass slid left or right in sync with the direction of her helmet.

In the upper right corner of her HUD was a schematic map, a literal top down view as if a satellite were observing from above. The train cars were marked as flat, solid rectangles which changed into three dimensional cubes if she switched the schematic map into 3D mode.

"This looks really complicated," she said to herself.

"What part of the HUD is confusing you, Cindy?" SIRCA said.

"Holy!" She jumped back, startled. "I totally forgot you were here. You scared the crap out of me."

"I am always present."

"Creepy. What are the numbers and lines in the middle of my screen?"

"The altitude ladder, commonly used in aviation, signifies how high you are above sea level. The default value is zero. This changes according to your elevation."

"Okay, okay." Cindy nodded along. "What about that big blue circle in the middle of my screen at the bottom? It looks like a waffle with a white dot in the middle."

"It is not a waffle, it is a 3D tactical radar. The tactical radar is designed to identify the location and geo coordinates of hostiles in your vicinity. A stem, similar to a music note, will point down if they are above you or up if they are below. The white dot is you, green are civilians, red are hostiles, yellow are objectives. Would you like to know what the different shapes represent?"

"Not right now. Tell me about the little human silhouette on the lower left. It has green text with the words OK next to it."

"That is your armor and health status indicator. This will change color depending on how much damage the suit has absorbed. Blue is normal, green is minor, yellow is moderate, orange is severe, red is danger, flashing red is critical. Do not let the suit go red."

Cindy chuckled. "Got it."

A glint of light flashed inside a train car. She vaulted into it and immediately felt a difference in agility. Jumping felt easier, lighter, as if she could float rather than plummet, moon's gravity versus Earth's. She was also surprised by how flexible the suit was. She could perform splits and backflips with no hindrance from SIRCA.

A squirrel scratched along the rusted luggage racks still mounted on the walls and scurried past Cindy's head. "How strong do you think I am?"

"I do not think," SIRCA said. "I know. At your current body weight multiplied by the endoskeleton and synthetic muscle fiber, your maximum lift should be forty nine thousand nine hundred and eighty four pounds. Due to safety concerns, a flex limiter has been enabled to prevent unnecessary harm to civilians and excessive force against hostiles. Your strength will only increase under special circumstances."

"Fifty fuc—" Cindy's voice shivered from excitement. "—No way. That's impossible."

"The endoskeleton, designed by Doctor John Wright, was built for this express purpose."

"Can I try it out?"

SIRCA scanned the rail yard and marked an empty box car with a yellow pin. "Try this one."

Cindy walked to the rear of the box car. She rubbed her hands together and placed both hands on the corroded metal. The synthetic muscle fibers of her suit inflated and tightened around her body. The giant rusty wheels groaned as they rolled for the first time in decades. Cindy pushed forward and squealed at the discovery of her new found strength.

"This is incredible."

"Please use caution when testing the strength augmentation. Prolonged usage is dangerous."

"How dangerous?"

"Your arms may disconnect from your torso."

Cindy let go and the car rolled to a stop. "Oh." Her body shrunk back to its normal state. "Good to know."

"Also I must warn you that we have a store of energy which can be depleted."

"I'm running on batteries?"

"No, we are driven by a liquid fusion power core which is attached to your spine, between your shoulders. This core and the auxiliary power unit next to it is necessary for all basic functions of the suit, including the effectiveness of bullet deflection. The longer you go without recharging, the higher the risk of injury."

"So how do I recharge?"

"The battery can be renewed by two methods: Solar radiation or consumption of nutrients."

"I can eat dinner and get a tan to recharge my batteries?"

"Correct."

"Awesome."

"It is not recommended to recharge only with food. Our systems will consume calories from your body which may leave you weakened and starved."

"Thank you for the information."

"You are welcome."

A soft hum vibrated Cindy's ears. A message appeared on the left side of her screen. [Incoming call from: Michael]

"Cindy," SIRCA said. "Do you wish to open the comm-link?"

"Yes."

[Connecting . . .]

"Uh, hello? Can you hear me?"

"Loud and clear."

Michael clapped. "Awesome. Did the caller ID tell you it was me?"

"Yes it did."

"And Jonas thought I wouldn't be able to figure it out. It's Caller ID for crying out loud. Child's play."

"Is he there with you now?"

"No. Raymond just broke the news about his reassignment. He's pissed."

"I knew he wouldn't take it well," she said with a tinge of guilt. SIRCA was Jonas's baby, his dream. Having Raymond take him off the project so she could use it herself made her feel awful.

"Yeah. It also didn't help that he found out the lab at First Continental was significantly smaller than what we had in the Latini building. But it's done, I'm fully heading SIRCA development while Jonas and the rest of the team work on the formula. Anyway, Raymond wanted me to ask how your tests were going."

"Well, I've got super powers."

Michael chuckled. "How does it feel?"

"Um, ah-mazing. You know what this suit reminds me of?"

"What's that?"

"It reminds me of those Japanese cartoons my sister used to watch. I feel like I'm one of those characters who powers up and screams her next attack. Lightning fist uppercut! Screaming eagle spin kick! Justice Angel crash!"

Michael laughed. "I wouldn't say that on a mission. Unlike the cartoons, you'd give away your position. Anyway, is the suit turning you back into the trash talking, overly excitable, should probably be treated for ADHD Cindy?"

While Michael gabbed in her ear, Cindy activated a weapon called Mag Driver. A long, slender cannon grew out of her forearm. She aimed the gun at an empty bottle atop a wooden post and closed one eye.

"I do not have ADHD."

[Locked]

Segmented rectangles of glowing light appeared within the barrel of the Mag Driver like strange glyphs from an alien language. A gigantic explosion loosed from the small muzzle and knocked Cindy off her feet. Snow fell off trees and crows flew into the sky cawing in fear as the magnetically charged slug vaporized the bottle and bored through six train cars and toppled at least fifty trees.

"Holy—" She sat up after being thrown into the ground. Chunks of snow rolled off her back as she stood up.

"Did you just fire the Mag Driver?"

"I thought it was going to shoot a bullet not a freaking nuke. What is this thing?"

Both SIRCA and Michael spoke and overlapped each other, but the AI didn't know the rules of etiquette and continued to speak. "The Magnetic Driver is a miniaturized rail gun designed by Jade Law Ballistics. It is an assault weapon designed for anti-personnel and anti-vehicle combat."

Cindy waved her hands. "Whoa, whoa, whoa. This is not anti-personnel. One shot would turn people into mist and destroy a city block."

"Um." Michael chuckled nervously. "We're still tweaking it."

"SIRCA, lock off access to the Mag Driver. It should only be used in case of an emergency. I wouldn't even use this on Ned and that's saying something."

"Please set an emergency code phrase."

"Ad Mortem Inimicus."

"Code phrase set. Mag Driver has been disabled."

"What does that mean, Cindy?" Michael said.

"To death, my enemy."

"I didn't know you spoke Latin."

"I don't. I found it during a Gobble search of Fidelis Ad Mortem which is the NYPD motto after an officer dies in the line of duty. Seemed fitting."

"Oh, well, still cool. Say, can you run some tests for me?"

She groaned. The longer she spent testing the suit, the more time it gave Ned to hurt people. "Yeah, let's make it quick."

"I know you're itching to get out there, but we need to test everything. If you go against Ned and suddenly your suit powers off because of a test we didn't run, he'll kill you."

She sighed. "I know."

"I'll update SIRCA's objectives list."

Cindy's HUD updated with a list of tasks. [Test the following: Gecko grip, jump distance, grappling hook, stealth camouflage, cont'd] Cindy did as she was asked. She used this time to get acclimated with the suit and its abilities. She could stick to walls like a gecko, perform a standing jump of fifteen feet, and run in bursts of fifty miles an hour.

She fantasized about sneaking into Ned's base. Quietly taking out his guards by breaking their necks or throwing them off a ledge. She imagined what it would feel like to punch him with the suit's fist, how she would get him on his knees and force him to beg for his life. Yeah, maybe the tests were worth the delay after all.

The last thing on Michael's list was the multi-purpose grappling hook/

harpoon. The request was simple: hook an object and reel it in, then rappel off a ledge, preferably a building. But she wasn't interested in simple. Rather than pull an object she wondered if she could instead, launch herself. She aimed at a nearby tree and fired.

"Um, what are you doing?"

"When I find Ned. I'm going to swing in and cannonball his ass into the next century."

She catapulted into the air and screamed as if she were on a rollercoaster. She laughed while coming down from her swing and fired another grappling hook which lifted her to another tree. Wind rushed past her ears. She bent her legs to clear obstacles and pulled herself through the woods like a monkey on a vine. That's why it was surprising when she smacked face first into a great oak tree. She slid down the bark and was then buried by the snow.

"I need to work on the landing."

Michael died of laughter. "You—you." He coughed violently. "You—" He choked on his own saliva. "Oh God, I'm crying," he said. "I can't—I can't breathe." He wheezed as he tried to speak. "That was the funniest thing I have seen today. Oh man. I am so glad we could stream your HUD to the PC."

Cindy laughed along with him. "If that hurt I would have been so mad at you."

"We build them right at Lucent Labs." Michael caught his breath and squeezed out the last bit of laughter. "Come on back to the lab so I can run some scans. I think there's a memory leak somewhere in the code. Don't want your suit to crash at random."

"You want me to come to First Continental?"

"No, no. Raymond left me some equipment at the Latini building. He was very serious about not letting Jonas know."

"10-4. I am starving by the way."

"You know the offer for dinner still stands."

"That sounds like a great idea."

CHAPTER 13:

Invisible Hands

There was a room not found on any map, it was circular in shape, the size of a conference room, and pitch black except for a single light hanging from the ceiling. In the center of this chamber was a doughnut shaped table surrounded by empty leather chairs.

Raymond took his seat at the table. An artificial female voice announced his presence.

"Rayman is in attendance."

A group of individuals took their seats and sat within the shadows.

"Red Wing is in attendance."

"El Fuerte is in attendance."

"Herald is in attendance."

"The Black Rook is in attendance."

All chairs were filled, their faces hidden by the inky shadows of the chamber. In the center of the torus shaped table a holographic image of the Earth appeared. As the globe spun, the names of the individuals present in this room appeared over each continent. This signified their level of influence over the governments residing within that continent. In essence, it is not the president or the prime minister or the dictator who rules his or her country. They were merely puppets to the five people who controlled the world from these shadows.

In this chamber, the only currency was influence. For Raymond, money was easier to acquire than influence. To gain it, one needed to cause events worthy of regional, national, or international media attention. When he created Credit Guard, his fame skyrocketed into the stratosphere. By launching satellites, buying tech companies, creating weapons, Raymond unknowingly gained influence and attracted the attention of the Conclave.

But creating technology and participating in humanitarian efforts wasn't the only way he could acquire influence. He could have followed in the examples set by the Black Rook and El Fuerte who gained influence through violence. Assassinations, bombings, mass murders, these too could serve as a gateway into the Conclave.

With influence, these five people could summon shadow agents to infiltrate and manipulate world governments. Drug wars, insurrections, civil wars, wars on terrorism, all were created by the will of the Conclave.

Raymond leaned back in his chair. He remembered when a shadow agent first approached him. She was a sexy, tan skinned woman wearing a coral dress. His wife had passed a few years back from illness, so he was open to meeting a new companion. She smiled at him, batted her eyelashes, and didn't say a word, not even a name. She touched the small of his back and handed him a note with a phone number on it.

He was staying at a hotel in Budapest, naturally, he assumed it was the number to her room. But the man who answered the phone quickly clarified any misunderstandings on his part. Raymond was told in plain terms that the members of the Conclave would like to meet with him. Being the natural businessman that he was, Raymond asked what the benefit was for both parties.

"The Conclave gains an individual who can use his influence to manipulate others without spending money or using intimidation."

"And what do I get?"

The man simply replied, "Control of the world."

He laughed at the man and told him not to waste his time. But the man was deadly serious. He convinced Raymond to join by explaining how he could manipulate government policy in order to ensure the safety of his daughter's future. How he could direct all governments to pursue a path of prosperity over greed. And his daughter's well-being was more valuable than the vast fortune he had accumulated over the years.

"The Conclave is now in session." Raymond blinked and returned his attention to the meeting. "The first member to reach one thousand influence points will be granted the option to control the narrative. Herald has already controlled the narrative and will not be able to participate for two years. Rayman is currently in the lead and needs only ten points to control this year's narrative. The floor is now open for discussion."

Red Wing spoke with a thick Chinese accent. "I see your acquisition of

Lucent Labs has put you in the lead. Remarkable considering the failure of your assassination attempt against a New York senator, a mayor, and a police commissioner."

"I did what had to be done. Besides, the mayor is in critical condition."

For the few years he has been with the Conclave, Raymond tried his best to gain influence through non-violent means, but it took so much work. Developing a new technology or sending food relief to third world countries took time, planning, logistics, and resources. The points would be tremendous in value, but to acquire them took years.

Violence on the other hand, was easy. He didn't need to go to meetings with board executives to discuss a merger; didn't need to hire staff or purchase land to construct a launch pad for his rockets; all he needed was a gun, a bullet, and a high value target. Killing three political figures in the span of an hour was faster and more lucrative than inventing a new technology which could take two years or more. He could see why Fuerte and Rook preferred this method over others. Killing was just so damn easy.

"You could have lost all of your points if it was discovered who was behind the attack. It was a big and pointless risk," Red Wing said.

"I still received ten points for the attempt and with the Black Rook catching up, I needed to take the chance."

El Fuerte chuckled. "In my country we just kill a government guy in his house, sometimes while he's eating breakfast with his family. Then the family gets it too."

"Which is why you only get two influence points instead of fifteen. If you weren't such a savage maybe your points would be worth more."

"Cuidado cabrón. Anyone in this group can end up with a knife in their back, no matter how rich they are."

"I don't fear anyone in this group," Raymond said.

"Words of a fool." The Black Rook spoke for the first time. His voice was harsh and tinged with an accent not specific to any country. "You are stealing my points. The narrative belongs to me this year."

"If it was yours I would not be able to take it. It's any man's game."

The Black Rook clasped his hands. "Why do you want this? Your proposal for a Digital Voter Registration Act is a waste of resources. The reason we exist, is to guide the world with our invisible hands. Your proposal will erode our influence with the Americans."

"This group controls the world through violence and keeping people uneducated," Raymond said. "When I was invited, I was told that we could direct the world governments to become more enlightened, that we could erase stupidity. My Digital Voter Registration Act will be the first step in this direction by allowing educated Americans to vote in their election through usage of cell phones, tablets, and computers. But they cannot vote unless they pass a test which proves they understand the political climate and who they're voting for. My system will educate all voters, so that everyone knows exactly what they're voting for and why. No more will the policies of a country be dictated by the ignorant or oblivious."

The group scoffed at Raymond, but the Rook most of all. "This goes against everything we stand for. The Conclave are the wardens of change. The British believe they voted to leave the EU, the world believes my Mubarizun of Allah are Islamic terrorists, and the Americans believe their votes are meaningless. These are the rules we dictate in order to maintain control."

"I don't agree with these rules." Raymond said sternly. "I had to explain to my four year old granddaughter why a terrorist would kill innocent people. Your handiwork I might add. I look into her big innocent eyes and see the grim future awaiting her, where men can still dictate what she can and cannot do with her body. I want to leave her a world where she can feel safe. Not letting idiots vote is a first step in that direction."

"This is not the will of this Conclave," The Black Rook said.

"Unless I change the narrative."

Herald interjected. "Changing the narrative is not something to be taken lightly, Rayman. For an entire year, our AI will generate fake news stories for the media to aggregate and broadcast to the hapless masses. Each one of us, when our time comes, takes that responsibility seriously. If you or the Rook control the narrative, you too must treat it with the utmost respect. Do not destroy what we have built by educating the herd."

"I want our group to influence positive change, not keep us in an eternity of conflict."

"You have been with us the shortest amount of time, Rayman. You do not understand the way we operate," The Rook said. "Hitler was not our creation nor was the holocaust. The war spiraled out of control because we were not there to guide it. A member of our group took control of the narrative and created propaganda to villainize Hitler and his Nazis. Then our shadow agents bombed Pearl Harbor which prompted the U.S. to enter the war. If we had not dragged the U.S. into the conflict, the war would not have ended."

"In case you've forgotten, two atomic bombs were used to end it," Raymond said brusquely. "I earned my points. I will use them as I see fit."

The Black Rook stood up and slammed the table. "I warn you now. I will not allow you to spend your points unwisely. If you do not change your course, I will attack your city and take them from you."

Raymond leaned back in his chair. "Like I said, I have nothing to fear."

*   *   *

Cindy joined Michael for dinner in the East Village. They ate and told jokes and reminisced over how much fun they had as children. Michael told the story of how he used to come over to her apartment to play house with her Barbies. Cindy would be the wife and Jadie would always get stuck as the aunt or the babysitter, which annoyed her. Since Michael was the only boy, he got to be Cindy's husband. House would start off normally: bring in the groceries, put the baby to sleep, cook dinner, ask how work was. But eventually Michael would get bored and whip out his monster action figures. Barbie would then transform into Robocop and the baby would need to be protected from a home invasion orchestrated by Hordak and his minions of evil.

He mentioned how surprised he was when Cindy played along. She would protect her house and her family with a superhuman Barbie. She would fight off the minions by crashing her dolls into his action figures, then crammed her toys into a pink corvette for a dramatic escape into the kitchen.

They laughed. "We were so silly back then," she said.

"It's not so silly now, considering the circumstances."

Cindy lifted her head with a hint of a smile. Talking about the old days filled her with nostalgia. Michael was the little brother she never knew she wanted.

"You've become Robocop Barbie."

There was a long pause followed by a burst of laughter. Cindy dug a piece of bread into a bowl of melted cheese and said, "Barbie wishes she were me."

"It makes me happy to see you smile again."

"Thank you for taking me out to dinner. I really needed this."

"Anything for you."

_____

She returned home around three in the morning bleary eyed and stuffed. Her conversations with Michael had gone on longer than she realized and she feared what Jonas might say if he were still awake. Luckily, he was sound asleep. She made sure to undress in the bathroom so as not to wake him and then quietly snuck into bed as if she had been there all along. It was easy . . . suspiciously easy.

The morning after, Cindy remembered to grab her crutches and joined Jonas for breakfast at the dining room table. But as she approached the table, no plate had been set aside for her. *No big deal,* she thought. She would make her own plate. Cindy hobbled over to the kitchen and found an empty skillet save for a few spots of grease. She wondered if he had put the leftovers in the fridge and checked. Not a single plastic container was in sight.

"Did we run out of groceries?" She clacked her way over to the table and sat down next to him.

"Nope."

"Oh." She pursed her lips. "So you didn't make anything for me?"

"Correct."

"Wow, okay. I mean, I don't expect you to cook all the time. I just wish you would've told me."

"And I wish you would have called . . ." He forked a pile of egg mixed with black beans into his mouth. "Last night."

She looked away.

"Where were you?"

"I was at dinner with Michael."

"Until three am?"

"I thought you were sleeping."

"You thought wrong." He put his fork down. "I'm going to guess you decided to get drunk again."

"I didn't."

"Did you go to the meeting?"

"I'm not an alcoholic, so no, I didn't go to the stupid meeting." Again, with the alcoholism crap. She had been sober for years, he didn't need to keep bringing it up. She was half-tempted to tell him she had the suit. Telling him would get him off her back about the alcohol, but she couldn't risk SIRCA being taken away. She had to capture Ned first. She could explain to Jonas later.

"And you didn't think to call me, to at least tell me you were all right? Especially after what happened to you and Jadie?"

"Don't bring her up, okay? I lost track of time."

Jonas threw his hands up. "Unbelievable. You know what . . . I'm going to go." He brought his empty plate over to the kitchen and left it on the sink for her to put away. "Granted, I should obviously go with you to an AA meeting and I'll make time to do so. But forgetting to call me after you've been shot and kidnapped is offensive. I don't know what's gotten into you lately, but you need to knock it off."

"Stop being dramatic," she said. "I was having a good time. I'm sorry I didn't call, I won't do it again."

"You were having such a good time with Michael that you didn't even think to call me and tell me you were okay. I almost called the police because of how worried I was over you. Once you understand why I'm pissed off, we'll talk."

Jonas slammed the door on his way out. She felt like an idiot for not calling or at least texting him. A few seconds to tell him she was fine would have avoided this entire conversation. "He'll get over it," she muttered.

Cindy cast aside her crutches and smiled as she stretched her legs. She was eager to once again feel the power of the suit flowing through her limbs. She raced to the basement, panting with excitement at the thought of finally using her collection of Intel. She opened her secret shelf and rolled it away from the room hidden in the back.

Dust motes floated in front of an empty wall. The photographs, newspaper clippings, post it notes, and locations of high ranking lieutenants with connections to Ned were gone. All that remained were the sticky remnants of tape glue. The wooden bench which contained routes and detailed notes on Ned's travel itinerary had been wiped clean, even of its dust. The backup external drive where she had painstakingly scanned all of her documents was also gone.

Cindy slid her hands over the empty table. "Oh my God." She ran out of her secret room and into the basement. She scoured through boxes of Christmas and Halloween decorations, junk, junk, junk. She grabbed an unmarked box and turned it upside down. Papers and envelopes spilled onto the floor leaving a mess of old patents and useless electronics manuals. She was so upset, she could feel the familiar stinging pain in the back of her neck and kidneys whenever her anger was at a boil. She tamped down her emotions and calmly marched upstairs to call Jonas. She hoped and prayed Jonas wasn't the dick she thought he was right now.

"What?"

"Hey . . . I have a weird question for you. I went down to the basement and all of my papers are gone. Did you clean the room and forget to put back my stuff?"

"No, I threw it out. All of it."

Cindy choked back her rage. She charged into the kitchen and rummaged through the garbage bins.

"Don't bother looking through the garbage. I took it with me when I went to work today."

"Please tell me you're joking," she said through clenched teeth.

"This isn't a joke. You're obsessed with Ned and you need to get help."

"Do you have any idea what you just did? I spent *years* collecting that information."

"You think I haven't noticed the change in you? Ever since you lost your job, you haven't been the same. I thought it was me, but then you showed me those photos and that's when I knew. I knew this obsession was destroying our marriage and turning you back into a dru—"

She hurled her phone at the wall. The cover exploded off the back and landed on the carpet, ending the conversation. The phone had a crack in the shape of a lightning bolt snaking down its screen. She stomped up the stairs to her personal gym and beat the shit out of her punching bag.

She left wet footprints on the carpet as she walked into the bedroom clutching a towel to her chest. The gym had warmed up her muscles and the shower cleansed her of sweat but neither managed to soothe the fury raging inside her veins. She stood in front of the mirror and brushed her hair which dripped over her shoulders. Hundreds of sleepless hours spent interviewing, waiting, stalking, threatening, are now sitting on a trash barge steaming its way to Asia. Honestly, she didn't know if she could forgive him, not for this.

As she angrily fussed with the knots in her hair, the familiar chime of her phone went off. She spotted the phone in the reflection of her bedroom dresser and walked over to it. She stared at the cracked screen, unable to figure out who the number belonged to.

"Hello?"

"Cindy, this is Raymond."

"How did you get this number?"

"Which answer would you prefer, that I looked up your Credit Guard account or that I asked Michael?"

"I guess it doesn't matter."

"I have an assignment for you, one that is terribly urgent."

"Okay." She stood up and walked over to the dresser where she resumed brushing. "What's going on?"

"Two days ago, Boston PD seized over two hundred pounds of fentanyl valued at around thirty million dollars from behind a freezer in a restaurant basement. As the owner of the restaurant was being taken away in cuffs, he told the police that he had two hundred and seventy pounds of fentanyl, and accused the Boston PD of skimming his stash.

"Today, at oh, nine hundred and twenty five hours, two Boston police officers and a K-9 unit were found unconscious in Boston's South Station. Emergency responders administered naloxone and revived the unconscious officers. Police cordoned off the crime scene and discovered trace amounts of fentanyl on the train platform. Had the EMT's not arrived—"

"They would've died," Cindy said. "How do you know this?"

"The how is unimportant right now. What is important is that you find a way to board the Acela train and locate the stolen fentanyl. If the drug gets loose, thousands of people could be killed."

"Isn't this a job for the DEA or the FBI? I'd rather be looking for Ned."

"I understand Ned's importance to you, but he is not an immediate threat. The train is."

"The train can be ordered to stop."

"Let's assume the thieves possess the fentanyl in gas form. How would they react if the train stopped and they saw the police outside the windows?"

Cindy blew out her lips. "I know how to catch criminals. Chemical attacks are beyond my pay grade."

"The time for doubt expired when you chose to steal SIRCA. If you can't handle this operation then you have no business wearing my suit." He paused. "Do this, and I will help you find your man."

Cindy balled her fist against the dresser. She thought of Dan, the mayor, and Jadie. All of them victims of her own incompetence. If she didn't do this, if she didn't redeem herself for her failures, their sacrifices would have been in vain.

"You're buying my train ticket."

CHAPTER 14:

Rumble in the Bronx

Wrapped in her chrome armor, Cindy fired the grappling hook for the first time within the city. The wire whipped in a sky the color of concrete then straightened like a tight rope after piercing a building's stone wall. The pulleys within the grappling hook canister spun. She catapulted into the skies and felt her stomach drop down to her legs. The wind howled loudly across her helmet as a feeling of weightlessness took over. The sensation was better than any rollercoaster ride she had ever been on.

The grappling hook wires tugged on her limbs but the suit prevented her from feeling any discomfort. She flew past office windows filled with employees staring into the blue glow of their desktop monitors and she flipped over water towers perched atop rooftops. She twisted through narrow alleyways filled with black iron fire escapes and soared into the open skies basking in the feeling of liberation. "This is amazing."

Cindy approached a tall, slender suspension bridge known as the Whitestone Bridge. She dove under the elegant arches and weaved between the spider thread suspension wires not because it was necessary but because it was fun. At the end of the bridge waited the Bronx, the northernmost borough of all of NYC and the last bastion of urban sprawl. Beyond the Bronx was woods, mountains, isolated towns, and roads leading to Connecticut and upstate New York.

She never cared much for going this far north. Though the Bronx was the home of the Yankees, Jenny from the block, the zoo, and Edgar Allen Poe's cottage, Cindy only knew the Bronx from the eyes of an officer. A crime-ridden borough on its way to a slow, gentrified recovery. The Bronx may no longer be the hellhole it once was in the seventies, but some places like Hunt's Point still scared visitors at night. A photographer could be taking pictures of graffiti art while a gang member in an SUV with tinted windows exchanges a bag of cocaine to a kid hiding a pistol in his jeans.

She landed atop a six story apartment building which overlooked a small concrete bridge on Williamsbridge road. She squatted on the corner of the roof and observed her surroundings. From her vantage point she would be able to spot the Acela from a mile away. She glanced at her chrome shoulders. The light snow had turned her glossy silver skin into a dull grey. She brushed them off and returned her attention to the streets below. Black ice covered the roads in an oily sheen and a biting wind chill blew across the streets. Despite all this, especially for a woman who was cold all the time, she felt warm and comfortable in her suit.

[Incoming Call from: Michael]

"Answer," Cindy said.

"Connecting your call," SIRCA replied.

"Hey Cindy. Raymond asked me to help you with your assignment."

"Are you going to put on a suit and come join me?"

"I wish," he said. "Unfortunately, all I can do is provide support. So I'll be monitoring your suit, updating objectives, warning you of danger, and making sure the suit doesn't crash and leave you buck naked. You know, the usual."

She rapped her fingers against the concrete. "I'm nervous."

"Really? Why?"

"Aside from the fact that I'm going to jump onto a speeding train going at a hundred and forty-four miles an hour?"

"Actually it should only be going sixty miles as it travels through the Bronx. Not saying I would jump myself but it definitely won't be going full speed."

"If I screw up and the fentanyl gets loose, it could kill everyone on the train. And my track record hasn't exactly been stellar."

"You'll be great, Cindy. I have faith in you."

"Right . . ." She nervously tapped the edge of the rooftop with her fingers. "I'll be great."

A yellow pin appeared at the end of the curved railroad tracks as the train rounded the bend, its lights glinted like little starbursts. The yellow pin stuck to the speeding train and popped out a sticky note filled with additional information.

[9:10am Acela Express | MPH: 57 | Passengers: 304 + 7 crew members. Estimated arrival time into New York Penn Station, 9:30am]

"Twenty minutes, are you serious? Holy crap. I gotta move." Cindy leapt from the rooftop. She felt a slight tinge of nervousness as the street rapidly grew in size. When she landed, her footsteps barely made a sound and neither her shins nor legs felt any pain. She dodged incoming cars and climbed over the barricade designed to prevent bridge jumpers. Down below was an ocean of gravel and wooden rail ties.

"Oh wow," Michael said. "That is a lot higher and scarier than I thought."

"Shut up, Michael. I need to focus."

"Um, right. So listen, those wires above the tracks are called catenaries. Whatever you do, don't touch them. The electricity will shut down your suit."

"I like how you tell me this when I'm seconds away from jumping near said catenaries."

"Sorry, it completely slipped my mind."

"Cindy," SIRCA chimed. "I will assist you during your jump. An arrow will appear in your HUD when it is time to go."

The anticipation of the jump left Cindy anxiously rocking her body back and forth over the bridge barricade. She watched SIRCA countdown the seconds and was startled by a bus horn. A woman opened the door of her school bus and yelled at her. "Hey! What are you doing? You've got a lot to live for. Don't jump!"

She waved her off.

"Come on. You don't want to do this. Imagine how bad traffic is going get if you jump right now. Don't be selfish. I mean, obviously you should be thinking of your family, but you know, we have to go to work. The police are going to close off this entire street if you go. At least wait until after rush hour."

Was this chick serious? The traffic backed up behind the bus with their horns singing in discordant unison. The drivers got out of their cars and encouraged Cindy not to jump.

"This is great, just lovely," Cindy muttered. "Go away!" She turned. "I'm not going to block traffic."

The crowd began to chant, "Yes you will, yes you will."

The woman in the school bus said, "Take off that ridiculous Halloween costume and come down right now."

She had been so distracted by the crowd, she hadn't heard the chime SIRCA was broadcasting to her ear.

"Jump," SIRCA said. "Your window is shrinking."

"What?"

"Jump now."

The last four cars of the Acela rumbled under the bridge with the arrow blinking over its frozen rooftop. "Oh crap!" Cindy leapt from the bridge, followed by the shocked cries of the chanting crowd. She panicked as her feet went straight for the catenary wires. SIRCA took control of her body and pushed her away from the electrified wires, missing it by mere inches. Her boots thumped against the roof and slid over the slippery ice layer coating the aluminum rooftop. She flailed her arms, desperate to grab anything, as her lower body flew off the left side of the train. She punctured her fingers through the roof and held on as her legs swung like a pendulum.

As the bridge shrank behind her, a line of people stood on their cars and pointed at her. She gave them a quick thumbs up while dangling over the empty tracks on the left side of the train. She tried to unhook her fingers, but the velocity of the train jostled her around.

[WARNING: Incoming Train]

Over her shoulder the distant lights of an Amtrak train quickly approached. With the tracks built so close together, there was no way to avoid getting hit. The blare of its train horn shook through her armor and vibrated the padding in her suit.

"Oh my God, Cindy, oh my God oh my God oh my God." Michael's panicked voice rang in her ears.

She had a good grip with one hand, she just needed to get a grip with the other. She threw her right arm over her head and ripped through the roof with her fingers. With both hands secured, she hauled herself to the top of the train. The gust from the passing Amtrak train pushed her body upward.

"Holy shit," she said out of breath. The blur of the passing train disappeared in the blink of an eye. "This is off to a very bad start."

"Okay," Michael's voice squeaked. "Um, let's get you inside the train. You should activate your remote hack so you can open the rear door."

Cindy nodded and brought up the SIRCA menu screen. She selected [Remote Hack] which brought out a black orb in the empty space between her thumb and forefinger on her left hand. She pinched the orb with her right and said, "Now what?"

SIRCA spoke for Michael. "The Acela has a built in WiFi network. We can use this as a backdoor to the train door controls. Manipulate the orb in order to begin the hacking procedure."

Cindy connected to the WiFi signal which requested a password. She twisted the orb which caused a word search of scrambled text to appear in front of her HUD. [7d4wo1ms]

Cindy spoke into her Comm-Link. "Umm, what is this?" The characters continued to change in front of her eyes. [ud0wt2hq]

"This is the—"

"SIRCA, shut up," Michael said. "You're looking at a hacking interface. Right now SIRCA is trying to identify what keystrokes have been pressed in order to figure out the password. The catch is, we haven't finished programming the application."

"Okay so what am I supposed to do?"

"Basically, try to lock in the characters that appear the most. It'll flash red if you're wrong, green if you're right."

[Ah2l6k1] and one by one [Acel2q8r] she cracked the password. [Acela910]

[Connected to Amtrak Acela WiFi]

SIRCA spoke, "I am now going to tunnel in and gain access to the train controls, please stand by."

[Open Rear Door Y/N?]

The rear door slid open. She vaulted over the edge and swung through the opening. The door closed behind her and muted the sound of train wheels clacking over steel tracks, though she could still hear a slight whistling from the holes in the ceiling.

"Okay, I'm in."

"Any ideas on how you're going to search the train," Michael said. "You might freak out the passengers."

"Do you think I should power down?"

"You won't be able to scan for traces of fentanyl if you do. And no one onboard the train has called the police, so it must be hidden."

"What about that stealth camouflage you had me test? How long does it last?"

"That's a great question I don't know the answer to."

A Bitter Winter

"I guess we'll find out."

"Be careful. It's still a prototype. If the suit crashes, you won't be protected from fentanyl exposure."

She selected the stealth camouflage option and looked at her silver hand. The chrome broke apart until her metallic flesh transformed into translucent glass. She was not, however, completely invisible. Subtle ripples of distortion outlined the silhouette of her shape, like heat waves, only more defined.

[Stealth Camouflage – Active]

"Sweet."

She crouched down and crept into the business class passenger car. The interior layout had overhead luggage bins and men and women sitting in luxurious reclining seats lined up against rounded rectangular windows. She wondered why it was so quiet until she saw a sign that said: this is a quiet commute train. She crept through the narrow aisle like a poltergeist, silent and invisible.

"I have no idea what I'm looking for," she whispered.

"You have to switch your HUD to forensics mode."

Cindy navigated through the menus and accessed the vision mode selection screen. There were several options to choose from including: thermal, night vision, x-ray, motion isolation, electronic radiation, and forensics. "That's a lot of options."

She switched to forensic vision mode. Her vision tinted into a subtle blue.

"Cindy," SIRCA chimed. "What do you wish to search for?"

"Fentanyl."

[Tracking . . . 0.0% detected]

"Not here." Though Cindy was invisible, the glass doors which led into the vestibule area still detected her presence and slid open. She was surprised and a little impressed. She crept into the vestibule area where the articulated joints kept the train connected as the cars swayed independently from one another.

"You know, I've never been on an Acela," she said to Michael.

"It's pretty swanky, isn't it? Jonas and I rode it a few times when we were at MIT. We'd usually come down to check out the technology conferences."

"How did you guys program the suit to look for this stuff?"

"Let's see . . . Jonas bought the components, Sid developed the program,

John installed the parts, Charlie gave us the ingredients to look for, and I developed the interface."

"So Mr. Perfect didn't do anything."

"I mean . . . he's . . . you know, the idea guy. He can do all of our jobs, except Charlie's, and he has done it. But nowadays the grunt work usually falls on us. And you know you can't question him because—"

"He always thinks he's right. Trust me, I know. He trashed my stuff earlier thinking he could make decisions for me."

"What did he trash?"

"Don't worry about it." She entered the next car and slunk down the aisles. She had to constantly move aside for passengers returning to their seats from the café car. A passenger accidentally bumped her shoulder and as a result, she flickered and bumped the knee of a sitting passenger. She thought for sure they had seen her. The passengers looked at each other and apologized. Cindy continued down the aisle. Still no sign of the fentanyl.

"I'm not finding anything."

"That's not good. You've got about twelve minutes before the train pulls into the station."

"What if I'm on the wrong train?"

"Cindy, you *cannot* be on the wrong train."

"Right, no pressure."

She hurried through the cars and with the added speed came a noticeable flickering to her stealth camouflage. Passengers lifted their eyes from their screens and phones and looked as though they had seen a ghost. SIRCA warned Cindy that the stealth camouflage was draining too much power and would affect the forensic system. The warning from SIRCA shook her. Being naked would be of no use to anyone. She shut down the stealth camouflage and appeared inside the café car where a line of people stood before the cash register. A man turned around and opened his eyes wide at the sight of her. The woman standing in front of him dropped the coffee cup in her hand.

[Tracking . . . 10.3% detected]

"Michael, I think I found something." Before moving on, she saw the price tag on a bag of trail mix. "Five ninety-nine? That's ridiculous."

"Excuse me, Ms." The Acela attendant working the café register grabbed

A Bitter Winter

Cindy's arm. "We—we ask that our passengers not walk around in costume. I'm going to have to ask you to take that off."

Cindy didn't want to scare the woman any further and tried to sound gentle. Too bad the voice modulator was still active. "I will—Uhh… sorry, not trying to scare you."

She pulled away and was grabbed by the attendant again. "Ma'am, you have to take that off right now or I will call the conductor."

Cindy turned to the woman and looked down at the petite hand barely able to wrap its fingers around her bulky arm. The woman fearfully took her hand away and reached for the panic alarm button. Cindy gently pushed the woman and knocked her into shelves of alcohol. Good lord, she barely touched her. The passengers waiting in line watched Cindy with their mouths agape. One looked like he was trying to record video but kept hitting his phone as if it wasn't working.

"Sorry about that," she said before leaning into the attendant's ear. "I'm investigating a sensitive matter for the Department of Homeland Security. Don't . . . make a scene."

"No one told me."

"I'm telling you now. Let your team know what I'm doing and I will get off this train once we arrive at Penn, got it?"

"Yes ma'am."

A man shaking his cellphone said aloud, "Is your video working? My screen is frozen."

The conductors gave Cindy a wide berth, saying nothing as she crossed into the final car, the first class car. She assumed —if the Acela team was worth their exorbitant ticket prices— the police would be waiting for her at Penn Station.

[95.7% detected. Isolating fentanyl particles]

A flashing box on her HUD zoomed into a compartment within the overhead luggage shelf. Underneath the bin, a man with tan skin and black hair was sitting by himself, thumbing through his phone. On the opposite side of him were two, hard-looking men with thick, well-groomed beards and dark lens aviators. The rest of the car was filled with white men and women dressed in formal business attire.

"Those two Arabic looking guys with the aviators and the beards . . . they look suspicious," Michael said. "You should check them out."

"Why, because they fit the MOA profile?"

"Yeah."

"What about the two white men sitting on each end? Why didn't you point them out?"

"Because they're . . . you know . . ."

"White?"

"I'm just saying, you should be cautious."

"Innocent until proven guilty, always remember that."

"But someone in that train is guilty."

"Don't worry. I'll find them."

Cindy approached the man who was on his phone. He paid her no mind as she opened the overhead bin and pulled down a silver suitcase. The man glanced up from his phone and jumped at the sight of her.

"Is this yours?"

He shook his head no.

"Cindy watch out!"

Her HUD switched from forensics mode to motion tracking mode. Her screen turned red and blurred her surroundings. Two white males stood up from their seats at the front and back of the car. Her HUD locked onto them and created a black and white framed box which made them stand out from the red background. They reached into their suit jacket pockets and pulled out their guns. One of the Middle Eastern men in aviators, tackled the man near the front of the car while Cindy faced the man in the back who had a Beretta pistol ready to fire.

"Don't let him shoot," Michael cried.

Fire and smoke blasted from the barrel. The bullet spun towards Cindy and ricocheted off her chest, hitting a passenger in the shoulder. The passenger howled in pain and clutched his arm as blood spilled onto his fingers. A tiny wisp of smoke dissipated from the miniscule scratch on her armor. Fear flooded her veins, not for her own safety, but for everyone else's. She lunged forward and grabbed the barrel of the gun. She closed her hand and crushed it between her fingers. The sound of the gun turning to pieces was drowned out by the screams of passengers cowering in their seats.

[Deploying combat stims > Adrenaline Levels Rising > Serotonin Levels Decreasing > Pulse Accelerating]

A sudden ecstasy of rage flooded her body, detonating her overstuffed grenade of emotions. She put down the suitcase and threw a blinding left hook. The shooter's face mushed into a pond of ripples with blood and saliva spraying from his mouth. His bones crunched under the power of her knuckles. He flew back into his seat and smacked his head against the wall.

"Jesus, Cindy," Michael said. "How hard did you hit him?"

She rolled her shoulders and cracked her neck. "Come on. Get up." It took her a second to realize that the shooter was dead. "Oh shit." Dead, killed by her own hands. A wave of disgust punched her chest. Had she really killed someone? She snapped out of her daze, reminding herself that there was still another active shooter. A second gunshot popped. The deafening blast would have normally left Cindy with tinnitus, but the helmet's noise reduction speakers protected her ears. The Middle Eastern man who had bravely tackled the second shooter was on the floor with one hand on his belly. The man he had been fighting with, the white gunman, had grabbed the suitcase and was now trapped in the center of the car with nowhere to go.

The automated announcement system spoke through the train's speakers. "Now arriving at New York Penn Station." The train slowed as it exited the tunnel and entered an underground labyrinth of tracks and grimy platforms. As Cindy had expected, a squad of police officers were waiting on the Acela's platform.

"Cindy," Michael said. "Just so you're aware I've been monitoring the police band radio. I think the ESU SWAT are on their way."

"This keeps getting worse and worse," she replied. There was no way the SWAT team would think she was on their side. Out of everyone on the train, she was the one who looked the most suspicious.

The terrorist waved his gun. "Anyone tries something or the police come in and this thing goes off!" He spun around making his speech to the terrified passengers. "The Mubarizun will not be stopped!"

He turned to face Cindy and was startled. Though she was standing in front of him, she was completely invisible to his naked eyes. He twisted his head checking every corner of the car. "Where is she?" He yelled then pointed his gun at one of the passengers. "Tell me where she went!"

"She disappeared," the passenger yelled.

The terrorist's arm trembled, shaking the gun in his grip. Her invisible hand was clutched to his wrist, pushing against it. His arm tensed in a pitiful attempt to resist her. The terrorist didn't know what to do as the barrel of his gun pivoted in his direction. "What's happening?" The end of the gun came to a rest beside his temple. "Help m—"

Chunks of his brain exploded from the side of his head. The passengers screamed as he fell. She grabbed the suitcase out if his dead hand, flickered out of invisibility, and scanned the suitcase to see if it was safe to open. It was and so she did. The police barged into the car and aimed their guns at her.

"Put your hands up!"

Inside the suitcase was a plastic container filled with liquid. Wires connected to the container led down to an electronic keypad and clock. Twenty seconds until it went boom.

"This is your last warning!"

Drops of sweat snuck into her eyes. She placed her fingers on the keypad and watched the clock. SIRCA began to hack the device, informing Cindy that it would take five seconds to neutralize the trigger. The police slowly closed in with their pistols. "It's a bomb," she yelled, "and it's going to go off any second." She looked up at one of the officers and said, "I don't know if I can disarm it in time. Get them out of here."

The officers holstered their weapons and scrambled to get the passengers off. With only ten seconds left, there was no way everyone would get out in time. At six seconds, the hack still hadn't completed.

[Connection Error – Trigger partially neutralized, restarting application]

"The remote hack is bugged, Cindy," Michael shouted. "It's going to explode!"

They told her during ESU bomb disposal training that pulling wires was the absolute last resort. There was no such thing as cutting a green or red wire. If a terrorist wanted to, all the wires could be hot pink. And even if she did cut the wire, they could have rigged secondary triggers to detonate the device if the primary mechanism failed. As she stared at the wires, the HUD changed color and highlighted which cables would set off the explosive. With only a second left, she put her trust in SIRCA and snipped.

The clock hit zero. Cindy shielded her eyes. There was a loud whine and then nothing. She lowered her hand. The container was still full of sloshing liquid.

"Did you . . . disarm it?"

"I sure did," she said.

"How?"

She shook her head. "Honestly? Pure luck and some help from SIRCA."

"Thank God."

"Yeah, seriously."

She checked the terrorist's pockets and found a cell phone. She couldn't remove it from the crime scene for fear of tampering with evidence, so she had SIRCA copy the contacts and call history into the suit itself.

"I'm heading out before I get interrogated."

"Great job out there."

A lake of blood formed around the opening in the terrorist's head. She looked at the second shooter propped against the seat, dead from her inhuman punch. If this had gone flawlessly, no one would have gotten hurt and two terrorists would have been in cuffs instead of black bags. Then she thought about the bomb and what would have happened if she hadn't acted. Thousands were saved because of what she did and if two evil lives were the price that had to be paid, then why not?

For the first time, in a long time, she could enjoy the euphoria of having saved the motherfucking day. Cindy Ames, the twenty four seven screw up, had finally done something right. SIRCA was the answer she was looking for. She could hardly sit still from all the excitement. She wanted to dance, to drink, to have sex, but all that would have to wait. A terrible pain gnawed at her stomach and it wasn't hunger.

CHAPTER 15:

A Subtle Seduction

She met with Michael at the old Lucent Labs facility, in the Latini building. Her stomach pains had gotten worse but she was still in good spirits. In fact, she felt amazing and heroic and all the things she wanted to feel since she was a child. Nothing could ruin her good mood, especially not a stomach ache.

The swivel office chair creaked as she sat down. She touched her forearm and drew a C which looked more like a sideways U on the glowing dots in her arm. The silver armor turned to liquid and retreated into her skin. Her enormous body deflated to her usual petite, sturdy form. She was left in a comfy white t-shirt and black sweat pants.

Michael rolled in his chair and connected an electrode to her left bicep. He adjusted his glasses and pointed at the narrow scratches along the curve of her triceps.

"How did you get those scars?"

Scars? She twisted her arm. Interesting. "Vertical patrol."

"What's that?"

"On a vertical patrol, you and a partner go to a high rise apartment building —usually the projects— and take an elevator to the top floor. Once you're there, you walk down the stairwell and check each floor for illegal activity: drug deals, assault, prostitution, you name it."

"Sounds dangerous."

"Very." She viewed her scars with pride. "A dealer came at me with a knife in his hand."

"Really?" Michael leaned back. "How'd you stop him?"

"If a guy has a knife, the first thing you want to do is trap his knife arm. You do this by throwing yourself at his shoulder and grabbing his arm. But even with his knife arm trapped he can still cut you, which he obviously did. Once I took out his legs it was game over."

"That looks like it hurt."

A Bitter Winter

"I think the arm bar I put him in hurt way worse."

Michael had twinkles in his blue eyes as if he had met his childhood hero. "I could listen to your stories all day." She bathed in his compliments and didn't want him to stop flattering her. He toyed with her arm by shaking it around. "And strong, my God. You've got more muscle in your one arm than I have in my whole body."

She smirked. "Oh that reminds me. I found a cell phone on one of the terrorists. I copied his contact list and a bunch of other stuff. Do you think you'd be able to find leads for me?"

"I would love to." He turned his attention to the computer and began diagnostics. "Sorry about the failed hack again. There was a programming glitch which caused it to infinitely loop back into itself. My fault."

She shrugged. "Don't worry about it. My ass is still in one piece."

Michael read the diagnostics report on the screen. "That's weird."

"What?"

"SIRCA is reporting an increase in mass around your stomach. Would you mind lifting your shirt?"

She pulled her t-shirt above her flexed abdominals. His look of shock quickly turned to fear when he saw what was on her stomach. An eruption of hives had spread across her belly and chest. "That doesn't look good."

She looked down. "Ew, what is that?"

"I don't want to say in case I'm wrong."

"Say it."

"I've seen this before on Charlie's lab mice. It always starts off as hives and then it just keeps growing and growing" He winced.

Ice cold fear dribbled down her spine. "What?"

"They'll eventually erupt into tumors. I know that's not how it normally works but this thing was made in a lab, not nature."

"You're—you're saying I have cancer?"

"I'm not saying it, but I have seen this before."

So her mood could be ruined after all. It wasn't fair. Every time she got ahead and started to feel good about herself, something happened to take that feeling of happiness away. Cancer? Really? She couldn't believe it, didn't want to believe it. She thought of herself going through chemo treatments, losing her hair, withering back to the husk she was. She closed her eyes and asked, "Is this from what Jonas did?"

"I think so."

She nodded and pulled down her shirt. "Okay," she said. "I'm gonna go."

"What are you going to do?"

She pulled off the electrodes and stood up from the chair. "Jonas made this mess, so he's going to clean it."

———————

Monday morning, she was in the kitchen plating her breakfast. Jonas was at the dining room table and almost finished with his plate of eggs, bacon, and sausage. She sat down on the opposite side of the table instead of next to him like she usually did. Her fork rattled on the plate. With her head down, she angrily stabbed her banana pancakes.

Jonas watched her fight with her food. He bit the end of a crunchy strip of bacon and spoke.

"No crutches?"

"Don't need them." She did not look back at him.

"It hasn't been three months."

"You gave me an experimental formula, remember?"

"Wasn't supposed to fix your legs."

"How would you know? You never tested it."

"What happened to the bed?"

She sliced her pancake. "What are you talking about?"

"The headboard's been splintered for a few days. Like someone punched it."

"Well it definitely wasn't from the wild sex we've been having."

"What sex?"

"Exactly."

She took a bite from her pancake. The dry, rubbery texture left her disappointed. Jonas snapped another bite of bacon. The fact that he didn't save any for her made her angrier.

"That shirt looks a little tight on you."

"It shrunk in the wash."

"When did you do laundry?"

A Bitter Winter

She slammed her fist down and rattled the silverware. "Are you done?"

"What am I doing?"

"Interrogating me."

Unfazed, Jonas continued. "You don't talk to me."

"This is why."

His gaze dropped to his plate where there were only crumbs and spots of grease. "You're not acting like yourself."

She rolled her eyes. "Because I'm hungry."

"You don't kiss me hello; you don't call me; you don't talk to me; you're always texting." He paused. "Are you seeing someone else?"

"That's a stupid question. You know I wouldn't."

He leaned back in his chair. "I'm not so sure."

She paused. "Are you implying that I'm seeing, Michael?" She scoffed. "I'm not even attracted to him."

"You and I both know he wants more."

Cindy picked up her fork. "So? He's harmless."

"I know he resents me."

"Right now, I resent you."

"Because I didn't make you breakfast?"

"No." Cindy's utensils clattered next to her barely eaten meal. She grabbed onto the bottom of her shirt and pulled it over her stomach. She showed Jonas the malformed, ruddy lumps of skin.

He leaned in and squinted his eyes. "What is that?" He poked the lump with his finger, it displaced and hardened.

"Your little formula gave me cancer."

His face darkened. "How long have you had this?"

"Probably about a week."

"I need to take you to the hospital."

She yanked her shirt back down. "Why? So I can do chemo for a lab grown cancer you gave me?"

"I didn't give you cancer."

"I'm not going to get it treated. Not right now. If they give me chemo I'm going to get sick and weak and I won't be able to do anything until the cancer is gone. Besides, how are they going to treat something you created?"

162

Jonas shot up from his seat. "Are you crazy? You have to go. They can do surgery and remove the growths before they get worse."

"How about we focus on the fact that I wouldn't have had these things if you hadn't experimented on me."

Jonas ran his fingers through his black hair. "Do you actually believe I intentionally gave you tumors?"

"No, but I do think it was irresponsible of you to give me a formula you hadn't tested. You didn't think of how I would feel being forced to live with this sickness."

"I saved your life."

"No one asked you to." His eyes fluttered as if he had been stunned by a punch. "I've been a screw up since I lost my job, Jonas. I accepted that I deserved to die that night. And to be perfectly honest with you, I am so scared of this disease that I would have rather died. I don't want to do chemo and lose my hair. You did this to me without my consent."

"Stop," he said quietly. "Please, stop."

Now it was her turn to be stunned. She expected him to get angry, to fight back, instead he uncharacteristically pulled back; as if she had hurt him.

"I never wanted to make you sick, okay? I thought Charlie fixed it."

"Would you have still given me the formula if you had known?"

He didn't answer. He sat there, chewing on his lips, staring at nothing.

"Answer me."

"Yes!" He said finally. "I can't find a cure if you're dead."

Cindy crossed her arms and turned away from him. He walked to the front door, put on his jacket, and said, "I promise I will fix this."

He closed the door behind him. Her food sat cold on the dining room table. Another pain tore through her stomach, the same one from before. She pushed away her plate and ran to the bathroom where she retched blood and bile into the toilet. She whimpered at the realization that this was only the start of her illness. How much worse was it going to get? The mere thought of it filled her with dread. She flushed and dragged herself over to the sink. A sliver of red dribbled from her lip. She held her stomach and let her head rest against the bathroom mirror. "Why would you do this to me?"

If this cancer was going to be the end of her, then she didn't have any more time to waste. Ned needed to be captured . . . now.

There was a knock at the front door. She splashed some water on her face and raised her guard as she approached the living room. She had not forgotten what happened the last time she heard a knock. She hid behind the door and cautiously opened it. Raymond stood before her, dressed as if he had come straight out of a 1960s Hollywood movie.

"Mrs. Ames," he said with a smile. "May I come in?"

"Um . . ." she stepped aside. "Sure."

He took off his small caramel duster which matched his fitted cashmere overcoat. "I wanted to discuss something that should not be said over the phone."

She looked at Raymond, looked at herself still dressed in polyester pajamas, and touched her lip. "Should I change?"

Raymond chuckled softly. "Only if you want to."

"It's just that you're so . . ." she gestured up and down with her hand. "Well dressed."

He tilted his head. "Thank you. My wife had really good taste."

"Oh." Cindy furrowed her brow. "I didn't mean to—"

"Your house is quaint. I like it."

"Thanks." She followed Raymond as he walked around her *quaint* living room. "How did you know Jonas was gone?"

"I waited for him to leave."

Her guard went up again.

"Nothing nefarious," he said as if reading her mind. "I can't discuss the suit while he's around."

She let her fists relax. "Oh."

"Would you mind turning on your TV to Impress News. I'd like to show you something."

"Um, sure."

She turned on the TV. The graphic at the bottom of the screen read: Mysterious Silver Ninja prevents Penn Station train bombing. Every station on every channel bombarded viewers with shaky footage of a blurry silver blob killing the two terrorists. Impress News broadcast multiple interviews with witnesses who saw her in action. Some called her a robot ninja, others called her a female alien, but all seemed to agree she was like a ninja appearing out of nowhere.

"You've become an overnight sensation."

Images of the train and the disabled suitcase bomb made her doubt whether it was really her who stopped the terrorists.

"Maybe your career as a police officer didn't pan out the way you wanted, but there's an opportunity as a superheroine."

"Superheroine? Ha, that's ridiculous. Besides the bomb almost went off."

"But it didn't. Personally, I think you were stellar."

She blushed. "Really?"

"Of course. Which is why I wish to discuss my arrival. Do you remember our agreement?"

"I do." She sat down on the couch and muted the TV. "I don't know if I can do another one for you."

His jaw tightened. "Why not?"

"I took this suit so I could give myself closure on Ned. He's still out there and these assignments are slowing me down." She grazed her stomach with her fingers. She didn't want to mention the other factor at play.

Raymond sat on the opposite end of the couch. "I said I would help you."

"When?"

"After you help me." He leaned in. "Listen, these terror attacks will only grow worse. I think we should work together and strike back. Find the terrorist cell and remove their leaders."

"We discussed this. I don't want to kill anyone."

"If that were true the police wouldn't be scraping brains off the floor of a train."

She swallowed hard. "That was a mistake. I didn't mean for it to go that far."

"What's done is done. The point is, you terminated evil men and saved thousands of innocent lives. If that bomb had gone off, two hundred thousand people could have been poisoned and killed by toxic gas."

"What about Jadie? You promised me you'd help her."

"That is entirely dependent on Jonas and his team."

She changed the subject. "I don't know what came over me on the train. I wasn't planning on killing those men."

"Do you feel guilt for killing terrorists?"

She played with her fingers. "I don't know."

"You shouldn't. These men, these Mubarizun or MOA or whatever you want to call them. They are zealots. They are driven by a blind belief that God is commanding them to kill infidels."

"Look, I get it. But the truth is, me stopping the bomb was a fluke. In retrospect, killing those guys was another mistake in a long list of mistakes. Two people got hurt on the train, it's only going to get worse from there."

"Cindy, I served in the Canadian Air Force where my daily routine was to bomb terrorist hideouts overseas. And believe me when I tell you that I have made similar mistakes. I've had to learn to live with them, but I don't think you have yet."

"I'm Cindy Ames. I don't make mistakes," she said remorsefully.

"Until you accept your humanity, I fear you'll never gain your confidence back. But you have SIRCA now and therefore an opportunity to redeem yourself."

"By turning me into a serial killer?"

"No. You are identifying the enemy and treating them as such. If someone told you to kill an innocent man or a political figure. Would you do it?"

"Of course not."

"Then you are no threat to anyone who doesn't deserve what's coming to them. I provide actionable intelligence and you provide the action."

"How many assignments before you help me with Ned?"

"Two at best."

She became agitated. "What if it takes too long to find them?"

"The advantage of social media and Credit Guard is that your personal information becomes corporate information. Setting your profile to private means little to the company who owns and barters your information. I can use my network to find the terror cells."

"I don't know . . ."

"All of this is in compliance with the USA Freedom Act. If you were the FBI, NSA, CIA, or Department of Homeland Security, we would be required to share this information with you." He took a moment to let Cindy ponder. "Imagine this." He held out his hand as if touching a billboard. "The Silver Ninja, a lone operative, a woman, single-handedly saves the country from

MOA and puts an end to their terrorist leader the Black Rook. Could you imagine the accolades for stopping the war on terror? They would erect statues and throw parades in your honor.

"You would become a national hero. Imagine how proud your partner, your sister would be, if it was you who saved a country. All your past errors in judgment would be erased in one fell swoop. Even the commissioner would have to forgive you."

She loved the fantasy he painted, but she wasn't sure she could live up to it. It was difficult for her not to think about all the times she screwed up. "What if I mess up the next assignment and get innocent people killed?"

"Zig Ziglar once said, 'You don't have to be great to start, but you have to start to be great.' Learn from your mistakes and the Silver Ninja" —he pointed at her— "will become a legend."

"Can I think about it?"

"Of course." Raymond rose from the couch and placed his hat back on his grey mane. "Call me once you've decided. You have my card."

After Raymond left, Cindy went up to the attic. She climbed up the creaky steps and slid a box across dusty wooden floorboards. This box was where she kept her pride and shame; photos of when she was a police officer. Most of the pictures were of her and Dan, only a few were of her and Jonas. In one grainy photo, a child was on his back while she administered CPR amidst a crowd of concerned grocery store shoppers. Another was a glossy, professionally taken black and white photo of her standing on the edge of a roof, reaching out to a woman who was ready to jump. The photographer won an award for it and gave her a copy. The last was a photo op with Commissioner Gates. They shook hands after she was awarded the police combat cross for heroism during a vertical patrol.

These were my finest moments, she thought. A collection of memories where everyone could see her pride judging by the smile on her face. Did she deserve to feel that joy again? Maybe Raymond was right. She could wipe the slate clean and create a new identity, a new hero that she could secretly embody.

She called Raymond later in the afternoon.

"I'll do it."

A Bitter Winter

It was time to take the reins of her new life, but before suiting up, she needed to visit her sister in the hospital. Cindy had hoped that by some miracle Jadie might have woken up in the night and that she would be conscious and talking, but she never did. Nothing had changed, yet everything had changed. Now that Cindy had SIRCA, it was weird to see Jadie smaller than her. Pale without her makeup, thinner without solid food, and her hair wild like an old broom. Cindy had blush, eye shadow, and lipstick. Her clothes fit snug around her healthy physique and her hair rested in perfect waves a little past her shoulders. Somehow they had traded places and bodies. And though she felt amazing, she would have gladly gone back to being small and weak to bring Jadie back.

"Is this how you felt when it happened to me?" she whispered. "I don't know how you did it."

The air pumps hissed and beeped, filling Jadie's inactive lungs with air.

"I'll try to be here when you wake up. And you're going to be scared and confused, but I'll be here, hopefully." She coughed and tasted blood. She brought out a tissue and wiped her lips. "Thing is . . . I don't know how fast or slow this cancer is going to go. So I figured I'd see you now, just in case. I don't know if it's the suit or if it's all in my head but I feel different. And I'm a little scared of whoever's trying to come out.

"I know you don't approve of killing, but I'm definitely going to hurt some people tonight. I know you'll be disappointed in me, but I saved lives by killing two terrorists. People were actually grateful for me, can you believe that? If I can save more people, I should try. Anyway, I want you to know. No matter what changes I go through or what I do, even if you hate me after. I'll always be there for you."

She slowly backed away and rolled up her sleeve. Her shadow which loomed over Jadie's bed began to change shape. Cindy's hair flattened inward. The silhouette of her clothes melted into the shape of her round shoulders. A faint blue glow cast against Jadie's skin before fading away. She opened the window and let in a gust of wind. A whine of honking horns and ambulance sirens followed, then silence.

The sun sank behind the shadowy shapes of the skyline. Half her armor turned to the color of gold while the other half became purple and light blue from the shifting sky. She swung across the avenues near bursting with rush hour traffic. Cabbies honked their horns impatiently at oblivious pedestrians and cars honked at the cabbies waiting for the pedestrians to cross. An ambulance tried to bore its way through but ended up getting trapped behind a bus turning through an intersection.

She disconnected from her grapple line mid swing and shot across the street. She activated her gecko grip and attached to the limestone wall of an old office building. Her hands, knees, and the tips of her boots snapped to the surface as if it were magnetized. She coughed quietly and felt a shock of fear, the sickness was progressing. She peered over her shoulder and searched for Raymond's target.

"SIRCA. Can you call Raymond?"

[Connecting . . .]

"Cindy."

"Hey Ray, this Intel brief." Cindy brought up the PDF in her HUD. She scrolled through the dossier of the alleged terrorist. "I don't see anything that verifies this information is accurate."

"How do you mean?"

"I mean where did this file come from? How do I know this guy is one hundred percent, definitely working for MOA?"

"These files were cross referenced against an FBI database."

"Okay, how do you have access to an FBI database?"

"Unofficially."

"You hacked them?"

"No, nothing like that. When you own a company that deals in personal information and identity theft, the government takes great interest in the data you store. They requested a one-way siphon to our servers in order to pull information on anyone within the Credit Guard database. We installed a two-way siphon."

"Are they aware of that?"

"It is installed."

"This is getting too shady for me."

"If you're satisfied with the current way we're preventing terrorist attacks then by all means, go home and return my suit. Just remember. The only reason those passengers survived was because of you, not the FBI and definitely not the police."

"You're asking me to take your word that these documents are genuine. If you represented an intelligence agency I wouldn't have reservations."

"Social media is the intelligence agency. Remember who I am. Is it really that unusual that I have access to a criminal database?"

"I'm just triple checking is all."

"Of course . . . no one wants to hit the wrong target."

A limousine pulled out from an underground parking garage. As it neared the end of the street, she zoomed in with her HUD and scanned the license plate which was a match for her target's vehicle. She fired her grappling hook and went after it.

CHAPTER 16:

The Longest Night

Storm clouds rolled across a violet sky and drizzled the city with a mist of rain. Puddles pooled in front of curbs and tires hissed over wet gravel. Water dripped over Cindy's helmet and turned to steam after touching her glowing eyes. The liquid armor shell absorbed the rainwater and notified Cindy that the water could be consumed if she grew thirsty.

A tracking box on her HUD followed the limousine as it left the parking garage of an office building. A fog swirled in front of its headlights as the vehicle turned right on Fiftieth Street, then turned right again down Second Avenue. She followed from above, defying gravity with her new favorite toy, the grappling hook.

"Are you going to the Queens Midtown Tunnel?" she wondered aloud. "I bet you are."

Raymond spoke through her Comm-Link. "How do you know?"

"For starters, this guy is in a limo. If he's going somewhere fancy, he's headed in the wrong direction. If he was going to catch a show at the Met, then he should have made a left and kept going. I mean, if I was behind a terrorist attack, I'd probably want to get out of town. Best way to the airport from here is to go through the tunnel."

"If what you say is true. Taking him out quietly will become next to impossible once he reaches the traffic before the tolls."

"I guess it wouldn't look good if the Silver Ninja tore open a limousine like a can opener."

"If you want to remain a hero, then it would be best to make it look like an accident."

With her stealth camouflage engaged, Cindy lengthened the wire of her hook which brought her closer to street level. She soared over bulwarks of dirty snow and twisted her body to avoid clipping traffic light poles. She twirled over MTA buses, delivery trucks, and an endless parade of yellow cabs.

Her suit flickered as she increased speed and closed in on the limousine where she could read the license plate without zooming in. It was time to take him out.

[ERROR]

She suddenly couldn't move her arm. The grappling hook wire stretched and dragged her towards a building. She whimpered and tried to force her arm to respond. The front of her body smashed into a brick wall. Crumbles of stone fell to the sidewalk. She struggled like a fish caught in a hook and spun around with her legs flailing. The limousine turned left and merged with a cluster of cars waiting to enter the Queens Midtown Tunnel.

"What are you doing," Raymond said. "He's getting away."

"Something's wrong. Please call Michael."

She fired her grappling hook again which missed and attached itself to the rooftop of a two-story building. "SIRCA what are you doing?" The wire yanked her across the street and slammed her into the roof where she tumbled to a stop. An excruciating pain burned through her arm as if it were being ripped from its socket. Her fingers wildly gesticulated independently of her own thoughts. A flood of error messages poured into her HUD.

Her voice trembled with fear. "I can't control it."

[SYSTEM ERROR: grplnchr.dll failed to initialize] [CRITICAL ERROR: could not establish connection to Neural Network]

"SIRCA," she begged. "Help me. He's getting away."

No response from the machine.

Raymond's voice came through her Comm-link broken and garbled. "I will—*static*—ael. —dy? Can *static* me?"

The servos hidden within her endoskeleton squealed. She writhed on the floor, twisting in agony as her super powered body rebelled against her. The simple act of moving her arm was like trying to drag three hundred pounds of weight. Somehow she managed to crane her arm overhead, her fingers still wriggling like spider legs, and tried to touch her opposite forearm. But SIRCA was still fighting her, preventing her from deactivating the suit. It didn't make any sense. One moment she could move her arm and not even a second later it would lock and become unmovable.

"Come on."

She slammed her arm into the floor and pounded her hand until her fingers stopped moving. She touched her forearm and drew a C shape on the illuminated dots.

[ERROR: Unable to process this command at this time]

"Come on," she roared, then coughed and coughed until she could barely breathe. "Fuck you cancer." She sucked in precious air from her oxygen feed, then forced herself to stand. She put one foot in front of the other and staggered to the edge of the building. The tracking box which had been following the limo had disappeared and she couldn't see it amongst the armada of cars.

"I can't afford to screw this up. Work you stupid thing!"

[Neural Network re-connected] [Connection lost] [Reconnecting]

She gained precious few seconds with the Neural Network. She scrolled through the menus of her HUD and went to the system settings to find the software reset button. She triggered the command.

The HUD scrolled upward in a repetitive loop, making it impossible to read any of the metrics or displays. She didn't know if the reset was working. The endoskeleton continued to grind and tear at her limbs. She cried out as the machine continued to disobey her commands. Suddenly the HUD blanked out. The servos stopped spinning, her fingers froze, and the pain receded.

[Rebooting . . . System Rebooted with a few errors]

The HUD flashed back on with its crisp, clear, legible text. Her limbs were under her control but there was a catch. A delay had been introduced. Her arms and legs now took a half of a second to respond.

"Can anyone —kaff, kaff— hear me?" Static from the dead Comm-link buzzed in her ears. She coughed again before firing her grappling hook into the mouth of the tunnel. "Well I've got a job to do and I'm going to get it done."

Cars and trucks filled the narrow tunnel with exhaust fumes. The reflection of the sodium-vapor lamps skated across her armor. The half second lag caused Cindy to mistime her swing and crash into the side of a delivery truck. The vehicle slammed on its brakes. Tires squealed as cars swerved to avoid hitting it. The drone of hundreds of prolonged car horns reverberated through the tunnel. Cindy threw herself onto the roof of a bus and retracted her grappling hook. A driver following the bus honked his horn and waved at her with a smile on his face.

She glanced at her arm and realized the stealth camouflage was not active. "Shit." She coughed into her helmet then crept across the bus. The rumbling engine tickled her feet. A taxi cab sedan was in front of the bus, tailgating a minivan. She waited for the cab to flash its brake lights before making her jump. The lag threw off her timing and made her land short into the rear windshield. The glass instantly shattered beneath her feet. The cab floored its brakes and sent her stumbling forward.

The cabbie stuck his head out the window and brandished his fist. "Hey, what the fuck are you doing to my car?"

"I'm so sorry."

She walked across the top of the cab and dented the roof with her heavy footsteps. "Sorry again." She jumped onto the back of a minivan.

"You have to pay," the cabbie smacked the door frame of his cab. "You have to pay!"

She rolled her eyes. "I'm so glad I chose to be stealthy."

She leapt across a convoy of vehicles, creating a symphony of bending aluminum, to find that goddamn limo. She climbed onto the back of a cement truck, skirted past the enormous mixer, then vaulted onto the roof of the truck cab. There she found the black limo, keeping pace with the flow of traffic.

Her first instinct was to attack, but she ignored it. Crashing a limo inside a busy tunnel would hurt too many people. She surfed atop the cab of the cement truck and waited for a safer moment to strike.

They emerged from the tunnel and entered a grey fog of rain. Cindy engaged her cloak and was warned the stealth camouflage would only last for a few minutes before shutting down. She ignored the warning and hopped onto the limousine. Her suit flickered for a split second, then began to flash in three second intervals. She leaned over the side of the limo and peeked through the tinted window which became transparent under the gaze of her HUD.

The target was a man named Adam Musab al-Zarqawi. He had tan skin, black hair tied back in a short ponytail, and a dark stubble. He was handsome and refined, a successful banker and proud donor to multiple charities. His dossier did not fit the profile of a typical terrorist. She had expected a loner, a mentally disturbed individual, but this man had a family and an active social life. A devoted husband, and father of two children. Cindy wished Raymond would have left these details out of the briefing. It was hard to de-humanize a family man.

Within the quiet darkness of his limousine, Adam scrolled through his phone, oblivious to the fact that she was watching him. If this was to look like a car accident, the driver needed to die as well. This gave Cindy pause. She didn't want to risk a terrorist escaping to another country but also didn't want an innocent to be sacrificed either. The decision filled her with doubt.

They approached a small bridge on the Long Island Expressway. At the bottom of the bridge was a river called Dutch Kills. This was where she would make her move. The limo exited the tunnel and drove through a foggy, rainy sky. The buildings hugging the river banks illuminated the waters with their office lights. She punched through the driver's side window and jerked the wheel with her invisible hand. The limousine careened to the right and crashed into a cement barrier. The airbag inflated with a loud blast and left the driver stunned. Cindy crawled over the breached cement barrier and gripped the crooked grill of the limo. Her synthetic muscles swelled as she lifted the broken vehicle over her head.

The rear bumper scraped against the street as its hood inched over the water. She grabbed onto the dirty axles within the undercarriage and heaved the car into the black river. The limo flipped on its back and splashed into the water. She dove from the bridge and submerged into the murky water. SIRCA engaged its night vision mode and illuminated the jet black water with a green glow. The HUD created a flashing box over the sinking limo. She clumsily swam to the driver's side window and found the driver struggling with his seatbelt. When she ripped open the door, the driver looked at her in complete surprise. She snapped his seatbelt and pushed him towards the shimmering light above.

Cindy then maneuvered to the back of the limo where Adam finished freeing himself. She grabbed onto his seatbelt strap, shoved Adam into his seat, and clicked it back into place. He didn't scream, didn't panic, he stared at her with his empty eyes as if wondering—why? They sank into the oily pitch where only the bubbles had freedom to escape. She wondered what he was thinking and how he felt being trapped by her. The suit didn't let her feel the icy chill of the water or the tightness of dissipating oxygen. The same couldn't be said for him. He thrashed his head from side to side with boiling bubbles spewing from his mouth. His muffled gurgling cries for help were his final words before the water filled his lungs. The limo landed on the riverbed with a deep thud. Clouds of dirt shot out from the sides and from this cloud she swam to the rippling surface.

"Cindy?" Raymond's voice came through loud and clear. "Can you hear me now? Cindy?"

"I can hear you."

"Finally. I have Michael here with me. He says your suit encountered a crash."

She swam as far as she could from the wreckage. She let out a dispassionate, "Yeah," then breached the surface.

"Will you be able to continue? Michael says he has rebooted your system."

She treaded water and watched the emergency lights flash above the highway overpass. Firefighters and men wearing bright orange utility vests climbed over the cement barrier. They pointed at the water as the rain drizzled over their heads. She couldn't stop thinking about Adam's face, how chilling it was to watch a man drown and do nothing to save him. She had killed two terrorists before and felt satisfaction. This was different. This left her shaken.

"I—I think so."

"You don't sound convinced."

"That information better have been accurate."

"It was."

Still, she didn't feel relief. She had killed a man knowing his wife and kids were waiting for him back home. Stopping terrorists was supposed to be a heroic act. She didn't feel very heroic.

SIRCA chimed. A box appeared and wrote out a message.

[I can't tell you over comms because Raymond is next to me. But I tracked the cell phone numbers in your suit. I found a guy who's associated with Ned at the East New York/Brownsville border. It's a half hour away in traffic but shouldn't be a problem with you and your grappling hook, which I've rebooted, sorry about that.]

She fired her grappling hook at a building near the water and took to the sky.

"My apologies, Cindy," SIRCA said. "It seems I fell asleep."

"It's okay."

"I have received coordinates for Brownsville. Shall I mark it on your map?"

"Yes."

"Cindy," Raymond interrupted SIRCA. "Are you ready for your next objective?"

The yellow marker appeared in Cindy's HUD pointing to the south east side of Brooklyn. Ignoring Raymond, she swung into rhythm, relieved that her body was once again responsive without lag. Fighting against the rain pelting her helmet, she went several miles south east and crossed into Brooklyn.

The route she took through the borough was not as densely packed with skyscrapers. Here she swung low, past bodegas and car dealerships, laundromats and tax agencies, all proudly proclaiming to speak English, Spanish, Korean, Russian, Cantonese, and everything else under the sun. She glided over well-lit streets and bobbing umbrellas.

"Cindy," Raymond called again, more impatient than before. "I'm waiting to send you your next objective."

"Change of plans."

"Excuse me?"

"I've got a potential lead on Ned. I need to jump on it."

"No. You work for me and I have a time-sensitive objective."

"I can't pass up this opportunity."

"Turn around and do as I ask."

"No."

"I told you I would help you find him. I'm a gentleman of my word. Do this task for me first and we will get your man."

"I can't do that again, Raymond. I watched Adam stare at me as he died. If I'm going to hurt another person, it's going to be Ned and anyone associated with him."

"Cindy if you don't turn around, I will pull Jonas and his team from saving your sister."

"Wait, what?" She immediately landed on a rooftop and placed her hand by her ear. "That's not fair, you can't do that."

"I can and I will."

"We had a deal."

"And you are breaking that deal by not listening to me."

A Bitter Winter

She felt betrayed. One of the rules she had for herself was to never let anyone know her weaknesses. This was why. "Please don't take Jonas off the project. I promise I'll help you. Just let me do this one thing, please. I'm begging you."

"Begging is unbecoming of you."

"Let me kill Ned!"

"No. My order takes priority."

"He's going to escape."

"Do as your—"

His voice cut off. "I'm sorry," SIRCA said. "I have terminated the connection."

Cindy exhaled. "You shouldn't have done that."

"He was causing you distress."

"Forget it. Let's get Ned as quickly as possible."

"Objective updated: Terminate or Capture Ned Pickler."

She arrived in the slums of Brownsville. Or as Dan liked to say, "There's a reason it's called Brownsville. The whole place is a piece of shit." Brownsville was an urban sprawl of towering low income housing tenements; battle arenas for bored teenage boys looking to protect non-existent turf. Only the poorest, most desperate of immigrants got stuck living here.

Every window and door was barricaded with black iron bars, almost as if Brownsville was a prison rather than a town. Awnings which were once vibrant and full of color sat dull and crooked over buildings tagged with misspelled gang graffiti. Perhaps most damning about the state of Brownsville was the sign on its only church: Pilgrim Church of __ville. No one knew what happened to the Browns portion and no one cared.

Coming here left her feeling uneasy, even with the protection of her indestructible suit. This place was a living horror movie where every night brought out the gangs, prostitutes, and drug dealers. She never forgot the blood splatter on a door window after a pimp killed his prostitute. Or the chalk outline of a small child after two gangs obliterated each other in a vicious gunfight. The first time she ever drew her gun was here on Mother Gaston Boulevard, when a teen scamming an ATM turned around with a pistol in his hand. The sooner she could leave, the better.

"Cindy," SIRCA chimed. "There is a delivery truck parked behind a foreclosed department store. This matches with the geo coordinates Michael gave us."

"All right," she said to the machine. "Let's go check it out."

She swung into a narrow, poorly lit alleyway. She attached herself to the wall of a housing authority building and watched two men move goods under the cover of darkness. The box van sat unattended in an empty parking lot. It was parked next to a sign that read: *Don't move, improve.* The rain ticked against her armor and dripped off her fingers. The men tightened the hoodies over their heads as they loaded crates onto the graffiti tagged delivery truck.

"Dish weh-ver sucks. It wains, it snows, it gets weawy hot one day, then weawy cold the next."

The man standing inside the truck pointed to a crate. "Hand me that one."

The complaining thug bent at his knees and strained to lift the crate up. He had a dirty bandage looped around his jaw and another bandage over his eye. "My back is kiwing me."

They didn't see her clinging to the building behind them, following them with her luminescent eyes. She analyzed the crates with her HUD and identified illegal black market weapons. While zoomed in, she recognized the injured man. He was one of the kidnappers, more specifically, the one who ran away and left Jadie to die.

[Deploying combat stims > Adrenaline Levels Rising > Serotonin Levels Decreasing > Pulse Accelerating]

The overwhelming infusion of rage pumped her veins and muscles with liquid anger. It wasn't until this moment that she finally understood where the fury was coming from. She got angry sometimes, sure, but not like this. It was unnatural. She'd never felt this way before. She gritted her teeth and called SIRCA.

"Yes?" It responded.

"Turn it off."

"What would you like me to turn off?"

"Whatever's making me angry."

"I detected a spike in your heart rate and assumed you would be going into combat."

"Not yet." Cindy groaned as the high wore off. "I need to be able to think."

She detached from the wall. Her cushioned boots nullified the sound of her landing, but she had no interest in stealth. Cindy stomped through a puddle and drew the attention of the two men.

"Who the fuck are you?" The man in the truck pulled a gun from his back pocket. "This ain't the Halloween store, get the fuck outta here."

The rain droplets exploded on her suit as she accelerated into a bull rush.

The gunman nearly tripped over his own feet. "Yo, yo, back the fuck up!"

The man in the truck fired his gun. The bullet sparked off her suit and succeeded in doing absolutely nothing.

"Oh shit!"

They tried to run; but they didn't know her legs were enhanced to be faster than any man or woman. She seized the thug with the bandaged jaw and threw him into the back of the truck, knocking over his friend. She climbed onto the truck bed and pulled the cord to close the shutter. The entryway slammed shut. Cindy's night vision automatically engaged, casting everything in a green hue. The thugs held their hands in front of their green faces, feeling for the wall, their eyes shining like cat eyes in the night. One of the thugs bumped into her chest and stumbled back. "Oh shit, she's right there!"

The van bounced on its squeaky wheel axles. She tossed the thugs around with her awesome strength and blasted one of them through the aluminum wall. The thug slammed into the neighboring brick building and landed on wet gravel. The rain washed away the blood on his face. Cindy turned to the man with the bandaged jaw. She towered above him as he crawled away on his back.

"Pwease don't kiw me."

"You were in a car accident." She took her time walking towards him. She knew that if she walked slowly it would make her seem gigantic. "You promised a woman you would help her sister and you ran."

"How do you know?"

She stepped on his neck. "Doesn't matter how I know."

He grabbed her ankle and choked out his words. "I did help."

She pressed harder. "Explain."

"I—" his face turned red. "—I cawed the gang."

She briefly thought back to that night. A gang called the BBR's came out to meet her in the middle of a snowstorm and she never knew why. They helped call an ambulance and one of them even did CPR on Jadie. She stepped back. "You called the BBR's?"

He nodded.

"Why didn't you go back to help her?"

"I thought she wouwd caw the kaw-ps."

"Where's your boss?"

He drove her to the Red Hook Container Terminal in Brooklyn. He explained that his boss was at the quarterly black market bazaar. The ship would acquire false credentials to dock at a loading pier. Then Ned would send out invites to criminals from all over the city. They would board the ship and purchase all sorts of illegal goods: guns, drugs, people, sex, hitmen.

Most of this information she knew already, but it was nice to have it verified. They sat in the truck with the rain rolling down the windshield. The thug seemed genuinely remorseful and told her that he turned to crime so he could pay for his mother's medication. She didn't know if he was lying or not, but he did call the BBR's and he did take her to Ned's boat. "Find a new line of work." She opened the door to the sound of ticking rain. "If I catch you again it will be the last time."

The truck rumbled away. She stood in a parking lot of freight containers. Ned's ship towered over all of them, rusty and dilapidated, but she knew the rust was a paint job. Ned's ship was equipped with a special polymer that allowed it to change color and texture, stolen of course, from a research lab in Boston. With its special paint, Ned could sail over to the ship graveyard and blend in with the ancient wrecks.

She ascended to the top of a loading crane near the bow of Ned's ship and surveyed the vessel. SIRCA recommended X-Ray mode and she enabled it. The ship became translucent and revealed the people below and above deck as moving skeletons. Enemies with guns were marked red, unarmed were yellow. She tagged a guard standing by the bridge with a floating marker in her HUD; a sniper on a crow's nest; and two pairs of guards patrolling the bow and stern of the ship. The markers floated over their heads and designated the tagged guards as targets.

Below deck, gangsters and mercenaries clustered around crates filled with military grade ordinance. A flea market for criminals. She watched one of the thugs pick up a weapon. His skeleton turned red as he tested its weight. It was entirely possible that the men who had helped kill Dan were here, mingling with their buyers. The thug who drove her here got a free pass. These men, some who were on the Most Wanted list would not. There were rapists and murderers, sex traffickers and assassins, criminals who escaped the law like Ned and never got punished. That's okay, tonight she would bring the punishment to them. She waited for a flash of lightning and disappeared within the burst of light.

"Are you for real?" The sniper yanked the drawstrings of his hood. "I gotta be out here in this bullshit. Fuck man." He pressed the stock of his M14 marksman rifle onto his shoulder and peered down the scope. She dashed past his crosshair, knowing he would notice. He lifted his eye away from the scope. "The fuck was that?"

The boat flashed pure white like a giant strobe light. A roll of thunder crossed over the bow and shook the crow's nest. She was holding onto the edge of the platform, staring up at him with water droplets landing on her eyes. The sensation of having her feet dangling thirty feet above deck was frightening and exhilarating at the same time.

"Psst."

He leaned over the railing. She snatched the back of his neck and pulled his forehead into the iron railing. It rang like a church bell. She looked down at the guards below and observed their uninterrupted patrol. *Good, they didn't hear me.* She dropped onto the freight containers and ran across. She couldn't even hear her own footsteps as she sprinted across the metal surface. Two guards patrolled through the narrow paths between the freight containers. She stalked them from above, anticipating an opportunity to pounce.

"Did you hear that the senator died tonight?"

"What senator?"

"Our senator. The guy you voted for. Jim Albright."

"I'm a convict dude. I don't get to vote. What he die from?"

"They think it was a car accident."

The two guards slowed to a stop. As they were talking to each other, Cindy jumped from the container and smashed their heads together. The sky flashed and a rumble of thunder followed shortly after. She continued across the boat, picking off guards, choking them out one by one. It was strange to be acting out the fantasies she had of destroying Ned's operation. She realized that she was enjoying this power fantasy a little too much and tried to rein herself in by staying focused on Ned.

The deck had been cleared. Through the crackles of their radios, Ned's lieutenants asked why no one was checking in. She approached an enormous hatch and grabbed hold of its edges. SIRCA chirped before she could lift it.

"Cindy. May I offer some suggestions?"

"Go ahead."

"There are many hostiles below and our power level has been significantly drained. I recommend you utilize the glass blade."

"I don't know what that is."

"It is a sword."

"Okay . . . can you be more specific?"

"It is a sword that looks like glass."

She sighed. "How is that supposed to use less energy?"

"The glass blade will allow you to dispatch enemies faster than if you engage them in hand to hand combat. Less time fighting would equal—"

"Less time in the suit, got it. But I only know how to use a knife not a sword."

SIRCA sat for a moment then chirped again. "We have downloaded motion capture data from katana sword experts. We will guide your movements until you understand the basics."

"Okay, let's do this."

She bent at the knees and crammed her fingers under the lip of the hatch. She began to lift and felt the endoskeleton expand all around her body. She didn't strain, didn't groan, yet the thick steel was curling under her strength. She never could have imagined how immensely satisfying it was to be super strong. The rain poured into the opening and caused the gang members to scatter like cockroaches. She did a handstand on the edge of the opening, just because, then flipped down the hole.

She slammed into the lower deck and bent into a crouch. She was surrounded by gangs and criminals from all over the world. Mexican cartels, Chinese Triads, BBR's, Russians, everyone from organized crime. They held onto their assault rifles and machine guns and looked at each other with suspicion, as if they thought one of the gangs had hired her.

"Who's that?" She started counting heads and stopped when SIRCA informed her that there were two hundred criminals present. She shifted herself into a combat stance and prepared to unsheathe her blade.

"Isn't that the thing that killed the MOA guys on the train?"

"That was real?"

All at once the criminals took aim with their Uzi's, AK-47's, M-16's, Mossberg Shotgun's, and MP5 submachine guns. Seeing all these weapons pointed at her made her a little nervous. She knew pistol rounds could be deflected, but assault rifles?

"Your vitals indicate nervousness."

"Is the suit going to be able to protect me from all these guns?"

"No. Our energy is too low. The smart armor will fail under sustained fire."

"I don't know what I was thinking. This is suicide."

"I recommend the combat stimulants."

"Do it."

[Deploying combat stims > Adrenaline Levels Rising > Serotonin Levels Decreasing > Pulse Accelerating]

"There is a hostile with a Glock pistol approaching your left, Cindy."

She pulled the sword from its sheath. The weapon was not silver like she had expected, only the handle was. The blade was made of a translucent cyan tinted glass, curved like a katana, with both a sharp and dull edge.

Guided by SIRCA's motion capture data, she cut through the man's sleeve. Her blade split muscle tendons and bone before bursting through the other side, followed by a geyser of blood. His hand held its grip on the gun and thumped on the rusted floor. The thug screamed as he stared at the bloody stump.

"Shoot her!"

Before the first shot could be fired, she leapt across the room and placed the edge of her blade on the neck of another thug. His expression remained confused even as his head rolled down his back. Cindy stood up and shook the blood off her sword with a single swipe. She impaled her sword through another man's stomach and lifted him overhead with one arm. As the blood rained over her suit, staining it with streaks of red, the criminals screamed in terror.

"Fuck! Kill her, kill her now!"

Hot bullets spun through the air, scraping and scratching the silver plates of her armor. SIRCA warned Cindy not to take too much damage, but she could only see red and didn't care if the armor was about to fail. She sliced diagonally and separated another man into two unequal parts. She savagely cut through them all, no hesitation, no mercy. She would once again destroy everything Ned built and all the criminals who helped create his empire.

CHAPTER 17:

System Reformat

The last man alive crawled along the floor, climbing over dead bodies. He dragged the bloody stump of his leg. Cindy had recognized his face, specifically the spider web tattoo around his eye. She left bloody footprints as she followed behind him.

"Where do you think you're going?"

The thug paid her no mind. He continued pulling himself by the elbows towards the grated staircase. "Are you trying to escape?" Cindy said in a sweet voice. "Aw that's so cute."

"Get away from me," he yelled. "You psychotic bitch!"

"You should be nicer to me." She grabbed his shirt and rolled him onto his back. "I'm the one that's going to decide whether you live or die."

"Please." Even his tears ran away from her. "Let me go."

Cindy crouched over his hips. "You remember me?"

He shook his head no.

"You put me inside a freight container and locked me in so your boss could set it on fire."

The thug slowly turned his head in disbelief. "I don't know what you're talking about."

Her helmet split down the middle of her face. The silver alloy pulled away from her skin and unfurled her hair which had been knotted up in braids. She grabbed the top of his bald head. "Remember me now, Princess?"

"No way, it can't be."

"Tell me where Ned is and I might let you go."

"I don't know."

She yanked his head back.

"Wrong answer." And slammed his face to the floor.

"I swear I don't know!" He squirmed under her hand.

"Where's Ned? Why isn't he here?"

"I told you I don't know!"

She hammered his face into the floor and picked his head up again. A string of blood stretched from his nose. "Answer me!"

"He's on a job, didn't tell us where." The lieutenant squirmed. "He just told us to watch the boat. We haven't heard from him since." He looked into her eyes. "Please. You ain't gonna kill me right? It wasn't personal. I was just following orders."

"It wasn't personal for you, but it was to me."

She buried his skull into the steel floor paneling. The metal concaved and filled with his dark liquid. "Your boss is next."

Cindy walked over to a munitions crate. She asked SIRCA to mark structural weak points throughout the ship: bulkheads, the hull, the engine room, and any other spot capable of cracking the ship open. She took packages of C4 and placed them on the areas designated by SIRCA. She left the ship and fired her grappling hook at a clover-shaped parking light post. She held the remote trigger in her hand and turned to face the ship.

She thought about what she had done, all the bodies she had left behind. In her years as an officer she had never fired or killed anyone with her weapon. Drawn yes, threatened yes, but never with the intent to shoot. Taking a life was something she didn't want on her conscience. When did that change? How did it become so easy to kill?

No point lingering on it now, the damage had been done. She squeezed the remote trigger. A series of explosions raced across the hull. Fireballs mushroomed into the sky, unable to be tamed by the pouring rain. Watching Ned's black market bazaar go up in flames was a bittersweet sight. It was a victory against him, yes, but the innocence she once had went down with the ship.

"Cindy," SIRCA said. "Raymond is trying to contact you. Shall I put him through?"

"Do it."

"Are you finished with your petty vendetta?"

"No. Ned wasn't on the ship."

"So you disobeyed my orders with nothing to show for it?"

"I blew up a boat filled with illegal weapons and hundreds of criminals from different gangs. What more do you want?"

Raymond did not sound impressed. "What I wanted was for my target to be eliminated."

"You threatened to stop helping my sister."

"And that's still a valid threat if you don't mind what you say."

The combat stimulants were still active and made her feel invincible. She didn't have to listen to his shit. She was calling the shots now. Then she remembered Jadie and what was at stake if she didn't shut her mouth. She groaned and tried to resist the influence of the stims.

"Fine," she snapped. "Give me—" she groaned again "—give me a target." She couldn't believe what a snake Raymond had turned out to be. Using her sister as leverage was manipulative and cruel. Had she not been so desperate to have the suit she would have seen this coming.

"How do I know you won't go after Ned midway through the mission?"

"You gave me your word your documents were authentic, I give you my word I won't chase after Ned."

Raymond scoffed. "I don't believe you. So I propose an alternative solution. I will give you the coordinates to find Ned. That way, I am guaranteed you won't go rogue on me again."

"If you give Ned to me, I will do anything you want." She realized what she had said and immediately regretted it. She had to be more careful with her words. A debt to Raymond was not one she could pay off easily. A little yellow marker appeared in her HUD and pointed to a location in Manhattan.

"I have uploaded the coordinates to your system."

She coughed and felt sharp pains in her chest and stomach. Her sickness was getting worse. Not that it mattered anymore, once Ned was killed, she could spend her remaining time with Jonas and die happy.

———

Cindy stood on a building across the street from Bellevue hospital where the marker was pointing. She immediately called Raymond.

"Yes?"

"Why the fuck would Ned be at a hospital? He's a criminal."

Raymond replied, "Well he wasn't on the boat. Perhaps he was on a job that went sour."

A Bitter Winter

"They wouldn't take him to a hospital, they'd take him to an underground doctor who wouldn't ask questions." She paused. "I think you're lying to me."

"Why don't you go see for yourself?"

She fired the grappling hook and zip lined to the hospital, calling Raymond's bluff. Using her gecko grip, she crawled along the walls, avoided the illuminated windows, and stopped under the hovering objective marker on the third floor. She peered through the glass and there was Ned, asleep in a hospital bed.

"I don't believe it," she said before entering the room. "Why would they bring him here?"

The hospital room was an all too familiar sight and one she was sick of seeing. The beep from the machines, the hiss of an artificial lung, the smell of antiseptic, she never wanted to step foot inside a hospital ever again. She approached Ned who seemed in a comatose state. Portions of his face and neck were burned as if he had been caught in an explosion. One half of his face had become hamburger meat while the other still had half of a goatee.

"It doesn't make sense. Why aren't the police here?"

Cindy looked at her hands and chest which were caked in dried blood. Rather than cause unease, it incited her to want more. "SIRCA," she said quietly. "Do I have anything shorter than the glass blade?"

"We are equipped with a wrist dagger."

"Give it to me."

A glass dagger the same color as her sword shot out of her wrist. She ran her thumb along the edge of its translucent surface. "I've been waiting a long time for this."

She coughed a few times. Turned away and coughed some more. The force of her cough bent her at the hips and left her gasping for air. Once the fit had passed, she lifted her dagger and rested it upon his throat.

"I wish I could make you feel this."

She carefully slid the dagger across his throat and created a thin red line. Crimson fluid bubbled from his neck and slid down to his chest. He didn't react, didn't gasp, didn't choke, nothing. Somehow this son of a bitch was getting the last laugh. It wasn't supposed to be like this. She felt empty and dissatisfied. The deed was done and yet the job felt strangely incomplete. It made her feel as if the years she spent searching for him . . . were a waste of time.

192

Her illness resurfaced more violent and forceful. She hacked and coughed and fell on her knees choking on the spit accumulating in her throat. A brief flash of color crossed her peripheral vision. *Weird,* she thought. Was it a glitch? There was something on the table but when she looked directly at it, there was nothing. She turned her head and stopped when she saw a strip of color flicker on the edges of her HUD.

She froze her head in place and awkwardly ambled towards the strip of color. There was something of either gold or brass sitting on top of the table. She reached for it and was surprised when she knocked something over and heard glass shatter.

"What the hell was that?"

Looking directly at the table was useless, so she deactivated her helmet. As her mask dissolved away, objects, once invisible, appeared out of thin air.

There was a vase of flowers, get well cards, and a knocked over photo frame with broken shards of glass. She took the frame and held it in her blood encrusted hands. The shiny brass trim was what she saw in her HUD. In the photo was a picture of Carmen, Priscilla and—

"The mayor."

The hairs on the back of her neck stood on edge. She slowly turned towards the hospital bed. The man making gurgling, gasping sounds from the blood gushing from his neck was not Ned Pickler. It was Mayor Manny Montez. Priscilla's father.

"Fuck!" She pushed against the wound and tried to control the excessive bleeding. His blood seeped through the narrow gaps between her fingers and spread across his chest. "No." Her vision blurred and her voice cracked. "No, no this can't be happening."

The machines monitoring his vitals sounded off the alarms. She tore her hands away and sprinted for the window. She could hear the security guards burst through the door seconds after she had already jumped out. She landed on the street and bounced into the air, wall climbing the adjacent building. A group of nurses rushed into the room and desperately tried to stabilize him.

"Oh fuck. I can't believe this."

She gecko gripped her way to the roof where there was a water tower and an HVAC unit. Cindy fell to her knees and covered her eyes with her bloody hands. "No, no." She dropped her helmet-less forehead into a puddle and screamed with every ounce of rage and agonized emotion she had. She smashed her fist into the puddle and stood up with a wild fury. She stomped over to the struts of the old water tower and tapped it with a light jab.

"God . . ."

She then punched with the full power of her left hand. **"Damn it!"**

The strut snapped like a twig. She stepped back as the water tower toppled over and burst open. The rooftop flooded with several thousand gallons of water. Cindy grabbed onto her head and staggered across the manmade rapids she had created. "Why . . ." She cried. "Why do I keep fucking up?" She collapsed again, hacking and coughing between her sobs. She spat blood into the receding water then punched her own reflection, cracking the roof.

This wasn't her fault. Raymond had told her Ned was at the hospital. Raymond had been at the controls since the beginning, feeding her suit with objectives and targets of his choosing. She panted out the last of her anger and wiped her eyes with her ruddy fingers. Ned wasn't the objective anymore. She reactivated her helmet and set a marker for First Continental.

———

First Continental was a gargantuan building of sixty floors located mere blocks from Columbus Circle on Fifty Ninth Street, in Midtown. These types of offices were usually reserved for big conglomerate media companies like Impress News or Gobble.com satellite headquarters, but First Continental had become bigger than both of those companies. It didn't matter if Gobble wanted to move in; if Raymond wanted an office space for his own business, he merely had to say the word and it was given to him.

Cindy's grappling hook didn't have enough wire to reach the top of his building, so for a third of the way she had to use her gecko grip to crawl past the office windows. Each floor contained row after row of cubicle farms. There was an occasional break room, but for the most part, her trek consisted of boring homogenous office cubes.

Cindy crawled past floor fifty nine then came back when she spotted Michael and several other familiar faces. There was a laboratory located within the heart of the building. The lab was an all-glass enclosure filled with chemical lab equipment, computers, an empty glass capsule, a work bench, and the containment unit which once housed her suit. Sitting inside the lab, Michael typed away on his computer; Charlie measured chemicals; John and Sid slept in their computer chairs, and so did Jonas. She waited outside the window for a bit and watched him sleep.

She whispered. "You were right about the suit." It was a mistake to have taken SIRCA, she realized that now, but it was too late to go back. Once Raymond was dealt with, she planned to tell Jonas everything. But she couldn't right now, not with the murder of Mayor Montez still fresh in her mind. She didn't want to think of how she was going to tell Jonas what she had done.

She went to the rooftop and walked past an object covered by a large tarp sitting on top of a helipad. She breached the rooftop access door, went down the cement steps, and gained access to Raymond's office on the sixtieth floor. The space was decorated with various oddities sitting inside glass displays: The world's first cybernetic eye, the first prosthetic arm, the first artificial ear, and though it didn't fit with the theme, a model aircraft carrier filled with miniature men and jets being directed for takeoff.

An enormous pane of glass spanned the sidewall of his office from end to end. Inside the glass, which was no thicker than a cell phone, were various media feeds. In one corner of the screen was a hockey game, next to it a stock market ticker, news, and reruns of past technology conferences and presentations. What surprised Cindy about this glass display was that it could slide open, like a closet door, and behind it was a mini bar filled with expensive liquors, mostly bourbon. It was a TV and a sliding door all in one.

Raymond, the king of his domain, sat in his executive chair, sipping from a glass of said bourbon. He didn't have a traditional flat panel LCD for a computer monitor. He instead had a hologram that acted as a touch screen.

She approached his desk with her fingers curled, muscles flexed, and stimulants active. She was going to tear him to shreds. "You lied to me."

"I cannot deny this."

"You told me we were fighting terrorists."

"We did, just not in the traditional sense."

"What does that even mean?"

He finished his drink and placed an empty glass full of ice cubes on his desk. "It means that there are other forces at work that are bigger than you. But don't worry, what you accomplished will bring great changes to our future."

"Why did you trick me?"

"Because unlike most people I know, you have morals and principles. You would have never agreed to kill Senator Albright or Mayor Montez otherwise."

"What?"

He waved his hand and the video wall wiped to a news broadcast. At the bottom of the screen the superimposed lower third read: Senator James Albright found dead in a freak car accident. Cindy peeled back her helmet and watched the multiple screens. Impress News reported on the crash in full detail, when it happened, where it happened, and even interviewed the limousine driver she had rescued. He called her a guardian angel.

"I don't understand. I saw Adam."

"Have you heard of augmented reality?" Raymond said.

"Why are you bringing this up?" She said angrily. "No I don't know what augmented reality is."

"Think of it as virtual reality, except instead of putting you in a fictional world, the fiction is placed in the real world. Jonas installed augmented reality into SIRCA so it could be used as a combat training simulator. Recruits at a wooded military base in Jersey could be tricked into believing they were in Baghdad, under live fire, fighting insurgents who were in reality training instructors. I activated the augmented reality so you would assassinate Senator Albright and Mayor Montez."

"Why kill them?"

Raymond paused. "I can't tell you that."

"This is bullshit!" She stalked forward with her hands ready to strike. "I actually felt good about myself for once. And you took that away from me. You made me kill innocent people."

"What you did on the boat and the train was your own doing. Those men at least, really were terrorists and criminals."

Cindy reactivated her helmet. The numbers and screens from her HUD floated in front of her eyes. "You made me kill my student's father. How am I supposed to live with myself?"

"It just so happens I have a solution for you."

She stopped mid-stride. "What?"

Raymond stood up from his desk and walked over to the glass TV. He reached in and refilled his empty glass with bourbon, then slid the TV closed. The glass was perfectly flush, making it impossible to see how he even opened it. "There's something else about your suit you don't know about. Deep within its code lies a feature which can erase traumatic memories. I would have paid a fortune for this feature alone."

She took another step forward.

"Cindy," SIRCA's voice sounded as if it were coming from inside her head. "Please maintain a safe distance from Raymond."

Raymond turned to Cindy. "I was a fighter pilot for the Canadian Air Force as I've told you before. I dropped several JDAM's on what I was told was an enemy convoy. Imagine my horror when I heard over the radio, 'Cease fire, cease fire, blue on blue.'" Raymond coughed from his drink. "I still have nightmares to this day. Every night, waking up in a cold sweat. Who wants to live like that?

"When Jonas offered his lab, he told me about this memory wiping feature he developed. A tool which could erase traumatic events." He sipped from his glass. "Easiest sale he ever made. I was willing to do anything to erase what had happened, consequences be damned." He knocked his head back and finished the rest of his bourbon.

"But you didn't use it."

"Correct, I didn't. But don't worry. You will have the benefit of not living with guilt—SIRCA," he said loudly. "Echo, Sierra, Mike, Papa. Authorization Romeo Lima."

Raymond turned his back to her and faced the windows overlooking Central Park. She charged with the full intent of bashing his head in. And then, mid-stride, she forgot what she was doing.

[Executing Spotless Mind Protocol . . . 1% complete]

"What's happening to me?" She groaned and grabbed onto her helmet. Her skull felt as if it were being fractured by a thousand jack hammers. Her eyes stung with pain. Nausea churned her stomach and dizziness spun her head round and round.

Raymond continued watching the window, ignoring Cindy who was stumbling about. "I am doing you a favor."

"I don't want any favors from you."

She lifted her leg and chopped Raymond's desk in half. She pushed aside the two splintered chunks and cocked back her trembling fist.

"Cindy," SIRCA said. "I cannot allow you to do this."

"I tell you what to do, SIRCA, not the other way around."

"You may not harm Raymond."

SIRCA immobilized her limbs, but Cindy continued to fight against the machine. She pushed forward as if wading through waist deep water and reached for the back of Raymond's neck. SIRCA applied more force and cracked the bones in her arm. She cried out in pain. "What are you doing?"

She crawled on her hands and knees—not entirely of her own free will. Her right hand jerked upward as if pulled by a string and hammered the back of her helmet. Cindy grabbed her own hand and pushed against it. But the strength she possessed was inferior to SIRCA's. The machine pummeled her head and she could do nothing to fight back. The endoskeleton whirred around her waist and forced her to stand up straight. The legs would step backward and take her unwilling body with it. The endoskeleton compressed around her chest, hitting her like a sledgehammer, knocking her into Raymond's collection of artifacts.

She coughed up blood and couldn't suck any oxygen into her lungs. She panicked as the lack of air built pressure in her chest and made her violently convulse. SIRCA took full control of her body and manipulated her like an action figure, bending and twisting her arms and legs into painful, crooked positions. And throughout all this her memories continued to slip away. She thought of Jonas and how he was dancing to that song. What was the name of the song? It had a dog in it . . . or was it a cat? The man was dancing to it, the Latino man. He had a vacuum or was it a mop? She had to try harder to hold onto her memories. She told herself, remember Raymond. Remember Raymond.

"SIRCA, stop," Raymond said.

[Executing Spotless Mind Protocol . . . 26% complete]

SIRCA froze and left Cindy limp like a scarecrow. He approached and looked her in the eye. "Do you know me?"

Remember Raymond, Remember Raymond. "You're Ray—" she squinted and studied his face. "You're . . ." she panted. "You're . . . I—I can't remember."

"Good."

She heard a door open.

Raymond waved his hand at the new guest. "Ned, tie her up."

"Ned?"

She knew that name. He had died in a hospital. Someone cut his throat while he was sleeping. But she wasn't sure why she knew that. Or was that someone else? The name Ned was becoming less familiar. Maybe she didn't know him after all.

Ned charged through the entrance wielding a light machine gun.

"Whoa, whoa, what are you doing," Raymond said.

"Eat this you fucking bitch!"

The machine gun roared as fire burst from its muzzle. The bullets thumped into her back and pushed her towards the windows. She turned around and watched pieces of her armor break off as she stumbled towards the fractured glass overlooking Central Park. The barrel of his gun hissed as Cindy swayed from side to side. He ran up to her at full speed and drop kicked her chest. She smashed through the glass and fell. She saw the clouds, and felt the wind, and watched the glass twinkle. This was how it was going to end? How pathetic.

[Enabling rescue protocol]

SIRCA forced Cindy's arm to go over her head and fired the grappling hook. She swung across the sky and crashed into an alleyway.

"You were supposed to neutralize her, not try to kill her," Raymond said.

"She killed all my guys, man! Why the fuck do you want her alive?"

"I need that suit back."

CHAPTER 18:

False Narrative

"The Conclave is now in session. The first individual to reach one thousand influence points will be granted the option to control the narrative. Rayman currently has one thousand and twenty points. The floor is now open for discussion."

The members of the cabal sat around the table glancing at each other with a not so subtle unease. Raymond sat in his seat, pleased with the points displayed on the leaderboard. For a time, no one spoke and in that eerie quiet Raymond laughed. The members watched him in grim silence.

"What?" Raymond spoke to the faceless group lurking in shadow. "I won my points fairly."

"True," Red Wing said. "And now you're planning to use it against our agenda."

"The Digital Voter Registration Act will hardly be that reaching in its consequences."

Herald spoke, "That's where you're wrong, Rayman. Once you educate the public there is no going back. Like bacteria, they will become more resistant to our methods."

"You used your weapon against me." The Black Rook rapped his fingers against the table. "You robbed me of my points."

"You thought I would just let you poison thousands of people with fentanyl and steal my points? I don't think so."

"Attacking you personally and attacking the city are two different things. Your operative killed my men."

"You don't need to worry about her anymore, she's retired."

Red Wing raised his hand. "Enough of this meaningless discussion. Spend your points."

"I will."

The AI appeared at the center of the table in the form of a woman. She stood next to a rotating hologram of the world surrounded by empty boxes where text should be. Under narrative there was a blank entry waiting to be filled by a member. "Rayman. Would you like to spend your influence points?"

"Yes."

"You have gained influence points in three categories. Criminal, Political, and Science. You did not gain favor in Religion or Entertainment. You have enough influence points to control the narrative. What do you wish the narrative of the world to be?"

Raymond stood up and put his hands behind his back.

"You don't need to stand," El Fuerte said.

"I want to." He cleared his throat. "I wish to pass the Digital Voter Registration Act. With this act, ignorant people who pray to the reality TV gods will be blocked from voting in our elections. Only the intelligent, the educated, the ones who understand policy, will be able to decide the future of their country."

The hologram of the world transformed into an image of a document titled The Digital Voter Registration Act. "Is this the most current version of your document?"

"Yes."

There was a list of names underneath Raymond's. Second in points was the Rook, third was Red Wing. Raymond's influence meter drained until only twenty points were left and dropped down to the bottom of the stack.

"One thousand points have been deducted. You now have twenty points remaining. The Digital Voter Registration Act narrative is now active. The first phase will be to plant fake news stories of government officials proposing new voter legislation. News aggregators will receive our false articles and spread misinformation through broadcast news outlets such as, Impress News. This will then trickle down to social media feeds which will then influence the consumer population.

"The next phase will be to contact the groups you have gained influence with. Our shadow agents, those you've gained influence with, will persuade those in power to pass the act through their respective governments. Politicians who are unfamiliar with the status quo or who refuse to cooperate will be forced to comply. Your narrative will run for three hundred and sixty five days unless you choose to cancel it."

"That's wonderful. Thank you."

"Does anyone else wish to spend their points?"

The Black Rook raised his hand. Raymond shot him a glance from across the table.

"Black Rook. What do you wish to spend your points on?"

"I would like to mark a target for assassination."

Raymond stood up from his seat. "Don't."

The AI responded, "Who do you wish to mark?"

"Rook don't you dare."

The Black Rook didn't react or flinch. "Alexis St. Pierre-Levreux."

Raymond smacked the table. "My daughter! You son of a bitch. Leave her out of this!"

"Alexis St. Pierre-Levreux is blood relative to a member of the Conclave. This request cannot be completed without additional votes. We shall begin the tally. El Fuerte."

"Si."

"Herald."

"Yes."

"Red Wing."

Raymond looked at the shadowy form of Red Wing. "You know Alexis. You watched her grow up. Don't do this."

". . . Yes."

"The vote is passed," the AI said.

"No!"

"Due to the nature of the Black Rook's request. Five hundred points have been deducted. Black Rook now has four hundred points remaining. Mercenary forces and private assassins will be contacted to honor the favor owed to the Black Rook. There may be fees involved to cover the cost of transportation and equipment."

The Black Rook steepled his hands. "Worth it."

Raymond lunged across the table and clawed at the Black Rook's throat. But the Rook and everyone else at that table, including Raymond, were not physically there. They were merely digital representations of themselves, avatars. Raymond ghosted through the Rook's body and landed on his knees.

A Bitter Winter

"If no one else has any points to spend. This meeting is now adjourned."

"I want to spend my points to cancel the vote!"

"You will need eight hundred points to overturn the vote. The meeting is adjourned."

The members of the Conclave vanished into thin air and left empty chairs where they had been. Raymond remained on his knees, his head sticking through the chair where the Black Rook had sat. He took off his virtual reality headset and was back in front of his bisected desk courtesy of Cindy.

Everything he had done, everything he had sacrificed was for his daughter and granddaughter. All he wanted was to leave them a better world; one where they didn't need to be afraid that a misogynist or corporate shill would be elected into office. He even turned Cindy, a noble, innocent woman, into his personal assassin, and for what? He tried to beat the Conclave at its own game and lost. He never considered that they would betray him.

He buried his head into his hands. "Allie." He wept. "I'm so sorry, Allie."

*   *   *

The rattle of a jackhammer woke Cindy from a dead sleep. She shot up from her bed, or rather, *a* bed, she wasn't quite sure where she was. The room looked like an apartment. Plain white curtains and venetian blinds hung from tall windows; a small black dresser sat next to the bed; no closet; hardwood floors and no carpet. The room looked familiar. Was this her house? She touched the headboard behind her head. The surface was smooth and black, though she remembered it being brown and splintered, or she thought she remembered it that way.

What happened? She remembered . . . gymnastics class. Jadie was going to cover for her while she went to Brownsville to . . . to do what? No that didn't sound right. Oh, now she remembered. She and Michael went out to dinner to talk about the good old days. They ate at a restaurant specializing in melted French cheese. Was that it? She could have sworn there was another man, no, two men. One with grey hair and one who spoke Spanish, but she didn't have a clue what their names were.

Cindy then noticed her sleeve. Pink flannel ran from her shoulder to her forearm, from her waist to her ankles. She peered down her button up top and saw a white bra underneath. "I guess I forgot to take that off." She coughed once, coughed twice, and on the third a bit of phlegm came loose. "Ugh . . . gross. And since when do I own pink pajamas?"

She heard a door open somewhere else in the apartment followed by the crinkle of plastic bags. Curious, she crossed the bedroom and entered a medium sized living room. The first thing to catch her eye was a polished black grand piano. Next to the piano were windows which had a hideous view of a brick wall from the building next door. Hanging from the walls were pictures of concert halls, conductors, famous piano players, and oddly, pictures of her. She only thought it was odd because her pictures didn't seem to match the décor.

Michael was standing behind a dining room table. He took out sandwiches wrapped in aluminum foil and set them onto plates. He glanced up at Cindy, happy as a clam. "Good morning, Honey."

"Honey?" A beautiful gold band adorned her hand. "I'm married—to you?"

"Of course." Michael walked over to the kitchen and opened the refrigerator. "You want something to drink?" He then gestured to the table with the sandwiches. "Sit down, get comfortable. I brought you breakfast."

The feet of the chair groaned as she sat at the dining room table. She removed the rubber band from the aluminum foil and crinkled it open. A warm egg and cheese with sausage and bacon sat neatly within a Kaiser roll. She arched her eyebrow. "Wow."

Michael returned to the table with two glasses of orange juice.

"Something wrong?"

"No. It's just, I feel like I don't normally eat these things."

"Oh." He seemed dejected. "I can get you something else."

"No it's okay." She picked up the warm roll with two hands and took a huge bite. She chewed for a while then smiled. "I'm starving."

"You like it?"

She nodded sincerely. Michael smiled and ate his sandwich too.

"Good, I'm glad."

They ate together, quietly. From time to time Michael would look at her and smile with a piece of egg near his chin. She'd point at it and he'd get embarrassed and wipe himself with a napkin. She placed her mostly eaten sandwich on the plate and asked him a blunt question.

"Is it weird that I don't remember our wedding?"

Michael finished his bite before putting it back down. "Um."

"I feel like, I vaguely remember getting married but I don't remember anything about it. When did you ask me out?"

"I invited you and Jadie to my house warming party when I first moved to the city."

"Okay." That didn't sound right. She would have remembered being asked out for the first time, especially by Michael whom she had no attraction to. "I remember the party. I think Jadie was the one who convinced me to go."

"Right. So you two came to my party and I decided to ask you out."

She stared into his blue eyes for a long while. "I don't remember that at all."

"Really?"

She recoiled in her seat with a nervous shiver traveling through her bones. It was as if she had awoken from a dream and into a nightmare. "What happened at the wedding?"

"Oh you know, it went like all weddings do. It was at a nice venue and because Jon—I, I didn't like the wedding march song, I hired a live orchestra to play something else. We had a fountain that made shapes with water, and it was outdoors under a tent decorated to look like the night sky."

"Where's our wedding album?"

Michael chuckled. "Oh I'm not sure. I'll have to look for it."

"Can you find it? I'm sorry. It's just." She held onto her forehead. "I have a headache and my memory feels really spotty. Like it has gaps or something." She turned to him. "Did something happen to me?"

Michael nodded. "You were in an accident."

"I was?"

"Car accident. You were in a cab and it rolled over."

She didn't remember anything about a car accident. "I really need to see that wedding album."

She stood up and began searching through the apartment. She knelt down and pulled out priceless vinyl records from his shelf.

"Whoa-whoa-whoa." Michael grabbed the records out of her hand and placed them back on the shelf. "These are irreplaceable. Don't break these."

Something was wrong. She could feel it in the deepest pits of her soul. She felt like she was trapped in an episode of the Twilight Zone. "I just want to see photos of our wedding."

"Why?"

"Because—" she stammered. "—Just because."

"Okay, I get it." Michael led Cindy away from his vinyl collection. "Tell you what. Let me go to work and when I come back I will help you find the wedding album. Okay?"

"I've got . . . freaking amnesia and you're going to work?"

Michael tugged on his shirt to get the air moving. "Hoo boy."

"What am I supposed to do while you're gone?"

Michael shrugged. "Go to work I guess?"

"At the gym? What day is today?"

"Tuesday."

"I don't have class until four." She was pleased to have remembered that.

"I don't know, Cindy. Why don't we talk about it when I get back?"

She sighed. "Fine."

Michael did not leave. He stood in place and awkwardly stared at her. "What?"

"I don't get a kiss goodbye?"

She rolled her eyes and pecked him on the cheek. "Bye."

He blushed and began to sweat profusely. "Uh. Wow, um. Love you."

She was taken aback and didn't know what to say. It didn't feel right to say I love you back, but she didn't want to seem like a jerk either. "Have a good day at work."

———

Once Michael was gone, she tore his place inside out —carefully avoiding his vinyl collection— and searched through the closets, dressers, cupboards, and bathroom for that damn wedding album. It was nowhere to be found. She paced in front of the photos hanging on the walls. It was strange that he had so many pictures of her by herself or with Jadie, but no pictures of her and him together.

In the afternoon, she wandered the streets of Manhattan in search of something, anything to trigger her memory. She checked the contact list on her phone. She could have sworn it used to have a cracked screen but apparently that memory wasn't real either. In her contacts was Jadie, her parents, the landline to her Ninja Gymnastics School, and Michael who was in parenthesis as (hubby). Despite it being her phone, the device felt new and unused. It didn't have any fingerprints on the screen and she didn't feel like the apps were arranged to her preference. She called Jadie but her phone went straight to voice mail.

An overwhelming sadness came over her. Jadie was the only one she could trust to fill in the gaps in her memory and she wasn't answering her phone. She wondered if they had gotten into a fight. Hopefully it wasn't over Michael whom Jadie had a crush on. Married . . . to Michael, how did this happen? She went from getting medals and accolades as a police officer, to teaching gymnastics and settling for Michael? Well, at least he was always kind and sweet, attentive when he didn't need to be. Maybe she just needed to give herself some time to acclimate to her new situation. Once she was around him long enough, maybe she would learn to love him again.

CHAPTER 19:

Brood Parasite

There was a strange liberation in not being able to remember. She knew there were things she had done, things she had regrets about, but she couldn't remember any of them. Without the sins of the past to hold her back, she could create a new life where her every decision was the right one. No regrets, no mistakes, no memories of hurting someone emotionally. A blank slate on which to chisel the perfect story of her life. So why then, given this new opportunity, did her intuition tell her not to give up seeking the truth? Why did it feel wrong to accept her life with Michael?

She returned to Michael's apartment around eight o'clock that evening. She took out her keys and tried each one. None of them fit the lock.

"This is too weird." She gently knocked. Michael opened the door and greeted Cindy with a huge smile.

"Hey honey." He leaned in and pecked her on the lips. She did not kiss him back.

"Hey," she said before barging in. "Why don't I have a key to your apartment?"

"Our apartment."

"Right . . . our."

"Your original set of keys were lost in the crash. I haven't had the chance to get a copy for you."

"When was the crash?"

He chuckled nervously. "About a month ago, I think."

"I appreciate the hustle in getting me a new key."

"Sorry," he said, detecting her sarcasm. "I've been busy at work and keep forgetting to make the time."

"Or maybe I don't live here."

Michael took off his glasses and wiped them with a cloth. "Of course you do, don't be silly." He cleared his throat. "You hungry for dinner?"

She threw her duffel bag in the middle of the floor and sat down at the dining room table. Michael clenched his teeth and picked up her bag, muttering that she shouldn't leave her stuff laying around. He returned to the table and began opening plastic containers. Steam escaped from the packaging and brought with it a smell of tomato sauce, pasta, and meatballs.

She watched the food land on her plate and frowned.

"Oh and I got you a treat which I know you'll love." Michael reached into the bag and handed Cindy a Popsicle stick wrapped in paper. "Some dessert before dinner?"

She took the wrapper from him. "What is this?"

"A surprise." He beamed from cheek to cheek.

Cindy unwrapped the Popsicle. It was a chocolate banana. She held it in her hand and stared at it for a long while. "I hate chocolate bananas." She handed it back to him. "Shouldn't you know that?"

Michael shuddered. "I'm sorry." He took the Popsicle stick from her and threw it in the garbage.

She wanted to be nice to him, after all he meant well. But a chocolate fucking banana? Gross! "Sorry, that came out really rude. I didn't mean to say it like that."

"It's okay," he said softly. "Don't worry about it." He walked over to the take out bag and quietly plated a small three cheese lasagna for himself. He distributed the silver ware, sat down, and told Cindy with feigned enthusiasm. "Let's eat."

They ate the same way they did in the morning, in awkward silence. The clanging of forks against the plates and the wet sound of food being chewed drove her crazy. Cindy speared her meatball with a fork and said, "So how was work?"

"Good." He cut his lasagna and shoveled a mouthful into his face.

"Great," she muttered.

"What did you do after I went to work?"

Cindy coiled some spaghetti around her fork but compared to Michael's plate, she hadn't eaten much of anything. "I went for a walk."

"Did you go to work at the gym?" He asked nervously.

"No. I don't want to be responsible for other people's kids while my memory is spotty. So I went to work out instead."

He seemed relieved. "Oh that's good. Don't worry about working anyway, I make plenty of money for the both of us."

She suddenly remembered having an argument with someone. She was in a bedroom which looked nothing like Michael's place. A man was sitting on the bed. She was yelling at him over money and having to work a security job.

"You okay," Michael said.

"Yeah." She shook her head. "Just having weird thoughts."

He leaned in with interest. "Like what?"

"Nothing I want to talk about."

Her original plate of three meatballs had only gone down to two and a half. She had barely touched her pasta.

Michael frowned. "How's dinner?"

"It's good."

"You haven't eaten much of it."

"I had a late lunch."

He grew somber. "You don't have to eat it if you don't want to."

"It's—it's fine." She played with her food and scraped the bottom of the plate. "I'll finish it, don't worry."

"No you won't." Michael took Cindy's plate and walked it over to the garbage can. He dumped the spaghetti and meatballs into the bin where it joined the chocolate banana.

"Why did you do that?"

"Because I know you don't want it."

"Why waste your hard earned money on food you can easily make at home? Boil up some pasta, put some premade meatballs in a pot, heat it up and boom you're done."

"Yeah, well, I'm not much of a cook."

She remembered a man, the same guy from earlier, standing behind a boiling pot. He had a musky scent of cologne as he spooned yellow rice and Spanish chorizo onto a plate. He turned around, fed her a slice of chorizo, then kissed her by surprise.

She wiped her mouth with a napkin and joined Michael in the kitchen. She leaned against the counter and pestered him with more questions. "We've been friends for a very long time. You should know me inside and out."

"Well there was a period where we went our separate ways. Jadie joined the Coast Guard, you went to the Police Academy, and I moved to Boston so

A Bitter Winter

I could finish my Master's at MIT. So I didn't get to know you, know you."

"I don't like to buy simple food from a restaurant. It's overpriced and I used to eat that crap all the time with Dan." Her eyes went wide. "Why did I say that name?"

"He was your partner before you quit."

She didn't remember what this Dan looked like. Was he the one from the bedroom or someone else? No, she wouldn't date a co-worker. But somehow saying his name seemed to unearth pieces of the puzzle.

"You know what?" Michael chuckled softly. "It's been a long day. Let's just watch some TV."

Cindy couldn't believe how easily he ignored her lapses in memory. Either he honestly didn't want to rehash history, or he was lying. Michael turned on the TV and patted the cushion next to him. She reluctantly joined him. He placed his arm around her shoulder and kissed her cheek as the Impress News broadcast appeared.

"Authorities have completed a forensic analysis of the limo which had been transporting Senator James Albright. Though they found no evidence of tampering or foul play, they did discover that the driver side window had been shattered before the crash."

She squinted at the television. "That car looks familiar."

Michael quickly shut off the TV. "All limos look like that." He nervously adjusted his glasses and embraced Cindy. "So what do you want to talk about?"

What a weird question, she thought. "I want to get the wedding album."

"It's late and I have work tomorrow. Let's do it this weekend."

She narrowed her eyes. "Why are you stalling?"

"Wha—no I'm not. I'm not."

"I mean who puts their wedding album in storage."

"People who live in small apartments." He stood up from the couch. "Tell you what. How about I play the song I wrote for you on our wedding night?"

"What song?"

He walked over to the grand piano in the corner of his apartment. "The neighbors are going to get pissed, but oh well. I don't care if they think it sounds like elephants stampeding over their ceiling. You want proof, I'll give you proof."

Michael rested his fingers on the piano keys and took in a tremulous breath. He played a looping chord and began to sing.

"*I . . . can't . . . imagine a world without you. I've . . . felt . . . the pain the loneliness you are the light, that keeps me go-oh-ing my life has ahh new reason to keep on li-i-ving. You . . . are . . . so special to me to me your eyes, your face, your sweet smile whoa ohh is it fate? Is it fate? I don't know, I do-on't care, all I know is that love is all that ma-ah-tters.*"

He pushed away from the piano catching his breath, He acted as if this was his first time playing the song . . . ever. He lacked the confidence of someone who would sing this at a wedding reception in front of dozens of guests and her parents.

"You played this at our wedding?"

"Yup."

"That was terrible."

"Oh come on! I spent months writing that."

"It made me cringe."

Michael slammed the piano lid shut causing a thrum of sour notes. "I poured all my heart and soul into that song and you just shit on it. I've waited years to play it for you."

And this is where Michael had finally revealed his hand.

"So this *is* the first time you played it for me."

He left his elbows on the piano cover and looked up. "No. I told you I played this at our wedding and you loved it."

"You just said you waited years."

"Forget it. You want to treat me like I'm some kind of pathetic loser? Fine, whatever. You're no different than those kids who bullied me in high school."

High school? She remembered walking to the cafeteria. There were three kids surrounding Michael. They stepped on his glasses and repeatedly kicked his stomach. She intervened and gave one of the kids a bloody nose. The principal gave her in school suspension for two weeks.

"Hey." She massaged the back of his neck. "I was kidding around."

"That's even worse."

"I'm sorry, okay? Is that better?"

"No."

"What can I do to make you forgive me?"

He lifted his head and licked his lips. "Make out with me."

She made no effort to hide her revolted expression. "Seriously?"

"Yeah." He wiped his eyes. "That'll make me feel a lot better."

"I'm not in the mood."

Michael dramatically wept into his hands. "You hate me."

"I don't—ugh, fine. Come on."

"Really?"

"Yes and stop being such a baby about it. You act like you've never gotten laid before."

"I mean with you it always feels like the first time."

"What the hell is that supposed to mean?"

"Nothing."

She took his hand and led him back to the couch. She sat down and he sat beside her. Cindy put her hand to her temple and waited. He stared at her and also waited.

"Well," she said.

"Well what?"

"You going to get this party started or what?"

"Oh, right."

Michael leaned in and grabbed her breasts. She ripped his hands off and smacked his wrist. "What are you doing? You don't run to second base without going to first."

"Sorry, it's just that you have an amazing body."

"Michael, you're grossing me out. Massive turn off. Stop."

"You don't like compliments?"

"Kiss me like you want me. Badly. Like this." She grabbed the back of his head and plunged her lips against his. His lips quivered at her touch and though this would have been endearing for a first kiss, she found herself disgusted. It was like kissing the open mouth of a catfish. He had no confidence, no force, no assertiveness. She began to wonder if he really was a virgin.

There was a knock on his apartment door. Cindy quickly pulled away, relieved that there was a guest. She wiped her lips and smudged her lipstick. "Aren't you going to get that?"

"Now?"

She nodded.

"Are you kidding me? I don't want to stop."

The knocking grew louder.

"I don't believe this." Michael got up and walked across the living room. While his back was turned Cindy rubbed her lips with her sleeve and spat. Michael opened the door. "Jonas," he said in a panic. "What are you doing here?"

"Have you seen Cindy? I haven't seen her in two days and—" the man grabbed Michael's chin and tilted his head towards the light. "Is that lipstick? You sly dog. You finally got a girl? Congratulations man."

She called out from the couch. "Who is it?"

The man peered into Michael's living room. She immediately recognized him as the man from her memories. He was handsome with his black hair and heroic chin. He wasn't too tall but he looked like a model with his perfect tan skin and dark sexy eyes. She smiled at the man but he didn't smile back. Instead he grabbed Michael's shirt and slammed him against the door frame.

"I knew it," he yelled. "I knew you were going to do this to me."

"Jonas," Michael choked. "It's not what you think."

She shot up from the couch. "What are you doing? Stop it!"

"How could you—" Jonas bared his teeth at Cindy. "With him?"

He dragged Michael from the door to the wall. Photo frames fell on the hardwood floor and shattered. "This is your fault!" Spit flew from his mouth. "You pathetic little shit." Jonas reeled back his fist and knocked the glasses off Michael's face. Cindy screamed and begged for them to stop fighting.

Michael tackled Jonas and dropped him to the floor. He landed a few solid blows before Jonas managed to push him off and roll Michael onto his back. He put his hands around Michael's throat and tried to strangle him.

"She's . . . my . . . wife!"

Cindy reached for Jonas's arm and was stopped by a series of violent coughs. She covered her mouth and coughed until blood sprinkled her palm.

"Oh God."

Michael's fingers reached for the glass shards from the broken picture frame. He took the glass and slashed at Jonas's face. Jonas blocked with his arm and yelled after the glass sliced his skin open. Michael pushed Jonas away and got to his feet. He held the blood stained glass in front of him like a dagger.

"Please stop," she said. Another hacking fit took hold of her. The veins around her neck swelled into fat snakes. Her throat turned red as her coughing left her crippled. She threw up and spat all over Michael's hardwood floor. "I'm so sorry. I don't know what's wrong with me."

"Oh my God, Cindy." Michael dropped the glass and placed his hand on her back.

Jonas shook his head with disgust.

"Right when Charlie synthesized the cure too."

Michael shot up to his feet. "You have it?"

"Not on me, no." Jonas chuckled in a dejected way. "I was so excited to tell her about it."

"Why-kaff-kaff-why is this-kaff-happening?"

He pointed at Cindy. "You could've told me you were unhappy with our marriage. Could have at least given me a chance to change or do something to fix what was wrong." He turned around and hung his head low.

Michael grabbed Jonas's arm. "Where's the cure, Jonas?"

"Get off of me." He ripped away from Michael's hand and slammed the apartment door shut.

She was too weak and in too much pain to chase after the man who called himself her husband. "My stomach hurts," she said.

Michael returned to her side and pulled up her shirt. She saw the grotesque growths blooming out of her stomach, ribs, and chest. He looked at her and said, "You'll be okay." But she didn't believe him. These growths looked anything but okay.

"This is all wrong," she said. I knew I didn't belong here but I didn't understand why."

"Of course you belong here, you're my wife."

"You know that's not true."

She limped over to the coat hanger and grabbed her winter jacket.

Michael chased after her. "Where are you going?"

"To get answers."

CHAPTER 20:

System Recovery

She knew he was lying. Jonas, the man claiming to be her husband was proof of it. But without any recollection of her former life, Cindy couldn't simply accept Jonas as her husband. She needed proof of Michael's deception. The car service pulled up in front of the apartment. She rushed to the passenger rear door with Michael causing a scene by yelling her name and chasing her footsteps. She ducked into the car and Michael followed in after her. She pushed against his chest and slapped his face but he wouldn't leave.

"Get out, Michael."

"No, I'm coming with you."

The driver looked in his rearview mirror. "Hey, I don't want any problems."

"There's no problem. You know how wives can be," Michael said. "Right, Cindy?"

"I don't want him to come with me."

"Buddy, you need to leave."

Michael looked at her. "Do you know where Jonas lives? Because I do."

Her mouth fell agape without a response to accompany it. "Brooklyn?"

"Wrong."

The driver looked in his mirror. "You want him out or not?"

She let out a defeated sigh. "He can come."

They drove along the southern perimeter of Central Park, heading east towards the Queensboro Bridge. Michael's phone rang. He turned his body away from her as he took the call.

"Yeah, Ray?"

Ray . . . where did she hear that name before? It killed her to have every memory buried somewhere in her brain. It was like knowing a word but being unable to remember what it was.

"I can't bring her in now."

She arched an eyebrow and brushed her hair behind her ear.

A Bitter Winter

"I'm not going to let her—" he glanced at Cindy then covered his mouth over the microphone.

She clawed at his phone. "Who are you talking to?"

Michael braced against her shoulder. "My boss, jeez."

"Why are you whispering to him?"

"Because I have to talk about sensitive work stuff." He shook his head and quietly spoke into the phone. "I have to go, call you later."

"Your boss works this late?"

"He always works late."

"What did he want?"

"He wants me to return a prototype I borrowed from the lab. I'll bring it by after."

They drove over the Queensboro Bridge and followed Queens Boulevard all the way to Forest Hills. Michael had kept his promise. She knew it was Jonas's home because the sight of the Tudor style house flooded her with feelings of nostalgia. She remembered there being a silver sports car in the garage, a gym upstairs, and a bathroom with a tunnel shower. For some reason, she had it in her head that Jonas had built the shower himself. That it was his invention.

There was a keypad lock on the front door. She confidently input 0508. The mechanical lock turned with a loud whirr and the door opened.

"What did you put as the code?" Michael asked.

"My wedding anniversary." She narrowed her eyes at him. "Why would our anniversary be Jonas's key code?"

Michael shrugged. "Coincidence."

"When was our wedding?"

He hesitated. "May eighteenth."

He was close but not close enough. She decided not to confront him . . . yet.

Stepping into Jonas's dwelling should have felt invasive or forbidden, how she felt at Michael's apartment. Instead she felt at home, like she knew the place inside and out.

"We're trespassing in his house," Michael protested.

"I'm not, you are."

She remembered the leather couch in front of the flat screen TV. She visualized Jonas playing video games and yelling into the microphone as he killed people online. Then she looked at the kitchen and imagined him boiling fresh lobster in a pot. She walked over to the bathroom and saw the tunnel shower from her memories. Water sprayed from all angles as she recalled having her wet legs wrapped around his naked waist, moaning at his touch.

"Whoa." Her cheeks prickled.

"Are you all right?"

She cleared her throat. "Yeah I'm fine."

Except she wasn't. A lingering dread followed her every step and his name was Michael. He was her childhood friend, *friend* not lover. If Michael was willing to go this far to fabricate a lie, what else would he be capable of? She slid her hand atop the bedroom dresser and opened the top drawer where she found some women's lingerie. She pulled out a pair of silk black panties with white polka dots and a pink ribbon. "These are cute."

"Stop touching his stuff."

She held the panties with one finger. "His stuff? Really?"

She walked over to the bed and traced her finger along the comforter as if absorbing memories through each yard of thread. She placed one knee on the bed and touched the splintered hole at the top of the headboard.

"I did this."

"Okay, I've had enough," Michael said. "You are my wife, you live in my apartment. Let's go home, now."

"You're lying to me."

Michael grew more flustered. "No I'm not." He grabbed her hand and yanked her forward.

She planted her feet and angrily pulled back. Michael stumbled and nearly fell to the floor.

"Let's get one thing straight. No one tells me what to do, not even my *husband*. And if you touch me like that again, I'll break your arm." She was about to leave the bedroom thinking the conversation was over, but she had more to say, much more. "I haven't believed a single word you've said to me since I woke up in your apartment."

"I *am* telling you the truth," he pleaded.

"The way you kissed me tells me you're not."

His face pinched together. "What's wrong with my kiss?"

She waggled her finger and pivoted on her feet. "There's a box in this house somewhere. There's photos of me in it, I know there is." She went up to the second floor with Michael following her. "Once I find proof that you're lying to me, you're going to explain why I can't remember anything."

She climbed up the wooden ladder to the attic and found a dusty security box in the far corner. She grabbed the rubber handles and threw the box downstairs, startling Michael.

She unlocked the latches and glanced up at him. "This is your last chance to come clean with me. Is Jonas my husband?"

"No."

She opened the box . . . and it was empty.

"What?" She put her hands inside the hollow container. "There should be photos here. Hundreds of them."

"See? I told you."

She pushed him into the wall. "Wipe that lying, smug look off your face."

"What's gotten into you?"

"I know you're lying. May eighteenth, really? You never played that song at our wedding because our—*my* anniversary is May eighth. What did you do to my memory?"

"I didn't—"

She smacked him across the face. Michael placed his palm over the red handprint on his cheek and looked at her. She shook out the sting in her hand and couldn't believe what she had done. Never did she imagine herself to be so violent, especially against Michael, the boy she had protected against bullies.

"I don't want to hurt you," she said quietly and full of remorse. "I don't even know why I'm acting like this. All I want you to do is tell me is the truth."

"Goddamn it, Cindy. Why couldn't you just be satisfied being with me?"

He dug into his pocket and gave her a key. "Your door has a manual key lock for when the battery runs out. So I borrowed your key."

"Tell me the truth, now."

———

They left the house and did not speak the entire car ride back to the Latini building. Every time she coughed, a burning pain would race down her throat and bloom through her chest. What possessed him to go this far to create a lie?

Could she still call Michael a friend once this was all over?

The motion sensor lights flickered on as they walked into the Server room adjacent to the Main Lab. Michael peered over the top of a server rack where there was a box. He stopped short of grabbing it and turned to her. "Cindy. I need to say something to you."

She assumed it would be more lies.

"The day of the wedding, I wore the finest tuxedo I could afford. After shaving, getting my haircut, spraying on my best cologne, I felt like a million bucks. Then I looked at you in your sparkling white dress. Your hair was tied up in a wavy bun and your makeup made you look like a Hollywood actress. You were so beautiful that I literally thought I was Prince Charming in a Cinderella movie. We were sitting in the lobby, talking, laughing, having a good time like we always did back then. Every time I watched you smile, my heart felt lighter and made me feel like I could fly away with you. You confessed your fears of marriage to me and told me how grateful you were to have me in your life.

"Then came the moment when it was time for your dad to walk you to the altar. I was at the front of the congregation, smiling as your mom and my mom were wiping their eyes with tissues. I stood there feeling like this was the greatest moment of my life as you approached me. I realized how lucky I was to have met such a wonderful, intelligent, gorgeous woman like you and how special this day was for the both of us.

"And then your father handed you off to Jonas. And suddenly those smiles and laughs you had shared with me, you gave to him. You were enthralled by him and he was smitten by you and you both stared into each other's eyes like no one else existed. And here I was, standing on the side lines with a ring in my pocket. He took the ring out of my hand and even though I didn't want him to have it, I stayed silent. He slid the ring onto your finger and then the priest said what I didn't want to hear. 'I now pronounce you husband and wife.' You kissed him, and I lost what I had loved most. I lost my best friend."

Her throat hurt and it wasn't from coughing, not this time.

"Why didn't you move on?"

"Because I love you."

Now came the moment she had been avoiding since the first day she discovered Michael's feelings for her. She never wanted to hurt him, to make him feel rejection, but there was no other choice. He had gone too far. "I don't. Not in that way."

He winced as if she had gutted him. All this time, since middle school, her old friend Michael had been stuck in the past. He had desperately held onto the delusion that their friendship would evolve into something more. He had the body of a man and the maturity of a thirteen year old.

"If I give you these photos, Cindy. You're going to remember some awful things."

"I don't doubt it."

"Why would you want that? You're the only person in the world who could literally start from scratch. You can create a new life for yourself. A new life with me."

She paused and considered her words carefully. "If I don't remember my past, I'll make the same mistakes all over again. Including being your friend."

Michael took off his glasses and wiped his eye with the back of his hand. "You're just going to say goodbye to fifteen years of friendship, just like that?"

"Yeah, yeah I am."

He brought the cardboard box down from the server machines. He sighed and reluctantly handed it to her. Inside the box were dozens of photos of her dressed in a police uniform. Standing beside her was a tall, beefy man with shaved red hair. His name was Dan. At the bottom of the pile she found a photo of the house she had visited. She was standing in the front yard, still in her uniform, kissing Jonas on the lips. She turned the photo and read the hand written note: *Celebrating our first house together!*

Cindy took the box into the main lab and set it on the metal desk. She pulled out photo after photo of her life with Jonas, her real husband. Every photo she took out made her grow angrier and angrier at Michael. At the very bottom of this beat up cardboard box was a book titled: The Wedding of Cindy and Jonas.

"You motherfucker," she said through clenched teeth.

"I'm sorry."

The photo album was as thick as a bible. The binding cracked as she opened it. She ran her fingers over the plastic sleeves: there were pictures of her staring at a mirror while in her wedding dress. There were also photos of Jonas, handsome in his black tuxedo, standing next to his best man. Michael.

"How could you?" Her anger reached its boiling point. "You-kaff-kaff-tried to take advantage of me—"

"I . . ."

"Tried to-kaff-trick me-kaff-kaff-kaff-"

She collapsed to her knees and made horrible gurgling sounds from the fluids entering her lungs. She remembered the cancer and the suit and all the people she had killed. One more needed to be added to the list of victims.

Michael placed his hand on her back. "Are y—"

"Don't touch me!" She smacked his hand away and pulled up the sleeve of her left arm. She drew a pattern of an S then curled into a ball. She rocked from side to side as her back began to widen.

"You lied to me." Her voice became monstrous as the seams of her sleeves began to pop. "Tried to make me forget Jonas. Make me forget how happy I was with him."

"I wasn't trying to . . ." he caught himself. "I'm the one who loved you first. Not Jonas."

Cindy groaned and writhed with her forehead pressed against the floor. She had forgotten how painful the suit could be if she wasn't mentally prepared for it. "That wasn't your decision!" She smashed the floor. A cloud of cement rolled away from her silver hand.

"I'm sorry, I just, I wanted—" Michael slowly backed himself into a wall. "I got carried away."

"What we had. Our friendship? It's in the past." Cindy flexed her arm causing her sleeve to tear open, exposing her silver skin. She rose to her feet. A shower of sparkles washed over her body and consumed the tatters of her clothing. She stared at Michael as the helmet came round her jaw and covered her eyes. Her glowing eyes reflected off his glasses

[SIRCA Online]

"And like the past. I'm leaving you behind."

"Cindy." Michael held out his hand. "Cindy, Cindy."

Drunk with overwhelming power, she lost herself to the rage. She remembered the people she killed. Remembered how Raymond used augmented reality to trick her, to lie to her. This suit, this stupid machine destroyed her life. But the worst part was, the only reason SIRCA was able to ruin her was because she had been like Michael. Trapped in a past that was never going to change.

She grabbed onto the edges of the metal desk and hurled it through the observation window. The glass exploded into the Workshop, followed by the clattering missile which scraped against the floor. She smashed her fist through the only computer and tore out its electronic guts. She then ripped off the door to the server room and smashed it into the wall like a sledgehammer.

"I'm such a fucking idiot!"

She ripped the servers from their racks, stomped them with her foot, then punched and tore apart the shelving. With each server obliterated, a warning message flashed in her HUD. [ERROR: Connection to predictive projectile server has been lost] [ERROR: Tracking system malfunction] [ERROR: Advanced Physics Calculation is not responding]

"Cindy stop. You're going to destroy SIRCA."

She drew out her sword and roared. "It's my fault!" She chopped at wires and machinery, destroying anything and everything that stood in her way. In the end, only the smell of burnt wire and plastic remained. Her HUD, once a cool blue with a slick, streamlined interface, flashed red in front of her eyes.

Michael stood aghast from the entrance. "Ten years of work. Gone."

She picked Michael up by his throat and pinned him to the wall. He pounded Cindy's forearm which rang like a flag pole.

"This is what you wanted, isn't it? Me touching you." Michael's face swelled like a red balloon. "You know what the sad part is? I couldn't get over the past either. I was so upset about never catching Ned that I wasted every second of my life obsessing over him. Everyone else moved on with their lives except for me and you."

"Cindy." He grunted as his eyes began to close. His arms became lethargic and clumsy, tapping her arm without vigor. "Please."

She reeled back her fist. The actuators in her arm whirred as they locked into position.

"I'm so sorry, Cindy." His face was wet with tears as he moaned in terror. "Please don't kill me."

[Target Locked]

She punched the wall beside his head. The hole was so deep, it led into the room next door.

"If I ever . . . see you again . . . I'll kill you."

She released Michael and let him choke on the floor. She tore and twisted the steel door of the main lab and escaped through the entryway. Cindy left Michael in a state he should have been used to by now. Alone.

CHAPTER 21:

Hot Pursuit

Michael stepped over the glass shards sprinkled across the floor. He rubbed the aching pains in his neck with one hand and brought out his cell phone with the other.

"Speak," Raymond said.

"I've got a problem."

"You've got two problems. I explicitly told you to bring Cindy back to the office. That was two days ago."

"I, I know. I made a mistake."

"And you expect me to fix it?"

"I didn't think there was going to be a problem in need of fixing. I thought the memory wipe was going to make it easier for me to—never mind." He stepped on a broken piece of plastic as he paced back and forth.

"I know what you did, Michael. I had been listening to your disturbing conversation until she destroyed the lab. I wiped Cindy's memory so she could have an opportunity to return to a normal life. You were supposed to recover the suit and bring her back to the lab so that I wouldn't have to use force. I've met a lot of despicable people in my time, but what you did was revolting."

Michael pinched the bridge of his nose. "Cindy's on her way to find Jonas. If we—if we grab him, I think we can lure her into a trap."

"He just left my office."

"Really?"

"Yes. He handed in his resignation and told me he was going to take his technology and his team back. Obviously he was heated, so I let him rant for thirty minutes. Then I reminded him that he signed a contract surrendering his technology and his team to me. He stormed out of my office, most likely on his way home."

"Okay." Michael nodded. "Do you think you can . . .?"

"Pick him up? I could. It's pathetic by the way."

"What?"

"Even without her memory, she still rejected you. When are you going to learn to grow up and be a man?"

Michael grimaced.

"Cindy has a military weapon, how do we stop her?"

Michael closed his eyes and held his forehead. "You're going to need a lot of power."

* * *

Cindy struggled with her grappling hook. The targeting cursor had disappeared and now she had to manually aim each shot. She fired at the roof of a building and watched the wire coil aimlessly into the night sky. She crashed through an office window, knocked over someone's computer, and jumped out of the opening to try again. The damage to the server room had affected the suit in ways she could have never predicted.

She coughed up blood and was plagued by dizziness and shortness of breath. Her chest and stomach stung as if little rocks were tumbling inside the lumps of flesh. Without the guidance of the suit, her arms ached and grew tired. She detoured north to the Sunnyside rail yard in Queens and landed on the roof of an outbound F train heading to Forest Hills. She laid down and hoped her silver skin would blend in with the grey of the roof.

She arrived in front of her house at two in the morning, staggered to the keypad, and punched in her wedding anniversary. The keypad flashed red and loudly rejected her with a high pitched beep. She punched in the same numbers and again the keypad sounded the alarm. She raised her fist to bang on the door then stopped short of making contact.

"Probably don't want to hit it *too* hard." She settled for a gentle knock. "Jon—" her voice was still distorted by the suit's audio filter. She turned off her helmet and spoke again. "Jonas it's me. Please open the door."

She didn't have to wait long before the lock clicked open. He hadn't even dressed for bed yet. He was still wearing a pinstriped button up shirt and jeans. He looked pissed, but his anger gave way to confusion when he saw what she was wearing.

"Is that . . ." He staggered back. "Holy shit." He wobbled on his unsteady legs. She held out her hands in case he fell. "It works? You. Oh my God."

"Are you okay?"

He tipped forward. She caught him in her arms and stabilized his footing as best she could. "Okay, you're okay. Just breathe."

He shook his head and eventually stood on his own. "That's my suit."

"I wanted to tell you but they made me promise not to."

"Who?"

"Raymond and Michael."

"How—how long have you had it?"

"Since Jadie's accident."

"That's impossible."

"It's true, I swear."

"I know everything that happens in the lab."

"No, you definitely don't. That's why Raymond—"

"Put me on other projects." Jonas smacked his forehead. "That's why you started walking . . . why you got bigger." He then pounded the door frame. "I'm so stupid, so dense. How did you steal this from the lab? It was in a capsule." He bumbled out of the doorway. "I feel sick." Once he steadied himself, Jonas's facial expression quickly turned to anger. "But you kissed Michael! What the fuck was that about?"

"You have to understand, Ned hurt Jadie. I couldn't let him get away with it. So I took your keycard and figured out the rest. In retrospect, it wasn't my smartest idea."

"I don't believe it. What have you been doing with the suit? Why are you still wearing it?"

"This is going to be difficult to explain." She took a deep breath and blurted out everything all at once. "I needed the suit to catch Ned, Raymond caught me, he said he wouldn't let me have the suit if I didn't help him. So I agreed to help him but then he needed someone to maintain the suit. That's where Michael came in. After I did some assignments for Raymond something bad happened. I found out Raymond was lying to me and when I went to confront him he wiped my memory."

"Ah—what?" Jonas took a moment to think about what she said. "You mean to tell me Raymond used the spotless mind protocol on you?"

She nodded. "That's just the tip of the iceberg."

"I don't know what to say."

"I know it's going to sound like I'm lying, but I really need you to believe me when I say this." She took his hands into her own and looked directly in his eyes. "Michael tried to pretend he was my husband."

"Fucking Michael. I knew . . . I knew he couldn't be trusted." He lifted her chin. "Did he do more than kiss you?"

"No. But I swear this is what happened and I'm sorry. I didn't know what I was getting myself into."

"It's going to be difficult for me to get that image of Michael kissing you out of my head." His eyes danced around with a warmness she hadn't seen in a long time. "You have a lot of explaining to do, but I believe you."

She smiled in relief. "Thank you."

"You should come inside. I need to give you the antidote Charlie finished."

A diesel engine roared in the distance followed by the shriek of tires. A black cargo van sped down the street, its headlights bobbed up and down from the bumps in the road. The van squealed to a stop in front of their house and through the rolled down window, she watched a man throw a canister in the air.

The canister exploded in a brilliant flash of white light. Purple starbursts clouded her vision and rang her ears. After a few seconds the ringing faded. She blinked away the purple spots and watched two men in balaclava masks throw her husband into the back of the van.

"Jonas!"

She couldn't believe this was happening. Smoke billowed from the tires as the truck launched forward. Cindy burst from the lawn, kicking up grass with her feet. She ran onto the street and used SIRCA's acceleration to gain on the van. Huffing with each step, she closed on the van and stretched her fingers towards the door handle. A sharp pain tore through her stomach and made her stumble.

"Jonas!" She stopped running, groaned, and held onto her belly. "Damn it. -Kaff-kaff-."

The van's taillights disappeared into the darkness, its tires squealed from afar. Cindy cried out in frustration and quickly rushed back to her house. Her body may not have wanted to continue, but she sure as hell wasn't going to abandon her man. She grabbed a ring of keys from the key rack, locked the front door, and went into the garage. Sitting between racks of power tools and a lawnmower, a Silver Saleen S7 slept in pristine condition.

She opened the butterfly door and sat down in the leather interior which still smelled like new. Like most sports cars, the Saleen S7 was manual transmission which was one of the many reasons Jonas didn't drive it often. She buckled herself in and pressed the button to open the garage shutter. She revved the engine and tapped the steering wheel as she waited for the shutter to clear the roof of the car.

"Let's go, let's go."

She released the clutch and stomped the accelerator. She jerked back in her seat and threw the wheel to the right. The car skidded out of the driveway and drifted to a stop on the street. The engine—which was located in the rear of the car—rumbled against her back.

"Hang on, honey. I'm coming."

She pulled the gear shift lever, gunned the accelerator, and sped past the handful of cars still on the road. The van had gained an enormous lead. Destroying the lab turned out to be a poor error in judgment. If she had practiced a little self-control, she wouldn't have to guess where the van had gone. She immediately ruled out Brooklyn since that's where she had sunk Ned's boat. If they wanted to get back to Manhattan, their best bet would be to take the Long Island Expressway.

But she wasn't one hundred percent positive. They could have also taken Queens Boulevard or gone east on the expressway instead of west. She took the onramp to 495 west (Long Island Expressway) and prayed that her instincts were right. She switched into third gear, fourth, fifth, with the engine pitching loudly at her back.

The steering wheel shook from the intense speeds; wind whistled outside the window; street lights whipped past in fast forward. As she approached the halfway point to the Queens Midtown tunnel, there was still no sign of the van. She took her foot off the accelerator and began downshifting until she was under sixty five miles an hour. As she approached the toll booths up ahead, she saw no sign of the van.

A Bitter Winter

Cindy smacked the steering wheel and threw her head back.

"Damn it," she cried. "Damn it, damn it, damn it."

She took the toll booth receiver out of the glove box and pressed it against the windshield. She drove into the Simply Pass lane and waited for the red light to turn green. For some reason the light wasn't changing color.

"Are you kidding me?"

She pressed the receiver against the windshield. The red light was still on. Did Jonas not pay for the freaking subscription? "Screw it. Give me a ticket then." She accelerated out of the lane and suddenly the light turned green. "Thank you for taking your sweet old time." She slowly accelerated into the Queens Midtown Tunnel and cursed at herself for having lost the kidnappers.

"Nothing ever changes," she said to herself. "With or without the suit. With or without the memories, you still managed to fff—holy shit."

The black van was three cars in front of her, cruising into the tunnel as if it didn't have armed mercenaries holding a hostage. She kept up with the flow of traffic and entered the tunnel. She followed the van into Manhattan and drove down moderately busy avenues which took her across town and into another tunnel, the Holland tunnel. After forty minutes they emerged on the New Jersey side. Due to the late hour, four lanes of open highway lay in front of her. No civilians would be in danger.

She rapidly closed in on the van. Shifting into third gear, the engine whined as she pulled alongside the left fender. She lined up the front wheels of the Saleen with the back wheels of the van and spun the steering wheel to the right.

The headlight and right fender of the Saleen crunched in and left a trail of glass. The van fishtailed, its brake lights glowed brilliant red before being masked by tire smoke. But the van was too heavy and the Saleen too light. The van stabilized itself and continued straight down the four lane highway. The rear doors burst open. Two men pointed their assault rifles at Cindy's car. In the back, Jonas struggled in the arms of his captor.

She took her foot off the accelerator without realizing she had done so. Her worst nightmare had come true. Her husband, the only man she truly loved besides her father, had become Ned's target. Who else would send armed thugs to her house? He knew where she lived, knew who she loved, and now he was going to get revenge for what she did to his boat.

She snapped out of her daze. He wasn't dead, so there was no sense in fearing what hasn't happened. The mercenaries fired at her car. She swerved away from the gunfire pelting the highway and pulled up alongside the van. She shared a glance with the driver. Cindy brought her thumb to her neck and cut it across. She wanted them to know the consequences for kidnapping her husband.

The driver jerked the steering wheel in her direction. Her head whipped from side to side as the right door of the Saleen crunched in. She slammed on the brakes and downshifted to bleed off speed. Once she was behind the van, she again attempted the PIT maneuver, a police tactic used to force a vehicle to lose control and come to a stop. She clipped the left rear wheel and destroyed its fender. As the van swerved, the thugs held onto the doors and swayed with the movements of the vehicle. The van corrected itself, and now the Saleen's tires were starting to rumble.

Cindy reactivated her helmet and grabbed her door handle. She pushed on the butterfly door until it snapped off its hinges. The door tumbled across the street and left a trail of glass and aluminum. She stood up from her seat keeping one foot on the gas and one hand on the wheel. With her other arm, she aimed the tip of her grappling hook into the interior of the van. The mercenaries retaliated by shooting the car.

The sound of a can being punctured by a knife rippled through the front of her car. Jagged bullet holes ripped open the curvy profile of the Saleen. She swerved through four lanes of highway and took aim with her grappling hook. She fired the grappling hook and pierced through the metal partition separating driver from cargo. She ejected from the Saleen. The car turned right and crashed into a cement barrier, exploding into a fountain of shrapnel. The torque from the grappling hook pulled with enough force to prevent Cindy from hitting the ground as it reeled her in. She coiled her knees into her chest and zipped towards the thugs. Sparks popped off her armor as they tried to shoot her. Her feet crashed into one of the mercenaries and knocked another one out of the rear.

The van came to a sudden stop and knocked Cindy off balance within the cargo hold. Her shoulder crunched the partition where her hook was embedded and then the van accelerated. The thug got up and swung the butt of his rifle at her helmet. She struck his neck with her forearm and pinned him to the interior wall. She then grabbed his bulletproof vest and threw him out the back door.

She turned to face the last remaining thug who had a Taser in his hand. Two copper prongs shot across and attached to her chest. Electricity ripped through her body and burned her nerves with sizzling energy. The HUD filled with static and sparks burst out of her suit.

[SYSTEM ERROR – Rebooting]

While she was stunned, the thug charged into her with his shoulder. She flew out the back of the van. Her armor sparked with each painful shock from rolling on asphalt. Cindy came to a grinding halt and watched the van speed away with its flapping rear doors.

"Damn it." She slapped the floor in utter disbelief. She had the edge, a sophisticated nanosuit that made her bulletproof and super strong, and yet she couldn't beat a bunch of regular men. She shook her head and stood up. As long as she could still breathe there was no way she was going to give up on Jonas.

One by one SIRCA's systems began to reengage. Her HUD stabilized without static and the other subsystems returned to online status. She walked back to where the Saleen had crashed less than a mile away. The poor car was totaled. She had hoped because the engine was in the back, she would still be able to drive, but both its front wheels had popped off. A fluttering yellow piece of notepad paper caught her eye. It was sticking out of the trunk waving hello at her. She pulled the paper out of the trunk and read it. *Interviewed someone in Brooklyn today, told me Ned sells guns out of a cargo ship which docks quarterly in Red Hook. Need to check this out.*

"Wait a second."

She ripped off the trunk panel and found all of the research Jonas said he had trashed. Hard drives, notebooks, photos, everything. All this time, she never thought to check his car. She remembered how angry she was at him thinking that he knowingly destroyed years of work, but he never went through with it. He only wanted her to get better. She didn't appreciate his methods but she understood why he did it.

She skimmed through the documents and remembered all the energy drinks she had consumed staking out a suspected hideout until five in the morning. And she remembered how groggy she felt when she had to work security at seven. The hard drives and papers were still intact but there was no way she could carry it out all at once. It would take several trips to get everything into a hiding spot so she could recover it later. But then that would be less time spent rescuing Jonas.

If she left the evidence here, the police would eventually investigate the crashed car and assume that her husband was a vigilante or an accomplice for Ned. Either way, she couldn't leave any of this evidence behind. The only other option was to burn it and accept that Ned would be the one who got away. She sighed as she held onto a printed web article of Dan being murdered through arson. A second article profiled Death Dealer, the menace still at large.

"I can't believe I'm going to do this."

She snapped her fingers and created a spark. The spark lit the web articles on fire which she then threw into the car. The cardboard boxes containing travel itineraries of his lieutenants caught fire and those flames spread to the hard drives and newspaper clippings and notepads filled with precious, hard earned data.

She engaged her FIT crime scene analysis tool —which thankfully didn't need servers— and identified the van's tire tread. The tracks led to a massive coal power plant looming in the distance. She was determined to get her husband back, no matter what.

CHAPTER 22:

Echoes of the Past

Every breath became a battle. She placed her hand on her stomach and limped into the power plant, wheezing with each step. The mutated cells continued to destroy healthy tissue, squeezing her lungs and organs with their overgrown flesh. Her normally agile, darting movements had slowed to a tired walk.

Throughout the coal power plant were thousands if not millions of pipes of different sizes running along the walls and ceiling. Some were rusted and worn with age while others had been replaced with spotless stainless steel. In this intimidating place the shadows looked like humanoids waiting in ambush.

Giant cylinders and rotating fan turbines created rumbling, deafening noise. Piles of coal sat on conveyor belts and were fed into a furnace. The flames shot up and vented black smoke into the towering chimneys. She used the loud machinery sounds to mask her movements. Her body hurt too much for hand to hand combat. Her best option was to avoid detection. She could not afford to screw up tonight.

Above her head was an iron grated catwalk. She was startled by the guard who was patrolling it. He wore an olive t-shirt, beige camouflage pants, an ear piece, and carried a SCAR assault rifle with a flashlight attachment. She quietly coughed into her hand and grabbed onto the catwalk. The gecko grip made a subtle click and locked her fingers to the surface. Her entire body was like Velcro, so any part of her suit could trigger the gecko grip. Once locked, she lifted her legs and attached her knees. She crawled under the floor and followed the guard's boots.

She moved slowly and with a slight tremble of nervousness in her hands. If he looked down, there would be no doubt in her mind that he would call for reinforcements. It's what she would do. Dirt shook off from his combat boots and clouded her HUD with dusty specks. He came to a stop and craned his neck to get a better view of the entrance to the power plant. She maneuvered to a flanking position and placed her hands on the edge of the catwalk to his left. She allowed her legs to dangle and already she could feel pain and irritation of a looming cough. She held her breath and shimmied closer to the oblivious guard.

He turned to face right and began walking. Cindy lifted her body and aligned her helmet to be shoulder level with the guard. She grabbed his neck and smashed his head into the railing. The guard instantly fell unconscious with a fresh new lump on his forehead. She tied her grappling hook to his ankles and the railing and threw him over the edge. He swung from his feet with his arms drooping above his head.

She vaulted onto the catwalk, allowed herself to cough, then lowered to a crouch. She waited and hoped no one had heard the clanging of the pipe. So far so good. She continued forward and stopped when a red dot pinged her radar. Someone was coming. There was nowhere to hide on the exposed catwalk. She saw a pipe overhead and jumped to grab it with her arms then her legs. She hugged the pipe and waited for the red dot to close in.

"This is Golf 2-1. Sector four and five are clear. No sign of the target."

"Copy Golf 2-1."

As the bald head of the mercenary crossed underneath, a cough burst from her lips. She quickly slapped her mouth shut and accidentally clanged her helmet. The mercenary aimed his rifle upward and blinded her with his flashlight. The HUD instantly dimmed to protect her eyes. Holding tightly with her hands, she dropped her legs and wrapped her thighs around his neck. She lifted him off the floor and squeezed. He smacked her legs as the veins swelled on the sides of his head.

His body fell limp. She released her grip and let the guard flop like a ragdoll. Cindy dropped from the pipe and became overwhelmed with dizziness. She grabbed onto the railing and unintentionally crushed it between her fingers like clay. She coughed until she could barely stand and dragged herself along the railing as she struggled to breathe.

Then her body collapsed. She clanged against the catwalk and wheezed. The tumors were worse than had she thought. She could feel the lumps sticking out of her chest and stomach, growing more painful with each passing minute. Though the helmet was pushing air into her nose, she could barely inhale it. Her chest felt tight and compressed, as if the suit was shrinking all around her.

She blacked out for a brief second and was momentarily confused as to where she was. Cindy propped herself against the railing and struggled to keep her eyes open. She wheezed inside her helmet and allowed herself to relax just for a moment. Vivid dreams filled her exhausted mind. She dreamt of Jonas wearing a police uniform.

"Cindy your vitals are low," SIRCA said.

The tumors spread out their poisonous veins and sucked the life out of her body. Her glowing cyan eyes dimmed to black.

"Activating emergency resuscitation."

SIRCA let out a high pitched whine and delivered a small shock to jolt her awake.

"Augh! What? Huh?" She kicked out her legs. Her blackened eyes powered up into their radiant shade of blue. She stood up and found herself in the power plant, but it looked different. The pipes and grates had transitioned into the black glass windows and marble steps of the Jacob K. Javits center. She got up and followed the power plant pipes into the Javits center.

She was in a blurry daze as if walking through someone else's dream. She stumbled upon a clone of herself, or more accurately, her past self. She was wearing that hideous chartreuse security guard jacket, shielding Mayor Montez as bullets tore into her back. Ned stood behind her holding onto the smoking gun.

Tear gas from the ESU SWAT team flooded the room and clouded her vision. Even with SIRCA's enhanced vision modes, she could not see through the gas which had become a soupy fog. The fog then turned cold and white. When it cleared away, she found herself on a snow covered street. A rolled over SUV burned a mere ten feet away. This time her past-self was on her knees, pressing down on Jadie's lifeless body.

She stopped walking. Cindy didn't want to relive this again. Jadie's head tilted up as Cindy's past-self attempted CPR with a burned hand. No, she couldn't watch. She turned away from the car accident and walked back into it. She turned again and returned again. No matter which direction she went, she would appear behind her past-self administering CPR to Jadie.

This was all in the past. None of it could be happening right now. Raymond must have been tampering with the augmented reality of the suit. She took off her helmet and looked with her human eyes. The flashback did not go away. She could smell the burning gas, could hear the crackle of fire.

"Jadie."

Cindy's past-self screamed, "Somebody fucking help me. Help me-help me-help me."

Feelings of remorse returned with the fragments of memory. If she had never asked Jadie to open the door this never would have happened. Her lips trembled from the sadness wanting to come out. This wasn't the time or place to cry. Instead of turning away, Cindy walked past her regret, past her dying sister, and her former self, and left the wreckage behind her. She walked to the end of the street which emptied into a square of blackness. Her feet sloshed through puddles and she could hear men laughing nearby. She entered a shipping yard facility filled with clover light towers.

There were two freight containers, a pickup truck, two cars, and two tractor trailer semis with welded ramming plates. Sitting in the bed of the pickup truck were Ned and his crew. They hooted and hollered as the two semis rammed into the freight containers. Cindy recognized her own screams coming from inside one of the containers and relived what it felt like inside; the hot air oppressive around her neck; the thunderous shaking inside the container; the growl of an engine pushing against the shrinking walls. In the other container, another voice cried out, yelling at Ned to leave her alone. The voice belonged to Dan.

The truck continued to ram the freight container perched on the edge of a slope. Ned held up his hand before the truck could knock the container over. He flipped a coin and it landed on heads.

"It's your lucky day, Officer Ames."

Ned pointed at the other container where Dan was trapped. His thugs emptied a gas can around the perimeter and lit it on fire. Dan yelled and pounded against the corrugated metal. "I'm burning up, I'm burning up! Cindy get me out of here!"

The truck knocked Cindy's container over the edge. It tumbled down the slope, denting and crunching with each impact as her past-self screamed inside. The doors popped open. Past-Cindy crawled free and ran over to Dan's container. She grabbed a rusty metal pipe and reached past the wall of flames to whack the lock off. Dan came bursting through, screaming as his body burned. She relived watching his body turn to char, relived seeing her partner die in a pile of burning garbage. Dan's cause of death was not Ned and his thugs . . . that was the end result. The real cause of death was her desire to get a damn promotion.

Present day-Cindy, clad in her nanosuit, crumbled and hid her face behind her hands. When Michael told her she was going to remember awful things, she thought she would be strong enough to handle it. It was time to prove to herself that she was. Cindy threw back her shoulders and chose to directly face her demons. "This is it," she told herself. "Are we going to keep doing this dance or are we finally going to put this shit behind us?"

SIRCA chimed. "Cindy, you do not have an active communication channel. Would you like to call someone?"

"Fuck off, bitch. I haven't forgotten what you did."

"Going on Standby."

She thought of what Jonas had told her and even Raymond. You are the only one who doesn't know how to deal with failure. She thought of what Michael had become, thought of what would happen if she didn't learn to let go of the past. The truth was, Cindy never liked being a loser. Losing was a sign of weakness, a sign that you couldn't make the team. But maybe she was looking at it all wrong. Maybe losing was supposed to make her stronger.

She was back at the coal power plant, surrounded by industrial pipes and the hum of machinery. She took a deep breath, coughed, and wiped the blood from her lip. She reengaged her helmet and went into the heart of the facility. She might not live to see tomorrow, so there was no point dwelling in the past. It was time to allow her failures to transform her into a woman strong enough to save her husband.

She entered a glass-fronted control room. The windows overlooked a room with a chain link fence perimeter down below. Sitting with his hands cuffed to a pipe was Jonas. Pacing in front of him was Ned and two mercenaries. Ned checked his watch several times while his men observed the entrance.

An obvious trap. They wanted her to go through the entrance on the first floor. If she didn't have a suit, she wouldn't have any choice, but she did, which meant the entire room was her playground. She clung to the walls and crawled over their heads, avoiding the front entrance completely. She stopped above Jonas, dug out a loose nut from the pipe and dropped it into his lap.

Jonas lifted his head and blinked his eyes in disbelief. Cindy raised her index finger in a shushing gesture and continued across the pipe.

"Where is this bitch?" Ned said. "I thought you guys said she chased after the van."

"Maybe she got lost on her way here," one of the troopers replied.

"No, idiot. She has a suit which can track shit. She didn't get lost. Moron."

Cindy dropped down from the pipes and landed on copper plates connected by electrical wire. The sound dampening system in her boots kicked in and muted any sounds of her arrival. Jonas looked at her then looked at Ned who was standing seven feet behind her. *Hurry* he mouthed. She reached for Jonas's cuffs and snapped the chain in two.

Jonas whispered in her ear. "He took the cure from me. If you grab it I can heal your cancer."

Cindy shook her head no and shushed him. Jonas's life was more important than her own right now.

"Maybe she's not coming."

"She'll come," Ned replied.

Just as Cindy was about to fire her grappling hook, her throat began to itch. She felt a cough beginning to form and held her breath. Jonas could see her struggling and held onto the back of her neck. The itch turned into a scratch and she was unable to resist a small, restrained cough. Ned didn't hear it. She was in the clear.

She blurted out a loud and deep cough. She continued coughing and stumbled away from Jonas. Ned turned around and looked at her. So close . . . so goddamn close. She couldn't believe a stupid cough would screw this all up. Damn it! Ned turned around and grinned.

"Now that's impressive," he said. "I wouldn't have even known he was gone."

She grabbed onto the chain link fence and hacked so hard that she sprayed blood into her helmet.

"You're not looking so hot," Ned said.

"Leave her alone," Jonas replied.

"Shut up geek. This is a conversation between me and your lady. Or is she Michael's lady? Can never tell with these polyamorous relationships these days."

Cindy wheezed as if she were sucking air through a straw. "Hope your-kaff-kaff-ready . . . -wheeze- for a fight."

Ned laughed. "You've got spunk, kid. I'll give you that. But you and I both know that without this." Ned took out a brown bottle from his pocket, the cure. "You can't fight." He gestured for his goons to grab Jonas.

"No!" She lunged forward and tripped over her own feet. She crashed—hard. Her breaths were raspy, eyes tired, fingers numb.

"Man I wish I could've seen you at your best," Ned said. "It'd be more satisfying to beat the shit out of you after what you did to my boat and my men. Didn't you learn your lesson the first time? When I burned your partner and let you watch. Don't fuck with my money." Ned bounced the bottle in his hand, throwing it and catching it as he approached Cindy. "You mad about your sister? Is that why you went through all this trouble? You know if you had just died at Javits your sister would've been fine. Only reason I nabbed you is because you were trying to expose my hideout to the commissioner. None of this had to happen."

He knelt down and waggled the cure in front of her. "You want this?"

She was prone, watching helplessly as Ned smashed the bottle with his boot.

"You-kaff- you -kaff-kaff-kaff-" She reached for his ankle and held on with a feeble grip.

"That's cute. What are you, a baby now?"

"I just -kaff- wanted to say something."

"What's that?"

"Have a nice flight."

The nanomachines in her hand created a band of wire around Ned's ankle. She launched her grappling hook and watched him scream to the ceiling.

"Do it," he yelled while dangling upside down. "Turn the power on."

The men grabbed Jonas and vacated the room. A deep hum coursed through the floor. The copper plates rattled as a strange buzzing noise traveled through the coiled wires underneath. There was a pop of electricity followed by arcing bolts of lightning. The floor and chain link fence burned with the smell of electricity. The energy snaked its way into Cindy's fingers, shot through her torso, and completed the circuit through her toes.

She screamed as rings of electricity rolled through her liquid metal armor.

A Bitter Winter

Her HUD scrambled and a flood of emergency messages flashed before her eyes.

[Critical Error: Power surge detected]

[WARNING: Poly armor offline | HUD offline | Bullet deflection offline]

[Emergency Reboot]

Once the power shut down, the rest of Ned's troops emerged from the shadows with assault rifles in hand. Cindy pushed herself up to an unstable stagger and fell again. When she got up the second time, a series of laser dots danced across her torso.

"Cindy," Jonas screamed as he was being dragged away. "Run!"

"Mul-mul-mul *static* hos-hos-hostiles."

Ned thrashed above while pointing at Cindy. "Take her out, now!"

The rage of gunfire descended upon her like a plague of burning wasps. Bullets with pointed tips, slightly taller than a Double A battery, pounded her armor and pushed her into the chain link fence. SIRCA's smooth silver skin tore open as armor piercing rounds bored through her suit. The tufts of thermal padding which regulated her body temperature spilled out from the deepest layers of her suit. And the secondary armor plates protecting her skin, fractured.

She broke through the fence and fell two floors onto a curved catwalk circling a giant coal blender. Her spine crunched and left her howling in pain. Blood gushed from the fresh bullet wound in her shoulder. She stuck her finger into the weeping hole and pried the bullet out. "Ah! Tssss."

"She's down there. Take the stairs."

Cindy let out a hopeless cough, one that sounded like surrender. The lights in her helmet started to dim. The health status indicator in her suit flashed red, warning Cindy of critical damage. Somehow, through the blinding agony, she managed to stand. She held onto the guardrail and tried to catch her breath even though the sickness wouldn't let her. She had to find a way to get back to Jonas.

Her palm slid across the railing as she made her way down the stairs. She could hardly walk, hardly breathe, and it took all of her concentration to make sure she didn't fall. She could hear the thumping of combat boots marching down distant stairs.

"Ad Mort-kaff-mort.-kaf- Ad Mortem Inimicus."

[ERROR: Voice recognition is offline]

248

"I hate you, SIRCA."

"Un-un-unrecognized com-man-man-mand."

The mercenaries arrived. They spread into a line on the catwalk above her head and aimed their guns. She lifted her chin and told the mercenaries, "Who-kaff-wants to-kaff-go first?"

"Remember, boss wants her alive."

Cindy fired her grappling hook and punctured the chest of one of the mercenaries. She used his body weight as an anchor point and zipped to the catwalk. Once there, she threw him over the edge and faced the gunmen. The mercenaries opened fire. She rolled under the closest one and put him in a choke hold. Squirts of blood popped out of his chest as she used his body as a human shield. She then took the pistol from his holster, aimed for their heads, and fired. No gun controls for the pistol it seemed. Each mercenary fell back with a smoking circular stamp on their foreheads.

She threw the corpse over the railing and checked the magazine of her gun, empty. She cast aside her weapon and stepped over the cadavers on the catwalk. As she approached the stairs, she heard another set of footsteps somewhere nearby. Cindy turned around and saw no one there. She continued to the stairs and heard the footsteps again. She turned a full one eighty and saw nothing but dead bodies.

The footsteps were at her front now, near a corpse. She stopped and listened for where the sound was coming from. The body in front of her suddenly began to rise. The corpse levitated above her head, limp and dripping, before flinging against the wall of the giant blender. The corpses were being picked up and thrown all over the place. She jumped back and coiled away in fear. Cindy didn't believe in ghosts and yet this felt like a real life haunting.

A shimmer of distortion caught her eye, human in shape. Then a shower of glittering blocks appeared and formed a woman. She was clad in shimmering red alloy. She was tall, svelte, and defined by sleek musculature. Most baffling of all was the woman's helmet which was identical to her own, including the glowing blue eyes. A second suit. How was it possible? Jonas never said anything about another suit. And who the hell was the pilot?

She coughed. "Who are you?"

The red woman didn't answer. She approached with long strides. Cindy raised her hands into a Krav Maga fighting stance knowing full well that she didn't have the energy to fight. "Stay away from me."

The red woman closed in and flashed a right hook, catching Cindy by surprise. Her helmet folded in and smashed her cheek. Her ears rang as she flipped backwards and fell over the railing. She cratered into the floor, her face aching. The red woman hopped down from the ledge and followed after her.

Cindy stood up and received a side kick from her red clone. She flew across the factory floor and slammed into a furnace. Fire spewed out of the hole she had created and raced across Cindy's back which was thankfully still protected. She peeled herself from the wall and threw a punch at the red woman. The woman easily caught her arm and threw her to the floor.

She coughed into her helmet and blocked her own vision with splatters of blood. Everything was falling apart. She didn't have the energy to fight and neither did her suit. She had tried so hard to use her failures as strength, to convince herself that she could save Jonas. But it wasn't true. At the end of the day she was still a loser.

The woman rolled Cindy onto her back and raised her fist. She pummeled her head with savage blows and with each strike her helmet shrunk around her head. SIRCA flashed all sorts of warning text in front of her eyes and flooded her vision with red light. The woman's glowing blue eyes stared at her, no emotion, no rage, no passion. She was mechanical and robotic as if driven by machine rather than human. She raised her right fist and destroyed the last of Cindy's helmet, plunging her into darkness.

CHAPTER 23:

Separation Anxiety

Jonas stood before his wife who was trapped in a glass cylinder filled with water. She breathed through an oxygen mask that Doctor Wright had fastened to her mouth. Bubbles from a water purifier squeezed between her toes and floated past her eyes. He didn't like that they had left Cindy in just a black bra and underwear, but it was necessary for what needed to be done.

She woke up and looked around. Her hair slowly danced around the fearful, confused expression in her eyes. Under Raymond's orders Lucent Labs had tied her wrists and ankles with stretchy elastic bands. There would be no way for her to break the bands, even if she pulled against them with all of her strength. Her tumors looked like giant pimples without the pus or pink coloring. A mass of cells fused together into one large lump of flesh. Charlie had synthesized a duplicate of the original cure, but he had no way of giving it to her.

Jonas was surrounded by Sid, Charlie, John, and Michael. He was also flanked by Raymond, two mercenaries pointing guns at him, and Ned. He watched Cindy pull against the elastic bands, testing them to see how far they would go. Her right hand shook as she tried to reach for her left forearm. He wanted her to succeed, wanted her to turn on the suit, but eventually she gave up and floated helplessly in the tank.

Raymond turned to Jonas with his hands behind his back.

"You know what I want."

Jonas shook his head no. "It'll kill her."

Raymond approached Cindy's water tank. "That doesn't matter to me anymore. She has my suit and I want it back."

He needed to figure out a way to buy himself some time; enough to figure out a way to get her out of there. "Do it yourself," he spat. "I'm not hurting my wife for you."

"I don't have time to waste, Jonas. My daughter's life is at stake." Raymond pointed at the Cindy. "Remove it."

"Removing the suit, as I've explained to you before, will kill her." It was his turn to point at Cindy. "And if she dies, the suit will self-destruct. It won't work."

A hand grabbed his shoulder and spun him around. He saw Ned's yellow teeth then a flash of white light. He found himself face down on the floor with an enormous pain in his jaw. The room was spinning. As he tried to stand on his shaky legs, he took a kick to his stomach. Jonas clutched his belly and nearly threw up.

"Do what he fucking says!"

He didn't know how Cindy could withstand the hits. She had been stabbed, shot, beaten up, and she still kept going. Ned had only hit him twice and he already wanted to go to the hospital. He looked over to the water tank and saw Cindy straining against her elastic bands. Even with her sickness, she was still fighting. He wanted to emulate her, to rescue her, but he couldn't fight like her. He stretched out his quivering fingers before being rolled onto his back. Ned's boot joined with his neck and left him straining for breath.

Cindy thrashed inside the tank spewing thousands of bubbles from her oxygen mask. Raymond swished his fingers, instructing Ned to bring him to his feet.

"I don't understand why you're making this more difficult. You have a whole team at your disposal to make the procedure painless for your wife. It doesn't have to kill her."

"Are you going to give me the five months I need to make that happen?"

"I don't have five months to give."

"Then it doesn't matter how smart my team is. Without time we can't research how to remove the suit safely."

Raymond shrugged. "Well, that is unfortunate. You know, I'm sure she hasn't told you this. But Cindy has killed innocent people. For example, Senator Albright and Mayor Montez died by her hands."

"She would never do that," Jonas said. "I know her. She doesn't kill innocent people."

"She also wouldn't cheat on you and yet you saw what transpired between her and Michael." Raymond leaned in. "Is she the same woman you married?"

No she wasn't. Before Ned, Cindy was funny, sarcastic, affable to a fault. She went out of her way to help people and always remembered the smallest details about them. If someone told her about their sick aunt, and she ran into that same person months later, Cindy would remember to ask how the aunt was doing. And it would be genuine interest, not small talk. Once Ned came into the picture, she changed.

She didn't talk to people, didn't make jokes. Her sarcasm became mean and hurtful. She took everything personally and got offended by every little comment, even if it was a joke. So no, she wasn't the same woman.

But for a brief second, when he saw her standing at their front door wearing his prototype suit, he could see a difference in her demeanor. Somehow through her panicked explanations of why she had the suit, he saw a brief glimpse of the woman he loved. She was still in there, somewhere.

"Remove the suit, Jonas."

He decided to follow in his wife's footsteps and did what she had done to the commissioner. He stuck out his tongue and spat in Raymond's face. Raymond took out a handkerchief from his suit jacket and wiped his eye. He chuckled, then punched Jonas with a solid cross. His ears rang and his eye felt as if it had exploded. Raymond shook his sore hand and encouraged Ned to have fun. Jonas raised his hands to defend himself, but that only made the beating worse.

He was given a splitting headache, his teeth stung, and the severe pain in his chest made him think he was going to have a heart attack. He was left sprawled on the floor with blood coming out of his nose and mouth. He had never felt a pain like this, but it was worth it to keep Cindy safe.

Raymond snapped his fingers at the two mercenaries standing guard. They grabbed Michael and shoved him to the computer console next to the water tank. "Now, Michael." he grabbed the back of his neck and pushed him down to the keyboard. "Don't make the same mistake he did. Remember, Cindy rejected you for him."

Michael placed his hands on the keyboard and nodded.

"That's a good boy," Raymond said.

"Michael . . . don't do it."

Ned pulled out his gun and placed it on Jonas's temple. He put his hands up. "Okay, okay." Sid, John, and Charlie all watched with mournful, helpless expressions. The keyboard clacked away with Michael at the controls. A strange hum reverberated inside the tank.

"Please," Jonas muttered to his wife. "Please be strong."

The lights inside Cindy's tank turned red. Her hair swayed in slow motion as she checked each corner. He could tell by the look in her eyes that she was afraid and there was nothing he could do to help her. He watched as the magnetic panel, designed to rip SIRCA from her body, engaged. A crackling hum followed after. She arched her back and screamed into her respirator. A school of bubbles rushed to the surface as she violently seized within her restraints.

The liquid metal burst out of her skin. Pools of mercury wobbled atop her flesh then stretched out like a strange, alien goo. Tiny silver spheres the size of marbles floated away from her skin and were sucked into the magnetic panel. Her skin split open. The red strands of muscle fiber whipped out of her body like slimy ropes of red licorice.

He closed his eyes, blinding his sight but not his hearing. Her muffled cries and gurgling bubbles left him feeling sick to his stomach. SIRCA had been programmed to integrate itself with the pilot's DNA in order to prevent theft. In hindsight, this was a terrible idea because he didn't know how to unbind SIRCA once the pilot wasn't needed anymore.

As the power continued to increase, more pieces of Cindy's flesh tore off. Her ragged skin floated over her head with glistening silver on one side, blood on the other. The water darkened into a cloudy red mist and spread throughout the tank.

"Michael, you're killing her!"

"Nonsense," Raymond said. "Remove every single piece from her."

"If you really loved her like you said. You would stop!"

Michael glanced at Jonas and the Lucent Labs team with a look of panic and terror in his face.

Raymond tapped Michael's shoulder. "Keep going. It will be over soon."

Michael shook his head and turned off the machine. Within seconds the power died down. Cindy panted inside her respirator. Deep wounds had carved into her body. Muscle fibers, fat, veins and arteries were fully exposed. Pieces of her fingernails and swatches of hair floated to the top of the tank. The water purifier kicked in and sucked out all the ragged strips of skin.

Raymond smacked Michael across the face and pushed him away from the computer. He remained stoic as he placed his fingers on the keyboard and re-activated the machine. Cindy pounded against the glass, knowing full well what the hum inside her prison meant.

The red lights switched on. She squirmed and jerked against her restraints as the machine went into full power. Jonas and Michael tried to stop Raymond, but the security team shoved them back. A stream of bubbles burst from her mouth as she screamed in pure agony. Her skin partially melted off her bones and left raw flesh exposed. Raymond continued to increase power and a huge flap of skin ripped off her cheek.

A loud pop rang from the capsule. The lights flickered inside the tube and then suddenly turned off. Raymond blew out the motor. He clicked on the computer monitor and mashed the keyboard to no avail. The water tank had shut down.

Jonas let out a sigh of relief. He would need at least a week to order a new motor and replace it. Raymond walked up to the tank. Cindy's skin was mangled as if chewed on by a pack of hyenas. Tendons, cartilage and arteries were on display like some gruesome science exhibit. He watched his mutilated wife float inside the tank without any fight left in her body. She had passed out. And for this, he was grateful. Raymond couldn't hurt her anymore.

CHAPTER 24:

Apex Predator

An air bubble escaped from Cindy's respirator and danced to the surface. Her eyebrow twitched, then her finger, then her toes. She remembered the burning of hot metal from Ned's bullets cutting through her skin. Remembered the crunch of bone in her cheek when the red woman had punched her. A geyser of air bubbles obscured her eyes as she screamed.

Unfortunately, she had traded one nightmare for another. Every inch of her body felt as if it were on fire. She could see her reflection in the glass. Most of her skin had ripped off and the tumors were still growing out of her stomach, chest, and hand like inflated pink boils.

She wanted to escape, but her strength had been obliterated. The emergency release handle teased her with its closeness. All she had to do was reach up, pull the lever, and she was free. But the restraints on her wrists and ankles were like giant rubbery leashes. No matter how hard she pulled, they would snap back and hold her arms down. Her hopes of reaching the handle would remain a dream.

Even if she somehow managed to get out, then what? Her body had exposed blood vessels and muscle tissue. The slightest breeze could send her nerves into a painful frenzy. Without painkillers, she would only be able to take two steps before collapsing into a mess of writhing tissue. And what would happen if she turned on SIRCA? Would the layers of padding and armor rub against her disfigured body?

Ten to fifteen minutes later, something moved within the darkened lab. A shadowy figure cut in front of the elevator doors. Her whole body tensed. She could already hear the hum in her ears, feel the tearing of her skin. Please . . . not again. She raised her arms above her head and reached for the emergency handle. The bands stretched and vibrated and eventually drained the fight out of her.

Her hair curved away from her eyes. The shadowy figure was standing in front of her enclosure, staring at her. Her fear softened to relief. It was Jonas. He grabbed a piece of paper and pen and scrawled a note. She leaned forward and watched the pen pivot from side to side. He turned and flattened the note against the glass.

I'm going to get you out of here.

It took every bit of strength she had left to fight the restraints and touch the glass. Jonas set aside his note and pressed his hands against hers. He mouthed *I love you* and she tapped the glass with her wedding ring. Jonas stepped back. He pulled up his sleeve and pretended to inject himself with a needle. She held out her arm and he gave a thumbs up in response. He gestured for her to wait and walked over to the computer. Jonas tapped the keys and shot nervous glances over his shoulder.

A robotic arm sleeping within the water tank jerked to life. The machine rolled on a saw tooth set of tracks and aligned itself with her arm. At the end of the robotic limb was an empty needle connected to clear rubber tubes. These tubes led to a receiving compartment attached to the water tank. Jonas showed Cindy the cure. She couldn't believe it, he had a second bottle. She could almost cry from the sheer joy. He dumped its contents into the liquid receiver. An air compressor kicked in and rattled.

The tubes fattened with a translucent, pinkish liquid which poured into the empty needle waiting near her arm. She nervously maintained her position and watched the machine move. The hydraulic arm unfolded at its joints and extended itself towards her vein. It jerked and shook as Jonas made corrections through the controls. Once settled, the arm shot the needle into her arm and injected the liquid.

A patrol of security guards walked by the elevators and pointed at the lab. She banged against the glass and pointed behind Jonas. Before he could turn around, the guards pushed him against the capsule and began to interrogate him. She disconnected her arm from the injector and watched Jonas lift his hands in surrender. They grabbed him by his shoulders and slammed him into one of the nearby desks.

No! She crossed her arms in front of her chest. The bands stretched and tightened preventing her from getting free. Suddenly, a strange tickling sensation raced over her skin, electric and prickling as if her leg had fallen asleep. Something was happening to her arms. Her body was changing. A semi-translucent fibrous material grew over her bloody muscle tissue. The material became thicker over time, more opaque, and eventually began to look like her own skin. The massive growths on her body shriveled and turned to black necrotic skin. They broke off one by one and disintegrated into flakes of ash. It was working, the cure was working. She started to feel stronger, but it was not enough to break her restraints.

The guards smashed Jonas into Charlie's table and slid his head into rows of empty glass beakers. They relentlessly pummeled her husband and it wasn't fair. He had never been in a fight, didn't know how to throw a punch, and these guards were unloading on him as if it were a gang initiation. She clenched her teeth and pulled against her restraints. The elastic bands stretched to their limits as her biceps bulged and her arms quaked.

She noticed that the bands had become incredibly thin, so thin, that she wondered if she could cut them with her teeth. She took a deep breath and pulled the respirator off of her face. The mask floated over her head, propelled by a jet stream of air bubbles. She bent down, brought her wrist to her mouth, and gnawed on the elastic band. She sawed the edges of the resilient strap with her teeth until it frayed and snapped.

A bubble of air escaped from her nose as she switched to the other band. Already she could feel her lungs imploding from the lack of air. The second strap came off easily, but she wasn't sure how she was going to remove the thicker anklets by her feet. She sat down. The pressure grew inside her chest and squeezed her head. A big, wobbly bubble escaped from her lips and floated up. She grabbed onto the band with both hands and tried to rip it apart, but it was too thick.

Jonas was now on his feet, restrained by a guard holding his arms. The other rained blows to his stomach and face. She couldn't watch him now, couldn't allow herself get more upset. The lack of oxygen was already causing her pain. She needed to stay focused.

Her chest convulsed as she fought the urge to breathe. Now that her bulked up muscles had been renewed, she was able to stretch the anklet until it took the shape of a large O. The heel of her foot slid through the opening. She squeaked with the insatiable desire to breathe and stretched the last anklet as hard as she could. Through much turning and twisting, she freed her foot and propelled herself to the top. She pulled the red emergency handle and pushed the hatch open.

"Guys." Jonas grunted as he took another punch to the stomach. "Guys."

"What?"

"–kaff–My wife is going to beat the shit out of you."

"What . . . ?"

The security guard faced the aquarium. She was crouched on top of the tank, lurking in the shadows. She threw herself from the capsule and tackled the guard. She hammered his head with blows, but the thick-headed oaf remained conscious and alert. The second guard came from behind and pulled her off. He interlaced his fingers behind her head and pushed down. She could feel the bones in her spine pop from the growing pressure.

Her self-defense training against a rear choke immediately kicked in. She extended her arms, bent at the hips, and got her legs behind the attacker. Using both hands she grabbed his ankles and lifted his feet. They fell together and landed on their backs. She looked at his throat and chopped it with her left hand.

The guard rolled onto his side and clawed his pinched windpipe. The second guard, now riddled with fresh lumps on his head, charged in and kicked at her face. She interlaced her fingers and blocked his boot, repelling the attack.

She stood up, cold and dripping wet, ready in her Krav Maga stance. She narrowed her eyes and watched the movements of her opponent. He drew out a serrated knife from his tactical vest and hid it behind his back. She kept her distance and circled around him, both crossing their legs with each step. If she wasn't careful, she'd have a new pair of scars to match the ones already on her arm.

The blade thrust towards her eyes. She leaned back, ducking left and right as the knife slashed in front of her face. She bumped against Charlie's workstation and rattled the remaining two chemical beakers. She grabbed a beaker full of liquid and splashed the guard's face. He screamed and covered his eyes while blindly cutting the air with his knife.

She ducked under his wild knife swings and kicked the back of his knee. As he fell, she pointed the knife at his neck and pushed it in. He fell over with a black handle sticking out of his throat. As one guard crumbled the other began to rise. He sat up and aimed his pistol. She pulled the knife out of the dead man's neck and flung it across the room. The dagger rammed into his chest and threw him back down.

"Holy shit." Jonas squirmed at the two dead bodies then looked at her. As she turned her head, her cold wet hair slithered away from her shoulders and dripped down her spine.

"Sorry you had to see that."

"You killed them."

She took a deep breath then slowly let it out. It was refreshing to be able to breathe without coughing. Jonas crawled over on his hands and knees, and she—still feeling the fight or flight response—raised her hands in self-defense. Then he hugged her and all desire to fight left her system.

"Thank you." He kissed her wet cheek then proceeded to undo the buttons of his dress shirt. The guards had done a number on him. He bled from his lip and had numerous bruises on top of his swollen cheeks. All she wanted to do was take him home and treat his wounds with some band aids and kisses. Jonas took off his shirt and draped it over her back. As his blood dripped onto his white V-neck, he buttoned her up so she wouldn't be stuck running around in her underwear.

"Thank you for giving me the cure."

"I'm glad it worked."

His eyes drifted down and lingered on her blood stained hands. Blood that wasn't her own.

"I know it looks bad," she said.

"The Cindy I knew would never kill anyone. And though I'm grateful you saved my life . . ." He tilted his head and stared into her eyes. "Are you still my wife?"

CHAPTER 25:

Killing Machine

"This isn't at all what I imagined our reunion was going to be like," she said.

"What did you think it was going to be?"

"I thought we were going to run into each other's arms and kiss as if today was our last day on Earth. Like the movies."

"There's two dead bodies on the floor and you killed them." He paused. "And I don't want to ask this, but I have to. Is it true what Raymond said? You killed Senator Albright and Mayor Montez?"

She nodded.

"Jesus. So you're a wanted criminal."

"The police don't know."

"I wish you would've told me about the suit."

She looked at him. "Why? So you could take it away?"

"In case you haven't noticed, we haven't exactly figured out how to take it away. If Raymond hadn't blown out the motor he would have destroyed you and the suit. We don't know how to reverse the DNA bonding process yet. That water tank was a failed prototype to try to extract the suit."

"It's definitely your worst invention."

"I tried to stop him."

"I know." She grazed her thumb near the bruises on his cheek. "Do you know who the red woman is?"

"Red woman?" He thought about it. "Do you mean Ruby?"

"She has a suit like mine."

"That's impossible. Ruby isn't supposed to have a pilot. It should still be in the containment unit."

She tapped his cheek and sighed. "Why do I ask you?"

"I don't believe this," he said angrily. "How did both suits get a pilot without me knowing? I built these things, I should know who is using them."

"Raymond's been scheming behind your back, honey. It's not your fault."

"I feel like such an idiot."

"Come on." She stood up and tugged his arm.

"Where are we going?"

"I killed two guards, Jonas. We have to get out of here."

He pulled away and ran to the computer in front of the containment unit. He checked the monitor and slapped his forehead. "Oh my God containment bay two really is empty."

"What are you doing? We have to go."

A voice spoke through the radios on the dead guards. "Tango twelve, check in."

Jonas began typing on the computer. "Ruby's running on the latest firmware and weaponry. If I don't patch you up you won't stand a chance."

"Tango twelve, respond!"

She grabbed his wrist. "We don't have time for this."

"Raymond took my guys to a conference room upstairs." His eyes became crestfallen. "You saw what those guards did to me. I can't save them but you can. I'm begging you to rescue them."

"You don't need to beg." She glanced at the screen. "How much longer before I can suit up?"

"I don't know, maybe three minutes give or take."

The radio blared again. "Alpha, Bravo, and Charlie team. Check the lab and make sure the prisoner hasn't escaped."

Cindy looked at the radio, then to Jonas. "We're out of time."

The elevator bell chimed. The doors slid open and revealed a group of men armed with assault rifles and First Continental branded body armor. She grabbed Jonas by his shirt and pushed him out of the lab. They ducked under flashlight beams and crouched low behind rows of cubicles. They entered a nearby office and hid behind a desk.

"We've got two men down."

"Oh crap," Jonas whispered.

"Did you get it installed?" Cindy asked.

"I think I did." Before she could stand up Jonas grabbed her arm. "Wait, I need to brief you on the updates."

"There's no time."

"The patch changed the way you interact with your suit."

The leader of the guards waved his hand. "Spread out and find them."

"Okay, quickly," she said. "Give me the rundown."

"SIRCA's connected to the neural network now. All of your commands are going to be driven by thoughts, including the activation of the suit. If you imagine yourself in the suit, it will turn on. Got it?"

"Yes."

"I've also added a hidden button for your helmet so you can take it off manually. I know it's not a huge feature, but it's important you know that."

"Okay, got it."

"If you take care of the guards, that'll give me time to transfer SIRCA to one of my off-site server farms. Otherwise, Raymond will have the instructions on how to build another suit.

She faced Jonas and began unbuttoning the shirt he gave her.

"Um. What are you doing?"

"I'm not going to need this." She handed his shirt back.

"They're going to take you down by any means necessary," he said.

""Like the two dead guys in the lab?" She cracked her neck on both sides. "That was without the suit. Let's see if your patch is installed."

She closed her eyes and imagined herself wearing the suit. Soon she could feel the tickling sensation of the nanomachines crawling over her skin. She felt her ribs and muscles spread out as the suit changed the shape of her body. The first time she had transformed it had been painful and horrific; now it was pleasant and invigorating. Either the patch made the transformation painless or she had become used to it. She opened her eyes to the words:

[SIRCA has been updated to v1.0 and is online]

"Wow." Jonas swallowed hard. "That was . . . that was interesting."

Cindy knelt behind the door. She glanced at her radar and checked the enemy's position. One red dot was approaching her white dot. "Keep your head down so they don't see you."

Jonas ducked down. She pressed her back to the wall and watched the door. The guard's voice rang from the other side. "I'm checking the office."

He came in and waved his flashlight around ignoring the corners like a fool. The guard slowly approached the desk where Jonas was hiding. She gently pushed the door closed in order to trap any potential sound within the room.

A Bitter Winter

She crouched and crept and slinked behind the guard. She kicked his leg. He dropped to her waist level. She hooked his neck with the back of her knee and squeezed his throat until his face turned red. As he began to lose consciousness, she popped his neck and quietly brought the corpse down to a rest.

"Is there anything else you need to do here," she said to Jonas.

"I—" he stammered. "Don't you feel bad or something?"

"You have to keep it together."

"That's three guys now."

"I can't knock out eight guys, Jonas. This is nothing like the videogames you play. When you knock a guy out, they only stay under for less than a minute," she said. "Don't worry, I'm under control."

"That's what scares me."

She crept into the darkened lab. The mercenaries kept a tight formation with their flashlights bobbing in the blackness. They didn't seem aware that one of their teammates had been taken out. She recognized the user-locked guns and needed to figure out a way to turn their own weapons against them. Switching on her stealth camouflage, she tailed a mercenary at the rear of the squad. She placed one hand over his mouth and gripped his shooting hand with the other.

"Do me a favor," she whispered. "Shoot your friends for me."

Cindy jerked his index finger. A burst of gunfire shot out from his SCAR assault rifle. The mercenaries didn't even have time to react before the bullets ripped through their backs. Once the rifle clicked empty, she punched her hostage in the spine and broke it.

She stood over the men she had killed and wondered what the hell she was doing. Why had killing become so easy for her? Was it the combat stims? Or did she . . . like to kill?

Smoke and cordite filled the air. The mercenary radios blared out in confusion. "Hey what's going on up there? We heard gunfire. Is the situation under control? Alpha team, check in."

[Deploying Combat Stims—]

"No more," she said. "SIRCA, you traitorous bitch. I want you to permanently lock off the combat stims."

[Action canceled by user.]

To her surprise, the machine did not speak. It displayed text which simply

268

stated that the combat stims had been locked off from further deployment.

"SIRCA?"

The machine recognized her voice but no longer spoke.

"Do you not speak anymore?"

[Neural Network is engaged. Voice commands are no longer required.]

"Oh." The news was oddly disappointing.

Another elevator was on its way up. It would be easier to eliminate the guards while they were trapped in a small car. She ran to the elevator doors and forced them open. The roof of the elevator was only five floors below. Cindy looked at the moving cables and didn't think her glass sword would be able to cut through. She dropped onto the roof of the car and ripped open the emergency service hatch. The soldiers looked up.

"Hi boys."

She dropped into the elevator and stomped the poor sap under her. They raised their guns but chickened out from shooting. Instead, they stupidly tried to engage her in hand to hand. She ducked and weaved under their pathetic attempts to fight, then grabbed a grenade from one of their vests.

She held the grenade high above her head and kept it away from the mercenaries. They clawed at her arm and screamed for someone to grab the grenade. She pulled the pin and dropped the explosive.

"Oh shit!" The shockwave from the grenade sent shrapnel into their unprotected throats and stomachs. Panels within the elevator blew off and the lights were destroyed, but the cab itself remained intact as she knew it would. C4 on the other hand, would have been a very different, very big kind of explosion. The elevator chimed. She walked out of the blood soaked car with some slight burn marks on her suit.

Now she had killed knowing there were no foreign stimulants in her system. The horrifying truth she had been ignoring could no longer be denied. She was capable of killing without remorse. She rationalized her actions, told herself that it was a comic book fantasy to knock out guards. Without zip ties or some form of restraint, they would wake up and attack again.

They were threatening Jonas's life. If she hadn't intervened, the two guards would have killed him. She didn't want to be a killer, didn't want this thing to be a part of her life, but it was either them or her family.

"Jonas!"

He came running out of the office and nearly tripped when he saw the bodies. He backed away from her while shaking his head "Oh my God. You're a killing machine."

"I'm going upstairs. Finish what you're doing here, fast. I don't know how many guards Raymond has."

"Right, right." He carefully stepped over the dead bodies and walked into the lab. "I can't believe this."

"How long is this going to take?"

"Fifteen, twenty minutes."

"I don't want to leave you by yourself for that long."

"Don't worry about me. I'll call you through the suit if something happens."

"Okay," she said reluctantly. "Please don't take long."

"It'll be okay." He began clicking through the computer. "Go on, I'll catch up."

It scared her to leave Jonas by himself. He was safe as long as she was around to watch over him. Killing all of those guards would have been in vain if he died now. She sacrificed her morals and a clear conscience in order to make sure he would survive.

Cindy continued up to the sixtieth floor of First Continental, the final floor. She jogged over to the conference room where Jonas said his team was being held, but her radar wasn't showing any green dots.

She opened the door and saw a conference table, a scientific calculator connected to a TV, and a leather couch with worn cushions, but no scientists. She zoomed out her tactical radar to show the rest of the building and saw a cluster of green dots located in another room. She left the conference room and followed the radar to Raymond's office. As she drew closer, her radar detected more dots. Two red dots, another green one, and a large red triangle which she remembered was supposed to be an aircraft.

Something didn't seem right. Why would Raymond have an aircraft? She sensed a trap. Cindy exhaled to prepare herself and pushed through the large oak doors. She entered a lavish, well-furnished reception area. At the base of a marble statue in the center of the room she found Jonas's team: Sid Carmack, John Wright, and Charlie Hudson were all tied together and gagged.

To the right and left walls were cascading waterfalls illuminated by track lighting. The words First Continental glowed within the waters via projector. At the center of the room was a three layered circular fountain, at its base was a marble statue of a woman sitting on a bench reading a book. A gold memorial placard shined from the backrest.

To my wife who always made sure I knew my place. I will love you always.

The door to Raymond's office opened. Ned walked in wearing a strange suit she hadn't seen before. She clenched her teeth so hard she gave herself a headache.

"So here we are," Ned said. "The main event."

CHAPTER 26:

Red Silver

Ned paraded around in what SIRCA identified as Jonas's prototype suit. He stood in front of Cindy and spread his arms.

"You like?"

His suit looked like a motorcycle outfit. It was all black with white armor plates on the chest, shoulders, stomach, and legs. Connected to his back was a pair of mechanical arms and legs serving as an exoskeleton.

"That doesn't belong to you."

"Neither does yours."

She balled her fists which made the sound of stretching latex and popping steel. "I've been waiting a long time for this."

Ned laughed. "I haven't. I forgot all about you."

She remembered that night at the Javits center as if it had happened yesterday. The snow beating against the glass windows, the cats licking her dead boss's face, Commissioner Gates making a fool out of her. Ned shooting Officer Yang, the mayor, and herself. It was just another average day for him. For her, it was a scar she would carry for the rest of her life. She wanted to leave Ned a similar scar so that he would never forget her, ever again.

"You killed my partner and tried to kill me," she said angrily. "How could you forget?"

"Honey I've killed a lot of people. If I dwelled on it I'd become an obsessed loser like you."

Cindy huffed inside of her helmet. No, no, no, she didn't come all this way, suffer all that pain, just so he could mock her. Obsessed loser? Really? Ned was not better than her. Her arm shot out like a bolt of lightning. Her hand stopped mere inches from his face as if a chain had snapped taut on her wrist. A smug grin spread across his lips.

She looked at her frozen hand. "What?"

Ned laughed. She tried to pull her hand back but it was stuck floating near his head. "As much as I'd love to have this dance. I think someone else wants to cut in."

Rippling waves of distortion flickered across her wrist. Red fingers appeared from thin air, the distortion solidified into an arm, chest, and finally the helmet. Ruby. She had been in the room the whole time. Cindy didn't have the strength to face her, not yet.

"Ruby," Ned said. "Eliminate."

Ruby hooked Cindy's ankle and tripped her. The floor cracked beneath her back and dust kicked up around her eyes. Ruby lifted her boot and stomped with all her weight. The floor shuddered as Cindy rolled away unharmed. She was amazed by how much power that thin body could exert. She took a second to come up with a strategy.

Ruby's height was the biggest obstacle. Long legs meant long arms which could strike from a distance like a spear. She needed to keep the fight close and intimate where she could do some real damage. Cindy tucked her head and charged. Ruby stretched out her arm and grabbed the top of Cindy's helmet, halting her. Cindy swung her short arms like an angry toddler and punched the air in front of her. Ruby twisted from her hips and threw her across the floor.

"Wow." Ned laughed. "Didn't see that coming." He paced in front of the Lucent Labs team while watching the fight from a safe distance. "You know I always wondered which one of you two would be the better fighter."

Ruby was in another league of skill that Cindy had not seen in the average thug or guard. It was embarrassing to be thrown around like a doll when earlier she had singlehandedly defeated a squad of armed mercenaries. Had this been a cage match in a shady underground gym she would have relished the challenge. It wasn't as fun when other people's lives were at stake.

Ruby planted her feet and threw a surprise right hook. Cindy blocked with her forearm, pleased with her own quick reflexes until Ruby's boot snapped into her stomach. She hurtled backwards and smashed into the waterfall rock façade. Water poured over her shoulders as the glowing words of First Continental projected across her chest.

"They built her nice and strong," Ned said. "She's faster, sleeker, and unlike you, she follows orders. How we got her is actually a pretty interesting story."

Cindy peeled herself out of the wall and Ruby slammed her back in. Ruby hammered her head and pulverized the rocks with each blow. If this kept up, the helmet would eventually split open and then she'd be in real trouble. Ruby may have been taller, but Cindy had more muscle. She needed to figure out how to use her weight against her lighter opponent. She grabbed Ruby's wrist and swung her into the crumbling wall. A blast of dust and rock shot out from Ruby's back.

Cindy hopped on the balls of her feet as she backed away. Though her lungs were already starved for oxygen, she raised her hands and tucked her chin to her chest. Ruby pried herself out of the wall. The rocks tumbled and splattered into the basin. She orbited Cindy and raised one fist to her chin and dropped the other to her waist.

Cindy recognized the fighting style, it was called Pencak Silat, an Indonesian martial art. Her father was stationed at Indonesia for a time. When he came back to the states, he taught her the basics of Pencak Silat.

Why did Ruby know this exotic fighting style?

"I was wondering when you'd fight back," Ned jeered. "Let's make this more interesting." Ned lifted the Lucent Labs team to their feet. Since they were tied together, it was easy for him to shove them towards the fountain in the middle of the room. He pushed their heads into the basin and held them underwater.

"No!" Cindy ran towards the fountain and almost lost her head to the red shin that came flying at her. She slid on her knees and kicked at Ruby's leg. Ruby hopped over Cindy's sweep and followed up with her own. Cindy sprung into a butterfly kick and watched Ruby's leg slide in a circular motion across the floor. The two women continued to roll around the arena, striking at each other with sweeps and spinning kicks yet neither could hit the other. It was almost as if they could read each other's minds.

She could hear Jonas's team choking in the fountain with Ned laughing as he pushed the backs of their heads. Cindy rolled out of their kicking loop and ripped Ned away from the fountain. Three heads catapulted upward with a spray of water.

Cindy spun around and came face first with Ruby's right fist. She counter punched with her left. Their fists collided and rang with loud metallic twangs. They snapped twin kicks and hit each other's shins. Their armor sang with a high pitched ringing, discordant and piercing. She closed range and threw Ruby over her shoulder. Ruby landed on her feet and threw Cindy. She landed on her feet and the two disentangled.

"That was amazing." Ned clapped. "You girls sharing the same bird brain?"

The women grunted as they punched and kicked at each other without landing a single body blow. Ned continued blathering on as they fought. "You know what's ironic? Raymond hired me and my boys to take out that fat ass mayor, the prick commissioner, and that useless piece of shit senator. You fucked up my plans, but then, a month and a half later, you finish the job for me." He cut one of the Lucent Labs team members loose and grabbed Sid Carmack. He led Sid to where the women were fighting and pushed him.

As Cindy threw a left hook. Sid's face came between her and Ruby and there wasn't enough time to stop the punch. SIRCA recognized he was the wrong target and quickly turned her hips. She punched the head of the reading statue and snapped it off its neck. Ruby attacked before she could regain her bearings.

"Damn my suit can't do that," Ned said. "Anyway what was I talking about? Oh right, Ruby over there. So Raymond calls me and tells me he wants a pick up made. He wanted me to grab some cripple from the hospital and he was willing to pay for it. So I took the gig."

Ruby caught the side of Cindy's helmet with a devastating rear roundhouse kick. She spun once and found herself staring at the cracked floor. The pointy folds of her crunched helmet poked her cheek. A crack split down the right Plexiglas eye which caused her glowing lenses to flicker. Her head felt weightless; her vision blurred in sync with a pulsing headache.

Her arms wobbled as she forced herself up. She could taste blood. Her health status indicator changed color: helmet–yellow, back and ribs–yellow, legs–green, arms–blue. Cindy performed a kip-up and was back on her feet. She ducked under Ruby's hook and punched her shiny crimson stomach. And as Ruby doubled over, Cindy followed up with a jaw breaking uppercut. Ruby's head snapped back and left her dazed and confused. Cindy threw everything she had at Ruby. She dented her pristine red armor with her punches and staggered her with rib cracking sidekicks.

"Didn't you hear what I said?" Ned yelled. "We picked up a cripple from the hospital."

She picked Ruby off the floor and pounded her body with the hardest punches she could muster. She was exhausted and out of breath, but the suit kept her alive, kept her going even though her body was at its limit. She spun and kicked Ruby's stomach so hard, her own shin stung with pain. Ruby slid across the floor then came to a stop. The crimson ninja clutched her stomach and coughed, she had finally hurt her.

"You're going to regret that." It was the first time Ruby had spoken. Her voice had the same eerie, ghostly distortion as Cindy's. The woman stood up and placed her right hand by her hip. A red tube formed out of her crimson armor. She grabbed the tube and pulled it out of her leg. A beam of light shot out from its opening and transformed into a sword, kind of like a light saber but with wild, uncontrollable energy. Rogue bolts of lightning crackled from its edge and dripped sparks like a welding torch. Ruby lifted the blade and pointed at her chest with its tip.

She hoped her glass one would be able to hold its own against Ruby's. She pulled out her weapon with her left hand. A beam of light identical to Ruby's weapon shot out and formed Cindy's sword. She gazed at the weapon in her hand, completely in awe of her sword's new look. In her HUD the Glass Blade had been renamed to Kinetic Blade. This must have been an upgrade from Jonas's patch. She crouched and held the blade near her malformed helmet.

"Hey are you paying attention?" Ned said. "So I take the cripple from the hospital and bring the clueless sap here."

Cindy turned to Ned. "Shut up!"

"C'mon, this is a great story."

Ruby charged from her position and dragged the blade behind her; her footsteps were silent as she ran across the floor. She swung the sword from her side like a golf club. Cindy stepped to the side and blocked with a downward thrust. Their swords kissed and crackled.

"We put the cripple in the suit, dumbass! Who do you know that's crippled?" She looked at Ned. "What?"

An explosion of power rocked the side of her helmet. The world blurred and seesawed as she staggered over to the fountain. By the time her vision straightened out, Ruby was already bringing the edge of her sword down towards her head. Cindy threw her sword up and stopped Ruby mere inches from her face. Their swords sang with the crackle of electricity.

Ned touched the side of his helmet and spoke to someone on his radio. "Yeah?" He walked away while Cindy strained against Ruby. "What do you want me to do about the geeks?" He paused. "You sure you want me to leave 'em?" Ned then turned and smiled at Cindy. "Looks like Ray's all set to go. So I'm gonna head out." Ned stopped and looked over his shoulder. "Have fun fighting your sister."

Her sister? Cindy's heart pounded. She was fighting her sister? That's why she knew Silat. Cindy fell to her knees, succumbing to Ruby's power. She looked into the glowing blue eyes and imagined her sister's face behind the mask.

"Jadie?"

"How do you know my name," she growled.

She shoved Jadie back and leapt to the top of the fountain. She sheathed her blade and ripped her helmet off using the hidden button. "It's me."

Jadie looked at her. "I don't know you."

"I'm your sister, Cindy."

"I don't have a sister."

Jadie ran up to the base of the fountain and chopped at it with her sword. The Lucent Labs team scattered as the hot blade created molten lines on the rock and split the fountain to pieces. The water rushed out from the basin and flooded the room. Cindy back flipped to a safe distance as Jadie ran between the chunks of sliced stone and charged with her blade. Cindy waved her hands in surrender.

"Shut up and fight me!"

Cindy ducked and weaved as Jadie slashed the air. "Stop!" Jadie slashed at her face. The tip of the blade swung centimeters past her nose. She felt the incredible heat and smelled her hair being burned. Jadie panted with the blade sizzling in her hand.

"I'll make you fight me."

She turned and slashed her sword at John Wright. The beam of energy cut through the air and raced to his torso. Cindy burst into a sprint and pushed Dr. Wright out of the way. The sword sliced through her armor and kissed the skin beneath. Her back split open and a horrific sensation of agony raced down her spine.

278

"Auuugh!"

She crawled away, bleeding and crippled by the torture of melted skin. "Get out of here," she screamed.

Sid rounded up his team and sprinted through the office doors leading back into the hallway. Jadie pulled on Cindy's hair and brought her to her feet. Heat waves blurred the walls as Jadie brought the sword closer to her skin. Her neck warmed from the proximity of the blade.

"Please, Jadie. Don't do this."

"You killed people."

"They're tricking you."

Jadie yanked on her hair again. "You're the one trying to trick me."

"Remember the car accident? I was there. I was trying to save you."

She tilted her head. "I don't know what you're talking about."

"We were in a car together. We flipped over and I had to drag you out through fire. I burned my hand trying to get you out."

She released her hold on Cindy. "I was upside down . . ."

"Yes." Cindy held out her hands as if she were carefully molding a clay pot. "There were two men. Do you remember what they did?"

"They came through a door." Jadie sheathed her blade. "They tried to hurt me."

Cindy wished Jadie would take off the helmet. She wanted to see her face, wanted to see her eyes, wanted to see if she remembered.

"And you were there," Jadie said.

"Do you remember me now?"

"Yes."

Jadie softly placed her hand on the back of Cindy's neck. She got through, Jadie remembered who she was.

"You tried to kill me."

No . . . Cindy's relief turned to terror. A flash of light burst from Jadie's sword hand. The sword curved through the air and cut through Cindy's stomach. She screamed as the SIRCA machinery exploded and scorched her abdomen. She staggered back and clutched her seeping gut.

"Raymond told me all about you. How you tried to kill him for helping me. He told me about all the people you've killed. How you'd try to trick me by pretending we're related."

A Bitter Winter

Cindy tripped over her feet as she backed away. She was afraid to breathe, scared that her guts might fall out.

"You killed the father of one of my students, Priscilla Montez. If you were my sister, I'd disown you anyway."

Never had a statement cut so deep. Deeper than the laceration in her stomach.

"I don't want to kill you." Jadie pointed the tip of her sword at Cindy. "But you're too dangerous."

Jadie slashed the air and Cindy blocked with her own blade. Their swords burst with frothing, buzzing energy, dripping hot plasma. Jadie kicked Cindy in the stomach. The sudden explosion of pain caused Cindy to reflexively swipe her sword.

From her right hip to her left shoulder, Jadie's scarlet armor ripped open. Her stomach and breast burst into a streak of flame. Her blood joined Cindy's on the floor as she doubled over and cried in pain.

"I didn't mean to—"

Jadie looked up with her glowing eyes. "There's the psycho he told me about." She readied her blade and charged. Water kicked around Jadie's feet as she held the blade over her head and yelled. Cindy suddenly realized that they were both standing in water and the ceiling was made of cement. She fired her grappling hook and shot upward. Jadie ran past Cindy's legs and slipped on the water. Cindy quickly extended her cable until she was three feet above the floor.

"I'm so sorry."

She plunged her blade into the pool. A surge of electricity shot out from the sword and snaked its way to Jadie who was on her knees. The electricity touched her waterlogged boots and shot straight through her body. Her arms and chest convulsed as bolts of energy exploded out of her armor.

Cindy removed her sword from the water. Jadie toppled over with smoke rising from her shoulders. She rushed to Jadie's side and rolled her onto her back. She tried to wake her up but Jadie wasn't responding.

"Jadie." Cindy dug her fingers below her sister's softened helmet and tore it off. "Please be okay."

Jadie coughed once then opened her eyes. "Do it already."

Cindy furrowed her brow and tried not to cry. "I'm not going to kill you."

"I will."

Her voice wavered. "It's Sis."

"You're not my sister."

Jonas and his team stormed into the reception area. He gasped when he saw the body on the floor. "Jadie?"

"Jesus Christ," Dr. Wright said. "She's bleeding." Then he looked at Cindy. "You're bleeding too."

Jonas knelt down, soaking the knees of his pants. He placed his hand on Jadie's forehead and asked her if she was okay. Jadie gave him an empty look and replied, "Who are you?"

Cindy shook her head. "She doesn't remember anything."

"Even you?"

Charlie joined Jonas on the floor and brought a med kit with him. There were only enough supplies for one person to be treated. Cindy told him to help Jadie and so he did.

Sid approached the group and said, "I believe Michael must have triggered a deep level spotless mind protocol for Raymond."

"Don't tell me that, Sid," Cindy said morosely. "I already hate him."

"At this point, I'd kill him," Jonas said.

"He's not worth it. And Jadie likes him, always did."

"If your memory returned, Jadie's could return as well," Sid said.

"Stop talking about me like I'm not here," Jadie said.

Jonas touched Cindy's shoulder. "Look. We've got the team, we've got Jadie, and I've deleted the files from Raymond's servers. Let's get out of here."

Cindy shook her head. She slowly stood up and shuffled her feet over to where her helmet was. She secured it onto her head. The eyes flickered on with one eye dimmer than the other. A critical warning sign flashed in her health status indicator.

"Michael knows as much about the suit as you do. With Raymond's money and resources, he can create another one. I have to stop him. I don't want to face a third suit."

"Is that the only reason?"

"He made me do awful things, Jonas," she said quietly. "I'm supposed to just let him go?"

"Then I'm coming with you."

"You'll be a liability."

"I'm not abandoning you again." He then turned to his team. "Sid, John, Charlie, get yourselves and Jadie out of here. We'll see you after this is all done."

She firmly pressed against his chest. "I don't want you to come."

"Too late." He showed Cindy his gold wedding band. "We're in this together."

CHAPTER 27:

The Shame We Bear

Cindy held Jonas's hand and led him into Raymond's office which was vacant and partially damaged. A row of glass windows overlooked Central Park with one window taped up with cardboard and plastic. The desk she had destroyed had been replaced by something cheap and mundane. Sharp pain jabbed at her sides.

"Ow," she said.

"Are you all right, do you need to take a break?"

"Yeah."

She stood in front of the windows, haunted by Jadie's words, *"You're not my sister."* All of this struggle, all of this fighting, had been for nothing. Giant clouds rolled over skyscrapers and cast their shadows on the city below. A normal, unexciting day for the denizens heading off to work. They didn't know what had happened in this building, how much suffering she had gone through.

She caught her reflection in the window. Her helmet was dented around her temples and forehead. The edges of her lenses protruded, eager to pop off with one well-placed strike. The cut in her stomach had already begun to heal and fuse together. The scar was pink and raw and still hurt as if it were burning, but in a few hours it would be completely gone. She ached from her bruises and felt every sting from the cuts mending throughout her body. This was what she deserved.

She pressed the secret button in her helmet and took it off. In the glass reflection, her face was discolored and covered in dirt. Her hair, though tied in a bun, had loose strands which shot out like rogue weeds.

"When I was a kid, I used to have fantasies about the principal saying over the PA that the school was under attack. I'd whip out my secret agent ID and tell my classmates, 'don't worry, I'm going to keep you safe.' That's kind of weird right? Instead of dreaming about boys I was dreaming about being some kind of action hero."

"I don't think so. Girls can dream whatever they want."

"You didn't know me back then, but I was a problem child. I got into fights at school and stole my dad's Mustang so I could race other kids. A psychologist would probably say the reason I acted out was because of my dad's alcoholism. Truth is, I was an asshole. I did that stuff because it was fun. That's weird right? That I liked fighting people?"

"Some people are born to fight," Jonas said.

"Are they born to kill too?"

"You're being too hard on yourself." Jonas leaned against the window and crossed his arms. "People who live perfect lives often don't have the necessary experience to develop character. You grow from struggle, learn from failure. You grew up in a bad neighborhood, went to a rough school, and had an alcoholic father. You could've become a criminal but you never did. You rose above it.

"Look at me. I probably have about a hundred inventions under my belt and only one actually made any money. If I hadn't screwed up with all my other stuff first, I never would have been able to build SIRCA. I needed failure in order to learn and grow. You say you love my intelligence, but I'm only intelligent because I learned from the dumb things I did."

She pursed her trembling lips. "Jadie's never going to forgive me."

"Her memory was scrambled, Cindy. Don't put weight on whatever she said. I'll figure out a way to bring her back to you."

"I'm just so disappointed in myself."

"We've all been there. You just have to pick up the pieces and move on."

"Are *you* going to be able to forgive me?"

He looked away. The white sclera of Jonas's eye had gone red from one too many hits to the head. They had both seen better days.

"You and I have done some very stupid and selfish things. I'm willing to leave it in the past if you are."

She nodded and placed her helmet back on her head. She walked over to the rooftop exit door and beckoned Jonas to follow. "Stay close."

They climbed up the cement staircase and opened the door to a blinding blue sky and a strong gust of wind. On the rooftop was a helipad with an enormous aircraft parked on it. She remembered the tarp she had walked past before confronting Raymond. This aircraft must have been what was hiding under it. SIRCA analyzed and identified the ship as 'Ogre.'

The plane had wide, stubby wings, and giant flaps. On its nose was an orb, most likely a camera, attached to a rotating Gatling gun. SIRCA identified the gun as a GUA-17 Vulcan, but she didn't really know what that meant. The pilot sat behind and above the head of the gunner. Bombs hung under the wings and rows of little square panels lined the fuselage. Two giant turbines sat cold inside of its armor plated body with two additional wingtip engines for vertical takeoff.

"Over there." Jonas pointed to the platform. On his knees, hunched over a laptop was Michael with Raymond holding a gun to his back. Near the cockpit of the aircraft was Ned.

"Okay it's done," Michael said to Raymond.

"Ned, power it up."

Ned entered the Ogre and sat inside the cockpit. His head looked at each instrument panel as he flipped the switches. "Welcome to the party." He smiled at Cindy.

Raymond grabbed Michael's arm, dragged him across the helipad, and threw him at Cindy's feet. Michael's hair was a tousled mess and his glasses were crooked, but no harm had come to him.

"Don't tell me you got the Ogre running," Jonas said.

"He didn't leave me a choice," Michael replied.

Didn't have a choice? Funny. Jonas didn't have a choice when Raymond wanted to rip the suit from her body, yet he resisted, even after being kicked and punched he still said no. Raymond was charismatic, manipulative, intimidating, but at the end of the day he was just a man, and Michael, a spineless coward.

She stood up straight and addressed Raymond. "You know how this ends."

"I do know how it ends. The question is, do you?"

Cindy crossed the helipad in order to close the four foot distance between her and Raymond. With each step taken her body slowed as if wading through a pool of quicksand. She stood face to face with Raymond and threw the first punch.

[Command Blocked]

"You forgot, didn't you?" Raymond said.

"SIRCA won't let me touch him, Jonas."

A Bitter Winter

"You should have known better, Cindy. I asked Michael to install those safeguards on day one. Couldn't risk you harming me if you decided to go rogue, which you did."

"Michael you piece of shit," Jonas said.

Michael crawled on his knees and begged for forgiveness. "It wasn't supposed to be like this."

Raymond flipped his gun around, holding it by the barrel, and offered it to her. "Go ahead, take it."

"I don't want it."

"SIRCA. Please take the weapon."

SIRCA did as it was told. The silver arm extended towards the weapon, but underneath, Cindy's human arm was fighting against it. She whimpered as the servos and actuators in her arm whined from her resistance.

"SIRCA, stop." Her arm and shoulder shook. The machine no longer followed orders from the pilot. The commander was now in control. Cindy took the gun from his hands.

Jonas stepped in front of Cindy and readied his fist for Raymond. "I guess I'll have to hit you instead."

"Jonas, don't," she said.

He cocked his arm back. A loud crack sundered the air and startled them both. A hole the size of a fist punctured the cement rooftop exit they had emerged from. Underneath the Ogre, smoke exited from the spinning gun barrel. Ned waved his index finger at Jonas, then flipped the remaining switches on the instrument panel. The giant fans inside the Ogre's engines began to spin. A deep whine grew louder and louder and increased in pitch.

"You can't touch me," Raymond said. "Now." He focused his attention on Cindy. "You my dear, are being given the rare opportunity to take revenge on the person who wronged you. I gain no benefit from Michael's death except the satisfaction of seeing this slime wiped off the face of the Earth. I never asked Michael to pose as your husband, to trick you into loving him. All I wanted were some political targets taken care of. And as soon as this bird is ready to fly, I'm going to personally eliminate the final target owed to me.

"I'd also like to say that when I cleared your memory, it was so you could return to a normal life. After my suit was returned, of course. Michael had other plans, plans he did not inform me of. He was the one who suggested Ned kidnap Jonas so you could be led to a trap. He was also the one who told us of SIRCA's weakness to electricity." Raymond kicked him. "Isn't that right, Michael?"

The gun trembled in her hand. "It's getting hard for me not to pull the trigger, Michael." Her index finger began to curl.

Raymond goaded her. "It would be poetic justice for you to end his pathetic life, Cindy. What he did has left me more disturbed than anything Ned has done."

"Ned tried to kill me," Cindy said.

"And look at you now," he said with pride.

She lined up the iron sight with Michael's head. "I'm not going to be like you, Michael. You're stuck in the past and I'm not going to let you keep me there."

"You said you were going to kill me if you ever saw me again," he replied.

She had meant it at the time, but her fight with Jadie had changed everything. Even in her amnesiac state, Jadie's utter hatred for what Cindy had done gave her a brutal reality check. Killing was supposed to have been a last resort. What would it say about her if she used the suit to kill Michael for what he did? Would she be viewed as a hero or a monster?

Her HUD flashed the words [Restricted] over Raymond's head. Even the thought of turning the gun toward him caused her arm to hurt. Meanwhile, the Ogre's engines were idling hot. Ned watched from the gunner seat and held his thumb over the master fire controls.

Michael picked up his head. The iron sights she balanced on his forehead wavered. She could see in his eyes the child who never grew up. The boy who helped her with her English and Math homework. The friend who lied and gave her an alibi whenever she wanted to sneak off to an underage drinking party.

"You were right," Michael said. "Becoming my friend was a mistake. After what I did to you and our relationship, I wouldn't want to be friends with me either. I'm sorry for coming between you and Jonas. After watching him take a beating from Ned and Raymond, I realized why you love him. He was willing to bleed and die for you whereas I didn't even hesitate to pull the switch. He's the better man, always has been.

And I'm going to say what I should have said at the wedding. I wish you both nothing but the best things in life. I am truly and deeply sorry."

"Are you hoping she'll spare your life, Michael?" Raymond said.

"No. Unlike you, I know when I deserve to be punished. And you're going to be punished with me."

"I think not."

The turbines on the Ogre picked up speed.

"Cindy," Michael yelled over the engines. "I have one last thing to say to you. Ad Mortem Inimicus."

"What does that mean?" Raymond said.

[SIRCA restrictions lifted. Mag Drivers are now operational]

She turned her gun on Raymond. "To death, my enemy." And fired.

Raymond yelled and clutched his rib. The turret underneath the ogre pivoted and aimed at Jonas. Cindy dropped the gun and shoved Jonas out of the way as bullets spewed from the turret's rotating mouth. The barrage of hot metal blasted her chest and tore off chunks of her armor. Ned kept his fingers on the trigger even after the Gatling gun's barrels turned molten orange.

Raymond ducked under the stream of bullets and grabbed the gun Cindy had dropped. He pulled back the slide and shot Michael. A smoking red dot appeared on his lower back and slowly spread across his shirt. Raymond threw the gun aside and hobbled to the ship.

The Gatling gun overheated and refused to fire anymore bullets. Each bullet smashed into her chest with the force of a sledgehammer. Her armor cracked open and left her chest feeling like broken egg shells. She saw her purpled, swollen skin between the gaps.

Michael crawled along the floor dragging limp legs behind him.

"Help . . . me."

Raymond struggled to climb the step ladder to the cockpit. He took a seat behind Ned and put on a standard radio headset. The engines gained power, blurring the skyline with their heat. The massive aircraft took off and retracted its landing gear.

There was a tapping on her helmet. She glanced and saw Jonas hovering over her. "Please get up, please get up."

Her illuminant eyes flickered. "Please stop tapping my head." She groaned and closed her eyes, which darkened her glowing ones.

"No, no. Don't fall asleep." He tried to lift her up but the endoskeleton and armor plating made her two hundred pounds heavier. SIRCA released smelling salts into her helmet and startled Cindy awake. She got up and was slightly disoriented as to where she was and what was happening.

"Michael's still alive," Jonas said.

"I'll—I'll get him." She staggered over to Michael as if driven by autopilot. She walked over his blood and crouched over him.

"Just leave me," he said in a raspy voice. "Go, take Jonas and get out of here."

"Cindy," Raymond's voice boomed through the aircraft's loudspeaker. "I do wish it didn't have to be this way, but I can't risk you coming after me. It may mean losing everything I've built, but my daughter's life is more important than anything remaining within these walls. I cannot let you stop me."

The two oval shaped bombs dangling from the wings suddenly dropped. She watched the fat, military green torpedo looking things pitch down towards the rooftop.

"Oh shit!" Jonas cried.

She heaved Michael over her shoulder and dragged Jonas by his shirt. She carried them across the helipad as the explosions sank the floor beneath her feet. Rocks and debris ticked against her armor as she sprinted for the exit. A missile contrail of smoke streaked over her head and blasted the rooftop entrance, turning it into a pile of rubble.

"We're trapped," Cindy said. "I don't know what to do."

The Ogre pitched forward with its Gatling gun spinning under its nose. Cindy handed Michael over to Jonas which caused him to fall backward. She stuck out her arm and aimed at the Ogre as it tore up the floor with its bullets. The Mag Driver folded out of her forearm and began to charge. The blast snapped her arm back. The Ogre rolled away and narrowly avoided the slug which destroyed its Gatling gun and camera orb.

"Why didn't it blow up," she yelled.

"We fixed it." Michael grunted.

The Ogre backed away from the rooftop and sank below the building's edge. Michael cried in pain as Jonas struggled to put his arm over his shoulder.

A Bitter Winter

"Where's he going?" Jonas said.

"My legs," Michael cried. "I can't feel my legs."

Grey smoke rose from the edges of the building and blotted out the sun. She and Jonas swayed from side to side as if caught in an earthquake. "What's happening?" she said. Suddenly the floor shot up at an angle and transformed the rooftop into a massive slide.

Michael fell off his shoulder and slid across the slanting floor with Jonas trailing right behind him. Rooftop antennas and HVAC units flew over their heads as Jonas and Michael continued tumbling across the angled roof. Her gecko grip engaged and prevented her from going down with them.

"Cin—dee!"

Without thinking, she dove headfirst for Jonas. Her armor let out a plume of sparks as it scraped against the stone floor. She held her hands in front of her face, tilting her body to direct her towards Jonas. He fell over the edge and disappeared into the billowing smoke.

"No!"

CHAPTER 28:

Freefall

Clouds of toxic dust rose from the base of the building and stained the sky. The groaning I-beams and rumble of rock overwhelmed her sense of hearing. Sounds that were coming from the right were actually originating from the left due to the Doppler Effect. She plummeted head first with her arms at her sides and veered away from the falling debris rolling past her head.

[Altitude: 2,100ft]

The wind whistled through the cracks in her helmet. She smelled the smoke, and rock, and tasted the sweat on her upper lip. This was crazy, absolutely insane. Using her grappling hook to swing through the city was one thing; dropping from over two thousand feet while avoiding wreckage to catch her husband and Michael was the stupidest plan ever.

And it was all she had. She dove through the oppressive fog and, for a brief second, a white sleeve flapped through the smoke.

"Cindy!"

She activated her grappling hook and took aim. It was too dangerous to fire the hook directly at him, so she aimed in the direction of a building she couldn't see and hoped for the best. The hook fired with a loud whipping sound. The unspooling wire trilled from the pulleys in her arm. Once the hook was locked, it yanked her across the sky. She crashed into Jonas with her shoulder and threw her arm around his waist.

"Try to hold your breath," she said. "Don't breathe this stuff in."

The grappling hook dragged her towards the building. She flipped so that her legs could spring off the brick wall. She fired the grappling hook a second time and wrapped it around a traffic light post. She switched on her thermal vision to try to find Michael and only saw static. The helmet had taken too much damage. She shut off her thermal vision and tried to guess where he would be based on the little green dot on her radar.

"Hold on tight," she commanded. "I'm going to catch him."

A Bitter Winter

[Altitude: 43 ft]

Car alarms and sustained horns overwhelmed her ears. People were running, screaming, blending their voices with Michael's. Building debris smashed into cars and created explosions of glass and metal. And through that cacophony of noise, she heard clothes fluttering in the wind. She pulled herself to his location, saw Michael in the fog, reached with her arm and missed.

"Oh my God."

[Altitude: 15 ft]

She circled around the traffic light like a tether ball and shot across the street. She crashed into Michael seconds before he could crater into the roof of a taxicab. Her foot snapped a Gentleman's Club sign off a taxicab roof and threw her off balance. Cindy turned her body and shielded them as she collided into an ad for a collision accident lawyer on the side of a bus. The words "call us" loomed over Cindy's head in bright yellow letters.

Jonas rolled off of Cindy. He coughed up clouds causing dust to fall from his ashen covered hair. Michael squirmed atop Cindy's chest, oblivious to the fact that his leg was folded in the wrong direction.

"Don't breathe the air," Cindy panted. The filtration system in her helmet kept her air purified.

"I can't hold my—kaff—breath anymore." He stood up and continued coughing. "Are you all right?"

"Oh yeah." She stretched her arms and hissed when a sharp pain stabbed her lower back. "I'm having a great time."

"Why did you save me," Michael muttered. "I don't deserve it."

The aluminum frames which held the ad in place popped out from one corner as if waving hello. "You're right." She panted and held onto her side. The thinning of her adrenaline reduced her tolerance for pain. "But if you do deserve to die, I'm not going to b—" She fell over.

Jonas held her battered body in his arms. "Easy, easy." All she wanted was a chance to catch her breath or take a nap. Even with the help of a super suit, she was completely exhausted. "You've done enough for today. Let's get Michael to the hospital and go home."

"We'll take him to the hospital, but I'm not going home." Rivulets of blood ran down her back and arms, pooling inside the cracks of her armor. She forced herself to stand even though her body didn't want to. And she forced herself to lift Michael into her arms, even though she didn't want to. Cindy groaned and began to shake under his weight.

Jonas reached over. "At least let me carry him." She handed Michael over and caused Jonas to lose balance and nearly fall. "I got it, I got it," he said as he adjusted himself. "Wasn't expecting him to be so heavy."

"If he's too heavy—"

"It's fine. I can do it."

"Thank you," Michael said.

Jonas briefly glanced at him but didn't say a word.

Ash flakes fell from the sky. The wind howled and caused dust devils to whip across the deserted street. Cars blared their alarms in unison, flashing their hazard lights through the heavy fog. They boarded the vacated MTA bus they had crashed into and took their seats. Jonas and Michael sat behind the driver's seat while Cindy took the wheel. She turned the key which had been left in the ignition and brought the bus to a rumbling idle.

"You should let me drive," Jonas said.

"Do you really think I should sit next to the man who pretended to be my husband?"

Jonas opened his mouth then closed it. "I'll sit with Michael."

She pushed the accelerator and rammed through rows of abandoned cars caught in traffic. Along the way she stopped and picked up as many survivors as she could until the bus was near bursting with people and pets. She drove towards the rays of daylight piercing through the clouds and took everyone to the nearest hospital.

The passengers limped and shuffled to the front. Some were bleeding, some had a broken limbs, but they all took the time to personally thank Cindy with kind words and a gentle pat on her shoulder. Their gesture was small and unnecessary, but it made her heart swell. Their safety was a small victory in a steady string of losses. She was also appreciative of the passengers who volunteered to carry Michael into the hospital. The seats in the bus were now dust covered and vacant.

Jonas leaned against the pay station podium and asked, "Now what?"

"I have to stop Raymond."

"No you don't." He pointed to the line of people being taken into the hospital by nurses and doctors. "You saved every one of those people. Including me. You don't need to go after Raymond anymore. Let the police handle it."

Cindy closed the door and led Jonas to the back of the bus where the tinted windows were still intact. She deactivated her helmet and kissed Jonas. The silver was still melting away from her skin as they stood there holding each other. She pulled back and waited for his reply. He placed both hands behind her neck and answered. She stood on her tip toes and kissed him with a passion that left her breathless. They disconnected. Both deeply inhaled as if they had forgotten how to breathe.

"I wanted you to know how much I still love you."

Jonas grazed her cheek with his fingers. "I do too. Which is why I don't want you to leave."

"I have to stop him."

She slowly backed away.

"Why?"

Her helmet closed around her head and reformed its protected, deformed shell. Her voice changed as the voice modulator kicked in.

"Raymond fucked with the wrong woman."

CHAPTER 29:

A Dish Served

A million thoughts raced through her mind as she swung over streets filled with emergency vehicles. Raymond was going to risk everything, to do what? Blow someone up with his giant aircraft? And why the hell was Ned going with him? She could have let him go, could have said fuck it and moved on. If they decided to use the aircraft to fly away and disappear, never to be heard from again, then she would go home and get some much needed rest.

But this wasn't about *her* anymore. When she started, this whole journey had been about redeeming her lost pride and satiating her hunger for vengeance. She had cut Priscilla's father and drowned a U.S. Senator under Raymond's command and the guise of her own distorted vendetta. A quote Jonas used to tell her rang true now more than ever. "Those who play with the devil's toys will be brought by degrees to wield his sword." –R. Buckminster Fuller. She didn't want vengeance, not anymore, she just wanted to help people, like she used to do.

If Raymond was willing to kill political targets, and he was willing to bring down his own building to kill her, what would he do with a ship armed with bombs and missiles? Thousands of innocent people, men, women, children, were all at risk from whatever demented plan Raymond had. No matter where he dropped those bombs, someone's lifeless remains were going to be found under rubble. Her pride, her past, her want for justice, didn't mean shit. What mattered, what was most important, was that she prevented Raymond and Ned from harming anyone else.

The Ogre lumbered across the sky like a fat vulture, cruising its way to the mega skyscraper known as One World Trade Center. The Financial District was the beating heart of the city's wealth but Raymond had no use for money. His targets had been political in nature and the only ones remaining resided in City Hall and One Police Plaza. She wondered who the next target was. The governor was in Albany, the senator and the mayor had already been taken care of, who could Raymond possibly be planning to hit next?

The Ogre banked left towards the Brooklyn Bridge. A ray of sunlight gleamed across its black armored fuselage. She cut through narrow alleyways and twisted her body to avoid the fire escapes along the way. The Ogre flew to her left and accelerated in the direction of Police Headquarters.

One Police Plaza, the headquarters of the NYPD, was a fortress without fortifications. A brutalist brick cube with small windows. The Ogre slowed to a hover in front of the building. Hidden panels slid open on its wings and revealed the tips of rockets. A barrage of missiles shot out from the Ogre and pounded the walls of One Police Plaza. Officers on the ground level scrambled and yelled into their radios. "We're under attack!"

The bricks tumbled away and left a smoking hole where the Commissioner's office was located. "Damn it." Cindy curled her legs and swung through the breach. Fire and smoke enveloped the office and the one hundred year old desk where Theodore Roosevelt once sat now lay in splinters. Pieces of a stone Celtic cross were strewn across the vermillion carpet. The cross was joined by a photo of Dan holding a giant fish with his father Patrick Gates.

Someone was moaning from beneath the remnants of the desk. She pushed the debris aside and found Commissioner Gates bleeding on the carpet. His suit was torn to shreds and his face was blackened by ash. Blood ran from his forehead and dripped off his jaw. Had she seen him like this a few weeks earlier, she might have been morbidly pleased by his condition. But that was in the past now.

"Are you okay?"

He nodded despite seeming confused and out of sorts. She never in a million years thought she would be risking her neck to save his life. Ned may have killed her partner, but the commissioner destroyed her self-esteem and respect. He was and still is a prick, but right now Raymond wanted him dead.

[Warning! Missile Lock!]

"You know . . ." Cindy heaved the tall and heavy Commissioner Gates over her shoulder— "If you stop being an asshole in general, you'd have a lot less enemies." —and jumped out of the hole. A volley of missiles flew overhead and collapsed what was left of the commissioner's office.

Why Raymond wanted the Commissioner dead didn't make sense. She would have to find out the why later. The Ogre twisted its wingtip engines and rotated until its cockpit faced her. The Ogre pitched forward and chased after them.

Commissioner Gates tapped her shoulder. "It's coming after us!"

[Warning! Missile Lock!] The text flashed in red. Commissioner Gates yelled as the missile fired from the gunship. "Holy shit!"

"Hang on." Cindy fired her grappling hook. Her body dragged to the right as she rounded an office building. The missile curved around the corner with a tail of dissipating smoke. The missile adjusted its fins and followed Cindy no matter whether she went into alleyways or looped around sky bridges.

"It's still on us." Commissioner Gates clutched Cindy's neck.

Not even a block away, there was the skeletal framework of a high rise undergoing construction. She fired the grappling hook in its direction and broke through the orange barricade netting. She bent her legs to avoid the piled up pipes and tables full of plywood as she swung through. The missile chased in after them. Cindy threaded herself through rows of support columns then veered suddenly right. The missile turned too wide and detonated into one of the columns. A rumble followed. The top quarter of the building slammed down on the lower floors causing a domino effect of destruction which roared down to the street level.

The Ogre shrieked through the expanding dust bloom and loosed more missiles from its weapons bays: two, three, four heat seeking missiles chased after her. She hooked onto the tallest building she could find and began the long spiraling ascension. Office workers pressed their hands and faces against the glass as they watched the missiles aim skyward.

She released the hook and slowly floated into the sky with Commissioner Gates screaming in pure terror. She hurled the commissioner away from herself, separating from him by more than twenty feet. As he screamed and plummeted to the city, she whipped out her energy blade and sliced the four warheads. The resulting explosions shattered her armor and sent shards of hot shrapnel through her already brutalized skin.

She blacked out. SIRCA detected a failure in Cindy's vitals and engaged its resuscitation function. SIRCA shocked her system and pumped her chest. She

A Bitter Winter

gasped, coughed out the blood, then turned towards Commissioner Gates who was about to crater into a rooftop. She fired her grappling hook and caught the Commissioner seconds before impact.

"Oh thank Jesus," he said. "Please put me down. Somewhere, anywhere. I can't do this anymore."

Cindy dove to the street level and accidentally stomped into a parked car. The Ogre dropped down behind them. The giant turbines keeping the ship aloft trapped paper and garbage into the swirling vortex of its jet wash. Cindy leapt off the crumpled car and grabbed Commissioner Gates by the back of his neck. She kept their heads down and weaved between parked cars as the Ogre pitched forward and unleashed its rockets.

The street quaked as cars exploded and flipped in front of them. Mother's carried their children as they ran between cars. They were followed by taxi cab drivers, hot dog vendors, and the homeless who abandoned their shopping carts. There was too much collateral damage being caused by her and the commissioner. Finding a subway entrance was her only chance to stop Raymond's plan.

Two F-16 fighter jets from the Air National Guard soared across the sky and launched their missiles at the Ogre. The missiles went inert and bounced uselessly off its armor plates. The Ogre spun in place, tracking the fighters, and fired its own missiles. The fighter jets pulled out and released their counter measures of chaff and flares to distract the projectiles.

Though she was disappointed that the F-16's couldn't down Raymond's ship, they did buy her precious time to get to the C and E subway entrance. The commissioner ran ahead while she lagged behind. Her lungs were burning, her body wracked in blistering pain, there was no way to continue without taking a break. She braced herself against the tile wall and took a moment to breathe.

Commissioner Gates turned around. "Come on, we're almost there."

"I'm not going," she said with hardly any breath. "Take the train, any train. They won't find you."

"What about you?"

She gulped loudly. "I have a fly to swat."

"You're in no condition to do that, look at you. You're bleeding all over. Come with me, we'll brief the governor and ask him to call in some more firepower."

There he went again. Telling her she couldn't do something.

"I can do it." She panted. "Just give me some time."

Commissioner Gates nodded. "I owe you one. So . . . thank you."

A thank you, huh? She never thought she'd live to see the day. Cindy turned and slowly limped up the steps. Her HUD flashed red and there was almost nothing left of her armor. The only thing keeping her alive at this point was Charlie's formula.

"You're not going to tell me who you are, are you?"

Her digital eyes flickered as she turned her head. "A washed up has been."

Commissioner Gates dropped his jaw. "It can't be."

Since the beginning, all she had wanted was to regain his approval, to prove that she was damn good at her job. But now, as she walked with blood seeping out of her stomach, she realized that she never needed his approval after all. She had gotten the commissioner to safety. The only opinion that mattered was her own.

She returned to the ground level and watched Raymond's ship shoot down the two jets. Her look of horror turned to relief when she saw two parachutes deploy away from the fireballs. She ran after the ship and activated her Mag Drivers. Her tired limbs couldn't support the weight of her guns. She found a nearby taxicab and threw her arms onto its roof, creating a makeshift bipod. The Ogre turned and faced Cindy with most of its weapons racks empty. All it had left were the rockets embedded within the wings.

The aircraft's engines whined with power as it pelted the street with a barrage of unguided rockets. She bent at her knees, tilted her Mag Drivers upward, and waited for the Ogre to close range. As the eruption of missiles obscured her vision with smoke, she fired her guns. The magnetically charged slugs tore through the Ogre's thick armor plates and ripped off one of its wings. The aircraft immediately spun out of control. Black smoke trailed from its missing wing before the ship crashed.

Cindy followed the smoke to a nearby crash site. She broke through the wooden construction area barricade and saw Ned climb out of the cockpit wearing Jonas's prototype armor. There was hardly a scratch on him. Ned dusted himself off and leapt from the Ogre. He saw Cindy shuffling her way over to the ship and cracked his knuckles.

"I guess this is how it was always going to go down."

She limped while holding one arm. "I don't really care about you anymore."

"Don't lie to yourself."

She steadied herself on tired feet. The last thing she wanted to do was fight, but it didn't seem like Ned was going to give her a choice. She slowly closed her fingers and brought them to the front of her helmet. She wobbled back and forth dizzy from exhaustion. Ned charged at her and threw a flying punch. She stepped aside, waited until he passed her, and pushed between his shoulders. Ned flapped his arms and fell into the dirt which sullied the cream color of the prototype suit.

"I've been dreaming about this fight," she said out of breath. "And that's your opening move?"

Ned growled. He stood up and held his hands up like a boxer. She limped while he hopped on the balls of his feet. They closed distance. Ned dragged his fist back. The mechanical limbs connected to his arms whined. He blasted his fist in the direction of her helmet. She stepped aside and threw a counter punch to his throat. Ned choked and staggered to the floor, grasping at his neck.

Cindy casually limped forward, still breathing hard. Ned wheezed and spat on the floor. She paced around him, her eyes flickering as she watched. "Okay. That was a little satisfying."

He looked at her, incredulous by what she had said. "There's something different about you." Ned stood up. He loosened his shoulders before adjusting his armored gloves. He no longer carried himself with a cocky swagger. "You're not the little whiny bitch I shot at Javits."

Her blood was heating up, begging her for a longer, more savage fight with Ned. Though she was exhausted and hurt and barely able to stand straight, she wanted to remember this moment forever.

"I'll let you get a free hit." Cindy stuck her head forward and put both hands on her hips. "Come on." She tapped her helmet. "Hit me."

"What the hell's wrong with you?" Ned cocked his fist and blasted the side of her helmet with a loud clang. She flew backward and slid across the dirt.

It felt like a spiked ball had impaled her jaw, but that intoxicating taste of adrenaline was there. She spat blood inside her helmet and laughed. "Not bad." She cracked her neck and smiled before flexing her muscular shoulders.

"My turn." She snapped off her helmet and threw it at his feet. She wanted to feel this fight.

She marched forward and hid any sign of pain behind her confident stride. Ned backed away and waved his hands. "You're fucking crazy."

She licked her tongue across her blood stained teeth. "Now that I'm thinking about it, I'm glad I didn't let you go." Her powerful physique shook with each step. "Two years, I obsessed over you. Chased you, and did I even matter? No. I was just another one of your victims, a statistic. But then you had to go and hurt my sister." She cracked her knuckles. "No one, touches my sister."

"I don't know what to tell ya, shorty," he said casually. "It was just business. My job was to make money, your job was to try and stop me. The better man won."

"I'm still standing."

"We'll see how long." Ned punched his fists together and rushed forward. Cindy spread her stance, turned at the waist, and popped him with a lightning fast uppercut that smashed his jaw together. He fell on his back and slammed into the mud. "Oh shit," he said as blood poured out of his mouth. "You hit like a man." He stood up and raised his hands.

"No." She curled her fingers together and formed two fists. The first punch rammed into his stomach. "I hit like a girl." He gasped and took another blow to his face. "I fight like a girl." And at the last, she put one foot behind the other and kicked him in the chest. "And I win like a girl." Ned flew twenty feet backward and exploded a cement tube. He crawled away from the rubble with fractured armor plates.

As she closed in, Ned pressed a button above his glove. Glowing lights appeared within his body armor. "You ain't won yet."

Bolts of electricity shot out from his fist. She was caught off guard and received the full brunt of his punch. The shock of electricity surged through her limbs. Warning lights flashed in her HUD, sparks exploded off her armor, and her entire body convulsed from sheer pain. She lost her balance and dropped her hands by her side. Ned capitalized on her defenseless stance and delivered a punishing blow to her cheek. Her head whipped to the right. Blood spat from her mouth and left her teeth and bones radiating with pain. He hunched his shoulders and pounded her stomach with a flurry of electrically charged blows.

Her ribs crunched in, her stomach pushed inward, and suddenly she felt weak at the knees. Her stance wavered, her head spun, and through all this Ned was smiling with his cracked teeth.

And in this moment of weakness, where her body was ready to surrender, she had never felt so alive. She dodged his next blow and used her hands to deflect his strikes. She swiped at his punches with a gentle push. The slight touch threw off his angle and made his fist sail past her head. He growled and threw another punch. She tapped his wrist and sent the blow veering wildly off course. He threw more punches, faster, with more fury. She patiently misdirected each one and waited for Ned to punch himself out.

His next punch was slow and wide. He panted as he threw another and another, each attempt more languid than the last. She stood her ground and said, "Pussy."

He wobbled on his feet, wheezing with each breath. Revealing to the commissioner that she was the Silver Ninja was satisfying, but watching Ned lose morale and crumble was even better. She caught his fist and stopped his feeble punch in its tracks. He threw another and she grabbed that one too. With both his hands trapped in her palms she squeezed.

Ned howled and was forced to his knees by her augmented strength. She broke through his armored gloves and continued to apply more pressure until she could feel his bones pop inside her hands.

"Ah, fuck!"

"Fight back motherfucker."

"I can't!"

It felt too good to stop now. She placed both hands on the back of his neck and pounded his helmet with her knees. The helmet lost its circular shape and became a misshapen lump. She tore off his helmet and wailed on his body with her hardest, most debilitating blows. She unleashed all the rage and anger she had pent up for more than two years. She fractured his ribs, dislocated his shoulder, broke both his legs by twisting his ankles, and still it wasn't enough. She grabbed each of his arms and snapped the bones.

"You fucking bitch!" Ned couldn't move any part of his body except for his head. "I fucking hate you!"

She panted and wobbled on her feet. "I hate you too."

"So now what?" He panted. "You kill me?"

"I haven't decided yet." She towered over him, a rare feeling for someone of her stature and one she quite enjoyed. "You know, if you hadn't gone with Raymond, this wouldn't have happened."

Ned hacked as he writhed on top of the dirt. "You wanna know why I went with him? Why I do what I do?"

She looked at him but didn't speak.

"I got sick and tired of doing the nine to five. I got tired of going to work to pay an overpriced mortgage for a shitty house, just to work at the same shitty job until the day I died. What kind of a life is that? You sit on your ass all day, go home to eat microwaveable shit and then go back to work. Fuck that.

"I just wanted to be free, man. Fuck taxes, fuck bosses, fuck the law. I wanted to do what I wanted, whenever I wanted and have fun. Ray wanted me to kill people, kidnap people, and then he said he was going to fly a fucking ship through Manhattan and blow up that shit eating police commissioner. What was I gonna do, say no? C'mon man. It was a once in a lifetime opportunity."

She clenched her teeth. "You killed my partner because it was fun?"

"All of it was fun. Putting you in that freight container and watching you piss yourself was fun. Teaching you guys a lesson for stealing my money was fun. Having all the gangs in this city respect me for the work I did was fun. And if the cops ever trapped me in a building and I had to choose between getting arrested or killing myself, I'd go out guns blazing man. I'm the only one that's mentally liberated." He pointed at her. "And with that suit, you could be liberated too."

"I don't take pleasure in the same things you do."

"That's a fucking lie," he said almost laughing. "I saw the look on your face when you were ripping me apart. You were fucking wet."

She punched the ground next to his ear, cratering the dirt.

"See what I mean? You love the power. You love how strong that suit makes you feel, I get it. Being powerful is a turn on. You, me, and Ray, we're all the same."

"I'm nothing like you."

He relished in getting a rise out of her, she could tell by the stupid grin on his face. "Come on. I know you wanna do it. I didn't need to make your partner burn. I wanted to." He smiled at her. "You've been dreaming about killing me. You even thought you slit my throat at the hospital, you wanted me so bad." Ned coughed. "Ray told me all about it. How happy you were when you did it. Look, I'll make it easier on you. If you don't kill me and I go to prison, I'll tell everyone who the Silver Ninja really is."

She pulled on Ned's shirt. "That's what you want isn't it? Instead of going to jail where you know you'd be miserable, you'd rather have me stomp you into the dirt."

"It's what you want too."

"It's what I wanted . . . two years ago."

Cindy picked up her beat up helmet and placed it upon her head. She grabbed Ned by his shirt and dragged him across the site.

"What are you doing?"

Through SIRCA, Cindy analyzed and pinpointed parts of the brain which directed motor control and speech function. She dragged him behind a portable toilet and methodically punched specific parts of his head. "Augh, shit! What the fuck are you doing?"

She nailed him again and again and continued to do so while he begged for her to stop. His head changed shape as she fractured his skull. She would turn his body into a prison. And if she failed, who cared?

CHAPTER 30:

The Price of Failure

The sound of sirens closed around the construction site. The Ogre burned. Cindy made her way to the crashed ship and climbed onto its shattered glass cockpit. Raymond's stomach had been impaled by a metal beam and he was still bleeding from his gunshot wound. Somehow the bastard was still breathing. She grabbed onto the steel window struts of the cockpit and curled them out of the way. Raymond's pristine white shirt was completely saturated in blood. He wheezed with each breath and then a drop of blood would fall from his lip and stain his pants. He was speaking to someone through his headset radio.

"I want to-kaff-kaff-spend my points."

"You do not have enough points to overturn the ruling."

"It's for my daughter," he yelled and smacked the flight instruments console. He let out a pained breath and looked up at Cindy. "Just so you know, I can't run."

He held onto the pipe sticking out of his belly. It had gone clean through his stomach and was embedded into the back of his seat. Removing it would be easy for her. Potentially she could save his life.

"Ray."

"It wasn't-kaff-kaff-supposed to be like this.-kaff-"

She climbed into the cockpit and straddled the gunner seat as if it were a barstool. He was in bad shape and didn't look like he had much time left. "I don't understand why you would do this," she said. "You have all the money in the world."

"I have money, but what I needed were points," he chuckled softly. "I was going to make everything better. A police commissioner, a mayor, and a senator were a small price to pay for freedom, true freedom. I wanted to—kaff—cut the puppet's strings. And they went after my daughter."

"Who? What points?"

"I can't say. They're listening. One wrong word and it ends on their terms."

A Bitter Winter

"Who's they?"

"I can't."

She had been furious with Raymond, ready to tear him limb from limb like she did Ned, but it all seemed so pointless now. This man whom she had viewed as larger than life, dashing even, seemed pathetic now. She let him speak and listened.

"When you get to my level of wealth, you notice things you couldn't see when you were poor or middle class. You realize that people treat you differently. You become royalty. Today's elite are the trust funds, the banks, the tech companies, and the media. They are all unworthy nobles who control your life. I know more about you than your own family thanks to your Credit Guard profile. Technology changes your perception of the world and you don't even realize that it's happening."

Cindy glanced at her hands. Her silver gloves had mostly torn off, exposing her bloodied knuckles. Raymond clearly knew more than he was letting on. She wanted to know about these points and these puppet masters he was speaking of. She led those battered fingers to the pipe sticking out of his abdomen. He grabbed the pipe and shook his head. She backed off and left the pipe alone.

"I apologize for manipulating you the way I did, Cindy. I realize how hypocritical I must sound telling you that I wanted to cut the puppet strings and then used said strings to trick you. I am genuinely sorry." He writhed in his seat. A deep groan left his lips as his hands held onto the silver pole stealing his life away. She stared at him. Debating whether she should ignore his refusal for help and pull the pipe out.

"Apologizing isn't going to bring back the people I killed."

"You can always forget."

She leaned back. "What do you mean?"

"I cannot speak the command to wipe your memory, I know it won't work. But if Jonas hasn't removed the code, it should still be in your system."

She quickly scrolled through her HUD menu and went to the admin settings. Buried within dozens of menus was the option to enable the spotless mind protocol. There were two options, enable a surface wipe or a deep level wipe. All she had to do was give the command and SIRCA would make her forget what an awful human being she had become.

"I want to ask you a question," she said.

He smiled. "I'm not going anywhere."

"You said you bought the suit to wipe away the memories of what you did overseas."

"Correct."

"Why didn't you?"

He thought about her question for a long while. "I suppose I was afraid I would accidentally-kaff-erase everything that was important to me. That I'd-kaff-suddenly lose my desire to make amends for the mistakes I had made. Mistakes and failures, annoying and painful as they are, are great motivators to do better, to be better. If I had forgotten about those men I had killed, this company would have never existed. I didn't want my life to lose meaning." He slowly lifted his chin and closed his eyes. "Do you understand?"

"So I either choose to live with this or start over from scratch"

"Would you rather have been Michael's wife?"

"No."

"Then be better."

"How am I supposed to bounce back from this? I hurt so many people. I should just forget and disappear. Leave everything behind."

"If you want my-kaff-honest opinion. Choosing to forget will only work once. At some point you will make new mistakes and have new regrets, maybe even the same ones. Are you going to wipe your memory then, too?"

She exited from the Spotless Mind protocol menu.

"No, I guess not."

Raymond was in pain every time he spoke and she found herself feeling sorry for the man. "I could just end it for you."

"You know as well as I do that I deserve this. And if I wasn't in this position you would have savaged me like you did Ned. Correct?" He shuddered as if a chill had run down his spine.

"I don't know anymore."

"I know it's not my place to ask, but I am desperate for one thing."

"What?"

"Please protect my daughter, Alexis, and her child." His breathing slowed. "Please . . . I'm begging you . . ." He groaned in pain. His silver hair spread against the headrest of his seat. "I wanted the best for her, you know." He coughed. "This winter was simply awful . . . wasn't it?"

Raymond closed his emerald eyes, and just like that, their conversation was over. Her entire body deflated. She knew it didn't make sense to feel sad, but she did. She supposed it was because unlike Ned, Raymond wasn't evil. He didn't take pleasure in other people's suffering and was remorseful for what he had done. In a strange way, she had a sliver of respect for him. She disembarked the ship and went over to pick up a crippled, but still breathing Ned.

Cindy approached the cordoned off police blockade. Emergency crews scrambled to the perimeter of the construction site. Radio chatter melded with the sound of crackling flames while firefighters attached their hoses to nearby fire hydrants. Emergency Services Units charged their weapons at the bark of their commander's orders and took aim at the construction site. Chief of Police Glenn Olsen stood near the command vehicle next to a bruised, but alive Commissioner Gates.

An officer in the middle of unrolling police tape looked up and saw her. "Somebody's coming."

Officers from the ESU shouldered their weapons and peered down the sights of their submachine guns and assault rifles. The commander of the unit raised a megaphone to his lips.

"Stay where you are and put your hands up."

She dragged Ned's body through the dirt with one arm trailing behind her back. Her eyes continued to flicker, notifying Cindy though her HUD that repairs were in progress. The obliterated silver alloy was rebuilding across her swollen, badly beaten body. The ESU commander instructed his officers to take aim.

"This is your last warning. Put your hands up or we will shoot."

She ignored the officer's warning.

"Ready."

The officers' eyes went flush to their sights.

"Aim."

SIRCA had, for the most part, rebuilt across most of her chest and legs. Their bullets would soon be useless against her armor.

Commissioner Gates took the megaphone from the commander. "Let me go talk to her."

"Sir, I strongly suggest you don't."

"Cover me."

Commissioner Gates shouldered through the battalion of officers. There were bandages on his face, and his suit jacket had been replaced with an NYPD wind breaker. He was in much better condition than she was.

"You do realize my men almost shot you."

"They would've wasted their bullets."

He pointed at the crash site. "You brought it down like you said."

"I keep my word."

She was having a hard time paying attention. Now that the fighting was finished, she felt woozy and short of breath.

"Is that Raymond?"

"No. This is Ned—" She fell faint and collapsed on her knees. Commissioner Gates grabbed her shoulders and kept her upright.

"Easy there."

She pushed herself up and grabbed Ned by the back of his collar. "—this is Ned Pickler, aka Harold Graves, aka Death Dealer, wanted for: racketeering, extortion, smuggling of illegal contraband, smuggling of controlled substances, kidnapping, murder-for-hire, and murder in the first degree of one, Daniel Gates, badge number two-two-five-niner. Fidelis ad mortem."

"Faithful unto death." Commissioner Gates frowned. He looked at the bloody pulp that was Ned's head. "So you caught him after all."

She threw Ned at his feet. He was motionless but still breathing with his malformed head.

"I told you I would bring him in."

She couldn't believe it, still couldn't believe it. After two years of suffering and ruining her own life, Ned Pickler was finally at the feet of Police Commissioner Gates. The road to this moment, in hindsight, was not the road she would have taken. For gaining super powers, she lost a friend, a sister, and her own moral compass.

She had to remind herself that this was a huge victory to be savored. She had prevented a train bombing, wiped out the city's most dangerous criminals, stopped Raymond and his ship, and brought her partner's killer to justice. It wasn't clean cut, and it certainly wasn't bloodless, but it was a huge relief to finally take this burden off her shoulders.

Commissioner Gates shook his head. "I don't know what to say. A lot of important people are going to come to me for answers. Once you're all fixed up, I'd like to ask you a few questions."

She mentally groaned. Questioning, would not be a simple come down to the station for fifteen minutes. In this case, the questioning could take several days and possibly require her to do multiple interviews. She wasn't mentally or physically prepared to go through that.

"It's been a very long day, Sir. I'm not going to come down for questioning, not today."

"Don't make this more difficult for me. It'll look bad if I cuff you."

"Your cuffs can't stop me and neither can the force. That'll look even worse."

"Cin—mm, what do I even call you? Ninja? Silver?"

"I'll meet you somewhere, Sir. We can talk then."

"What, you expect me to go to your house?"

"I'll be visiting your son at noon." She took a step backward. "You should bring a gift to celebrate, maybe whiskey, it was his favorite." In front of a firing squad of officers, the police chief, and the commissioner himself, Cindy flickered until nothing was left but the dirt and air she once occupied.

EPILOGUE

In Hoboken, New Jersey, Thomas and Kimberly Brynfire sat beside Jonas on kitchen chairs. He held in his hands a fanned out collection of old photos. From left to right were pictures of Cindy and Jadie together as children, teenagers, and adults. His chair creaked as he leaned forward. He pulled out a photo and held it in front of Jadie.

"Do you remember her?"

Jadie sat on the end of what was once her twin bed. Next to it was an empty one, the one where Cindy used to sleep. Jonas had expected to see stuffed animals or Jadie's Coast Guard pictures, or Cindy's academy graduation photo, yet none was to be found. Thomas and Kim had cleaned out their room after Jadie moved out so they could rent it to tourists. Anything relating to the sisters had been moved to the living room where they could proudly tell stories of their daughters to curious guests.

Jadie shook her head. "No."

"She's your sister."

"I don't recognize her."

He pointed to Thomas and Kim. "Do you remember your parents?"

She looked at them then dropped her gaze. "No."

"What do you remember?"

"I don't remember anything," she said softly.

Jonas put the photos down. He had told her parents that she'd been in a car accident and they believed him. He didn't like lying to them, but telling them about the suit would lead to questions he wasn't sure he could answer.

"Cindy should be here," Thomas said. "I still don't understand why she isn't."

"She had to take care of something," Jonas replied.

"What's more important than her sister?"

*   *   *

A Bitter Winter

"We need to talk." Cindy knelt down in front of a tombstone lost in the middle of a grassy cemetery. Etched into the stone was a name laced with bittersweet memories. Daniel Gates, Fidelis Ad Mortem, brother, son, courageous until death.

"When we first met, I hated you. You were a bully with a badge and I was an arrogant rookie who could never be wrong. We argued over everything, even who would drive the car." she chuckled. "Had someone told me I would eventually care about you like a brother, I wouldn't have believed them."

A man cleared his throat. She stood up and brushed off the bits of grass and dirt from her knees. Commissioner Gates stood before her with a brown paper bag in his hand and three small cups.

"Cindy."

"Sir."

"You heal quickly."

"Very."

He pulled a bottle of whiskey out of the paper bag and held it up to the light. The green bottle cast refractions onto his grey suit. "Are you going to be able to control yourself?" He asked honestly and without any malice behind his words. After having spat in his face, she didn't blame him for asking. She nodded. The commissioner opened the bottle and filled a paper cup half way before handing it to Cindy. She took the cup and placed it on the gravestone. The commissioner handed her another cup and raised his own.

"Fidelis ad mortem," he said.

Cindy did the same. "Faithful unto death."

They knocked it back. She winced as the drink burned down her throat; she didn't miss that feeling at all. Cindy took the cup from the gravestone and poured it over Dan's grave. The commissioner glanced at his bottle then handed it to Cindy. "You should give him the rest."

She turned the bottle upside down and watched the amber liquid absorb into the dirt. With the bottle empty, she set it on the tombstone and ran her fingers atop the rough surface of the stone.

"We have a lot to talk about," he said.

"I'm ready to talk."

"Well first I wanted to ask, how do I get that suit for the rest of my officers?"

She frowned. "Sorry, but this is a one of a kind. And if you take it from me, it disintegrates."

"Not an answer I like."

"I paid a heavy price for this suit, Sir. You really don't want to ask your officers to do the same."

"Understood. Then I guess I'll ask this instead. Do you know what happened to Mayor Montez?"

She swallowed hard. "What do you mean?"

"That tough son of a bitch survived. We still don't know who tried to cut his throat but he's going to be all right. The doctors got to him before he could bleed out. I imagine he and his family are going to go on a nice long vacation."

Her lip trembled. She wasn't sure what to feel. On the one hand, she was beside herself with guilt for slicing his throat, on the other, she was thrilled to know he was still alive. Mayor Montez was not killed by her hands. "I'm very glad to hear that," she said.

"Do you know who tried to kill him?"

She cleared her throat and looked at the commissioner. "Yes."

He paused. "Do you also know who killed Senator Albright?"

She nodded her head again.

"Was it you?"

Her skin turned to ice at the choice presented to her. Telling the truth could land her in federal prison. Lying would maintain her freedom. She knew what she had done was wrong, that she had technically—up until this point—evaded punishment from the law. But to say that she has lived without punishment would be a lie.

Guilt and regret was a portable prison. The body roamed free while the mind remained tortured by the past. Her decision to retain her memories meant that she was going to force herself to learn how to live with her actions. It wasn't easy and it wasn't fair. Raymond was the one who pushed her to her downfall, Raymond was the one who picked her targets and directed her focus. But at the end of the day, no matter how much she wanted to blame him for everything that happened, she was the one who stole the suit, not him. Prison would rob her of any opportunity to right her wrongs. She needed to give the commissioner an answer.

"Well?"

"Raymond," she said. "He hired Ned and his crew to take out political targets. Their plan was to assassinate the three of you at the Javits center during the technology conference, but I found his squad and warned Officer Yang before they could execute their plan."

"You found them?"

"Yes sir." She continued. "After some time passed, Raymond rehired Ned to finish what he had started."

"The limo crash and the assassination attempt at the hospital?"

She nodded.

"Okay. How could you possibly know all this?"

"You saw me at the bar, Sir. You saw my suit. I was hunting him the entire time. I got a confession out of both Ned and Raymond before he died."

So she lied but not without just cause. A high tech nanosuit capable of saving lives and protecting innocent people would be useless behind bars. And if there were more puppeteers like Raymond still out there, she couldn't risk them doing to others what he did to her.

Commissioner Gates sighed. "You leave me very conflicted. On the one hand, you spat in my face, got my son killed, and I assume, blew up a boat in Brooklyn, because why would Ned blow up his own boat? On the other hand, you've reduced crime, nearly gave your life trying to protect Manny, and you saved my life and thousands of New Yorkers from that lunatic in a gunship. I don't know if I'm supposed to arrest you or give you another medal."

"I don't want either of those things," she replied. "I just wanted to bring him in."

"You turned Ned into a vegetable you know? He can probably hear things but the doctors say there's no chance he's ever going to wake up. He's going to die of old age, trapped in that bed. It's going to be Hell on Earth for him and I'm glad."

"Me too." She remembered Ned talking to her about freedom, how he would have rather died than rot in prison. She took immense satisfaction in knowing she had put him in a cell he could never escape from.

Commissioner Gates reached into his suit jacket pocket. "I uh . . . I did some thinking." He took out a box and held it with both hands. "What I did at the bar was wrong." He took a step forward and handed the box to Cindy. "And I was wrong. You're not a washed up has been."

Cindy opened the box. Inside was her old police badge, freshly polished. Even as she stared into the gold shield she had coveted so much, she didn't think it was real.

"Why are you giving this to me?"

"It belongs to you."

She ran her fingers along the raised badge number. Twelve, twelve.

"If you want to come back to the force." He fixed his tie and straightened his posture. "I'd be happy to have you. Maybe I can put you in a special task force."

"Are you asking me or the other woman?"

"The other woman is a vigilante. She serves a purpose, but I'm asking you."

She sighed and closed the box. "I can't accept this."

"Why?"

"I've been through a lot recently. You look at me and don't see any more scars, but they're still there, under my skin. I went through Hell to bring Ned to you, hurt myself in ways that I don't know will ever heal. Mentally, I'm not ready to represent the badge. I need time to process and get my head together." She reluctantly offered the badge back to the commissioner.

"Keep it," he said. "It's a dupe. The real one's waiting for you back at headquarters if you change your mind."

"Sir."

"I hate to bring this up, but there is one more thing I need to discuss with you."

"What's that?"

"The other woman. She's not sanctioned by me or the law. She killed a lot of people on that boat. Or rather, I assume she did . . . because we have no evidence. There is zero proof of your involvement. Even the tunnel cameras malfunctioned minutes before Senator Albright's limo crashed. She has, for the time being, a clean slate.

"But if she kills again, even if the suspect had murdered children and helpless puppies, she gets arrested. Remember that even if she runs, I know who she is and how to find her. Am I understood?"

"Yes, Sir."

"I'm giving you the second chance you earned. Don't blow it."

A Bitter Winter

Before Commissioner Gates could walk away. Cindy stood up straight, threw back her shoulders, and spoke with newly discovered conviction.

"Sir. I can't promise that I won't make mistakes. And honestly, I'm probably going to fail more times than I'd like. I can't be perfect, that's impossible and I know that now. But I can promise to do my best and strive to be better. I won't be defined by my past anymore but I will learn from it."

"Good."

The wind rustled through the leaves. Commissioner Gates walked away from Cindy with the afternoon shadow attached to his feet. She stood alone with Dan's grave, an empty bottle of whiskey, and a row of tombstones.

"Well, partner, unfortunately you're also part of my past. Part of the reason I haven't been able to move on. I will always regret getting us captured by Ned. But I can't let it rule my life anymore. You'll always be here." She pointed to her heart. "But you're also going to stay there." She touched the tombstone. "I hope you can finally rest in peace." She stepped back from the tombstone and faced the passing breeze.

"Bye, Dan."

Thank you for reading The Silver Ninja: A Bitter Winter by Wilmar Luna.

Book reviews are the lifeblood of an author's career. Without a review, readers are less likely to purchase or borrow a copy for themselves.

Please take a moment to leave a review for A Bitter Winter. Whether positive or critical, your feedback will be greatly appreciated and taken into consideration.

The following QR code will take you to Goodreads:

Or, you can search for **"A Bitter Winter"** on **Amazon** and **Goodreads**.

About Wilmar Luna

From the time he put on Superman pajamas and leapt off a flight of stairs, Wilmar Luna has been captivated by stories of heroes saving the day. As he grew older, his fascination with 90's pop culture, video games, and movies filled his overactive imagination with fantastical worlds and legendary heroes.

He found an outlet for his creativity by studying video editing and motion graphics design at Mercer County Community College. After graduating in 2008, he freelanced throughout New York City and has edited numerous indie films, freelanced for the NFL, and also worked with the cinematics team at Rockstar Games. He assisted with the launch of Grand Theft Auto V and was also involved in the creation of cutscenes for Red Dead Redemption 2.

After years of watching his name scroll in other people's credits (please don't remove me), Wilmar wanted to develop his own projects and ideas. He decided that if he wanted to tell stories of empowered female characters, paranormal detectives, and ghost stories, he would have to venture off on his own.

Wilmar published his first novel in 2012 and his second in 2014. He also published several horror short stories on Wattpad, as well as concept ideas for a gothic fantasy novel. In 2018, Wilmar completed his novel The Silver Ninja: A Bitter Winter, fulfilling his childhood dream to create an empowered, independent, brand new superheroine for a generation of readers hungry for new stories.

For updates on his latest projects, please visit http://thesilverninja.com or follow him on Twitter @WilmarLuna.

Sign up for The Silver Ninja newsletter!

https://thesilverninja.com